# BETTER THAN NEVER

# BETTER *than* NEVER

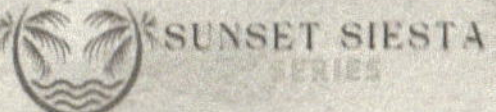

# BETTER THAN NEVER

## Sunset Siesta Series

ERIN BROCKUS

GREEN SAGE
PRESS

# Chapter One

## ELI

MY LIFE PHILOSOPHY WAS SIMPLE—IF you couldn't fix it with duct tape or solve it with a beer, you were probably overthinking it. I was currently working on the latter as I studied my little brother Braden. The way he served drinks, with that easy smile and a wink here and there, was like watching a magician pull rabbits from a hat. I leaned back in my chair, soaking in the buzz of Tropical Hops around me. The cheerful pale turquoise walls, the laughter spilling from the bar, and the clinking of glasses personified Dove Key in the lower Florida Keys on a Friday night.

Braden's eyes flicked to me and caught my upraised fingers, a signal for two beers. He nodded and withdrew two pint glasses from the freezer. As he expertly poured them from the tap, I rolled my head around on my neck. I dragged a hand through my messy dark-blond hair, which was still stiff from saltwater. The day had been long, filled with the usual ups and downs of running the dive shop and lining up scuba classes, and I hadn't had time for my usual post-dive shower at the shop. But now, as I sat at a relatively quiet table, surrounded by the familiar sights and sounds of Braden's brewpub, it was time to relax.

Chase Ashworth strode through the door, his face drawn tight with an interesting mix of fatigue and exasperation. His normally neat dark-brown hair was tousled, and the crispness of his button-down shirt and slacks seemed at odds with the expression on his face. But the moment he spotted Braden heading our way and carrying two frosty mugs of beer, a flicker of hope danced across his features.

"Thank God for small miracles," he muttered, collapsing into the chair across from me.

"Rough day?" I asked, leaning forward with a grin that threatened to widen. Chase and I had been best buddies since we were kids, a friendship that had held steady into our mid-thirties.

"More like a rough week. Lacey is driving me insane with her wedding plans—or lack thereof." He scrubbed a hand over his face, his hazel eyes narrowing. "She's got less than three months, Eli! And she hasn't even picked a venue yet."

"Maybe she thinks a tropical beach wedding is too cliché," I teased, raising an eyebrow. Chase's sister was thrilled about her upcoming nuptials but not known for her solid planning. Hence, her penchant for turning to her big brother.

"Yeah, well, if she keeps this up, I'm going to need more than a beer," he grumbled, but a hint of a smile tugged at his lips.

Braden set down the beers with a flourish. "Two cold ones for my favorite professional man and the king of carefree living. I'll leave it to you two to decide who is who."

"Thanks, brother." I lifted my glass in a toast.

After saluting with two fingers, he returned to the bar.

"At least you dodged groomsman duties," I said to Chase, trying to lighten the mood, then took a sip of Braden's latest IPA—cold and hoppy, perfect to wash away the last remnants of the workday. I had to admit he'd found his calling.

"Thank God, but I still have to listen to her whine about color palettes and floral arrangements." Chase groaned, his expression helplessly perplexed. "I have no idea why she even asks me for input."

"Just tell her you think white clashes with the whole tropical paradise vibe. That should keep her busy for a while."

"Oh, sure. I'd just throw fuel onto the fire." He shook his head but was unable to suppress a laugh. "I can picture it now. Lacey in a frenzy over my so-called fashion advice."

"Hey, look on the bright side," I continued, leaning back in my chair. "At least you won't be stuck in an ill-fitting suit sweating bullets while trying to keep a smile pasted on."

"Right? Small victories." He took a sip of his beer, and the tension from earlier ebbed away, replaced by the casual camaraderie we always shared.

"Just remember, if things get too overwhelming, I'm always here to distract you with tales of my thrilling life as a beach bum." I rested my chin in my palm, feigning a dreamy expression. "Today, I swam with gorgeous tropical fish and caught some rays. Oh wait, that's every day."

Chase laughed. "Sounds about right. While I'm stuck in the land of spreadsheets and architectural renderings, you're out there living the dream."

"Someone's got to keep the Coleridge legacy alive," I shot back. Beneath the banter, though, a flash of unease seized me. It was easy to joke about my relaxed life, but under the surface, the weight of expectations always loomed large. We Coleridges were a large clan. I had five brothers and sisters, and our slightly ramshackle resort had been an anchor in Dove Key for well over a century.

Behind Chase, the door swung open, and my sister Harper walked in. Her chestnut hair danced around her shoulders, though tension coiled in her tight shoulders and the furrow between her brows. At thirty-four, she was a year younger than me. When she spotted us, she gave us a smile that didn't quite reach her eyes.

I waved to her. "Come on over. You look in need of a beer too." I signaled Braden again as Harper dropped onto the chair next to Chase.

"Hey, you two," she said. "I'm not crashing some private boy talk here, am I?"

"Nah," I replied. "You're a welcome distraction from Chase's constant bitching."

"Up yours," he said mildly before taking a drink.

I grinned as Braden set a frosty beer in front of her.

"Here you go, sis. Just what you need after a long day."

"Thanks, Braden. Isn't that the truth." She took a sip, and I could almost see the weight of the resort's financial struggles settling onto her shoulders like a heavy winter coat.

"How's our lovely Sunset Siesta treating you?" I asked.

"About the same, I suppose." She glanced down at her drink. Harper had been the general manager of our family resort for ten years, and she wore the mantle of responsibility like an albatross around her neck. "Though we've got some serious issues to tackle. The repairs are piling up, and I'm starting to think we need a nose-to-tail remodel of everything."

"Renovations? What kind of fun updates are we talking about?" Chase probed as he leaned in slightly, his curiosity piqued at the architectural subject change.

"Everything from outdated furniture to kitchen equipment that belongs in a museum," she replied, shaking her head. "I mean, we can only patch things together for so long."

"Sounds like a blast," I said with a slightly smug grin. "Nothing says beach vacation like a new toaster."

"Very funny, Eli," she groused. "I just wish I had more resources. We've been scrambling to make ends meet, and it feels like I'm chasing my tail half the time."

"Maybe it's time to take a page from my book and focus on the essentials—sun, sand, and a cold beer," I joked, clinking my glass to hers. "Who needs fancy renovations?"

"Right, because that's the answer to everything." She rolled her eyes, but her tiny smile told me she appreciated the distraction, even if just for a moment.

"Seriously, though," Chase interjected, turning to face her. "Have you thought about reaching out for outside help? You know, maybe bring in someone who can take a fresh look?"

"Believe me, I've considered it," she replied. "But every time I think about it, I get stuck worrying about costs. It's like walking a tightrope without a safety net."

"Look, if anyone can figure it out, it's you," I said. "You're basically the heart and soul of this place."

"More like the person holding it all together with duct tape," she quipped with a rueful smile.

"Hey, at least it's colorful duct tape."

"True, but I'd still prefer solid foundations over flashy colors."

"Solid foundations, huh? Sounds like a fancy way of saying boring," I teased, but there was a twinge of seriousness in my voice. As I glanced around Tropical Hops, I couldn't shake the feeling that the entire resort mirrored our conversation. Braden's vibrant bar was a burst of life, laughter, and creativity, while the rest of the resort felt… well, tired. The faded paint and worn furniture spoke of better days, though I had to admit I liked things the way they were. Change was rarely a good thing in my experience.

"Eli," Harper said, shaking me from my thoughts, "the resort is overdue for some serious renovations. We can't keep pretending everything's fine when it clearly isn't."

"Hey, let's not get too dramatic. A little faded paint adds character."

"Character or not, we need to face facts." She turned, her warm brown eyes narrowing slightly. "Chase, what do you think? You've seen more resorts than anyone here."

Chase blinked, visibly taken aback. "You truly want my opinion?"

"Yeah. You're the architect, right?" Harper asked.

"Uh, well, I mean—" He rubbed the back of his neck, a bit of color creeping onto his cheeks. "I'd say you need to address the structural integrity first. Roofs might need reinforcement, and those air conditioning units are ancient. They probably suck energy like a black hole."

"Great, and how much would that cost us?" The lines in her brow grew deeper. "A fortune, I bet."

"Well, it won't be cheap," he admitted. "But maybe it's worth it to prevent bigger issues down the line."

"Jeez, you two are downers. May I remind you that it's Friday night?" I added, ready to change the subject. "Do we have to discuss business crap?"

"Economics aside," Harper said, sighing softly as she ignored me completely, "renovations are something we have to consider. Maybe Julianne has some ideas."

"Julianne." I grimaced and gave up on happier topics. Just her name soured my mood. "Oh, joy. If the conversation is anything like the last chat I had with her, that should be a fun time."

"Come on, Eli," Harper said, a teasing smile forming on her lips. "Just think of it as a chance to show off your charm."

"Charm? With Julianne?" I snorted. "Please. She's completely charm-proof. The woman is made of ice. Nope, count me out for this fight. Besides, I have my own battle to wage with her Monday morning."

That made Chase's ears perk up. "Oh? Do tell."

I scowled as I recalled the dive I'd led that morning. "I need to talk to her about authorizing new dive computers. They're practically antiques at this point. I mean, we might as well strap a sundial around our wrists and call it a day. Divers are complaining left and right—lost signals, glitches, you name it. It's like we're sending them down there with one foot in the stone age."

"That doesn't sound like the image you want to portray," Chase said before taking a sip of beer.

"Exactly! But you know how she is—joyless killjoy mode activated." I huffed and forced my hand to relax around my beer glass. "Last time I asked for new wetsuits, she dragged me into an endless lecture about the budget and unnecessary expenses. She's totally impossible. You should have never hired her, Harper."

"Oh, stop!" Harper added with a laugh. "You're just pissed off because she's the one woman you can't bat your pretty blue eyes at and have her melt. She's damn good at her job."

I leaned forward, lowering my voice as if sharing a secret. "She runs the place like it's a military operation. 'Expenses must be justified!' More like 'Eli must be punished at every opportunity!'"

"Okay, okay." Chase laughed, shaking his head. "But

maybe you're exaggerating her nature a tad? Don't forget I know her too."

"Exaggerating? Me? Never!" I grinned, spreading my arms wide. "I'm a beacon of rational thought."

"More like a beacon of drama," Harper added with a smirk.

"Fine. Maybe I'm a little melodramatic," I admitted, shrugging. "But she's relentless. If there's one person who can turn a casual chat into a miserable financial audit, it's Julianne."

"She's just doing her job," Harper said. "You know she cares about this resort as much as we do."

"I doubt that. Plus, she could tone down the accountant-from-hell vibe a bit," I argued. "I mean, can't a guy just ask for a few upgrades without feeling like he's entering a courtroom?"

"Look, Eli," Chase said, leaning closer. "Just try framing it differently. Instead of asking for money, present it as an investment. Show her how it could attract more divers, maybe even increase profits."

"Investment, huh?" I mulled that over, picturing Julianne's skeptical face. Her black hair pulled into that no-nonsense bun that fit her perfectly. I narrowed my eyes at him. "That sounds suspiciously like something a responsible adult would say."

"Exactly!" Chase encouraged, then blew it by adding, "Julianne does have a point. It's not like you're exactly known for your budgeting skills, Eli."

"So what? You two both manage to be responsible adults without carrying your own personal black cloud everywhere. God, I can't stand that woman."

"Well, she's not exactly your biggest fan, either," Harper added, her expression softening into a knowing smile. "Just remember, sometimes it helps to be more professional. You might surprise yourself."

"Professionalism is overrated," I replied, waving a hand casually. "What's wrong with a little charm? I thought I was running a dive shop, not a Fortune 500 company."

"Charm can only take you so far," Chase said, then heaved a sigh. "Well, whatever happens, I'll be there to listen to your melodrama afterward."

"Aw, thanks. You're the best." As I glanced over at Harper, who was staring into her beer again, guilt twisted inside me. She carried so much for everyone else, and I hated to add my burdens to hers. So I raised my glass in a toast, determined to lighten the mood. "To diving, family businesses, and maybe even new computers!"

"To new computers!" they echoed, clinking their glasses against mine.

I was glad to see those lines disappear on Harper's brow as she grinned. As I laughed along, my humor felt a little forced. But hey, it was better than facing the reality of the battle with Julianne. That would come soon enough.

# Chapter Two

## JULES

THE NUMBERS on the spreadsheet flickered as I squinted at the screen, but they didn't change. Then they went sideways, and my screen went dark.

"Oh, dammit. Guess it is Monday."

I reached behind the monitor and fiddled with the cord, saying a little prayer that the magic trick would work. Some days it did and other days I had to smack my monitor to get it to behave. Today the gods smiled on me. My numbers came back to life, but that didn't change the stark reality in front of me.

I had hoped for a bounce back after last quarter's dismal performance, but there it was—red ink creeping dangerously close to the bottom line. My stomach knotted tighter with each passing second. The resort's financial health dangled by a thread, and I could almost hear the ominous ticking of a clock in the background.

Approving some requests while denying others was part of my job. Not the most enjoyable part, but I wasn't here to be everyone's best friend. And I applied a rigorous review process to every request, even my own. I had put off getting a new desktop for the last three years. The thing on my desk was a relic and made my already challenging job frustrating beyond measure. But my persistence and patience were about to pay off. I was a department of one, and even though we could use a second person to help me out, I had used the savings to carve out some funds for my desperately needed replacement. That was the one bright spot on the report before me. In another month, I wouldn't have to cross my fingers every time I turned on my computer.

My office was a haven of order amidst the sunny chaos of a beach resort. A tidy desk with neatly stacked folders, a succulent plant that somehow managed to thrive despite my lack of attention, and the faint scent of coconut from the air freshener. Bright sunlight spilled through the panes, casting playful shadows on the walls and mocking my serious mood.

I tugged at my crisp white button-down shirt. My raven hair was coiled into its usual bun at the nape of my neck, and I itched to loosen it. I sighed and poked the blunt end of my pen into my scalp to relieve the pressure as I waited for the file to save. I could just picture the hamsters inside the CPU running on their little wheels.

Just then, a sharp knock sounded on my doorframe. I glanced up, expecting another staff member with a question about linens or towels. Instead, Eli Coleridge sauntered in and my day immediately went from bad to worse. Even though his casual smile lit up the room like the sun itself, our resort dive instructor was my least favorite person on the island.

"Julianne!" he called, his breezy tone instantly setting my teeth on edge.

"What do you want, Eli?"

"Well, I thought I'd drop by and discuss our dive equipment."

He perched on the corner of my desk like he owned the place, all relaxed charm with his artfully messy hair catching the light. His indigo eyes sparkled with a hint of something. Was it mischief or just confidence? Either way, it grated on me. The man was infuriating and never took a thing seriously, which was ridiculous at his age. Though he was six years older, there was no doubt which of us was more mature.

"Isn't this a bit too early for your daily dose of smarm?" I shot back, folding my arms.

"Too early? Nah, it's never too early when you're in paradise. Besides, it's almost closing time." He grinned wider, undeterred by my frosty demeanor. "Ready for the details? Come on, don't tell me you're not even slightly intrigued by the idea of upgrading our dive gear."

"Intrigued? More like concerned," I replied with a sinking in my gut. "We're barely scraping by as it is. Don't you think we should focus on keeping the lights on before splurging on new toys?"

"Not toys. Dive computers! New gear *is* what keeps the lights on, Julianne." That ridiculous smile finally faded as he stared at me evenly. "Don't look at this as an expense. It's an investment. Look, our dive computers are obsolete. All the divers in my group today remarked on it, which was embarrassing because they were absolutely right. We need new ones STAT."

"Look, Eli, we can't afford it," I insisted, my voice firm. The large, ugly figures on my monitor still stared at me. "Maybe in a quarter or two, once I sort out the budget. Until then, we have to stick to basics."

"Right, basics. I get it. But when things go south, you know who they'll blame, right?"

"Of course they will blame me," I snapped, frustration boiling over. "But I'm doing my job, unlike some people who think life is just one endless beach day!"

He stared hard at me, all traces of charm gone. "I take my job seriously, which you would know if you ever came by the dive shop. Believe it or not, people can have fun and be good at what they do. Which is how I know that old, outdated dive computers are a problem."

I sighed and rubbed my forehead. "I understand that. But can't you just use those... pressure gauge things for a few more months?"

"Oh sure. Why don't we just use horse collars instead of BCDs while we're at it?"

I blinked, the reference sailing right over my head. My lips pressed into a thin line. Every discussion I had with this man was a battle. "What does that even mean? I have better things to do than argue with you, Eli."

He shrugged, feigning nonchalance. "I'm just saying, if we keep using outdated gear, we'll be stuck in the past. And our guests will move on. Somewhere else."

"Maybe if you focused on numbers instead of jokes, we wouldn't be having this conversation." The words slipped out before I could stop them. I hated how he had this ability to unravel my focus.

"Numbers, right. The ever-comforting embrace of spreadsheets." He glanced around my office, taking in the happy green plant and my meticulously organized bookcase. He cocked his head to the side as his eyes stopped on a shelf, puzzlement appearing in his lowered brows. "Why do you have old copies of *Robinson Crusoe* and *Journey to the Center of the Earth*? Planning an escape? Works for me."

"Those b-books are classics," I shot back defensively,

my cheeks warming despite myself. Now I was completely flummoxed. I stood and drew myself up to my full height, which wasn't very impressive compared to his. Dammit. "And I enjoy a good adventure."

"Yeah. Sure you do." His laughter rang out, rich and teasing, and my anger flared hot.

"Don't mock me, Eli."

"Wasn't mocking. Just calling it like I see it. You, an adventurer? You're more like a… what's the term?" His eyes lit up with victory as he leaned in, his face insufferably smug. "A safety net enthusiast."

"Excuse me for wanting to ensure financial stability!" I nearly shouted, my hands clenching into fists. "This resort is barely afloat!"

"Right. Because investing in better dive gear is such a wild risk." His tone shifted, frustration creeping into his words as he rose to his feet. "It's not like I want to provide the best experience for our guests or anything. Perish the thought."

"Experience doesn't come before budget!" I snapped, reeling from the heat rising in my chest. I couldn't believe I was getting worked up like this. This ridiculously handsome guy standing in front of me—the same one who made everyone laugh—was a complete ass when it came to serious matters. And only I seemed to notice that. It wasn't like I was intentionally denying his request. As much as I despised Eli Coleridge, the dive operation was actually helping our bottom line. But people seemed to have the idea that I could conjure money out of thin air, and it didn't work like that. I took a deep breath and composed myself. "I can't approve your request at this time."

"Fine." He crossed his arms and squarely faced me. "So when exactly will you work this expense into my budget? When hell freezes over?"

"That's not fair."

"Yeah, but—"

"Look, Eli," I interrupted, forcing calmness into my voice. "We can't afford new dive computers right now. Not ever if things keep going like this."

"Whatever you say, Julianne." His face was icy, his eyes narrowed. "Guess I'll just make do with what we've got. Freaking gauges. Perfect."

"Thank you." I nodded, feeling both victorious and frustrated. And guilty.

"Wish me luck," he snarled before turning toward the door. It rattled in its frame after he slammed it shut behind him.

I jumped, placing a hand against my chest. Seeing it trembling, I scowled and flopped down into my chair and studied the spreadsheets before me. Each row and column was a stark black-and-white reminder of our precarious financial situation. My stomach twisted at denying him a reasonable request, but it didn't matter. The resort's future depended on rational decisions, not impulsive purchases.

I glanced at the clock and was relieved to find less than an hour left of my shift. Dinner with my best friend Lacey loomed on the horizon like a beacon, promising laughter and distraction from the frustration of my day. I had always appreciated her flighty nature, a refreshing contrast to my own rigid tendencies. Lacey drifted through life like a dandelion seed in the wind, while I was anchored to solid ground. With a long, extra-deep breath, I shoved Eli Coleridge from my mind and turned my attention back to the financial reports.

Two hours later, I stepped into Conch Republic Brewpub, the familiar scent of yeasty beer and French fries wafting through the air like an old friend. The place buzzed with chatter and laughter, a lively mix of locals and tourists soaking up the island vibe. Exposed ductwork and worn wooden planks enhanced the feel of the converted cannery. It felt good to be surrounded by a sense of community rather than isolation.

"Jules!" Lacey Ashworth's voice cut through the bustling noise, drawing my attention. She beckoned from a cozy corner table, her sun-bleached blonde hair catching the light. A smile raised my lips as I made my way over, and the weight of my encounter with Eli lifted with each step. The server approached, balancing a tray with two frosted beers that Lacey had already ordered, setting them down before us.

"Hey, Lacey! After today, a drink sounds absolutely divine," I remarked with a grateful sigh as I settled into the chair opposite her. We clinked our glasses together and took a healthy sip of the brew made on the premises. After smacking my lips, I inquired about our favorite topic —the progress of her wedding plans. As her maid of honor, I needed to keep on top of the ever-changing details.

"It's all absolutely fabulous!" she exclaimed, her brown eyes sparkling. "Daniel has been such a sweetheart about everything. You know how he is, always looking for ways to surprise me."

"Surprise? As in keeping you on your toes?" I tilted my head, knowing Lacey well enough to anticipate a whirlwind of ideas.

"Exactly! At first, we wanted an outdoor ceremony right on the beach at sunset." She leaned closer, her voice dropping to a conspiratorial whisper. "And then a reception under twinkling lights with tropical cocktails! Doesn't that sound dreamy, Jules?"

"Extremely," I replied as I pictured the admittedly lovely scene. Being a CPA, I also pictured the bill. Lacey and I had had several conversations about how to keep their big event from bleeding them dry and looked at several venues. But she needed to book something soon.

"But wait until you hear the idea he mentioned the other day."

"Okay, I'm listening." I braced myself for whatever wild idea was coming next.

"He was talking about wanting to learn scuba diving, and my mind just took off! How about an underwater wedding ceremony?" Her eyes widened with glee as if she'd just discovered a hidden treasure.

"Underwater?" I repeated, wanting to confirm I had heard correctly.

"Yes! On scuba. Doesn't that sound incredible? Think of the stories we'd have."

Diving was something I had wanted to do since moving to Dove Key but had never gotten around to. Lacey wasn't certified either. "It's certainly an unusual idea. How is that going to work?"

"Everyone in the wedding party would need scuba certification, which is perfect considering you work with the best dive instructor on the island!" Lacey clapped her hands, delighting in her own brilliance.

"Best dive instructor?" I repeated absently, my stomach already plummeting to the floor.

"Of course! Chase has told me over and over what an amazing teacher Eli is."

"Right," I muttered. "He's an amazing asshole. That's what he is."

She frowned but was too excited for the expression to

last. "Oh, stop it. We live on a tropical island! I think we have an obligation as locals to know how to scuba dive."

Before I could say anything else, a shadow fell over us as someone walked by. Chase and Eli strolled past our table, their casual talk rising above the lively hum until Eli's voice stopped suddenly. His gaze sliced through the air like a sharp knife. The moment our eyes met, that familiar irritation surged within me, amplifying the pulse in my temples. His furious glare was completely at odds with his usual expression and took me aback for a moment. Eyes pinned to me and hard enough to wound, he remained silent as he strolled on, completely ignoring Lacey.

"Good evening, ladies," Chase said, stopping mid-stride. He flashed his easy smile, completely oblivious to the charged atmosphere spiraling around me. "How are my lovely sister and her BFF doing tonight?"

"Fantastic," Lacey drawled at him.

He turned to me. "Jules?"

"Don't call me that!" I hissed, panic fluttering in my chest. I craned my neck to look around his large form, where Eli was sliding into a booth on the other side of the room. That made me feel a little better. "Don't call me Jules around him!"

"Seriously?" Chase rolled his eyes, crossing his arms in disbelief. "You're making too much of it. You always have. It's just a nickname."

"Easy for you to say. You're not the one who'll have to endure endless taunting from Mr. Comedy over there." I felt ridiculous pleading with Chase, but there was no way I would allow Eli to turn my nickname into fodder for his relentless teasing. Jules was reserved strictly for friends, not business associates. And absolutely not for enemy dive instructors. "It's Julianne around Eli, okay?"

"It's hard to call you Julianne," he added with a frown. "You don't even seem like a Julianne."

I paused, because what was I? A responsible, serious accountant? An uptight librarian-type who only found adventure in books? I had no idea, but I certainly wasn't ready to embrace any part of me that might make Eli smirk. "You've managed it quite well for years, Chase. Keep up the good work."

"Okay, okay!" Chase held up his hands in mock defeat. "I won't say a word. Just chill, will you? I'm going to grab a seat before Eli thinks I ditched him."

"Thanks." I forced a smile before he turned away. He settled across from Eli, and a wave of frustration crashed over me. I turned back to Lacey, who was sipping her beer with an innocent look on her face.

"There!" I snapped and pointed at their table. "Now do you understand why we need to find another instructor? Did you see that look Eli shot me? It was like I had just set fire to his favorite wetsuit."

She waved her hand at me casually. "That was nothing. Eli is the obvious choice, and he'll be flattered to do it, I'm sure. All you need to do is ask him, okay?"

"I'd rather eat a ten-course meal of crushed glass and kerosene."

Lacey shrugged, her attitude unwavering. "Let me point out that you're my maid of honor. It's practically your job to make my wildest dreams come true."

"Sure, because that's how weddings work."

"Exactly! So we're settled then?"

I leaned forward. "Hell no! Why me? Chase is your brother and Eli's best friend. Why can't he ask Eli?"

"Chase isn't even in the wedding party, silly," she chirped, unfazed by my irritation. Her enthusiasm was usually infectious, but right now, it felt anything but.

"Which leaves you, my dear. And I know you want to help."

"Right," I grumbled, shoving a lock of hair behind my ear. As soon as I'd left the resort, I'd unwound my bun to let my hair fall over my shoulders. "This is less about help and more about me being thrown into shark-infested waters. Lacey, we hate each other!"

"Daniel loves the idea of an underwater ceremony," Lacey continued, her tone sweetly persuasive. "You know how much he adores the ocean. This will make him so happy, and besides, it's not like you'll be spending a lot of time with Eli. Just think of it as a fun adventure."

"Adventure?" I repeated, my voice dripping with sarcasm. "You mean torture?"

"Come on, Jules. Please?" She clasped her hands together, her expression earnest. "We're talking about my wedding here! It would mean so much to Daniel. And to me."

I sighed, helpless to resist those puppy-dog eyes and knowing when I was beat. "All right. I'll ask Eli about the dive certification, but I need to figure out how to approach him without getting into another argument. Maybe I should wear combat gear or something."

"Yay!" Lacey squealed, her delight ringing like a bell.

I couldn't help smiling, wondering just how many more surprises awaited us on this journey to her big day. And how I was going to survive Eli as my instructor.

# Chapter Three

# ELI

I'D LEFT the windows open in the dive classroom to let in the morning breeze. I moved with purpose, my fingers deftly arranging scuba gear on the long table standing at the front of the room. Tanks gleamed like polished treasures, each one waiting for a new adventure beneath the waves. I double-checked the straps on the buoyancy control devices, methodically checking every inch. This wasn't just my job. It was pure passion, a love letter to the ocean that had always been my home.

But even as I focused on the equipment, my mind drifted back to two nights ago at Conch Republic when I'd walked by Lacey and Julianne's table. Despite being mad as hell at her and not trusting myself to speak, I'd noticed her, all right. How her dark hair flowed freely over her shoulders for once instead of the tight bun, framing green eyes. Dressed casually in a white sleeveless blouse, she looked damn attractive, almost disarming. I would have never admitted it to anyone, but I couldn't help noticing how gorgeous she was when she let her guard down.

How different.

That thought made my stomach sour and I scowled. She didn't deserve my admiration. Not after what happened with the dive computers. They were a vital piece of equipment that I *needed*, and now I was out of ideas on how to get them. I'd set up the rental gear with the old dive gauge consoles that morning—each twist of my wrench a reminder of her role in this mess.

But Julianne was the last thing I should be thinking about. Hell, I didn't even like thinking about her. So I grabbed a clipboard and jotted down notes for this morning's scuba lesson plan, trying to push aside the simmering irritation. In front of me, rows of sturdy plastic chairs faced the front of the room behind tables, each one positioned for optimal viewing of the whiteboard, where I'd scrawled my class notes and the upcoming schedule. A tall bookcase stood against one wall, filled with fish identification books and scuba certification course packs.

Just then, the familiar ring of the dive shop bell above the glass entry door broke my concentration. I perked up, recognizing Harper's voice mingling with my nephew Finn's excited chatter. I stepped out of the classroom and into the main dive shop area, the vibrant aquamarine walls greeting me like an old friend.

"Guess who just got a new mask?" Five-year-old Finn's voice rang out, filled with glee.

"Let me see it!" I called out as I entered the large room. "Uncle Eli needs to make sure it passes muster."

I leaned against the glass counter as Finn handed me a neon green mask. Like his mother, his hair was medium brown with a light wave, but his eyes were blue instead of brown.

"I don't remember discussing this purchase, Finn," I teased, but a quick inspection revealed it was solid quality. "Did you get a mask without my okay?"

"Yep, Mom surprised me with it today," he declared, spinning around like an underwater superhero before stopping in front of a wall of fins. He picked one up and turned it around in his hands. The sight warmed something in my chest. He reminded me so much of myself as a kid, filled with wild dreams and boundless energy.

"Island Market had them on closeout, and I couldn't resist," Harper added with a smile and a shrug.

As I nodded and handed the mask to her, I caught sight of my mother entering the shop. She surveyed the area, her silver-streaked auburn hair swaying slightly as she moved. Her warm brown eyes scanned the racks of gear. "Everything looks great, Eli. You really kept this place organized."

"Thanks, Mom. That's the idea." I flashed her a smile, but I wondered at the flicker of concern in her gaze.

"Diving is the one area of his life he doesn't allow to fall to rack and ruin," Harper added with a broad grin.

I reached up to scratch my cheek with my middle finger and her smile widened.

"Do you need anything before your class?" Mom asked, still studying the shelves lined with BCDs.

"Nope. I think I'm good."

"Good to hear." She smiled, but I could tell her mind was somewhere else entirely.

"Can we snorkel now? Can we, can we?" Finn tugged at Harper's arm, his excitement bubbling over like a shaken soda can ready to explode.

"Soon, okay?" Harper kneeled to meet his eager eyes.

Finn took the mask from her and slipped it over his eyes, pretending to peer into the depths of the ocean as he twirled around once more in front of a wall with an aquatic scene painted on it. This was what diving was all about—freedom, exploration, being part of something totally unknown to most people.

"All right, little explorer," I said. "You'll make a fantastic diver one day."

"I know!" he shouted, puffing out his chest proudly. "I've got you to teach me."

"That's my man." I turned to Harper. "Escaping the lobby this morning?"

Her smile faltered as she straightened up and brushed a few strands of hair off her forehead. "Yeah. A guest complained about a pothole in the parking lot, so I had to get a repair lined up. We need to grade the whole thing. Or better yet, pave it."

"Sometimes it feels like we're stuck between a rock and a hard place," Mom added quietly, folding her arms across her chest.

"Maybe we just need to find a balance," I suggested, trying to play peacemaker. "We don't have to change everything. But… a little upgrade wouldn't hurt, right?"

"Fixing potholes, yes. But upgrades wipe out history," Mom replied, her tone measured.

"They can, but we can't be afraid of progress," Harper interjected gently. "The world is changing. We have to adapt or risk losing what we love."

"I agree. But at what cost?" Mom's voice dropped, almost wistful. The familiar clash brewed between them, each holding tight to their beliefs. Mom had been at the reins of the resort since our dad walked out nearly two decades ago, leaving all of us behind. It had been a terrible time, but we'd pulled together as a family and persevered.

I wanted to support Harper's vision for a modernized resort, but honoring Mom's attachment to our roots weighed heavily on me. She was our rock and anything that stressed her out made me worry.

The dive shop door opened again, and an excited trio stepped through, my students. All three pairs of eyes were filled with excitement, which was what I liked to see.

"We'll let you go, Eli." Harper placed a hand on my shoulder before she, Finn, and Mom headed toward the door. She turned her smile to the prospective divers. "Have fun, guys. You're learning from the best."

"All right, team! Welcome to the dive shop!" I called. "Today, we're going to explore the basics of scuba diving in our first classroom session. By the end of our class, you'll all be ready to take the plunge. Literally!"

Laughter sounded from my students as we headed to the classroom. I grinned, the rush of adrenaline kicking in. Forget the parking lot debates. Right now, it was all about the ocean and sharing that love with others. With my family fading into the background, I focused on my role as an instructor—a task that brought clarity. And there was nothing better than the sound of laughter and the promise of adventure ahead.

LATER THAT AFTERNOON, I was alone in the shop and working on dive trip assignments for my two divemasters and myself. Though I taught a fair amount of the time, I never missed the opportunity to lead dives on our daily two-tank trips for certified divers. The hum of the air conditioner filled the dive shop as I typed away. I assigned myself my fair share of beginner groups. I never made my divemasters take the newbies while I cherry-picked the experienced divers.

But my focus shattered like glass when the door opened. I raised my head, expecting another eager student or perhaps Finn looking for an excuse to try out his new snorkeling gear.

Instead, Julianne stepped in.

She hesitated at the threshold, her navy pencil skirt and fitted white button-down contrasting starkly against the backdrop of wetsuits and colorful snorkels hanging from the walls. Her eyes darted quickly around the room before settling on me. She took a deep breath and quietly shut the door behind her before walking along the wall of fins. Hands clasped behind her back, she inspected them closely.

"Julianne." I tried to inject some levity into the air, thick with sudden tension. "Lost your way to a board meeting?"

"Very funny."

"Can I help you with something, or did you come to deny me something else?" I waved a hand toward the neatly arranged dive gear.

"No denials today." She strode toward me, the heels of her shoes clicking against the non-slip floor, each sound echoing like a reminder of our different worlds colliding. "Um. Yeah. I need to discuss your upcoming class schedule."

That floored me. "Really? You know you can't dive in a business suit, right?"

She glared at me, and I sent back a blinding smile, knowing it would irritate her more. I was right. Her eyes narrowed and she opened her mouth. But before she could say anything, she snapped it shut and took a big breath.

"Thank you for the information. I am aware." Her voice was steady but held an edge that hinted at her discomfort. She remained quiet, shifting from one foot to the other, and I was both intrigued and tempted to mess with her. It was like watching a fish swim against the current. She was trying to navigate, yet clearly struggling.

"Well"—I broke the silence— "as much fun as it is chatting with you, let's get down to business. What do you need from me?"

"I need to talk to you about Lacey's wedding plans," she said haltingly.

I wasn't sure I'd heard her correctly. "Come again?"

Her face flushed scarlet. "You know who I'm talking about. Chase is your best friend."

"Yesss," I drawled. "But I'm having a difficult time figuring out what any of that has to do with me. Or my dive class calendar."

Julianne primly laced her fingers together in front of her. "Lacey and Daniel have decided on an underwater wedding. The wedding party—four of us, that is—all need to get certified to dive."

"What? You're in Lacey's wedding?" Chase had never mentioned anything about that to me. But then again, why would he? I was there to listen to him bitch about the wedding, not get the finer points of it.

She took a big step forward to stand on the other side of the glass counter, her eyes blazing. "Is it so impossible to imagine that I have a friend? Or that she wants me to be her maid of honor?"

Frankly, it was hard to believe, but I managed to wrangle my mouth into not saying that. "I guess not. You caught me off guard, okay?" Then it dawned on me why she was here, and my eyes went wide. "Hold on. Do you want *me* to certify you guys?"

"You're the natural choice," she asserted as she fidgeted with the hem of her sleeve.

"Natural choice, huh?" I leaned forward, unable to

resist a smug smile. "So you're finally admitting my exceptional diving skills?"

"Very funny." She shifted from foot to foot, and I tried not to notice how her high heels showed off her legs. "The wedding is important to Lacey, so we all have to get certified. And Chase has assured her you are the only guy for the job, damn him."

"Right, because nothing says romance like bobbing around in the ocean with a tank on your back." I laughed, getting ready to refuse. There were plenty of instructors around. Calypso Key Resort came to mind first. I was about to tell her to try her luck there because I'd rather certify a thirty-foot great white shark than her when my mind exploded with the most brilliant idea I'd ever had. It was the answer to my prayers. I struggled to keep an even expression. "Let's say I agree to do it."

She nodded. "Thank y—"

"I'm not done yet," I interrupted. "If I do this favor for you, I expect you to do one for me. Quid pro quo. Got it?"

Her brows drew together, suspicion flashing in those bright green eyes. "What do you want?"

"You know what I want. Approval for my new dive computers." The wicked grin finally escaped to spread across my face. "You sign off on them, and I'll give you guys, including the bride and groom, a thorough course on how to properly sink at their own wedding."

"How dare you!" Her face turned beet red, which only made me smile more. "You should be happy to do this. It's your job, Eli!"

I shrugged, leaning back again and folding my arms. "Think of it as a win-win. You get a certified wedding party, and I get my shiny new gear. What do you say?"

"You're unbelievable," she replied, staring at me like my head was covered in slime.

"Only in the best way," I quipped, relishing the moment. "C'mon, it's practically destiny. Underwater weddings need certified divers, and I need dive computers to keep my operation afloat. I'll even volunteer to keep a watchful eye from afar during the ceremony to make sure no one freaks out. We both know I'm the best man for the job."

She actually bared her teeth at me. The weight of her decision hung in the balance, and I was dying to find out if she'd say yes or no. As much as it killed me to stay silent, I kept my mouth tightly closed.

"Is that all this is to you? A business transaction? You've known Lacey for years! I would think decency alone would make you thrilled to help!" She parked both hands on her hips, and I had to admit the flush on her face didn't detract from her looks at all. I had known Lacey since she was a grasshopper, but I'd never paid her much attention or cared at all about her friends.

I met Julianne's furious gaze head-on, not giving in. "Four certifications in exchange for ten new dive computers. Take it or leave it."

Her eyes narrowed, and for a moment, I thought she might actually explode. "You are such a complete, manipulative asshole!" she spat, her voice rising as she took a step closer. "You'll stoop to anything to get your way, won't you? This isn't just about equipment for you—it's about power. You know how important this wedding is to Lacey, and yet here you are, holding it hostage like some kind of pirate."

I lifted one shoulder, feigning innocence. "Pirate? That's a little dramatic, don't you think?"

"Dramatic?" Her hands shot up in exasperation. "You're using my best friend's wedding as leverage! And your best friend's sister. What kind of person treats their friends like bargaining chips?"

I didn't respond, keeping my arms crossed tightly over my chest. Her words stung more than I wanted to admit. But I couldn't back down now. Not when I had her right where I wanted her.

"Go to hell, Eli!" Julianne spun around with military precision, and her heels echoed in the room as she stormed out of the dive shop.

# Chapter Four

# JULES

THE EVENING SUN illuminated the open-plan living area of my townhouse in hues of amber and gold. I smoothed a nonexistent wrinkle from my soft-gray linen sofa, my gaze sweeping over the organized bookshelves and the tasteful beach accents that adorned the walls. Everything in its place, just as I liked it. The residential district of Dove Key was in the northwestern section of the island, which made for an easy commute to work, even if I couldn't afford an oceanview home.

A rapid series of knocks at the door broke my moment of quiet contemplation.

"Jules! Open up!" Lacey's muffled voice called from the other side.

I barely had time to turn the handle before she burst in, a whirlwind of blonde hair and infectious enthusiasm. "Oh my God, I can't believe we're doing this! How did it go with Eli? When do the lessons start? I need to know everything!"

I forced a smile, trying to match her excitement. "Hello to you too, Lacey. Why don't we sit down first with a glass of wine?"

She bounced on her toes, following me to the kitchen. "Sorry, I'm just so pumped! This is going to be amazing."

"Glad one of us thinks so," I muttered under my breath, reaching for a bottle of Pinot Grigio. As I poured two generous glasses, a twinge of guilt pinched at my conscience. Two drinking sessions in one week? Not a regular occurrence for me, and something else I could lay right at the door of Eli Coleridge.

"What was that?" Lacey asked, accepting her glass.

I shook my head. "Nothing. Let's head out to the patio."

We settled into the wicker chairs on my covered rear patio, the salt-tinged breeze ruffling the potted palms that lined the space. Lacey took a sip of wine, her eyes dancing with anticipation. "So spill! When do we start?"

I swirled the wine in my glass, buying time. "About that… there might be a slight hiccup."

Lacey's face fell. "What? Why? Jules, you know how important this is for the wedding!"

"I know, I know." I pinched the bridge of my nose. "It's just, uh, I may have had a bit of a disagreement with our esteemed dive instructor."

"Disagreement?" Lacey's eyebrows shot up. "What happened?"

I took a long sip of wine before answering. "We got into a fight. He agreed to do the class only if I approve his requisition for new dive computers. Expensive ones."

At first, she just stared at me, then she bit the side of her cheek. I narrowed my eyes at her, but she finally couldn't keep her laugh inside. "Really? That sounds like Eli."

"It's not funny!"

She chewed on her lip. "It kind of is."

"He was dead serious when he gave me his ultimatum. Not amused in the slightest."

"Well, new computers don't sound so bad," Lacey said, becoming serious again. "Don't we need those for diving anyway?"

I set my glass down with more force than necessary. "That's not the point. It's the way he went about it. He's trying to manipulate me, Lacey. Hell, he's blackmailing me! Using you and your wedding as leverage."

"Yeah, you two have always been oil and water. But, Jules," Lacey leaned forward, her voice taking on a pleading tone, "if he needs them for safety—"

"I know the equipment is justified," I cut her off, my frustration climbing to the surface. "But the resort's finances are already stretched thin. We can't just throw money around because some charming dive bum bats his eyelashes."

Lacey's lips twitched. "Charming, huh?"

Heat crept up my neck. "That's not... I didn't mean—"

"Uh-huh." Lacey grinned, clearly enjoying my discomfort. "So what exactly happened with this charming dive bum?"

I sighed, slumping back in my chair. "I stormed out on him."

Lacey's eyes widened. "Jules!"

"I know, I know." I groaned, covering my face with my hands. "It didn't go at all like I'd planned. But you should have seen him, Lace. All smug, then serious, acting like he had me over a barrel."

"Didn't he, though?" Lacey asked gently. "I mean, we do need those certifications for the wedding."

I lowered my hands, meeting her gaze. The excitement in her eyes had dimmed, replaced by a mixture of concern and disappointment that made my chest ache. I'd known Lacey since moving here seven years ago. She'd been there through every up and down, always my steadfast cheerleader. And now, when she needed me the most, I was letting my own hang-ups get in the way. "Why can't we just get certified by someone else? There are loads of dive shops around!"

Lacey's face clouded. "Honestly? Because even though Eli comes across as a goofy slacker sometimes, I trust him. I've known him since I was a little kid. I'm not sure I'm going to be real great at this scuba thing, Jules. And I want to learn from someone I know, not a stranger."

That tugged on my heartstrings. "You'll do great at this, though the person you just described doesn't sound anything at all like the Eli Coleridge I know."

She tilted her head to one side and regarded me seriously. "Maybe that's because you don't really know him. Jules, please talk to him again. It's not like he's asking for complete new sets of scuba gear."

"Yeah, I guess it could be worse," I admitted, then reached over to squeeze her hand. "You'll have your underwater wedding. I'll figure something out in the budget, Lace. I promise."

Lacey beamed at me. "I know you will. You always do."

I managed a weak smile, even as my mind raced with the implications. How was I going to justify this expense? Especially when other repairs were needed too?

And more importantly, how was I going to face Eli again and agree to his demands without throttling him?

"So"—Lacey's voice pulled me back, a mischievous glint in her eye as she held out her empty glass—"tell me more about how charming you suddenly find Eli. I've known him for a long time, you know. He's not such a bad-looking guy."

"Don't even start with that." I groaned, reaching for the wine bottle. It was going to be a long night.

---

THE NEXT AFTERNOON, I sat in my office at Sunset Siesta, staring at the quarterly budget. I'd been crunching numbers all morning, trying to find a way to justify the expense of new dive computers without completely derailing our budget. Dammit, delaying my new desktop was not an option. I'd waited too long for it. After combing through several resort departments, I found a way to depreciate some assets and move some debits forward. I blew a big sigh of relief.

Raised voices from Harper's office next door jolted me out of my financial fugue state.

"Mom, we can't keep putting this off!" Harper's exasperated tone carried clearly through the thin walls.

"I know that, so let's grade the parking lot. But where do you suggest we get the money for these renovations you want?" Helen's voice was sharp.

I winced, shrinking lower in my chair. This was exactly the kind of argument I'd been dreading.

"Maybe if we actually invested in some upgrades, we'd attract more guests," Harper shot back. "We can't keep relying on nostalgia forever."

"I understand that. But we have to find balance with what we decide to repair."

I closed my eyes. The Coleridges' argument felt like a perfect metaphor for the war raging inside my own head. Tradition versus progress. Safety versus risk. The irritating devil I knew versus the very talented dive instructor I kept hearing about but had never seen a glimpse of.

"Lupe came to me this afternoon with the name of the housekeeper I'd requested," Harper said in a quieter voice. "After last month's numbers, I had to do something. So we'll cut Annie's hours and housekeeping will just have to stretch."

I buried my head in my hands. Annie was a sweet young woman who loved her job. She was a bright ray of sunshine, shining on everyone she came in contact with. Even me. I stared at my old monitor, the keyboard with its lettering rubbed off on the home row. And there was no contest. Annie had a young child to support. I opened the budget projection spreadsheet again to rework the figures. My new computer could wait.

"Oh, Harper," Helen said gently. "I know this is the worst part of the job. I've done it myself. But you don't have to talk to Annie tonight."

Harper's voice softened. "No, you're right. It's the end of the day. Let's put work aside and make dinner together."

"That's my girl. You take too much on, sweetie. Let's collect Finn and we can make fish and chips. He loves that."

As their voices faded down the hallway, I slumped forward, resting my forehead on my folded arms. How was I supposed to justify Eli's expensive toys when we couldn't even afford basic maintenance? When we were cutting staff hours?

"This isn't about me and Eli," I murmured to myself as I lifted myself upright again. I stared at my ancient monitor, resignation settling within me. "It's about taking care of others. Like Annie and like Lacey. I'm helping a friend out. That's all. This old computer will limp along another few quarters, and I can put up with Eli for a couple of weeks."

But I couldn't quite silence the traitorous little voice in the back of my mind whispering that this felt very personal indeed. Hearing the two women leave provided an unwelcome reminder that the day was drawing to a close. I had been avoiding the conversation with Eli all day, but now I was out of excuses. With a resigned sigh, I pushed my chair back.

"Guess it's time to face the firing squad."

The walk to the pier felt interminable, giving me plenty of time to repeat to myself that I wasn't going to let Eli affect me or get me riled up. As I passed the two hotel room blocks, their cinderblock walls painted a cheerful seafoam green, I couldn't appreciate the tropical vibe. Vines of bougainvillea cascaded over railings, splashes of magenta contrasting with the soft greens of palm fronds swaying gently overhead.

As usual, the pool area was busy with once vibrant but now faded umbrellas dotting the sun-soaked deck. Sunbathers lounged on chaise lounges, sipping fruity cocktails garnished with mini umbrellas. A group of teenagers dove off the diving board with gleeful shrieks, their laughter echoing against the backdrop of soft reggae music drifting from Tidal Hops. Each step I took heightened the knot of tension coiled in my gut and finally I climbed the three short steps onto the pier and marched down its length to face my doom. As I neared the end of the faded but solid wooden structure, I froze.

Eli was hosing down *Sunset Diver*. Shirtless. His broad, muscled back glistened with a light sheen of sweat as he carefully swept the deck of the boat clean from saltwater and accumulated debris from the day.

I swallowed hard, telling myself that hot flush creeping

over my skin was just the sun. "Oh, for heaven's sake," I muttered and marched forward. I stepped onto the fiber-glass boat, hoping he wouldn't blast me with the hose. "Eli!"

He turned, flashing that infuriating grin as he blessedly shut off the water. "Julianne. To what do I owe the pleasure?"

I pointedly averted my gaze from his very defined chest and abs. "You can start by putting a shirt on. We need to discuss business."

Eli held that sunny smile as he reached for a nearby staff T-shirt. "As you wish, boss."

"I'm not your boss," I snapped, then exhaled a long breath through my teeth. So much for him not affecting me.

"Could've fooled me," he replied, pulling the shirt over his head. "So what's on your mind? Come to tell me how much you're looking forward to our dive class?"

I took a deep breath, steeling myself. "I've decided to approve the purchase of new dive computers."

Eli's eyebrows shot up, genuine surprise crossing his face before morphing into that insufferable smirk. "Well, well. Look who came around."

"Don't get cocky," I warned, my jaw clenching. "This isn't a blank check."

"Hey, I'll take what I can get." He held up his hands in mock surrender. "So are you excited to get your feet wet? Literally?"

I narrowed my eyes, fighting the urge to roll them. "Let's not get ahead of ourselves. I'm doing a favor for my best friend. That's all."

Eli leaned against a raised platform in the rear part of the boat, crossing his arms casually. The movement drew my attention to his biceps, and I quickly snapped my gaze back to his face. His grin widened as if he'd caught me looking. Damn him.

"Come on," he cajoled. "Admit it. You're at least a little excited about learning to dive."

I scoffed, ignoring the tiny flicker of anticipation in my chest. "I'm excited about maintaining our resort's reputation and keeping my best friend's wedding on track. Nothing more. Certainly not being around you any more than absolutely necessary."

"If you say so," Eli replied, his tone light. "But I bet I can change your mind once I get you in the water. Diving is irresistible, and with me there, you can double that."

The casual confidence in his voice sent an unexpected ripple through me. I tamped it down, reminding myself of the headaches this man had caused me.

"When can we start the class?" I inquired, my tone filled with a touch of impatience I couldn't quite conceal.

Eli paused to think about it for a moment. "I've got some availability opening up next week if that suits you."

I gave a brisk nod, maintaining my professional demeanor. "That's fine. Lacey and Daniel are eager to start. And Daniel's best man, Randy, will be joining us also. I'll make sure the schedule works. The sooner we start, the sooner we'll finish."

Eli's grin widened, and dammit if he didn't have a dimple on his right cheek that only appeared when he smiled. "Aye aye, captain. Promise I'll be on my best behavior."

I found myself fighting a smile of my own. No, absolutely not. I would not let this infuriating man charm me. "We'll see about that." I stood squarely and inhaled a deep breath of the salty air, determined to regain control of the situation. "About the lessons. I expect nothing but the most professional instruction. This isn't some beach party, Mr. Coleridge."

Eli's eyes sparkled as he nodded. "Of course. I promise you the best certification class ever. You'll be a pro in no time."

I raised an eyebrow, skeptical. "That remains to be seen."

"Oh, ye of little faith." He laughed lightly as he bent over to swoop up a wetsuit. "Trust me, by the time we're done, you'll be as comfortable in the water as you are crunching numbers."

The mental image of myself gliding effortlessly through crystal-clear waters was admittedly appealing. But I squashed that thought immediately. This was business, nothing more.

"Speaking of numbers," I said, my accountant's instincts kicking in, "let's talk dive computers. I need you to choose something practical and affordable. Think Honda, not Lexus. Ten of them maximum. Is that understood?"

"I can work with that. Sometimes the top of the line isn't the best, especially for rental gear." His tone had become less arrogant and more approachable. "I'll find us the most reliable, cost-effective option out there. No flashy bells and whistles, just good, solid tech."

His easy compliance surprised me. I'd been prepared for an argument, for more of his usual charm offensive. This cooperation was unexpected.

"Good," I managed. "Send me the receipt after you order them."

"Consider it done," Eli said with a mock salute that should have been irritating but somehow wasn't. "Anything else?"

I shook my head, suddenly eager to escape before I did

something ridiculous like actually smile at him. "That's all. Good night, then."

As I walked away, he called out, "Sweet dreams, Julianne! Don't forget to pack that sense of adventure you told me about for our first lesson!"

Ignoring him, I quickened my pace. I strode down from the pier, my heels clicking against the wooden planks with a rhythm that matched my pulsing heartbeat. The breeze whipped tendrils of hair free from my bun, and I resisted the urge to glance back at Eli.

I paused at the edge of the beach, kicked off my pumps, and sank my toes into the cooling sand. The setting sun painted the sky in brilliant oranges and pinks, but I barely noticed, too caught up in my swirling thoughts.

"Why do I let him press my buttons?" I muttered to myself, trying to figure out why he made me so flustered. "It only encourages him. I need to work on that, or this will be a complete disaster."

I huffed in frustration, then vowed to study all the class materials in depth. That way I could minimize interacting with Eli and giving him any more material to use against me. Obviously, the two of us were a combustible mixture and I had to be careful. I bent to pick up my shoes. As I straightened, I caught sight of Eli in the distance, his tall frame silhouetted against the colorful sky. He was still watching me.

I quickly turned away. It was going to be a long few weeks.

# Chapter Five

## ELI

I OFTEN KEPT the windows open in my bungalow. Dove Key had very little crime and I didn't have much worth stealing. My slice of heaven was a two-bedroom oasis of sun-bleached wood and faded beach landscapes. Grabbing a mug of fresh coffee, I headed to my makeshift office—a sturdy mahogany desk I'd salvaged from a local shipyard. The rich wood bore the marks of its maritime past, and it was one of my few treasures.

"All right, then," I muttered, sorting through four neatly stacked piles on the desktop. "Let's get you guys ready to dive."

I carefully packed each student's materials into zippered pouches—textbooks, handouts, and thumb drives loaded with both the required video from the certification agency along with informal videos of me demonstrating skills underwater. Maybe I went a bit overboard sometimes, but I wanted my students prepared.

I'd been pretty shocked when Julianne agreed to find

me the money for the dive computers. Her obvious discomfort at the transaction had almost made me feel sorry for standing my ground and being a dick about it. Almost.

But I was going to have a wonderful time burrowing under her skin for the next few weeks…

As I stuffed everything into my backpack, my eyes landed on an old family photo sitting on a battered set of shelves. From before the divorce. I quickly looked away. The picture of all six of us kids with both Mom and Dad was a reminder to me. A souvenir of happier times and a reminder that forever was for chumps.

I snagged my helmet and headed out. The morning air was thick with humidity and possibility as I hopped on my mountain bike. I always rode unless the weather was too awful. Pedaling down the sandy path, I let the joy of a tropical morning fill me. This was living—wind in my hair, sun on my face, heading toward a job I was born to do. I wove between palms, their fronds painting dappled shadows across the trail. In the distance, the ocean sparkled, already beckoning.

I rode through the bumpy parking lot of the resort, grateful for my bike's suspension and acknowledging that Harper might have a point about paving it. As I neared the pier, I dismounted and carried my bike up the three steps onto the structure. I walked it beside me as I headed down, then rested it against the wall at the back of the dive shop.

Walking to the front, I strode into the shop, and the familiar, sharp scent of neoprene greeted me. One of my divemasters, Andrea, was already hustling around, her curly brown ponytail bouncing as she checked in divers for the morning trip.

"Morning, boss," she called out, flashing me a grin. "Ready for another day in paradise?"

"You know it," I replied, tossing her a playful salute. "How're our divers looking today?"

Andrea jerked her thumb toward a group of excited resort guests gathered near the counter. "Raring to go."

I laughed, making my way over to the group. "Morning, folks! Who's ready to swim with the fishes today?"

A chorus of enthusiastic responses met my ears. I launched into my usual spiel, peppering it with jokes and reassurances. By the time I finished, even the nervous-looking diver was smiling. As I helped a couple adjust their masks, my mind wandered to the upcoming class. Julianne's stern face flashed in my mind, and I couldn't help but smirk. This was going to be fun. She always made me feel inadequate, like I couldn't measure up, and I was more than looking forward to being the professional between us for a change.

With the morning trip ready for success, I gave the guests a jaunty wave and headed toward the classroom. As I entered through the open door, the energy in the room hit me like a wave. Lacey was chattering excitedly to Daniel and Randy as they sat abreast behind one of the tables.

"Good morning, eager students," I announced, flashing my most charming smile. "Ready to take the plunge?"

Groom-to-be, Daniel Greene, and his best man, Randy, turned toward me. Daniel, his blue eyes alight, couldn't seem to stay still. "Man, we're so ready!" he exclaimed, his arm wrapped around Lacey. "I've always wanted to try diving. Not sure how practical an underwater wedding will be, but I aim to make my bride happy."

Randy, Daniel's slightly shorter friend and best man, nodded in agreement. The movement caused a lock of dark hair to fall forward, and he swept it back casually.

"Yeah, and Daniel here needs all the practice he can get before the big day. Can't have him floundering his way through, right?"

I laughed, appreciating their easy camaraderie. That made teaching much easier. "Don't worry, we'll have him diving like he was born doing it."

As I removed the class packs from my backpack and set them evenly on the table before me, Julianne's voice rang out. "Good morning, everyone." I glanced up, expecting to see her in her usual buttoned-up attire. Instead, my jaw nearly hit the floor.

She strolled in wearing a faded blue T-shirt and white cargo shorts, her black hair pulled back in a messy ponytail. Gone were the severe bun and crisp business attire. This Julianne looked… relaxed. Almost approachable. And her T-shirt and shorts were tight-fitting, enough for me to get a good hint that a gorgeous body lay underneath.

I blinked, trying to reconcile this image with the uptight accountant I'd been sparring with. "Well, well," I drawled, covering my surprise with a smirk. "Looks like someone got the *casual Friday* memo. Except it's Tuesday."

Julianne pursed her lips tightly. "It's called dressing appropriately for the activity, Coleridge. I'll change into work clothes afterward when I start my workday."

I glanced down at my own board shorts and light-blue Sunset Siesta Dive Team shirt, then back at her. "I'd say we're both nailing the dress code."

She took a seat next to Lacey. "At least you're on time."

I flashed a smile, happy for the opening. "I believe you were the last to arrive, not me."

Lacey held up a hand. "Knock it off, you two. Eli, I've known you for a long time, so don't think I won't call you on your bullshit."

"What bullshit?" I asked, full of wide eyes. "Did I lie?"

Lacey sighed. "I only meant it will be a very long class if you two snipe at each other the whole time. So call a truce, okay?" She stared straight at Julianne, who inclined her head.

"Agreed. Let's start, Eli."

She raised her head to meet my eyes, and for some reason, my heart skittered a little. Had her eyes always been that green? The conversation I'd had with a thoroughly irritated Harper yesterday flashed through my mind. I'd been bitching about having to certify Julianne and how it should be as much fun as a trip to the dentist when my sister had rounded on me.

"Eli, shut up. Maybe you don't know Julianne as well as you think."

I'd huffed. "I think I do. She's a neurotic miser who only cares about numbers. What else is there to know?"

"Did you know she deferred a new computer she's been wanting for several years so we don't have to cut Annie's hours? Does that sound like a dragon queen?"

I stood there completely speechless, which was new territory for me. Now I stared at this... almost easygoing Julianne, and I had to wonder if maybe there was more to our uptight accountant than met the eye.

Blinking, I handed out the four packets. "Let's dive in!"

I settled into my element, the familiar rhythm of teaching washing over me like the gentle waves lapping at our shores. "All right, folks, let's talk about the most crucial aspect of diving—buoyancy control."

My hands moved animatedly as I explained, my voice carrying the passion I felt for the underwater world. "Think of it as your superpower down there. You control it via your buoyancy compensation device." I moved to the table at the front of the classroom with a disassembled scuba kit neatly laid out in a row and lifted the vest-like

BCD with its interior air bladders. "Too much air in your BCD, and you're a cork shooting to the surface. Too little, and you're sinking like a stone."

I caught Julianne leaning forward, her eyes focused intently on me. I had emailed all of them an introductory document that listed some of the very basics of diving. Hardly anyone ever read the thing, but it was always a good idea to find out who my real, interested students were. "Now, who can tell me the first rule of scuba diving?"

To my surprise, Julianne's hand shot up. I nodded, curious.

"Never hold your breath," she stated confidently.

I blinked, caught off guard. "That's absolutely correct. Care to elaborate?"

She launched into an animated but concise explanation of lung overexpansion injuries that had me raising an eyebrow.

As the class progressed, I found myself consistently impressed by Julianne's quick grasp of concepts. She asked insightful questions that even seasoned divers often overlooked. As I went over the material, covering Boyle's Law and symptoms of decompression sickness, Julianne paid close attention, taking notes in her textbook. I tried to hide my growing admiration behind quips and jokes, but internally, I was begrudgingly impressed.

*Damn, she might actually be good at this.*

The realization irked me more than it should have. It was easier when I could dismiss her as just a boring number-cruncher out of her depth.

With a wide smile, she high-fived Lacey after a particularly tricky question. Lacey grinned back. "Nice one, Jules! You're crushing this!"

Julianne stiffened and her happy expression dropped

like a stone, her eyes darting to me for a split second before she pasted a smile back on. "Thanks, Lace. But let's stick to Julianne, okay? I am at work, after all."

My eyebrows shot up, a flicker of curiosity running through me. She had a nickname? "Aw, come on," I teased lightly, unable to resist a playful jab. "Jules has a nice ring to it. Very… casual."

Julianne's gaze met mine, her expression frostier than an arctic breeze. "It's Julianne, Eli. Shall we continue with the class?"

Raising my hands in a mock gesture of surrender, I concealed my racing thoughts behind a mask of nonchalance. There was something about that name, something on the edge of my memory that eluded me at the moment. "As you wish, Ms. Julianne Verne. Now let's move on to the scintillating mechanics of regulators…"

AFTER THEY LEFT, I cleaned up the classroom, and all day my mind ran over the nickname. *Jules…* It repeated over and over inside my head. For some reason it made me think of books, but I didn't know why.

Fortunately, I knew someone who would.

As SOON AS work was over, I made my way out of the dive shop and rode my bike along Main Street. Good thing the tourists were driving well today—one of the reasons I never rode without my helmet. As I rode by Corner Scoop, I waved to Brynn Mercer who was sweeping her front stoop. She was a smashing success as the new owner, and her recent hubby wasn't doing too shabby with his financial planning business, either.

Stopping before the quaint, cozy Bookshop in Paradise,

I leaned my bike against the large glass window. The familiar jingle of the bell greeted me as I entered, mingling with the comforting aroma of old paper and freshly brewed coffee.

"Well, well," my sister Brenna called out from behind a stack of new arrivals. Her long auburn hair hung like a curtain as she leaned out, and her soft-green eyes held a teasing glint. "To what do I owe the pleasure of my big brother gracing me? Did you get bored lounging around all day?"

I laughed as I weaved through the cozy maze of book-shelves. "Ha-ha. I'll have you know I've been up and productive for hours."

"Teaching resort guests how to breathe underwater hardly counts as productivity," her husband, Hunter, chimed in, appearing from the back room with a box of books. He set them down on the check-out counter, the heavy box looking almost comically light in his muscular, tattooed arms. He oozed ex-military—dark short hair and beard, everything neat and clean.

"Says the guy who gets paid to stand around and look intimidating," I shot back, grinning.

The bookshop was warm and inviting, shelves upon shelves creating little nooks that practically begged you to curl up with a good story. Brenna's personal touch was everywhere, from the hand-painted signs to the mismatched, overstuffed armchairs.

"So," Brenna said, eyeing me suspiciously. "What's up? You're not exactly my most… literary customer."

I leaned against the counter. "Can't a guy drop by to see his lovely sister?"

"Well, it would be a first," Brenna deadpanned. "Plus, you've got that look."

"What look?"

"The *I'm up to something* look," Hunter supplied help-fully. The gigantic man moved to wrap an arm around Brenna's shoulders. "It's the same one you had right before you talked me into that drinking contest."

I winced at the memory. Neither of us had won that one. "Okay, fine. I might have a question."

Hunter glanced at the clock and planted a kiss on Brenna's head. "As much as I'd like to hear this, I've got that security detail to get to. See you tonight, baby. Take it easy, Eli. I'll say hi to Ben for you."

"Do that," I said. "And tell him he needs to come around more. And for more than just to trim the hedges." Our oldest brother worked for Hunter part-time and spent the other half doing landscaping work at the resort.

Hunter clapped me on the shoulder as he passed. "Will do, man. Don't you two get into too much trouble."

As the door jingled shut behind Hunter, Brenna turned to me. "So what's your question?"

"Okay, here's the deal," I began, leaning in conspirato-rially as if sharing a state secret. "I've got this… acquain-tance? Coworker? Friend?—no way, more like a frenemy if I'm being generous—who's super uptight and serious. Oh! You know her. The accountant at the resort, Julianne Verne?"

Brenna frowned. "She's not super uptight. She's nice. You two are just complete opposites, is all."

"Yeah, well, I'm teaching her and some friends to dive —long story. It turns out she's got this hidden nickname that she didn't want me to know about. It rings a bell, but I can't place it. But if she doesn't want me to know about it, that means I must know every detail. I thought it might have to do with books, and you're our resident bookworm extraordinaire. So here I am!"

She ignored my attempt at flattery. "So what's the nickname?"

"Jules."

Brenna just stared at me. "Her last name is Verne?"

I nodded.

"Eli, you're a complete idiot. You know that, right? You seriously don't know who Jules Verne was?"

I scowled and threw my hands up. "I'm a dive instructor, not a librarian. So *ixnay* the insults, okay?"

She finally burst into laughter and grabbed my arm, dragging me toward a section under a sign that read Science Fiction Classics. "Jules Verne was one of the most important novelists of the nineteenth century. He wrote incredibly imaginative stories that changed literature forever. He practically invented science fiction." She plucked out a hardcover and placed it in my hands. The title was *Journey to the Center of the Earth.*

"Hey!" I exclaimed. "She has this in her bookshelf inside her office."

"Gee. I wonder why? And why do you care, anyway?"

My mind was racing with the possibilities. I wasn't sure why the nickname was important to Jules—I was never referring to her as Julianne again—but I knew this was a gold mine as a way to needle her.

"Earth to Eli." Brenna's voice cut through my plotting. "I asked why you care so much about it."

I shrugged, trying to play it cool. "No reason. Just... wanted to know."

"Uh-huh," Brenna said, clearly not buying it.

I felt a flicker of something in my chest. Annoyance? Excitement? I pushed it aside. "Please. I'm just looking for new ways to get under her skin."

Brenna's eyes danced with mischief. "Sure, big brother. Keep telling yourself that."

I narrowed my eyes, but something in her tone made me uneasy. "What's that supposed to mean?"

"Oh, nothing," she said, innocently reorganizing a stack of books. "Just that you seem awfully fixated on someone you claim is your frenemy."

"I'm not fixated," I protested, but even I could hear the defensive edge in my voice. "She's just… interesting to mess with, that's all."

Brenna raised an eyebrow. "Interesting, huh? That's new. What happened to her being a stuck-up number-cruncher?"

I opened my mouth to argue, then closed it again. The image of Jules in her casual clothes, effortlessly picking up diving theory, flashed through my mind. "She's, well, surprising. There might be more to her than I thought," I admitted reluctantly. I'd been trying to forget that she'd given up her own delayed computer upgrade to ensure that Annie's hours didn't get cut. That image definitely did not mesh with my image of the cutthroat CPA.

"Mmm-hmm," Brenna hummed, a knowing smile on her face. "And that has nothing to do with why you rode your bike halfway across town at the end of the day to ask me about the name?"

I ran a hand through my hair, suddenly feeling exposed. "Look, it's not like that. It's a puzzle, okay? She's irritating and I like messing with her."

"A puzzle you seem very eager to solve." Brenna wore a huge grin now.

I shook my head. "Whatever. Thanks for solving the mystery for me. I should get going." I held up the book in my hand. "Can I take this?"

"Sure." She plucked the book next to where it had been on the shelf and gave it to me before tapping the new book. "Read this one, *Twenty Thousand Leagues Under the Sea*. It's more your lane."

I brightened. "Hey! I've heard of that one."

"Will wonders never cease? Love you, brother."

"Love you, too. Thanks for the info and the books."

As I headed for the door, Brenna called out, "Anytime. Have fun with Julianne!"

I paused, my hand on the doorknob. "It's Jules," I corrected with a broad, shit-eating smile. Begrudging admiration was no match for ammunition like this that I could use anytime the fancy struck me. "And I'm going to call her that at every opportunity."

# Chapter Six

## JULES

THE NEXT AFTERNOON, I was knee deep in payroll when Eli sauntered through my office door, his artfully disheveled dark-blond hair still damp. A waft of clean scent like fresh rain drifted toward me, letting me know he'd just showered after his ocean adventures. I tried not to notice how good he smelled.

He leaned casually against the wall. "Hey there, Jules. Working hard or hardly working?"

I bristled at the nickname, my fingers tensing on my keyboard. "I go by Julianne while at work. Because unlike some, I take my responsibilities seriously."

Eli's grin widened. "Come on, Jules. Why the secrecy? What's the story behind that nickname, anyway?"

I exhaled slowly, willing myself not to rise to his bait. "If you must know, my mother gave me the nickname as a child, as a nod to Jules Verne. I used to devour his books when I was young."

"No kidding?" Eli's teasing tone softened, curiosity

creeping in as he moved to inspect the books in my bookcase.

"*Twenty Thousand Leagues Under the Sea* was my favorite growing up," I continued. "Something about exploring the unknown always called to me. I dreamed of having adventures like that."

"So what happened to that adventurous spirit?" Eli asked, settling into the chair across from my desk.

I stiffened, kicking myself for revealing even that small tidbit. How did he manage to slip past my defenses? "Life happened. The need to be a responsible adult and find a career. I went to Ohio State for accounting, and it was a good choice for me."

"You're a Buckeye, huh? So where did Jules grow up?"

I was tempted to respond with something icy and acerbic, but despite him using my nickname, I couldn't detect anything other than curiosity in his manner. "Columbus," I replied neutrally. "Not exactly a hotbed of adventure, you know."

"Maybe not, but it sounds like you had a pretty lively imagination," he said, crossing one ankle over the other knee. "What was it like growing up there?"

I could see the flicker of interest in his eyes, and it unsettled me. I didn't trust this sudden interest, but it couldn't hurt to be on more civil terms. "It was fine. Lots of books, a best friend, one younger sister."

"How come you left Ohio?"

I stilled, and when I saw my fists had clenched over my keyboard, I forced them to loosen. I wasn't about to get into that story with Eli Coleridge, of all people. "I was ready for a change. I'd had enough snowy winters to last a lifetime, so I chased the sun and it led me here. Why are you so friendly all of a sudden?"

He smiled, though there was an edge to it. That dimple

appeared on his cheek again. It made me want to grind my teeth. "I'm a friendly guy, Jules. You're the only one who has never seemed to notice that."

I sighed. "You're not going to call me Julianne, even if I ask. Are you?"

"Nope." Then his smile softened, became something almost endearing. Almost. "Besides, we're spending more time together, right? Time to bury the hatchet and all that. Using your nickname is just my way of getting to know you."

"Huh. And I could have sworn it was to get under my skin and irritate me."

"Are you irritated?"

Admitting that would be a huge mistake. I straightened my blotter. "Irritated? No, Eli, I'm just marveling at your ability to turn every conversation into a comedy sketch. It's truly a unique talent."

His grin became devilish. "Oh, I'm just getting started. Stick around, and you might even get a front-row seat to my one-man show."

"A front-row seat? Not if we were the last two people on earth. I'm sure watching paint dry would be far more entertaining."

"You know, Jules, for someone who claims to be uninterested, you're surprisingly good at keeping this conversation lively. Admit it, you're having fun."

"Fun would be a stretch. And there's my nickname again. Guess I'd better get used to it." It really was a miracle that Chase had kept it from him all this time. Lacey's brother was a paragon. It was baffling how he and Eli could be best friends.

"Oh, absolutely." Despite his exaggerated casualness, there was no denying he spent many of his work hours in hard, manual labor. It showed.

*Dammit. Why couldn't he be physically repulsive?*

"I can live with it if you can." I shrugged, feigning nonchalance. "But if we're admitting to being surprised, I guess I should say that you're a much more prepared and professional instructor than I anticipated. That introductory document you sent was very thorough."

He laughed, and the sound was so unforced and honest that I nearly found myself smiling back.

"I'm pretty sure you're the first student I've ever had who actually read the damn thing. Well done."

I arched a brow. "Did you just compliment me?"

His smile fell as he screwed one eye shut in concentration. "Oh, shit. You're right. But I think you said something nice to me too. About me being such an amazing instructor and all that. Ready for the first pool session?"

The four of us were scheduled for our first underwater breathing session later in the week, and I couldn't feign boredom about it. "I am. I'm realizing I haven't done much in the way of excitement in a while, so I'm looking forward to it."

"Ah, there's that sense of adventure again."

"Some of us take different paths in life. You seem to be living your adventure every day under the water."

Eli lit up like Times Square, and this time I couldn't help the smile that rose on my face. "That's a good way to put it! Nothing beats being out on the ocean. You discover something unusual or unexpected all the time. It's amazing. But trust me, there are days when leading dives is a very tough job." He paused and studied me for a moment. "You might think about diving into something more than just numbers someday. Life's too short to stay tethered to a desk."

Heat rose across my cheeks as he leaned back, clearly enjoying our exchange. And just like that, he broke the mood. Eli Coleridge was the last person I was going to take career advice from. I picked up a stack of papers and straightened them. "Right, because you're such an expert on responsibility."

"Fair enough," Eli conceded, holding up his hands in mock surrender. And not acting at all upset that I'd needled him. "But maybe there's room for both adventure and responsibility. You might surprise yourself."

I arched an eyebrow. "I think I've had quite enough surprises in my life, thank you very much." His gaze sharpened, and a pang of vulnerability twisted my gut. I'd already shared much more than I'd intended. Pressing my lips together, I tried to regain control of the conversation. "You're lucky, you know. To have grown up here, with such a big family, and with Sunset Siesta at your doorstep. It must be nice having such deep roots."

A crooked smile grew on his lips. "Oh, we've got roots all right. More like weeds, if you ask some of the locals. The Coleridge clan has a bit of a reputation for stirring up trouble." He laughed again, shaking his head. "You should hear some of the stories about my oldest brother, Ben. Let's just say for years, he made it his personal mission to keep the island gossip mill running."

I couldn't help but smile at that. "I've heard some of those rumors."

"Hey now," Eli protested, but his eyes were twinkling. "We're not all bad. Just... colorful. Makes life interesting, you know?"

I felt a twinge of envy at the obvious affection in his voice. "Ben has been making a determined effort to turn his life around. I think that's obvious to everyone now. Still, you should appreciate what you have. Not everyone is so fortunate."

Eli's expression softened. "You're right. I do appreciate

it, more than you know. Well, Dove Key, and maybe even Sunset Siesta, does need its share of responsible folks. Keeps the chaos at bay, I suppose."

I blinked, thrown by the sincerity in his voice. Once again, he'd disarmed me. For a moment, the air between us felt charged. I cleared my throat and tore my eyes from his, scrambling to regain my professional demeanor. "Yes, well. Someone has to keep this place running smoothly."

Eli leaned forward, bracing his forearms on my desk, a playful smirk creeping back onto his face. "And you do that very well, Jules. But I'm starting to suspect there's a little adventurer hiding in there somewhere. I dare you to let her out."

I crossed my arms defensively, trying to suppress the flutter he sparked with those words. What happened to that child who used to plan elaborate adventures and treasure hunts with her best friend? The college girl who was the first to suggest a new place to explore?

*You know what happened to her. Life happened. Travis happened. Kala happened.*

I straightened in my chair. "You think coaxing me into the water is going to unleash some hidden mermaid? I hardly think so."

He laughed, and the sound warmed the air between us. "You said it yourself. That it's past time to have a little adventure, and I think diving is just the thing. Plus, I've got a secret weapon. Me!" He wiggled his eyebrows suggestively.

I bit my cheek to keep from laughing. "I guess we'll find out Saturday, won't we?" The idea of spending more time with him made my stomach twist in an unusual, fluttery way. "You've already done enough today. I need to get back to work, assuming you'd like to get paid."

"All right." His eyes danced as he stood and headed

toward the door. "See you at the pool session, Jules. Don't worry. I promise not to let you drown."

I managed to delay until he was out of sight before I let my full smile escape. And with a lighter mood, I turned back to the payroll reports.

---

THE POOL at Sunset Siesta glittered under the afternoon sun. A chorus of excited chatter and splashing filled the air, but the resort guests were in a section entirely removed from where the five of us were. I stood at the edge, tugging self-consciously at my one-piece swimsuit as Eli strode confidently to the center of the group.

"All right, future merpeople!" Eli called out, his voice carrying easily over the din. "Today, we're going to take the first step to becoming bona fide scuba superstars. Or at least get you comfortable enough not to panic when a curious grouper decides to say hello."

A ripple of nervous laughter spread through the wedding party. I fought the urge to groan but couldn't help noticing how at ease Eli seemed, his tanned skin practically glowing as he gestured animatedly.

"Now, we've got some key skills to cover," he continued, his gaze landing on me with a mischievous glint. "I'm sure Jules here will be a natural at the fine art of regulator recovery. After all, it's only fitting for our resident Verne to lead us on this underwater adventure, right?"

I groaned out loud. "Coleridge, your jokes are horrible."

"Oh, come on, Jules," Lacey murmured to me between giggles. "It's kind of cute. And he's not wrong."

Eli was already moving on, outlining buoyancy control techniques with a series of exaggerated gestures that had the group in stitches. Despite myself, I found the corner of my mouth twitching upward.

"And remember," Eli added. "If you start to feel overwhelmed, just channel your inner Captain Nemo. Though maybe skip the part about battling giant squids."

I couldn't hold back a snort. "I'm pretty sure we're fresh out of krakens in the resort pool."

"Never underestimate the perils of the deep end," he shot back, grinning. "You never know where a rogue pool noodle might be lurking."

As Daniel and Randy burst into laughter, a smile raised my lips. Eli's enthusiasm was infectious, and even I couldn't maintain my professional façade in the face of his ridiculous antics.

"All right, all right," I said, turning to my disassembled scuba kit lying on the pool deck. "Fewer squid jokes, more actual instruction. How do you actually breathe off this thing?"

He moved over to demonstrate how to put the contraption together, making it look easy. All four of us just gaped.

I folded my arms. "You'd better go over that again. Slower this time, Coleridge."


I SLIPPED beneath the pool surface, the water enveloping me as I tried to focus on Eli. We settled on our knees in a semicircle around him in about six feet of water. The regulator felt alien in my mouth, a constant reminder that this wasn't my natural element. But I couldn't suppress the thrill—I was breathing underwater!

As Eli demonstrated the proper technique for regulator recovery, I felt a spark of the old rush I used to get from trying new things. He let the mouthpiece fall from his mouth to his side, then made a long sweeping stroke with his right arm to lift the long hose up, following the tube to the mouthpiece with his hand. Tapping it deliberately, he pressed the purge button to dispel the accumulated water with air from the tank before placing it in his mouth and taking a breath. His entire ballet of movement looked as effortless as… well, breathing.

Eli motioned for me to give it a try. I took a deep breath, steeling myself, then deliberately let the regulator slip from my mouth. Panic flared instantly as I fumbled to recover it, my fingers clumsy and uncoordinated. My lungs immediately reminded me I was in water, not air. Just as I was about to surface in defeat, a strong hand grasped mine, guiding the purged regulator back to my mouth.

Eli's eyes met mine, crinkling at the corners in a reassuring smile. There was no trace of his usual cockiness now. He gave me an okay signal, his touch on my shoulder somehow reassuring and not irritating. I nodded, my heartbeat slowing as I took a few deep breaths.

As we surfaced, I couldn't help but laugh, the tension dissolving as I pushed wet hair from my face. "Well, that was graceful. I think I just redefined flailing. Time for a new nickname, I guess."

"Nah." Eli grinned, standing before me. "You should've seen me when I first started. I looked like a cat trying to escape a bathtub."

I snorted, picturing the image. "Now that I'd pay to see."

"Sorry, Jules." He winked. "That footage is locked in the Coleridge family vault, never to see the light of day."

As I laughed in response, I realized with a jolt that I was actually enjoying Eli's company. The charming troublemaker act was still there, but beneath it, I caught glimpses of genuine passion and expertise. His teasing and joking were reassuring and put us all at ease, and his competence was obvious. It was intriguing.

"Ready to give it another shot?" Eli asked, his voice gentler than I'd ever heard it.

I nodded. "Might as well. Can't let a little water get the best of me, right?"

"That's the spirit, Captain Nemo," he said, his smile warm. "Trust me, you've got this."

And as we submerged again, I was surprised to find that I did trust him, at least in this.

When the group surfaced after the next skill, Eli moved to work with Daniel. A splash and a muffled cry drew my attention. Lacey was flailing to find her feet, her mask askew and the regulator bobbing just out of reach. Her eyes were wide.

I swam over, my own nerves forgotten. "Hey, easy there," I said, steadying her. "You're okay. Let's fix that mask."

Lacey clung to me, gasping. "I-I can't—Jules. I'm not so good at this."

"Shh, you're fine," I soothed, adjusting her mask. "Deep breaths. Remember what Eli said about the mask? Just get used to the water in it, exhale through your nose, and clear it."

She nodded. I pantomimed the motion, and when she nodded again, this time it was a little more confident.

I smiled. "You've got this, Lace." As Lacey calmed, warmth spread through my chest. I caught Eli's eye, who was watching carefully from afar, and he gave me a subtle nod of approval.

The rest of the session flew by. Before I knew it, Lacey, Daniel, and Randy were climbing out of the pool as I stood in the shallow end in the heavy gear and inspected the second stage of my regulator more closely.

"So," Eli said, shaking the water out of his wet hair. "How'd it feel?"

I glanced up, considering. "Good and bad. I got pretty good at the regulator recovery, but my buoyancy was all over the place."

To my surprise, Eli's face lit up. "That's great!"

I snorted. "My utter lack of control is great?"

He laughed. "No, that you noticed it. Most people don't even realize they're struggling with buoyancy at first."

"Oh." I smiled, oddly pleased by the compliment. "Well, noticing and fixing are two different things."

Eli's expression softened. "Hey, everyone struggles at first. It's all about practice and finding your rhythm. You'll get there."

"I definitely need more practice then," I said as we waded out of the shallow end and dumped our scuba kits on the pool deck.

Lacey, Daniel, and Randy moved off to stand in a cluster, talking as they toweled off.

Eli cleared his throat. "Listen, Jules." His usual cocky grin faded into something more hesitant. "If you want, we could do a private session after work early next week. Just to focus on your buoyancy control."

My breath froze. The smart-ass veneer had slipped, and as his deep-blue eyes held mine, uncertainty flitted through them.

"Am I that awful?" I asked with a smile.

Eli shrugged, but this time the casual gesture seemed forced. "Not at all. Uh, I just want everyone to love diving as much as I do."

I studied him, intrigued by this glimpse beneath the surface. "I… That would be really helpful. Thank you, Eli."

A smile, smaller but somehow more real than his usual

grin, spread across his face. "Great. How about Monday at six? We can have the pool to ourselves then."

"That works." I nodded, turning away to gather my things.

"Hey, Jules," he said, and I looked back. "Good job today."

"Thanks, Eli. See you later."

As I headed toward the changing room, my mind whirled. I paused at the door, glancing back. Eli was coiling a regulator, his movements practiced and efficient. There was more to him than I'd given him credit for, clearly. And I'd realized something else. I didn't mind him calling me Jules. Because there was no trace of mockery in his voice anymore when he said it.

# Chapter Seven

## ELI

THE POOL WATER was crystal clear around us as I demonstrated buoyancy control, my arms out and my body remaining absolutely still. Jules watched intently, her eyes narrowed in concentration as she tried to mimic my movements. Her raven hair was coiled into a bun like usual, but underwater, it looked natural, not severe. The mask amplified her green eyes, making the various hues even more compelling. She really did have gorgeous eyes.

After several rounds of practice, I gave her the thumbs-up. We surfaced, and I couldn't help but grin at the determined set of her jaw. "Not bad for a beginner. You're getting the hang of it."

"I think I understand now. What you meant about popping up like a cork if I add too much air to my BCD."

"Exactly. It's all about finding that sweet spot." I winked, unable to resist a little flirtation. "Kind of like life, right?"

To my surprise, a smile tugged at the corners of her

mouth. "I suppose so. Though I prefer my balance sheets to be precise not… sweet."

I laughed, treading water easily. "Come on, Jules, admit it. You're having fun breaking free from those spreadsheets."

She rolled her eyes, but there was no real annoyance behind it. "I wouldn't go that far. But it is oddly freeing."

"That's exactly what it is. You're literally weightless. Let's work on it some more."

As she practiced the technique again, I found myself watching her with growing interest. There was something compelling about the way she approached each new challenge I threw at her—meticulous, focused, but with a sense of adventure I hadn't expected from our by-the-book accountant. It was a different side from the driven, detail-oriented woman I'd known, but it suited her to learn a very unnatural skill. Most kids took to scuba naturally, but adults were another story. She was continually surprising me. And impressing me.

"I gotta say, you're a natural," I said when we resurfaced. "Must be all that number crunching giving you ninja-like precision."

Jules splashed water in my direction, her eyes glinting. "Very funny. I'll have you know there are plenty of things I'm good at."

"Oh really?" A flood of images flashed through my mind. Images involving her and me doing things that had nothing to do with work. Or scuba diving. Yeah, I was definitely seeing her in a new light, but I didn't want to push our newfound common ground too far. "Care to put that to the test? I bet I can hold my breath longer than you."

"That's hardly a fair competition," Jules protested, but I could see the competitive glint in her eye. "You're a professional diver. Suppose I challenged you to depreciate next quarter's expenditures?"

I shrugged, grinning. "Scared, Verne?"

"Not even a little. I'm just keeping you sharp for your family dinner tonight."

I frowned at the reminder of what I had coming up after our pool session. "A collection of Coleridges is absolutely a reason to stay sharp. I take it you're not up to the breath-holding challenge?"

"You wish. You're on."

As we both took deep breaths, preparing to submerge, it occurred to me how things had changed between us. The razor-sharp accountant I'd first met was still there, but beneath that professional exterior lurked a woman full of surprises. And humor. And damn if that combination wasn't becoming more appealing by the minute.

After our impromptu breath-holding contest—to her credit, Jules gave me a run for my money—I glanced at the brilliantly lit western horizon and reluctantly called an end to our practice.

"See you at the next classroom session?" I asked, hauling myself out of the pool. Water cascaded off my body as I offered Jules a hand up. She hesitated for a moment before taking it, her fingers warm against mine.

"I suppose I can pencil you in." A definite smile played at her lips.

"Careful, Jules. That almost sounded like you enjoy my company."

"Don't let it go to your head. It's a requirement, remember?"

As we gathered our gear, I found myself wanting to know more about my unexpected student. "You know, you're picking this up really fast. Maybe we should celebrate your progress at Tropical Hops."

Jules paused, towel in hand. "Are you asking me out, Eli?"

"What? No, I—" I backpedaled, suddenly aware of what I'd said. My mouth always ran away with me. It was a terrible habit. "Just a friendly offer. You know, instructor to student."

"Mm-hmm," she hummed, clearly unconvinced. "Noted. But don't you have a dinner to get to?"

I groaned dramatically, grateful for the subject change. "Don't remind me. We have two family activities once a month or so. The bonfires, which are a lot of fun, and the family dinners like tonight. Which are usually less boozy and more minding our manners at the table. I'd much rather stay here and get waterlogged."

Her smile changed her whole expression. Her teeth were white and even, her lips round and generous.

"I imagine you could spend most of your time getting waterlogged. See you tomorrow, Eli."

As I headed toward the dive shop, I couldn't help but glance back. Jules was still by the pool, wringing water from her hair. The setting sun bathed her in amber, illuminating the beads of water on her shoulders and chest. That very un-accountant-like chest. That very womanly, curvy chest. For a moment, I forgot how to breathe.

Shaking my head, I turned away. What the hell was happening to me?

---

I ARRIVED at Mom's house, a sprawling four-bedroom ranch that discreetly overlooked the resort like a watchful parent, yet was screened by foliage to remain mostly unseen. The familiar scent of sea salt and gardenias hit me as I stepped onto the wraparound porch. This place held a lifetime of memories. Some good, some… well, let's just say I was glad to have my own place now.

Pushing open the door, I called out, "Anyone home? Or did you all start without me?"

Mom's voice drifted from the kitchen. "In here, Eli!"

I found them settling around the large oak table, the one that had witnessed countless family dinners and heated discussions. Harper was helping Mom set out plates, while Finn entertained himself with a toy boat.

"There's my favorite nephew," I said, ruffling Finn's hair as I passed.

Harper laughed. "He's your only nephew."

"Details, details." I grinned, then turned to Mom. "Need any help?"

She waved me off. "Just sit down. Austin should be here any minute."

As if on cue, the back door opened, and my younger brother walked in. Austin's rugged face was etched with the day's sun, his movements deliberate as he hung up his jacket.

"Hey," he said quietly, nodding in my direction.

"Look what the tide dragged in," I quipped as I rose to grab some steaming serving bowls from the kitchen. Despite Mom trying to shoo me, I wasn't going to let her and Harper do all the drudge work. I set a platter of rolls in front of Austin. "How was the fishing?"

His gray eyes brightened as he smoothed his dark hair. Our fishing charter captain, Austin had loved fishing since he could hold a rod. "It was a great day. Had a family out, and the dad hooked a two-hundred-pound tarpon. You should've seen it, Eli. The fight lasted nearly two hours."

I leaned forward. "No kidding? Did they land it?"

Austin launched into the story, his usual reserve melting away as he described the battle between man and fish. I found myself grinning, caught up in his enthusiasm. It was moments like these when I saw glimpses of the brother I'd grown up with before everything changed. Before he changed. But despite that and our very different personalities, we had a lot of similarities too. We were less than three years apart. And when it came to the ocean, we spoke the same language.

"Sounds like quite the experience," I said when he finished. "Maybe I should trade in my scuba gear for a fishing rod."

Austin's mouth twitched in a quick smile. "You tried that, remember? You don't have the patience for it."

"Isn't that the truth." I laughed as I carried over a bowl of mashed potatoes and another of roasted zucchini Mom grew in her garden. "But at least I don't have to sit still for two hours waiting for a fish to decide if it wants to join me for dinner."

Harper chimed in, "You know, if you focused on other things as much as you do diving, you'd probably be running this resort by now."

I shrugged, tossing a glance at Mom. "Not everyone can handle the pressure of being the perfect child like you, Harper. Some of us have chosen the path of least resistance."

Mom sighed but couldn't hide her smile. "Oh please, Eli. Your path of least resistance keeps us all smiling."

I slid into my seat, the worn wooden chair creaking beneath me, a sound that felt like home. The table was a feast of colors and aromas—a perfectly cooked roast, buttery corn on the cob, and a vibrant salad bursting with greens from Mom's garden. My mouth watered as I grabbed a plate and piled it high.

"Wow, Mom. This looks amazing!" I exclaimed. She always had a knack for turning simple ingredients into something magical, just as she had turned this house into a safe haven over the years.

"Only the best for my family," she said modestly, but her smile betrayed how much she liked the compliment.

As we dug into the meal, I took a moment to soak it all in—the warmth of my family, the food that felt like a hug, and the memories intertwined with every corner of this house. Jules's words echoed in my mind—*appreciate what you have*. And in this moment, it was easy to do that. Easy to forget the bad times.

Harper set her fork down, her warm eyes sweeping around the table. "You know, we've been discussing the projects around the resort lately. When there's so much to do, it's hard to know where to start."

"What do you mean?" Austin asked as he took a sip of iced tea.

"I wonder if we should get some professional help on what to tackle first," she replied.

I sat back in my chair. "That's not a bad idea. Even better, I know the perfect guy."

Austin arched a brow. "Who?"

"Chase. He's got the expertise we need, and he knows the place inside out. This is what he does all the time."

At the mention of Chase's name, Harper nodded eagerly. "He's certainly qualified."

"Eli, honey…" Mom's eyes narrowed slightly. "Bringing in an outsider for something this big makes me nervous. After what happened with Russell… with that whole fiasco… I need to know we have complete oversight. I agree the time has come to remodel, but we need to manage the scope. It's a huge risk."

I leaned back in my chair, aiming for a relaxed posture. "Come on, Mom. Chase practically is family. He's been around since we were kids."

"That may be true," Mom countered, her tone gentle but firm, "but there's a difference between being like family and actually being family."

I could feel the familiar tightness in my chest, the one that always appeared when Mom and I butted heads. She had been hurt so much, and I tried not to give her too much grief, which was a damn sight easier now that I was older. "I get that, Mom. But sometimes fresh eyes make all the difference."

Mom's lips pressed into a thin line. "It's not just about boundaries, Eli. It's about the potential for things to go wrong when you trust someone outside the family with decisions that could sink us. We barely survived the last time we faced that kind of financial exposure."

Harper leaned forward. "But we did survive. Thanks to you."

I couldn't help the mischievous grin that spread across my face. "Well, Mom, if you're worried about boundaries, I can promise I won't get romantically involved with Chase. Wouldn't want to break that no-workplace-romance rule, right?"

The tension in the room dissolved as Harper let out a surprised laugh and Mom cracked a smile. But as the others joined in, a pang of guilt ran through me. Mom only had one ironclad rule. No workplace romances. They were too messy and wreaked havoc after the breakup. The resort had personal experience of that with Russell and Lucia, a couple who had become romantically involved and it went south. Very south. The fallout left ripples we still felt.

Which naturally caused my thoughts to drift to Jules and her determined face as she'd practiced buoyancy control in the pool earlier. And those big green eyes. Then I firmly pushed those thoughts aside. No point in worrying about things that didn't exist. And if things did start to blossom between us?

That was a problem for future Eli.

"I think a consultation is a great idea," Harper said. "Chase does have a great mix of knowledge and personal history. Great idea, Eli."

I bowed over my plate. "I'm not just a pretty face, you know."

After the laughter faded, the conversation went back and forth. Harper talked about updated booking systems and eco-friendly renovations, while Mom emphasized the charm of our Old Florida aesthetic.

And I was torn.

Part of me sided with Harper. I knew we needed to evolve to survive. But I also got where Mom was coming from. The resort's history was our history, and changing too much felt like losing a piece of ourselves. The good part.

"Maybe there's a middle ground?" I commented as I idly stirred my mashed potatoes. "We could update some things behind the scenes but keep the look and feel people love?"

Mom and Harper exchanged glances, and I held my breath, hoping I'd managed to bridge the gap between them, at least for now.

I caught Austin's eye across the table. "We could start small," he offered, his voice low but steady. "I like the idea of Chase's input. Maybe have him suggest changes and repairs that are inexpensive first. See how it affects our numbers."

I raised my eyebrows. "Look at you, coming in with the voice of reason."

His lips twitched in a rare smile. "Someone has to balance out your wisecracks."

"Ouch." I laughed, clutching my chest in mock pain. "*Et tu*, Austin?"

Harper, ever the peacemaker, jumped in. "See, Mom? We can figure out how to do both. Modernize and keep what makes Sunset Siesta a place people want to return to, all while keeping the budget in mind."

As Mom considered, I watched the family dynamic unfolding before me. Harper, the eternal diplomat. Austin, the unexpected voice of reason. And me? Well, I was the comic relief, I supposed. It was a role I'd perfected over the years. But as I watched them, a familiar weight settled in my chest. They all seemed so… sure. Of their place, their purpose. Meanwhile, I was still trying to figure out where I fit in this family puzzle. Other than Braden, who was married to his brewpub, only Ben and Brenna were missing tonight. They were the two Coleridges who felt their destinies lay elsewhere than the resort, though Ben was still figuring that part out.

"Well," I drawled as I pointed to the *Hang Loose* T-shirt I'd pulled on after Jules's and my pool session. "As long as we don't update my stunning wardrobe of threadbare shirts and shorts, I'm on board."

Finn laughed out loud, bless his heart. Harper groaned, but I didn't miss the smile she tried to hide. "God forbid we mess with your carefully cultivated beach bum aesthetic."

As the laughter rippled around the table, that weight lifted a little. Maybe this was my role after all—keeping us all from taking ourselves too seriously.

LATER THAT NIGHT, I flopped onto my bed, the springs creaking in protest. My eyes landed on the battered copy of *Twenty Thousand Leagues Under the Sea* on my nightstand. I was halfway through it, and I'd meant to keep reading tonight, but my mind was too full of… well, Jules.

I exhaled a long breath. How had this happened? One minute she was the uptight accountant making my life miserable, and the next …

I couldn't shake the image of her in the pool today. The way her eyes lit up when she performed a perfect helicopter turn. The little victory dance she did when we surfaced. It was… unexpected. Charming, even.

I rolled over, burying my face in the pillow. This was dangerous territory. Jules was all about rules and order. I was anything but. We were as different as a shark and a sea turtle. And holy hell, could we set off a detonation with Mom. Could I even consider this?

And yet…

Yet I wanted to spend more time with her in a very non-teacher, non-student kind of way. The urge was so strong I'd asked her out after our pool session, though I hadn't meant to. I'd managed to walk it all back, but my mind kept returning to one solid fact—surprise had been clear on Jules's face and her response, but no anger. No refusal. Instead, she'd deflected by bringing up my family dinner.

So what did that mean?

After a long moment of watching the ceiling fan spin above me in its endless circles, I lifted my arm and made a flicking gesture with my right fingers. "All right, universe. I'm putting this one in your hands. If Jules and I are meant to be more than reluctant coworkers, I'll leave it to you to figure out the details."

I paused, half-expecting a bolt of lightning or something. When nothing happened, I shrugged and reached for the Verne book. If I was going to let fate steer the ship, I might as well enjoy the journey.

# Chapter Eight

# JULES

THE GRITTY SMELL of stale beer and peanut shells hit me as soon as Lacey and I walked into Salty's Tavern. I wrinkled my nose, noting the contrast to the polished mahogany and craft beers of Conch Republic, the usual haunt. Though Tropical Hops was a great hangout, my need to separate my business and leisure personas prevented me from spending my off-duty time there. So Conch Republic had been our setting for get-togethers for years.

But not tonight.

Eli's teasing about my nickname made me remember that I *liked* adventure. But somewhere along the way, I'd forgotten that. So I suggested the local dive bar with a dubious reputation for our girls' night out. Lacey had paused over the phone, then agreed. It was dark inside, with old playbills adorning the walls, and plenty of locals were celebrating Friday night. And my natural caution was seriously considering whacking my adventurous side over the head with a hammer.

"All right, Jules. This place adventurous enough for you?" Lacey grinned, dragging me toward a sticky-looking bar.

"That's one word for it," I said, gingerly perching on a barstool. But as I sipped my beer—admittedly pretty good —my shoulders relaxed. The jukebox was playing an old Jimmy Buffett song, and the salty air drifting in from the open windows reminded me why I loved living on Dove Key.

"So." I turned to Lacey. "Getting excited for the big day?"

Lacey's smile faltered. "About that… I've been think-ing. Are we sure about this whole underwater thing? I mean, what if I panic? Or flood my mask? Or—"

"Oh, no." I groaned. "Lacey, please tell me you're not getting cold feet. We've put so much work into this."

"Not about marrying Daniel!" Lacey bit her lip. "It's just, scuba diving isn't exactly my forte. Maybe we should rethink—"

"Nope." I cut her off and pointed a stern finger at her. "You are not backing out now. We'll practice more, okay? Eli can give you some extra lessons if you're nervous, and you'll be a pro in no time."

At the mention of Eli's name, my traitorous heart gave a little flutter. I pushed the feeling aside, focusing on Lacey. "Trust me, it'll be beautiful. Daniel will cry manly tears inside his mask when he sees you."

Lacey laughed, tension easing from her shoulders. "You're right. I'm just being silly. And hey, if we add another session, that means more time with Eli, right?" She waggled her brows at me.

I gave her a stern stare but couldn't quite suppress my

smile. As much as I hated to admit it, I was thoroughly enjoying our scuba lessons. And Eli. He was a patient teacher and watching him glide effortlessly through the pool water was… distracting, to say the least. We'd had to postpone our next set of classes due to a conflict in Daniel's schedule, and I hadn't been able to deny the disappointment I'd felt.

A band strolled onto the makeshift stage in one corner and started tuning their instruments. Lacey glanced around the dark bar and smiled. "This place isn't so bad. Maybe its reputation isn't deserved, kind of like a Coleridge?"

I swept my gaze around, taking in the neon beer signs, the worn pool tables, and the eclectic mix of locals. There was something oddly comforting about the bar's unassuming charm.

"It's got character," I replied, tracing a finger through the condensation on my glass. "And sometimes it's good to step out of your comfort zone, right?"

Lacey nearly choked on her drink. "Who are you and what have you done with Jules?"

I laughed, surprising myself with how genuine it felt. "Hey, I can be spontaneous."

"Sure, if by spontaneous you mean color-coding your planner instead of alphabetizing it."

I opened my mouth to argue, but the truth was, she had a point. I'd been so focused on work that I'd let a whole side of my personality fade away. Maybe this change of scenery wasn't such a bad idea after all.

"I'll admit, it's nice to do something different," I conceded. Then I narrowed my eyes. "But don't go spreading that around. I have a reputation to maintain."

"Don't worry. Your secret's safe with me. Now, how about we order another round?"

I nodded, and Lacey flagged down the bartender. On impulse, I ordered a scotch on the rocks as a nod to stepping outside my usual beer or wine. As I tried not to choke on it, my mind drifted to Eli during our private scuba session. How he was continually surprising me. The way his humor, which used to irritate me to no end, now relaxed me when I was unsure about a skill. The way his dark-blue eyes crinkled when he smiled. How his strong, assured hands had steadied me when I'd wobbled…

"Uh-hmm." Lacey's loud throat clearing brought me back. "You're thinking about him again, aren't you?"

I straightened, adopting my most professional tone. "I don't know what you're talking about."

"Oh please." Lacey gave me a saucy grin. "You get this dreamy look whenever Eli's name comes up. It's cute, really."

"I do not," I protested, even as a traitorous blush crept up my neck, and I took another gulp. I was feeling pleasantly buzzed now. "Eli and I have a strictly professional relationship."

"Uh-huh. And I'm the Queen of England."

I sighed, knowing I couldn't fool my best friend. "Fine. I'll admit he has certain appealing qualities. But nothing's going to happen. We're too different, and you know our history."

Lacey just smiled, a knowing glint in her eye. "I wouldn't be too sure about that. You two have come a long way these past couple of weeks. And let's be honest, I've seen you checking out his fully certified muscles."

I exhaled a long sigh, remembering how distracting Eli's lean body had been. "Okay, yes, he's attractive. I like how he doesn't flaunt it, you know? It's just… there. A side effect of his job, I guess."

"A very nice side effect."

I couldn't help but laugh. "You're impossible."

Just then, the band struck up a lively tune, the twangy guitar and upbeat drums filling the air. I felt a sudden surge of energy, my body responding to the rhythm before my mind could catch up.

"Let's dance!" I called out.

Lacey laughed out loud. "Now you're talking!"

We pushed our way onto the dance floor, the press of bodies and the pulsing beat washing away my usual inhibitions. And maybe the scotch too. I let my hair down, shaking out my bun and the strands whipping around my face as I moved. For once, I didn't care about looking professional or put-together. I just danced.

"Woo!" Lacey cheered, twirling beside me. "Look at you go, girl! Friday night agrees with you."

The music thrummed through me, and I gave in to the moment, swaying and spinning without a care in the world. Lacey took a step back and a couple stepped between us, then moved on. I closed my eyes, feeling freer than I had in years.

That is, until a pair of unfamiliar hands touched my waist.

"Hey there, beautiful," a gruff voice said near my ear. "Haven't seen you here before. How about a dance?"

I stiffened, turning to face a stocky guy with bloodshot eyes and a too-wide grin. The smell of cheap beer wafted off him.

"No, thank you," I said firmly, putting some distance between us.

He followed, undeterred. "Aw, come on, don't be like that. Just one dance."

My good mood evaporated, a crawling sensation of discomfort replacing it. "I said no," I repeated, louder this time.

The guy's grin turned ugly. "Playing hard to get, huh? I like that."

He reached for me again, and I dodged, my heart racing. Where was Lacey? I scanned the crowd, panic starting to set in, but I couldn't see her.

"Look, asshole," I snapped, trying the direct route. "Back the hell off before I make you regret it."

A tall figure materialized between us, broad shoulders blocking the creep from my view as he knocked the guy's arms away from me.

"I believe the lady said no." Eli's voice rang out, low and dangerous.

I'd never heard that tone from him before, and it made me blink twice. Gone was the easygoing charm, steel-edged assertiveness in its place. A ripple ran down my spine that had nothing to do with fear.

The guy sneered, puffing out his chest. "This ain't your business, pretty boy. Why don't you piss off?"

Eli didn't budge. "I'm making it my business. Now back away before things get ugly."

"Or what?" the creep taunted, shoving Eli's shoulder.

In a lightning-fast move, Eli grabbed the guy's wrist and twisted it behind his back. The man yelped as Eli towered over him.

"Or I'll break your goddamn arm," Eli growled. "Now apologize to the lady and get lost."

"Okay, okay!" the guy whimpered. "I'm sorry! Jesus, let go!"

Eli released him, and the asshole scrambled away, shooting us a venomous glare.

I stared at Eli, my heart pounding for an entirely different reason now. Where had this protective side come from? And why did my body like it so much?

"You okay?" Eli asked, his voice softening slightly as he turned to me.

I nodded, not trusting myself to speak. All I could think was how different Eli looked in that moment—dangerous and compelling in a way that made a pulsing, hot wave roll through my core.

"Thanks," I finally managed. "I had it under control, but… I appreciate the backup."

Eli's lips rose in a half-smile and just like that, the Eli I knew was back. "Anytime. Can't have some drunken idiot ruining ladies' night, right?"

I laughed, the tension breaking. "Right. My hero."

Lacey sidled up to us, her eyes darting between Eli and me with undisguised interest. "Well, that was quite the show." A sly grin spread across her face. "You two make quite the team."

Heat flashed across my face, and I avoided Eli's gaze. "It was nothing."

"Mm-hmm," Lacey hummed. She checked her phone and yawned dramatically, patting her mouth with one hand. "You know, I think I'm going to call it a night. Early morning tomorrow."

I narrowed my eyes at her. "It's barely nine, Lace."

She shrugged, already adjusting her purse. "Beauty sleep is important when you're the bride. You don't mind walking home, do you? It's only a few blocks. I know you'd prefer to walk under the lovely night sky than huddle in my car, anyway. You two have fun!"

"Lacey, what are you—"

Then she gave us a salute. "Nighty night, folks." With a wink that was about as subtle as a foghorn, she sashayed toward the exit, leaving me alone with Eli.

# Chapter Nine

## JULES

I TURNED TO ELI, mortification warring with a secret thrill as I smoothed my decidedly messy hair. "I'm sorry about her. She's not known for her acting."

Eli laughed, his eyes crinkling and that damn dimple showing up again. "No need to apologize. She's right, though. I'm not sure I want to leave you by yourself. Want some company?"

My heart did a little flip. "Well, I guess it'd be a shame to waste the night. Want to grab another drink?"

"Thought you'd never ask." Eli shot me a lazy smile that made my lungs freeze mid-breath, then led the way to the bar. As we parked ourselves on two stools, the atmosphere buzzed again with laughter and upbeat music. The bartender, a tattooed guy with an infectious smile, greeted Eli like an old friend and poured us two cold drafts without needing to ask.

"Here you go." He slid the frosty mugs our way. "On the house for the hero of the night."

Eli inclined his head, lifting his glass in a mock salute. "Guess I should come in here more often if this is how I get treated." Turning to me, he clinked his glass to mine and leaned closer. "By the way, I've got some good news on the work front. The new dive computers came in today."

"That's good. Are you happy with them?"

He nodded. "They'll be perfect for what we need. And you guys might even be the first to use them, in the final pool session."

I grinned back at him, unsure if the buzz had anything to do with the alcohol. "Then I'm grateful that you've given me this honor."

"Only the best for Ms. Jules Verne."

As we sipped our beers, the conversation flowed surprisingly easily. We talked about everything from our favorite spots on Dove Key to what he used to get up to in high school. Unsurprisingly, he spent a lot of time getting in trouble. I found myself laughing comfortably at his stories. And very aware that we were interacting on a completely new level. Our old animosity was ancient history right now.

The night air was balmy when we left Salty's, a gentle breeze providing the perfect cooling touch. The bar occupied a prime lot on the primary corner of town, and it had always been a bit of a mystery why the place had never been spruced up. Eli and I fell into step as we walked beneath the ornate lampposts of Main Street, their riotous flower baskets lit softly.

"So," Eli said, breaking the comfortable silence. "You mentioned earlier that you're not usually a dive bar kind of girl, thank God. What's your usual scene?"

I laughed, a bit self-consciously. "Lacey and I usually go to Conch Republic, where you saw us several weeks ago.

But honestly? Most nights, you'd find me curled up with a good book and a glass of wine. Thrilling, I know."

"Hey, no judgment here." Eli held up his hands. "Sometimes a quiet night is exactly what a person needs."

Something in his tone made me glance over. His easy smile was there, but his eyes held a hint of… something. Weariness? Longing?

Before I could stop myself, I asked, "Is that what you need? A quiet night?"

Eli's steps faltered for a moment. "Sometimes," he admitted. "I felt like a little solitude tonight, which is why I went to Salty's. I'm not as well known there."

"Guess you didn't get much solitude."

He laughed, that relaxed, easy sound. "That place can get a little rough. I'm glad I was there."

"Me too, Eli. Even if it wasn't what either of us planned on."

He pressed a hand against his chest. "Don't get me wrong, I love the whole beach bum lifestyle. Though being a dive instructor is a lot more work than people think. But occasionally… I don't know. It can feel a bit hollow."

I couldn't resist looking up at him. Seeing how the moonlight painted his face in shades of silver and shadow as we walked along the sidewalk, transforming the carefree dive guy I thought I knew into someone different. My gaze traced the sharp angle of his jaw, the relaxed set of his broad shoulders. There was a quiet strength there I'd never noticed before, an intriguing depth beneath his easygoing exterior.

I quickly looked away when Eli darted a glance at me. "Can I ask you about something?"

My heart did this strange little flippy thing. "Sure."

"Harper mentioned you gave up a new desktop you

needed so Annie could keep her hours." His voice was gentle, probing.

I stiffened, surprised he knew about that. "It was nothing," I said quickly, adopting my best no-nonsense tone. "Just a simple reallocation of resources. Annie's ability to pay her bills took precedence over updating my hardware. Basic cost-benefit analysis."

Eli's eyebrows rose slightly. "You could have let Harper handle it. You didn't have to get involved."

I bristled at his probing, feeling strangely defensive. "It's my job to manage the resort's finances. I was just doing what needed to be done."

Eli's gaze was warm, curious. "You care about the staff, don't you?"

I swallowed hard, fighting the urge to retreat behind my usual walls. "Of course. They're good people. They deserve better than what we can offer right now. What I can offer them."

A small smile played at the corners of Eli's lips. "Sounds like there's more to Jules Verne than just spreadsheets and budget reports."

I hesitated, my heart pounding. This wasn't me— sharing personal thoughts, especially with Eli, of all people. But something in his gentle probing made me want to explain.

"I don't like… the attention," I confessed. The admission surprised even me. I rarely acknowledged my own discomfort with vulnerability.

Eli cocked his head, his indigo eyes thoughtful. "The attention?"

I took a long breath of the sultry air, running a hand over my loose tresses. "When people make a big deal out of, uh, kindness. It's uncomfortable. I-I just…" I struggled to find the right words. "I don't want people to see me as soft."

Eli's brow furrowed. "And that would be bad because...?"

I let out a humorless chuckle. "Because soft gets you hurt. Soft doesn't keep a struggling resort afloat."

The words hung in the air between us. I realized I was giving Eli a glimpse behind my carefully constructed persona—the meticulous accountant, the by-the-books professional. And I wasn't at all sure that was a good idea.

"Plus," I added, "I felt guilty about approving those new dive computers for you when we're facing staff cuts. It didn't seem fair. And adding a new desktop for myself was just the cherry on top. Delaying my new computer was an easy decision."

Eli's eyes widened, a flash of—was that admiration?—sweeping across his face. "I had no idea that side of you even existed."

I shrugged. "There's a lot about me you don't know, Eli."

"I agree." The moonlight caught the curve of his jaw as he nodded, the corners of his mouth lifting. I smiled back, warmth blooming in my chest that I couldn't squash.

"Guess that goes both ways," I said as we strolled under the pink canopy of Sweet Dreams Bakery. "You've got more depth than I gave you credit for."

Eli's smile widened, but before he could respond, I forged ahead, desperate to regain some semblance of control over the conversation. And my emotions. "Look, I know my approach to life and work can be rigid. It keeps people at a distance, but that's kind of the point."

"What is?"

I took a deep breath. "I've learned the hard way that emotions can be a liability. Logic and order? Those are things you can count on in this world. A math problem always has the same solution." I let out a self-deprecating laugh. "I know how it sounds. The accountant finding comfort in spreadsheets and financial projections. But that control? It's a hell of a lot safer than the alternative."

As soon as the words left my mouth, I wanted to snatch them back. I was sure a patented Eli Coleridge zinger was about to come my way.

I was wrong.

Eli's expression softened, his smile fading. "I get what you're saying. We all have our ways of dealing with… stuff." He ran a hand through his hair, a gesture I'd seen a hundred times before, but now it seemed different. Vulnerable, almost. "Mine is humor."

My breath caught. There was a depth to his words, a hint of old pain that resonated with my own.

"Humor, huh?"

"Yeah." He laughed, but it lacked his usual easy sound. "Crack a joke, deflect with a witty one-liner. It's easier than facing things head-on sometimes, you know?"

I nodded mutely, shocked at the admissions both of us were giving tonight. At how honest they were. And how similar.

"But I'm glad I got to see the real Jules tonight," he added, his gaze softening even further.

"And I'm glad I got to see the real Eli. Bar fight and all."

He held up a finger. "*Near* bar fight. The guy slinked off, remember?"

"I haven't forgotten." I sighed. "That was a good example of why I stay away from men. I seem to attract troublemakers."

He grinned as he walked with both hands in the pockets of his shorts. "Present company included?"

That made me laugh. "Oh, yes. Absolutely." Both smiling, we walked along for a few steps before I found myself opening up again. "My walls and the poor choices in men are related, as you might have guessed."

Eli nodded, his expression softening as he stared at me. "What happened? If you don't mind me asking."

I took a deep breath. "It was during college. I thought we were serious—forever serious. Until he cheated on me. Real cliché, right?"

"Damn," Eli muttered. "That's rough. I'm sorry."

"It was a long time ago." I shrugged, trying to ignore the old ache. "Close to ten years. But it made it hard to trust people for a while. Still does, if I'm being honest."

Eli's gaze held steady on me, a flicker of understanding igniting in his eyes. "I understand. Trust is a funny thing." He paused, as if weighing his words carefully. "My parents had a… rocky relationship. They fought a lot, but everyone thought they were just one of those couples who dealt with crap like that. I thought that's what love looked like. Until my dad walked out one day and never looked back. At first, I thought I'd be fine with it, you know? But then it messed with my head."

I tilted my head slightly, intrigued. "Messed with your head how?"

His shoulders slumped a little, and he raised a hand to the back of his neck and rubbed. "I guess I just started to think that love was always going to end up in disaster. I mean, I obviously have no idea what a healthy relationship looks like."

"What about Brenna and her husband? They look like a great couple." Though Eli's sister had her own life away from Sunset Siesta, she was still a regular visitor, and now Hunter with her.

He lifted one shoulder uncomfortably. "Yeah, and

that's great for them. But what if they're the exception? Hell, most couples I know end up tearing each other apart. So I avoid anything serious. I like to keep things light, fun… you know?"

"Like your dive classes."

Eli laughed, and that made me feel better. I liked the sound of his laugh. "Exactly! It's all about making sure no one drowns while I show them the perfection of diving. If they get scared, I tell them to focus on their breathing and enjoy the ride."

"You're a really good instructor, Eli. I'm sorry if I was harsh about that."

He shrugged. "I dished it out pretty good myself. So I'm sorry too."

"Look at us now! Talking like two grown adults."

"Not an insult to be found! Could be dangerous, Jules."

I took a deep breath. Dangerous, indeed. Because now I was seeing the man next to me in a completely new light.

We rounded the corner onto my street, the soft glow of streetlights illuminating the palm-lined sidewalk. My town-house loomed ahead, and a strange mix of disappointment and anticipation swirled in my stomach.

"Well, this is me," I said, gesturing to the modest two-story building.

Eli's eyes wandered over the neat facade. "Nice place. Very… Jules."

I raised a brow. "Is that a compliment or an insult?"

He grinned, and that dimple appeared again. "Definitely a compliment. It's orderly and welcoming but not stuffy. Kind of like you."

I burst out laughing and fumbled for my keys. "Thanks. I think."

We reached my front door, and my stomach fluttered as I turned to face Eli. He stood completely still, both arms at his sides as his eyes met mine. They were inscrutable, not the open book he usually was. The air between us became charged, electric. And for an endless, breathless moment, I wondered if he was going to lean in and kiss me.

My heart hummed in my chest. Did I want him to?

The responsible part of my brain said *no*.

But every other fiber of my being was screaming *yes, please*.

Eli shifted his weight and gave me a slow nod, breaking the spell. "Well, good night, Jules. Thanks for the chat."

"Right." I blinked, trying to hide my disappointment. "Thanks for your help tonight. Good night, Eli."

He flashed that easy smile and turned to go. I watched him stroll down the sidewalk, his broad shoulders silhouetted against the streetlights. And it occurred to me I didn't even know where he lived. There was so much I didn't know about him.

And now I wanted to.

# Chapter Ten

# ELI

"YOU GONNA EAT that or just rearrange it?" Chase pointed at my plate with his chin.

I shrugged, not putting much effort into the motion. "Not super hungry, I guess."

I leaned back in my chair as I surveyed the cheery turquoise walls of Braden's pub on a Sunday afternoon. Across the table, Chase was demolishing his fish tacos with surgical precision. I picked at my own club sandwich.

"Uh-huh. Since when are you not hungry?" He set down his half-eaten taco.

I rubbed the back of my neck. "I've got a lot on my mind, okay?"

"Like what?"

"I think…" The words stuck in my throat.

Chase's gaze sharpened on me. "You think what?"

I ate a fry, then whipped my head back and forth. "Nah, forget it."

"Eli, what the hell is eating you? Whatever it is, it's recent. You weren't like this last weekend."

"No, I wasn't." I took another swig of beer for liquid courage and looked him in the eye. "I think I'm falling for Jules."

Chase's eyebrows shot up. "Huh. That's not what I expected."

"Yeah, well, join the club."

"I take it the scuba lessons are going well, then?" He looked like he was trying not to laugh, damn him.

"She's…" What? What exactly was Jules?

"I thought you two hated each other." He finally started laughing and I threw a fry at him. That only made him laugh harder.

"Well, things have changed."

"Damn, you must be some scuba instructor."

I smiled smugly at him. "That goes without saying." Then my face fell. "But Jules has surprised me a lot. I think she'll be a great diver." Unlike Chase's sister, who I had serious doubts about.

"Right. So you're not torturing her with her nickname? She's been forbidding me to tell you about it for years."

I snorted. "I did a little at first. But she explained it, and… I dunno. It was like she revealed a side I never knew existed. But you're still a dick for hiding that from me."

"Caught in the middle, bro. Nothing I could do about it. But you and Jules are getting hot and heavy?"

"No. At least not yet." I laughed, but it turned into a groan. "God, I'm such an idiot."

"Why's that?"

"Because I almost kissed her the other night, but instead, I bolted like a scared teenager." The memory made me cringe. "I literally chickened out, too afraid of rejection."

My whole reaction had been weird. Stepping in at Salty's to protect her hadn't been something I'd even needed to think about. Then, while walking her home, we'd had by far the most insightful conversation ever. Yet I couldn't seal the deal at the end. The funny thing was, I was pretty damn sure she wanted me to kiss her. She was giving off that vibe for sure.

Chase's expression softened. "I admit, that's not your usual move. This clearly means something to you."

I nodded, my chest a tight ball. "Maybe. I'm still trying to figure it all out."

I'd been sitting on a bar stool when I saw her on the dance floor and was stunned at how her hair was loose, how *free* she looked. I froze in place, unable to look away. First, the sight of her had made me want to slide my fingers through those silky tresses, then it had made me want to grab a double handful, yank her head back, and kiss her until she melted into a puddle.

"Did you two go out?"

I shook my head. "Friday night I decided to go to Salty's. I was tired and wanted to be invisible. Salty's is a good place for that."

Chase nodded. "Go on."

I explained about the asshole and how seeing that Jules was clearly not into him had made me go full-on caveman. I'd been so full of testosterone, I'd been ready to punch the guy into the next county.

Chase listened intently, his hazel eyes thoughtful. When I finished, he leaned back, a slight smirk playing on his lips. "You know, I'm not sure I've ever seen you this worked up over a woman before."

I rolled my eyes, but my stomach did a little flip. "Come on, man. It's not like that."

"Isn't it?" Chase challenged, his voice gentle but firm.

"Eli, you've been my best friend since we were kids. I've seen you with plenty of women, but never once have I seen you this… contemplative. You're actually concerned about her feelings. That's new for you."

His words hit me like a punch to the gut. I took another swig of beer, buying time as my mind raced. Was Chase right? Was Jules different?

The thought didn't please me.

I didn't want different. I liked my superficial, fun relationships with no strings.

I stared at the condensation dripping down my beer glass, memories of my parents' bitter divorce flooding back. Mom's tear-stained face as Dad packed his bags. Her thunderous silence in the weeks that followed. The way Mom had retreated into herself, becoming a shell of the vibrant woman she'd once been. It had taken all of us as a family to pull her out of that, while we were dealing with our own pain over the fallout.

"You don't get it, Chase," I said quietly. "Commitment changes people. Look at what happened to my folks. One day they're a steady force in my life, the next they're done. He's gone. And Mom never recovered from that. She just… gave up."

I could feel Chase's concerned gaze on me as I stared at the table. "That doesn't mean it's going to happen to you, Eli."

I shrugged, trying to shake off the heavy memories. "Maybe. Maybe not. But why risk it? Things are good now. Jules and I are finally getting along. For the first time ever. Why rock the boat?"

But even as I said the words, I knew they rang hollow. Because deep down, a part of me—a part I'd been doing my best to ignore—wanted to rock that boat with Jules. Wanted to rock it like hell.

Before Chase could respond, a whirlwind of light hair and enthusiasm burst into the pub.

"Uncle Eli!" Finn exclaimed, bounding over to our table with a grin that could outshine the Florida sun. "Guess what? I'm on a super important mission!"

I couldn't help but laugh. "Oh yeah? What kind of mission, buddy?"

Finn puffed out his chest, clearly relishing the attention as he bounced his gaze between us. "Mom asked me to bring this to Uncle Braden, and it's very delicate." Pronouncing the last word carefully, he held up a small electronic device. "It's for the sound system, I think. Pretty cool, huh?"

"Very cool," Chase agreed, ruffling Finn's hair. "You're quite the responsible little man."

I watched their interaction, struck by how natural Chase was with kids. Finn had taken to him practically from the moment he could walk.

My nephew looked at him with more than a little worship in his eyes. "Have you built any more skyscrapers lately?"

Chase laughed, a warm, rich sound that filled the brewpub. "Not lately, bud. Not since that big one in Fort Lauderdale."

"Whoa," Finn breathed, clearly impressed. "That's so awesome! Can you teach me?"

"Maybe someday," Chase said with a giant grin and pointed at the sound card. "For now, better finish that important mission of yours, huh?"

Finn nodded seriously, cradling the device against his chest. "You're right. Gotta get to it. Bye, Chase! Bye, Uncle Eli!"

As Finn scampered off, I turned to Chase. "Speaking of building things, I didn't ask you here to talk about my love life. We need to talk about the resort. The family has been talking about getting a formal consult on which repairs and renovations to prioritize."

"That's a solid idea." Chase tapped his chin. "What do you have in mind?"

"We want to hire you officially. To get your take on what we need to focus on first. Maybe some structural assessments or whatever else you think might be necessary."

He nodded slowly, contemplating my words as he swirled the dregs of his beer. "I could definitely do that. Sunset Siesta has so much potential, you know? That Old Florida charm is worth preserving."

I leaned forward, excitement rising in my chest. "Exactly! And with the right updates, we could attract more guests and keep the resort afloat. It's just, I want to make sure we get it right."

Chase gave me an encouraging nod, his eyes steady as he listened intently. "This means a lot to you."

"Yeah, well…" I shifted in my chair as I glanced around the pub again. "It's not just about business. It's our home. Our family built this place from the ground up."

Chase tapped his jaw as he considered my words. "It's a lot to think about. Anyplace specific you want me to start?"

"Since you're here now, could you take a preliminary look around? Maybe check in with Harper first for specifics?"

He barked a laugh, shaking his head. "Nah, I'll just start. She's got enough on her plate."

"What do you mean?"

"Come on, Eli," he said, a teasing smirk creeping onto his face. "She's the general manager of a resort and a single mom. I can handle the resort priorities without putting any more work on her."

"She lives for chaos. Always the calm harbor in the storm, that girl," I replied, but my mind was already moving on to the upcoming week. "I'm looking forward to a Monday morning for once. I'm leading a group tomorrow. No classes." My heart took off at the thought. Leading dives made me forget all my worries. "It'll be choppy. A storm is supposed to hit, but not bad enough to cancel the dive."

"Should keep things interesting," he said. "You love it when it's challenging."

"True," I admitted, already picturing myself beneath the surface, surrounded by vibrant corals and swaying sea fans. The way light filtered through water was like magic. The sunbeams formed stained glass in my own cathedral.

He stood up. "I'll poke around a little and get a sense of what the immediate priorities are. But don't expect my report right away. If the resort is officially hiring me to consult, I'll do a thorough job."

Folding my arms, I grinned up at him. "You're such a Boy Scout. Fine, I'll be the slacker for you. Don't worry, I'll think of you when I'm enjoying myself tomorrow."

***

I'D JINXED myself with my big, fat mouth yet again. As I surfaced in the churning waters, I scanned the slate-gray horizon. Angry clouds loomed overhead, and a steady rain and wind pelted the group surfacing around me.

"All right, folks," I called out, my voice carrying over the wind. "Let's wrap this up nice and easy. Remember the procedures we went over before the dive, stay close, and we'll be back on the boat in no time."

I did a quick head count as my collection of six divers bobbed around me. Five calm faces, and one that looked like he'd just seen a shark sharpening its teeth. That'd be Lou, the newbie of the group.

"Hey, Lou," I said, paddling closer. "How are you holding up, buddy?"

His eyes were huge. "I'm, I'm okay. It's just…"

"The weather?" I finished for him, flashing my most reassuring grin. "Don't sweat it. Mother Nature's putting on a little show for us. I deal with weather all the time. We've got this."

The tension in Lou's shoulders eased a bit like I'd hoped. Years of guiding divers through their first underwater adventures had honed my ability to read people quickly to a fine art.

"Now let's get you dry," I continued, gesturing toward *Sunset Diver*. "I'll be right behind you."

As we made our way back, I kept a watchful eye on Lou and the others. The waves were getting bigger by the minute, but I'd dealt with worse. Lou was finning on the surface much too strenuously and his BCD was underinflated. "Add air to your BCD. Float on the surface and take it easy. Let the gear do its job, not you."

Lou's head bobbed in acknowledgment. As he added a burst of air to his BCD, a flicker of pride crossed his face. Moments like these reminded me why I loved this job. Sure, the endless summer and laid-back lifestyle were nice, but nothing beat the feeling of helping someone conquer their fears.

As we neared the boat, I allowed myself a small sigh of relief. Despite the challenging conditions, another successful dive was almost in the bag. I finned ahead to check on the other divers, making sure they were all doing okay. They were in a neat line, watching the boat carefully as they boarded one by one. That's when I heard a splash and a panicked gasp behind me.

"Help! I can't—" A mouthful of seawater cut off Lou's voice.

I spun around, my heart racing. Lou was flailing, his eyes wide with terror. Obviously, he hadn't added enough air and was struggling in the heavy waves. Before I could react, he reached for his BCD release, fumbling with the buckles.

"Lou, don't—" I shouted. I lunged for him, but it was too late.

I heard the click of the buckle opening even over the wind, and Lou's entire scuba kit plummeted into the depths below. Shit. We were in deep water here. This was bad. Really bad.

I surged through the water, my muscles burning with the effort. "I'm coming, Lou! Just stay calm and float on your back!"

As I reached him, I could see the fear etched on his face. "I'm sorry," he sputtered. "I couldn't figure out the inflator and I panicked—"

"It's okay," I said, keeping my voice steady despite the adrenaline coursing through me. "I've got you now. Your wetsuit provides plenty of flotation, so relax. Let's get you to the boat."

I slipped my hands around under Lou's armpits and started towing him while I moved backward, using the rescue technique I'd practiced countless times. "Deep breaths, buddy. We're gonna take this nice and slow."

As we made our way to the boat, I kept up a stream of casual chatter, anything to keep Lou's mind off the situation. "You know, my first time in rough seas, I hurled all over my instructor. Trust me, this is way less embarrassing."

A weak laugh escaped Lou's lips. Good. A relaxed diver was a safer diver.

Finally, we reached the boat. As I helped Lou up the ladder, I could feel the collective sigh of relief from the other divers. Deke, our boat captain, promptly put an arm over his shoulders and steered him safely to the side bench. Crisis averted.

Well, the crisis involving Lou anyway. The kit? That was another story.

"Everyone okay?" I called out, doing another head count. Six nods from my group, and Andrea's group was already on board. Perfect.

Except for the thousands of dollars of gear lying on the bottom of the ocean.

As we rode back to the resort, the adrenaline from the rescue slowly ebbed away to leave room for a gnawing worry to settle in my gut. I glanced at the empty spot where Lou's gear should've been, and an internal groan escaped me.

Shit. This was going to be expensive.

I ran a hand through my wet, salty hair, trying to push away thoughts of the conversation I'd have to have with Jules. Our almost-kiss still lingered in my mind, a bittersweet memory now tainted by the dread of this upcoming financial discussion. I had no doubts which Jules would be present for this conversation.

"You saved my life back there." Lou's shaky voice pulled me from my thoughts as he sat next to me.

I turned to him, mustering up a reassuring smile. "Nah, you were fine. Like I said, the wetsuit did the work, not me. How're you feeling?"

"Better." He paused, staring at his fidgeting hands. "I'm sorry about the equipment. I'll pay for it, of course."

I waved him off, even as my stomach twisted. "Don't worry about it. Safety first, always."

We had insurance, but the deductible was huge—more than the cost of a new kit. And we'd never make a guest compensate us for what was an accident. As the shoreline of Dove Key came into view, I couldn't shake the dread. Jules was going to freak out when she saw the numbers. God, why did this have to happen now?

I could already picture her face—those amazing eyes narrowing, her full lips pressing into a thin line. As we docked, I helped the still-shaken Lou off the boat, my mind racing. How the hell was I going to explain this to her without derailing whatever fragile connection we'd started to build?

# Chapter Eleven

## JULES

I BLINKED HARD, trying to refocus as the lines on my screen swam out of focus. Staring at my empty coffee cup, I contemplated a refill. Even though it was afternoon. This was ridiculous. Budgets were my bread and butter. Fiscal responsibility was practically my middle name. And yet here I sat in the same old office, staring at my temperamental computer screen, yet my mind was a million miles away from quarterly projections. My brain was fixated on one thing and one thing only.

Eli Coleridge.

The man who'd rubbed me the wrong way since the moment we met. The man who had walked me home Friday night and who I'd opened up to. The man who had almost kissed me.

I dropped my head into my hands. What was wrong with me? I hadn't seen or spoken to him since Friday night, but I couldn't get him out of my head. This was exactly why workplace romances were forbidden at

Sunset Siesta. They led to nothing but distraction and disaster.

A soft ping sounded from my computer. New email. Probably another tedious request from the **PR** company asking for approval for their bloated ad budget. I glanced at the sender and my heart skipped a beat.

*From: Eli Coleridge*
*Subject: Need to meet ASAP*

*Jules,*
*Can you swing by the dive shop when you get a chance?*
*Something I need to discuss with you.*

*Thanks,*
*Eli*

I REREAD the terse message twice, my curiosity piqued. Eli rarely emailed and had never asked to see me like this. What could be so urgent? And why did the thought of seeing him again send slow tendrils reaching through my abdomen?

Before I could think, I was on my feet and striding out my door. I stepped out of the resort's main building, my mind so preoccupied I barely registered the dreary weather. The rain pattered against my face and dampened my blouse as I rushed down the path toward the pier. Dammit. My raincoat hung forgotten on its hook by my office door. At least the storm had lessened this afternoon. It had been pouring buckets when I drove to work.

My heels clacked a staccato rhythm on the damp wood

as I hurried along the pier, my thoughts a whirlwind. What could Eli need to discuss that couldn't wait? And why did the thought of seeing him again make my heart race like I'd just sprinted a 5K?

I reached the dive shop, pausing for a moment to catch my breath and smooth my rain-soaked hair into some semblance of order. As I stepped inside, I glanced around for Eli. But Andrea looked up from behind the counter, her usual cheerful smile tight-lipped.

"Afternoon, Andrea. Where's Eli?"

"Hey, Julianne," she said, her voice strained. "He's in the classroom. But, uh… heads-up. We had a rough one out there this morning."

My footsteps paused as I headed toward the hallway. "What do you mean, rough?"

Andrea shook her head, glancing toward the classroom. "You'd better hear it from him. Let's just say it wasn't exactly smooth sailing."

A knot of apprehension formed in my stomach as I nodded and continued. I stepped into the classroom, my eyes immediately drawn to Eli. He stood in front of a computer terminal, his usually relaxed demeanor replaced by a tense, almost rigid posture. His sun-bleached hair was a chaotic mess as if he'd been running his fingers through it. When he looked up at me, his eyes were stormy with frustration.

"Jules. Thanks for coming."

I stopped before his teaching table. "Sure. What's going on? Andrea mentioned something about a rough morning."

He exhaled sharply and rubbed his tired-looking eyes. "Yeah, you could say that. We had an accident during the dive. Everyone's okay, but…" He paused, jaw clenching. "A diver panicked at the surface, and we lost a full scuba kit. It's at the bottom of the ocean now. We have to replace it."

My heart sank. "Oh, no. Is the diver okay?"

He nodded distractedly.

"Are you okay, Eli?"

A fleeting smile cracked his face. "I'm fine. He just lost his head, and I had to rescue him and tow him back to the boat."

"I'm glad you're both all right." The situation was another reminder that there was much more to Eli Coleridge than I'd ever given him credit for. But it didn't change the current facts. "This is terrible timing, especially after the dive computer expenses. How much are we looking at to replace it?" I chewed my lip, mental calculations already running through my head.

Eli turned to the computer and pulled up a page. "I just looked it up. It's going to be around two thousand dollars. He was using one of the new dive computers, of course."

The blood drained from my face. Two thousand dollars! "Eli, I'm sorry, but there's no way we can swing that right now. The budget is already stretched thinner than a rubber band as it is."

His eyes flashed. "Jules, this isn't optional. I've been cobbling together gear for months. Hell, years. We don't have any spares, okay? If we don't get a new set of gear, we'll have to start canceling divers. That'll cost us even more in the long run."

My practical side warred with my sympathy. "I understand that, but I can't just magically make money appear. We're barely staying afloat as it is."

"Believe me, I know. But we've got to come up with it somehow." He looked me up and down, his gaze appraising. "Look, I know you're damn good at your job. I might not have admitted that out loud before, but I'm aware of it. So I need you to wave your magic wand, okay?"

Ignoring the warmth that wanted to spread over my abdomen at his compliment, instead, I planted my feet and squared my shoulders. "Eli, I get it. I do. But we can't just throw two grand at this without considering the bigger picture."

His jaw set hard as he straightened to his full height. "The bigger picture? Jules, I am. Without proper equipment, we don't have a dive operation. No dive op, no dive charters. It's that simple."

"Nothing about running this resort is simple," I shot back, my voice rising. The dive operation was one of the resort's strongest earners, but it wasn't the only area I had to worry about. "Every department is screaming for more funding. I've already bent the rules for you, so where does it end?"

Eli stepped closer. "This isn't about bending rules. It's about safety."

"There's no room to carve out an expense this big."

He raked a hand through his messy hair. "I'll have to charge it on my own card, then. It's pretty much maxed out, but—"

"Absolutely not." I was shocked he'd even suggest that. "That is strictly against policy. And Harper would never sanction it. Neither would I."

"What the hell are we supposed to do then?" His voice was rising. "This expense will increase revenue, dammit."

My breath caught. I'd never seen him like this, all intensity and determination. Except the other night. Goose bumps rippled down my arms. Part of me wanted to keep arguing, to stand my ground. But another part—a part I was trying to ignore at the moment—was finding this passionate version of Eli extremely attractive. My heart hammered, and not just from the heated discussion. I quickly shoved that back. My attraction to him didn't matter right now.

I swallowed hard. "It's not about future revenue. Your request isn't unreasonable, but—"

"No buts," he interrupted. "We replace the gear or we start canceling divers. And guests. Those are our options."

I stepped forward, my frustration boiling over. "Goddammit, Eli! You're right. I am damn good at my job. Because I'm fair. I do the right thing, even when it pisses people off. You can't just demand things, Eli. I'm not going—"

That was the last word I got out. Eli closed the distance between us in two swift strides. He gripped my shoulders, and before I could process what was happening, his lips crashed into mine. For a split second, I froze. The clock ticked on the wall. His lips were so warm, so smooth.

Then something inside me snapped.

I threw my arms around his neck, kissing him back with a ferocity that shocked me. His tongue swept into my mouth, and I groaned, pressing myself against him. I plunged my fingers into his hair, the thick strands sliding between my fingers as I pulled him closer, deepening the kiss. The taste of him was everything I'd been fantasizing about, and I couldn't get enough.

Eli's hands moved from my shoulders to the small of my back, pulling me flush against him. His body was hard and warm, radiating an energy that made my head swim. I could feel the tension in every muscle as I rubbed my hands across his shoulders, down his back.

In one fluid motion, I jumped up and wrapped my legs

around his waist. Eli grunted in surprise, his hands moving to support my ass. He spun us around, pinning me against the wall with a thud that knocked the breath from my lungs.

"God, Jules," he panted against my mouth, grinding his hips into mine. The friction sent shockwaves through my body, and I arched into him, desperate for more contact. My fingers closed in his hair, gripping him as I devoured his mouth, all thoughts of budgets and propriety forgotten.

Andrea's voice rang out from the main room. "Hey, guys, I'm heading to the gear room to check on those tanks I've been filling!"

Eli sprang back as if electrocuted. My feet hit the floor, and I stumbled, chest heaving. Eli's eyes were wide, his hair even more of a mess from my hands. We stared at each other, the realization of what we'd just done crashing over us like a tidal wave.

"I... uh..." I stammered, smoothing down my skirt with trembling hands. My lips felt swollen, and my whole body hummed with desire.

Eli was wide-eyed as he cleared his throat, looking equally shell-shocked. "Right. I, um, didn't expect to do that."

I nodded mutely, unable to form a coherent thought. The tension in the room was thick enough to cut with a knife.

"We should probably..." Eli gestured vaguely.

I took a deep breath, trying to regain some semblance of composure. "I-I shouldn't have done that," I said, working to keep my voice even. "It was completely unprofessional and—"

"Yeah," Eli cut in. "Me neither. It just happened." He

paused and shook his head as if to clear it. "But we need to focus on the gear situation. It's urgent, Jules."

I bit my lip, weighing the options. The accountant in me screamed about budget constraints, but a bigger part—the part still tingling from Eli's touch—wanted to help him. I was glad we'd stepped back from the brink, but the last thing I wanted was to go back to being adversaries. "Look, I can't promise anything, but… I'll see what I can do. Maybe we can reallocate some future charges or buy it on credit somehow."

Relief washed over Eli's face. "Thank you. I really appreciate it."

"Don't thank me yet," I warned, but I couldn't help a small smile. "I'll look into it and get back to you."

As I turned to leave, Eli's hand brushed my arm. The touch was light, but it sent electricity through my body. "Jules," he said softly. "About what happened…"

I shook my head. "Let's just focus on the dive kit for now, okay?"

He nodded, understanding in his eyes. I turned and almost stumbled out of the classroom. My legs were wobbly.

I pushed open the door of the dive shop, welcoming the cool drizzle that hit my face. My mind replayed the intense encounter with Eli over and over. All of it. The kiss, the passion, the way my body had responded without hesitation. It was all so unlike me.

"Forget it," I muttered, rubbing my still-tingling lips.

The rain picked up, soaking through my crisp button-down shirt. I hardly noticed. My thoughts raced between expense allocations and the feel of Eli's hands on my waist. The hardness between us as we ground together. There were a million reasons to keep my distance, to maintain that professional wall I'd so carefully constructed.

And yet...

I couldn't deny the pull toward him or the desire to help him out of this jam. It wasn't just attraction, though God knows that was there. His passion for his work, his unwillingness to compromise on safety, resonated with me.

By the time I reached my office, I was drenched and disheveled. I sank into my chair, wiping raindrops from my face with trembling hands. My reflection in the computer screen showed flushed cheeks and wild eyes. I barely recognized myself.

With a deep breath, I woke up my computer and pulled up the resort's financial records. "Okay," I whispered, fingers flying over the keyboard. "Let's see what we can do here."

I threw myself into the task, grateful for the distraction. Numbers were safe. Numbers didn't make my heart pound or my knees weak. So I combed through line items and juggled figures. Two hours later, a plan began to take shape. My phone buzzed with a text.

Eli: Any luck?

I STARED AT THE MESSAGE, my resolve wavering. It would be so easy to give in, to let myself fall. But I couldn't. Eli and I were as opposite as two people could get. Not long ago, we couldn't stand to be in the same room with each other.

So I typed back.

Jules: Working on a solution. Give me through tomorrow, okay?

His reply came almost instantly.

I set the phone down, my hand still shaking slightly. Tomorrow. I had until the end of tomorrow to get my head on straight and face Eli with a solution.

God help me.

# Chapter Twelve

## ELI

MY FOOTSTEPS WERE wooden as I walked the familiar route from my bungalow to Mom's house, my mind full of conflicting emotions. The taste of Jules's lips lingered, a ghost of sweetness and passion that refused to fade. Hours later, I replayed every moment of that unexpected kiss.

I sighed heavily and muttered, "It was just a kiss. A really hot, mind-blowing kiss that I absolutely can't stop thinking about. No big deal."

But it was a big deal. I couldn't shake the feeling of Jules in my arms, and it scared the hell out of me. I had a feeling Jules had been pretty shaken up too, even though she quickly backpedaled. At the time, I'd agreed that we needed to forget that kiss ever happened, but now?

Now I couldn't stop thinking about it.

I'd spent so long avoiding real connection, convincing myself I was happy with my unattached lifestyle. But now? After a single kiss, I wasn't sure of anything anymore. I felt more like a tortured teenager than a thirty-five-year-old man.

As I approached the house I'd grown up in, that all of us had, I spotted Harper on the porch, hunched over her laptop and her frown lit up by the screen.

"Hey, sis," I called out, plastering on my best easygoing grin. "You look about as relaxed as a lobster at a seafood festival. What's got your claws in a twist?"

Harper's attempt at a smile quickly faded. "Hi there, Eli. I'm feeling a bit overwhelmed."

I plopped down in the swing next to her, concern replacing my forced cheer. "Talk to me. What's going on?"

She sighed and closed her laptop. "It's this whole modernization thing. We need to do it, but I can't see how."

Seeing Harper so stressed hit me hard. "You know you don't have to do this alone, right?"

"I know," she said softly. "But sometimes it feels like the weight of Sunset Siesta's entire future is on my shoulders. I'm the manager of the resort. What if I mess it up?"

I wanted to reassure her, to say something profound yet witty that would chase away her doubts. But my own insecurities about the future, not to mention my conflicted feelings about Jules, left me fumbling for words. "Sometimes you've gotta take risks," I finally offered, thinking of the way one kiss had shattered my carefully constructed façade. "Even if it's scary. You never know what might happen."

Harper gave me a curious look. "That's surprisingly insightful and serious coming from you. Are you feeling okay?"

I couldn't help laughing. "Just channeling my inner fortune cookie, sis. Don't get used to it."

As Harper launched into the details of the budget forecast Jules had given her, and which certainly didn't include the new scuba kit, the porch steps creaked with footfalls. Our oldest brother, Ben, marched up, his muscular frame silhouetted against the fading light. His green eyes, usually sharp and alert, were tired, but there was a satisfied set to his jaw.

"Look what the kitty cat dragged in," I quipped. "How's the big, bad world of corporate security?"

Ben grunted, dropping into a nearby chair. "Successful. Stressful. Long."

I studied my brother, noting the tension in his shoulders despite his claimed satisfaction. "You thinking of another line of work?" I asked.

He lifted one shoulder in an uncomfortable shrug. "I don't know. I'm grateful to Hunter for hiring me, and the work is rewarding. I like helping people. But it's not what I want to do long term. I like being outdoors, but I don't exactly want to do landscaping for the rest of my life, either."

"You used to talk about becoming a paramedic," I said as I sprawled in the swing. "Whatever happened with that?"

The change was instantaneous. Ben's posture stiffened, his eyes darting away. "Nothing to tell. A dead end."

Harper leaned forward, her voice gentle. "Ben, you were so passionate about that. You'd be amazing at it."

"It was a stupid idea," Ben replied, his words clipped. "The resort needs me here. KeyMark pays well. It's fine."

Ben's walls went up, brick by brick. This was a topic I brought up from time to time, just to let him know I hadn't forgotten about it. About his desire to make a new start as something other than Dove Key's resident troublemaker. His insecurity was palpable, and suddenly, I saw a reflection of my own fears in his stubborn refusal to dream.

"No one's saying you have to change everything all at once," I said, treading carefully. "But don't sell yourself short."

Ben's laugh was bitter. "Right. Because book smarts are my strong suit. I barely graduated from high school. I know my place, Eli."

"That was a long time ago," Harper added quietly.

"Doesn't matter." You could have bounced a quarter off Ben's shoulders. "Half of Dove Key only sees me as the guy who used to love to get drunk and fight, while the other half refuses to acknowledge that I'm not twenty-five anymore."

The Coleridges had always had a reputation for trouble, though our reconciliation with the Markhams had tempered that a little. But Ben had always been the poster boy for *troubled local*.

Harper closed her laptop and faced Ben squarely. "They might see the past, but *we* see the man sitting here now. The one who shows up, works hard for Hunter and the resort, and helps Mom without being asked. People notice change, even if it takes time for perceptions to catch up. The EMT idea sounds like *you* taking control of your story."

"If only it were that simple, huh?" Ben pushed to his feet and headed to the door. "I'm going to see if Mom needs help."

"Well, that's probably our cue also," Harper said, standing up. "I don't think Ben is a battle we're going to win in one night."

The clink of silverware against plates filled the silence at our family dinner table. I stabbed at a piece of grilled dorado, my mind drifting back to the feel of Jules's body as I ground my hips into her.

"Eli? You've been awfully quiet tonight." Mom's voice snapped me back to reality.

"Sorry, just daydreaming about my secret plan to turn the resort into a nude beach." I flashed her my most charming grin. "Think of the money we'd save on towels."

Harper huffed but gave up and grinned. Ben let out a snort, nearly choking on his water. Even Mom cracked a reluctant smile.

"Always the comedian," she said, her tone the usual mix of exasperation and fondness I brought out in it.

I glanced over at Finn, who was quietly pushing his vegetables around his plate, lost in his own world. Poor kid was probably bored out of his mind with all this adult talk.

"Speaking of plans," Harper chimed in, her eyes meeting mine across the table, "how's Chase's consultation coming along? Any progress?"

"He's still working on it," I said. "Done a lot of the preliminary stuff, though. You know Chase—thorough to a fault. We probably won't get his report for another two months."

Mom dabbed at her mouth with a napkin, her movements deliberate. "About that," she began, her voice careful. "I've been thinking…"

The air in the room seemed to thicken, and I found myself holding my breath.

Mom slowly scanned our faces. "This resort is our legacy, and I want to leave it to you kids someday. I just want to be clear that we need to manage the extent of this. You all witnessed and experienced the fallout from our last financial crisis. We almost went under, your father's and my marriage shattered irrevocably. It nearly broke us. Not just the resort, as a family."

Mom's words hung in the air. She toyed with her napkin, her fingers betraying a nervousness I rarely saw.

Harper leaned forward. "Mom, we understand why this scares you. But most of us kids are involved with the resort now, and we can bear most of the burden. I believe we've reached the point where we can't afford *not* to do this."

I nodded, surprising myself. "Harper's right. Chase has a unique perspective on this whole thing. He knows all the history but can still approach this with new vision. And change isn't always bad, Mom." The words tumbled out before I could stop them, my runaway mouth betraying me once more. "Sometimes it's exactly what we need."

Harper shot me a grateful look, and I felt a surge of solidarity with my sister.

"Eli." Mom's voice wavered slightly. "I understand the need for repairs. I'm not blind to how things have slipped around here. But renovating a resort is a big task. A very big financial risk... it brings back memories I'd rather forget. And you've always been against wholesale change around here too."

I swallowed hard. "I know. But maybe it's time I learned to embrace a little change. And it can't hurt to see what Chase has to say. If we don't like it, we don't act on it."

Mom stared at each of us, her eyes filled with lingering doubt. Then at last a smile raised her lips, like the sun peeking through the clouds. "All right. And I know you're right, Harper. All of you are doing a wonderful job here. There's no reason for history to repeat, is there? Let's hear Chase out."

I let out a breath. "That's all we're asking, Mom."

Harper reached across the table to touch Mom's hand.

"Thank you. We know how much this place means to you. And it means the same to us."

Mom nodded. "Just… promise me you'll all be involved every step of the way."

"Of course," Harper and I said in unison, exchanging a quick glance.

Mom continued, "Harper, I'm sure you'd like to be the point person on any remodel that might happen."

Harper gave her an eager nod. "I'd consider it my personal responsibility to be the resort's representative on all remodel plans. You're not doing it all yourself this time."

Mom let out a deep breath that was a little shaky. "And I can't tell you what a relief that is. Thank you. All of you."

Ben had been quiet during dinner, but now he wore a small smile. "I'm just glad to hear we're not bulldozing the place and turning it into a water park," he said, his voice lightening the mood.

"Hey!" I pointed my fork at him. "Leave the jokes to me, buddy."

Ben just smirked and took a bite of roast, clearly pleased with himself for stealing my thunder. We settled back into the meal, the immediate hurdle cleared. Bigger questions remained, but maybe they felt less daunting now.

After dinner, Harper and I cleared the dishes. The knots in my shoulders eased, only for a new kind of restlessness to replace them. I kept replaying Mom's words in my head, *"You've always been against wholesale renovations."*

Had I? Or had I just coasted along, too lazy to imagine it any other way?

"Thanks for backing me up like that." Harper handed me a plate to load in the dishwasher. "I know you've had mixed feelings about modernizing."

I shrugged. "Yeah, well, even a broken clock is right twice a day."

She shook her head and gave me a side-eye. "Is that all it is?"

I rinsed a bowl excessively, buying time. "I don't know. What if Mom's right? What if we make all these changes and it blows up in our faces?" Jules's face flashed in my mind as much as I tried to prevent it.

Harper was quiet for a moment. "That's a risk we have to take, Eli. Nothing worth having comes without some kind of fight."

I nodded. "Yeah, but what if you're not cut out for the fight? What if you're better off not even trying?"

Harper's hand on my arm made me turn. "Eli," she said softly, "are we still talking about the resort?"

I forced a laugh. "Of course we are. What else would I be talking about?"

She didn't push, but her eyes broadcast her concern. As I resumed rinsing, I wondered how long I could keep pretending that a single kiss hadn't turned my entire world upside down.

As I walked home, the warm night air clung to my skin. The cement sidewalk was solid under my feet, but each step felt heavier than the last. Because our family was discussing the most important decision we'd had in decades, and my mind kept drifting back to Jules. The softness of her lips, that passion she'd shown that damn near undid me.

I groaned, scrubbing a hand over my face. "This is insane. You don't do relationships, remember? Especially not with someone you're not supposed to be involved with."

Yet something kept pulling me toward her, like a tide I couldn't resist. As I reached my bungalow, I paused at the door. I was playing with fire here, no doubt about it. But I had to wonder if getting burned might be worth it this time.

# Chapter Thirteen

## JULES

I SNUGGED the two Conch Republic IPA cans I'd just taken from the fridge into two Sunset Siesta cozies, wondering if Braden was missing out on revenue by not having the ability to make cans of his beers. Then I snorted, realizing I was trying to distract myself.

From that kiss.

And the fact that I'd *jumped* Eli Coleridge.

As I recounted the kiss to Lacey, I left out that last tidbit. Surreptitiously, I wiped my sweaty palms on my shorts and made sure my face was neutral as I handed her the beer.

"And then we both agreed to step back," I said, pleased at the steadiness of my voice. "It meant nothing. We got carried away in the moment and both agreed it won't happen again."

Lacey pressed her lips together to hide a smile. "Sure. And I'm the Queen of England."

I shot her a glare. "I'm serious, Lace. We can't… I can't…" I trailed off, unable to finish the thought.

"Can't what? Have some fun? Live a little?"

I flopped onto the couch, opened my beer, and took a long pull. "You don't understand. This isn't about fun. It's about my career, my future at Sunset Siesta. I can't afford to lose sight of my priorities. What if I let myself get swept away? What happens if things go wrong?"

"Jules, you realize that worrying about what-ifs is one of your superpowers, right?"

"Ha-ha. Very funny."

She sighed. "Jules, honey, you're allowed to have both. Fun and a career."

I looked up, meeting her gaze. "Am I? Because from where I'm sitting, it feels like I have to choose. And I've worked too hard to throw it all away for… for what? A fling with Eli?"

Lacey slowly spun the cozy in her hand, reading it, then stared me dead in the eye. "We're totally ignoring the elephant in the room here."

I frowned. "What are you talking about?"

"The fact that Eli is the first guy I've seen you get this distracted over. Which means it's probably the first time since college. Since Travis. How could this whole situation not bring all that bad juju up?"

I stared at the fronds of a palm tree dancing outside my window. She wasn't wrong. "Yeah. That's part of it. I've spent years protecting myself. I've gone on plenty of dates and had a fling or two, but I don't like to get close. And now I'm having a… a…"

"Non-relationship?" Lacey added helpfully.

"Not even that." I pointed at her. "I'm not going to get close to this guy. My God, Eli Coleridge's picture is in the dictionary next to *Commitment-phobe*. No more kissy face—therefore no getting hurt."

"Sounds very logical and well thought out," she said, and I ignored her sarcasm.

The memory of his lips on mine, the feel of his very obvious arousal grinding against me, flashed through my mind. I pushed it away, clinging to logic like a lifeline as I stood and began pacing. "It's not just about the resort. Eli's family. He's not going anywhere. But my job? That could disappear in an instant if this goes south."

Lacey sighed. "Possibly, but isn't that a bit dramatic? You're overthinking this."

"I'm being practical," I countered. "I'm good at practical. It's what I do."

"And how's that working out for you?"

I ignored her question, focusing instead on the dive kit. "There was an accident this morning and now Eli needs a whole new scuba kit. Which is a huge expense but an important one. The dive operation is one of the few profitable parts of the resort. So I spent hours doing financial hocus pocus to find the money while rejecting other purchases. And I'm still not finished."

Lacey's eyes grew sly. "Sounds like a purely business decision."

I nodded, guilt gnawing at me. "Exactly."

"Uh-huh," Lacey said, unconvinced. "And it has nothing to do with a certain dive instructor?"

I squared my shoulders. "No! Besides, Sunset Siesta has a rule against workplace romances, so there's another reason we need to keep our hands off each other. I can handle this. It's just a matter of compartmentalizing. I'm good at that."

Lacey shook her head, a sad smile on her face. "If you say so, honey. But remember, relationships have a way of forming whether you want them to or not. And no amount of logic can change that."

"It's not that complicated. We're adults. We can be professional."

Lacey's gentle laugh made me raise my head. "Oh, sweetie. When has anything involving the heart ever been simple?"

I opened my mouth to retort, but she cut me off with a sheepish smile.

"And speaking of complications… I have some news."

My stomach dropped and I stopped pacing. I knew that look. "What did you do?"

She twirled a strand of blonde hair around her finger. "So Daniel and I were talking, and we decided we don't want an underwater wedding anymore."

"What?" I blinked, processing. "But the dive lessons, the planning—"

"I know, I know," Lacey rushed to say. "We're thinking of a nice park ceremony instead. More practical, you know?"

"So are you guys finishing the class with me?"

Lacey shook her head. "No. Sorry, Jules."

I groaned, pinching the bridge of my nose. "Lace, do you have any idea how much time we've already invested in this?" *And what I had to go through to make it happen?* I added silently.

"I know, and I feel terrible." She grabbed my hand and pulled me down to sit next to her on the couch. "But isn't it better to change plans now rather than later?"

I wanted to be mad, but one look at her earnest face and my irritation melted. This was classic Lacey—impulsive but always well-meaning.

"I suppose," I conceded. "But we're so close to finishing. The open water dives will be incredible, Lace. Are you sure you don't want to continue?"

She shook her head firmly. "Nah, even after extra practice in the pool, I don't feel like I've got the hang of it at all. I keep having nightmares about panicking during my wedding, and that's not the vibe I'm going for at all. But hey, you should totally finish! You've worked so hard."

I bit my lip, unable to deny that she had struggled with many skills. I was torn between practical concerns and the traitorous flutter in my chest at the thought of solo checkout dives with Eli. "I don't know…"

"Come on." Lacey nudged me. "It's obvious you love diving, and unlike me, you're good at it! When's the last time you did something just for you?"

I couldn't remember, and that realization hit harder than I expected. "You're right. I'm not even sure."

"Daniel and I just have too much going on right now, and Randy only signed up because he had to. This is fate stepping in, Jules. You need to stay in the class."

I nodded firmly, decision made. "You know what? You're right. I'm going to finish the certification."

Lacey clapped her hands. "Yes! That's my girl!"

"It's only logical," I explained, ticking off reasons on my fingers. "I've already invested the time. And the class is nearly over—it'd be wasteful not to see it through. Plus, it's a valuable skill."

Lacey's smile turned knowing. "Absolutely. And the fact that the class is only you and Eli now?"

"Please," I scoffed, hoping my voice didn't betray me. "This is about finishing what I start."

"Sure, sure," Lacey said, clearly unconvinced. "Eli isn't quite the guy you thought he was, is he?"

I sighed, unable to deny it. "No, he's not. He's skilled.

Rescued a guest in trouble today. And he's passionate about diving."

"And hot," Lacey added helpfully.

I rolled my eyes. "That's irrelevant."

"Is it?" Lacey challenged.

I stood up, needing to move. "Look, I can acknowledge that Eli has… qualities I didn't see before. But that doesn't change anything. We're utter opposites. Coworkers, nothing more."

"Just coworkers. Got it. So when you see him next, you'll be perfectly calm and collected?"

"Of course. There's no reason things should be awkward."

Lacey's skeptical face spoke volumes, but I ignored it. I had to believe my own words. The alternative was far too dangerous to contemplate.


THE NEXT MORNING, I stood before the bathroom mirror, methodically twirling my hair into a bun as I practiced the conversation about the underwater wedding being off. Each precise movement was a silent mantra.

*Professional. Composed. In control.*

"It's just another day at the office," I told my reflection. "I'm simply informing a colleague about a change of plans." But as I fastened the last button on my neat white shirt, my fingers trembled slightly.

The drive to the resort was a blur of rehearsed phrases and steely determination. I was able to distract myself for a few hours by finishing my financial wizardry to allocate the money for the new scuba set. Nothing out of bounds or illegal, but my new desktop was looking like a distant pipe dream now.

As I approached the gear room, a sweltering, glorified

shed next to the dive shop, my carefully constructed façade began to crack. I hesitated at the door and the muffled sounds coming from within. Andrea had already informed me where Eli was, so with one last steadying breath, I pushed the door open. The dim room was stiflingly hot, the whir of fans doing little to dispel the oppressive warmth. A sheen of sweat broke out on my skin immediately. And there was Eli, bent over a row of tanks, his damp T-shirt clinging to his back. The giant air compressor, quiet now, stood on one side of the room, and neat rows of BCDs and regulators were lined up like soldiers across the back wall.

"Morning," I called out, wincing at the slight waver in my voice.

Eli straightened, turning to face me. His easy smile faltered for a moment as he stared at me, and I felt a ridiculous surge of satisfaction that I wasn't the only one affected.

"Jules." His tone was carefully neutral. "What brings you to my humble domain?"

*Professionals, colleagues, coworkers…*

I clasped my hands tightly, willing them not to fidget. "I needed to inform you of a change in plans." My words were clipped and formal. "Lacey and Daniel have decided against the underwater wedding, and they no longer want dive certifications. And Randy is dropping out too."

Eli's eyebrows shot up. "Seriously? After all that work?"

"Indeed. It's rather, uh, frustrating."

He shrugged, some of the tension dissipating as he swiped a forearm over his brow. "Classic Lacey, huh? Chase is always complaining about how she can't make up her mind."

I allowed myself a small smile as I took a step forward, like I was being pulled toward him. "You have no idea."

There was a beat of silence, and I couldn't tear my eyes from him. How his sweaty shirt clung to his chest. I cleared my throat. "Anyway, I wanted to let you know that I intend to continue with the certification. Solo."

Eli's gaze sharpened, and heat crept up my neck that wasn't exactly due to the room's temperature.

"Oh?" His tone remained maddeningly steady.

I forged ahead, the words tumbling out like rocks. "It would be a waste to stop now, after all the classroom work and pool sessions. I believe in finishing what I start, and… well, I'd like to experience the ocean dives. You've told me so much about them."

Eli nodded slowly, his eyes never leaving mine. "Makes sense." There was a hint of something in his voice I couldn't quite place. Amusement? Skepticism?

I raised my chin but held his eye. "Maybe I remembered what it's like to have an adventure. Maybe I remembered that I like it. Maybe I want more of that."

Eli's expression changed, softening and becoming assessing and… approving. "I like the adventurous side of you. The one I've seen in class and outside. I agree you should let it out more often. Good things might happen."

I shifted on my feet, acutely aware of how close we were standing in the cramped room. The male scent of clean sweat wafted off him. The air crackled with tension, a stark reminder of our last encounter. "Then we should continue."

"You're right." His tone was low and smooth. "Stopping now really would be a mistake."

My pulse quickened. Was he talking about the certification, or…?

"I mean," he continued, a hint of a smile playing at the corners of his mouth, "you've come this far. It'd be a shame not to see it through."

I swallowed hard, willing my voice to remain steady. "Exactly. That's… that's what I was thinking."

Eli took a step closer, and I caught another whiff of his scent. The intensity of his gaze sent a jolt of desire through me. My carefully constructed composure threatened to crumble.

"Tell you what." His words were soft and persuasive, like honey poured over velvet. "Why don't we move the open water dives up to this weekend?"

This weekend? My mind raced. That was so soon, and yet…

"This weekend?" I echoed.

Eli simply nodded. My heart hammered in my chest. I should say no. I should take the extra week to make sure I was immune to him. But as I stood there, drowning in those indigo eyes, I realized I didn't want to wait. I wanted to be with him. And that was both exhilarating and terrifying.

"I… I'll have to check my schedule," I managed, clinging to the last shreds of my self-control.

"Of course," Eli replied, his tone maddeningly casual as that sexy smile raised his lips further. He stepped back toward the tanks, completely in control, damn him. "Just let me know."

I turned to leave, my knees wobbling and panic fluttering through my chest. But as I hurried down the pier, I already knew what my answer would be. I glanced at the gentle ocean, imagining the world underneath. Would finishing the class with Eli—only Eli—plunge me deeper into chaos?

# Chapter Fourteen

## JULES

SUNLIGHT DAPPLED the ocean floor around me, casting shimmering patterns across a coral reef teeming with life. Eli and I were diving near Sunset Siesta's beach on the small reef that stretched just offshore. Schools of neon-bright fish darted between swaying sea fans and intricate coral formations. My heart hummed inside my chest. I still couldn't get over that I was breathing underwater, surrounded by this aquatic paradise. Despite my turmoil at the time, agreeing to move up our check-out dives had been the best decision I'd made all week. In fact, my hesitancy was now a distant memory, replaced by the very real present.

We were midway through our fourth and final ocean dive, and I only had one more skill to demonstrate. I glanced at Eli, his powerful form gliding effortlessly beside me. He flashed me an encouraging okay signal and gestured toward a broad sandy patch. I nodded, recalling the final skill I needed to demonstrate.

Carefully, I adjusted my buoyancy, hovering just above the rippled bottom without touching it. After catching Eli's deliberate nod of approval, we settled on the white sand on our knees, facing each other. My fingers trembled slightly as I removed my regulator and let it fall to my side, but I forced myself to remain calm. *One… two… three…* I counted silently before replacing it and clearing it with a forceful exhale. Relief flooded through me as I took a deep, easy breath.

Eli applauded me. He scrawled on his dive slate.

*Perfect form! You're a natural.*

I flushed at his praise. As we continued exploring the reef, I found myself mesmerized not just by our spectacular surroundings, but by Eli himself. He moved through the water with a fluid grace that I envied. When a graceful sea turtle swam past, Eli's entire being lit up with wonder. He gestured excitedly, pointing out how the turtle's flippers propelled it effortlessly through the water.

I saw him with new eyes now. Here was a man utterly in his element, radiating competence and passion. It was magnetic. Eli caught me staring and raised an eyebrow. I quickly averted my gaze, pretending to be fascinated by a nearby tube sponge.

A flash of vivid blue and yellow caught my eye. Two queen angelfish, each a foot across, flitted near a coral outcropping, their movements mesmerizing. The turquoise crown surrounding the top of their heads gave the stunning fish their name, while the mottled, bright yellow and blue body hardly seemed real. I tapped Eli's shoulder and pointed. He scribbled on his dive slate:

*Courtship dance. Watch.*

The pair of fish circled each other in an intricate ballet, their fins flaring in dazzling displays. As they twirled and swooped, I marveled at the beauty of their dance and how few people got to experience something like this.

I smiled around my regulator, enjoying myself immensely as my eyes met Eli's. He gestured forward, and we swam on. The reef began to thin, giving way to scattered coral heads. Then, suddenly, the seafloor dropped away entirely. Deep below, hazy white sand shimmered like a mirage.

My breath caught. The sheer magnitude of the ocean stretched out before us, beautiful and terrifying all at once.

I felt small, insignificant… and utterly alive.

A sudden movement caught my eye. Eli grabbed my arm, his touch sending a jolt through me even through the wetsuit. He pointed into the blue expanse, his eyes wide.

Three diamond shapes glided into view, their movements effortless and graceful. Eagle rays. Their wingspans must have been at least six feet across, their bodies sleek and beautiful. They soared through the water, undulating in perfect synchronization with long tails following behind.

I turned to Eli, goose bumps rising on my arms beneath my wetsuit. He met my gaze, his eyes sparkling with shared wonder. In that moment, words weren't necessary. The beauty surrounding us, the thrill of discovery, we were experiencing it together and forging a connection deeper than I'd thought possible.

As we began our ascent toward shore, my mind reeled. The dive had been nothing short of magical, and yet I'd almost not gone through with the class. Would I have had this experience with a different instructor, as I'd originally wanted? I doubted it. Eli's patience, his passion for the ocean, the way he'd put me at ease throughout my training. It all coalesced into a realization I couldn't ignore.

I had feelings for him.

Real, heart-pounding, stomach-fluttering feelings that went far beyond mere physical attraction.

But as we broke the surface and stood in the shallows, pure joy overcame me. I pulled off my mask, grinning widely. "That was incredible!"

Eli's answering smile was radiant as he gave me a gallant bow. "Welcome to the underwater world, Jules. You're officially a diver now."

"Thanks for being so patient with me," I said, softer now. "I was a bit of a mess on the first dive."

"Nah, no more than anyone else their first time in the water. It's a pretty unique skill and something that takes time. You were great by the fourth dive."

I laughed, the sound blending with the gentle lapping of waves against the shore. "I really appreciate you, Eli. You make this whole diving thing feel easy."

"That's the goal." His tone was serious now, yet still warm. "You deserve to enjoy it. Everyone should have a little wonder in their lives."

"Especially when surrounded by all that," I added, motioning to the ocean, the sun's reflection dancing on the surface. "I had no idea we'd get so close to the fish!"

"Exactly. I've got the best job in the world."

As we waded back to shore, I couldn't stop sneaking glances at him. The way the water droplets clung to his eyelashes, how his muscles rippled with each stride, was intoxicating. As my feet touched dry sand, I didn't want this moment to end. For once, I wasn't thinking about spreadsheets or resort renovations.

I was simply happy.

I couldn't wipe the grin off my face even though the sudden reappearance of gravity made the kit I was wearing awkward and heavy as we trudged up the beach toward the shore diving shack. Salt-and-pepper sand clung to our neoprene booties. I'd always loved the beach here—the mix of colors made it unique as well as soft and luxurious.

"Let's get this gear off," Eli said, already unclipping his BCD.

I nodded, fumbling with my own straps. As I peeled off my wetsuit, I caught Eli doing the same out of the corner of my eye. He was all hard muscle and sun-kissed skin, with a smattering of freckles across his shoulders.

"Not bad for an accountant, huh?" I quipped, attempting to mask the heat flooding my cheeks.

"Not bad at all. I enjoy this new side of you." Eli grinned and pointed with his chin at the empty pier. "Next step is getting you on *Sunset Diver*. You can join one of our regular trips."

"Maybe I will."

"Seriously, Jules. You were great out there." Eli's tone shifted, earnestness lurking behind the banter. "You really took to it."

"Thanks." The warmth of his praise washed over me. It wasn't just the compliment. It was how effortlessly he put me at ease, coaxing out this playful spirit I'd buried under layers of work and responsibility. "I couldn't have done it without your... charm."

"Charm is my specialty." He winked, and now I didn't find a thing annoying about it.

I hesitated, then decided to throw caution to the wind. "I'm appreciating this new side of you as well."

"Oh yeah?" His voice deepened as his eyes became serious. "And what side would that be?"

I met his gaze, hyper-aware of how close we were standing. "The patient teacher. The passionate diver. The man who sees beauty in the world and wants to share it."

He took a step closer. "Careful, there. Keep talking like that, and I might start to think you actually like me."

I laughed, but it came out breathier than I intended. "Because I do. I mean, we're friends now, right?"

My eyes darted around, and I realized how secluded we were. The dive shack screened us from view. A thrill of anticipation coursed through me.

Eli's lips lifted in a half-smile. "Friends. Is that what we are?"

I stepped closer, feeling the heat radiating from him. "Of course. I'm glad we've moved past… you know. That kiss." I waved my hand dismissively as if it hadn't been seared into my memory. "Clearly a mistake. Water under the bridge."

"Clearly," Eli agreed. He reached out, his fingers ghosting along my cheek. I leaned into his touch. "We're much better off not getting involved."

I couldn't breathe. Couldn't think. All I could focus on was the warmth of his skin against mine, the way his eyes had darkened to the color of a storm-tossed sea.

"Absolutely," I whispered, not even believing myself anymore. "Nothing more than friends."

I leaned in closer, my lips brushing his jaw as I rested a hand on his shoulder. "Besides, workplace romances are forbidden here, aren't they?"

He was completely still, his skin warm and smooth beneath my fingers. The words hung between us, both a warning and a dare. I pulled back slightly, searching Eli's face. The expression in his eyes made my knees weak.

"Absolutely forbidden," Eli murmured, his voice low and rough. He stepped forward to obliterate what little space remained between us. "Good thing we don't need to worry about that."

Before I could respond, he lowered his head to cover my lips with his. All thoughts of rules and consequences evaporated as I melted against him. My arms wound around his neck, pulling him closer. His mouth was hot, demanding as our tongues slid against each other. It felt so good. I lost myself in the kiss, in the feel of Eli's strong arms around me, in the intoxicating blend of salt and sun that clung to his skin.

Finally, we had to break apart to breathe. Eli rested his forehead against mine, his eyes closed as he tried to catch his breath.

"We probably shouldn't do this," he murmured, but it lacked conviction.

"I know," I whispered back.

Before I knew what was happening, he grabbed my ponytail and yanked my head back. His lips crashed into mine and we were lost in each other once more. Everything else faded away as I leaned back against the dive shack. I ran my hands down Eli's chest, drowning in the heat radiating between us.

And my inhibitions evaporated.

I pressed my lips to his ear, my entire body thrumming. "Eli. I want you. Now."

He stiffened, pulling back just enough to meet my gaze. His eyes widened, surprise and hunger swirling in their depths. "Here? Now?"

# Chapter Fifteen

## ELI

HOLY SHIT.

I stared at Jules to ensure I'd heard her correctly—this was our resort accountant in front of me. Yet she was also someone completely new. I let my gaze slowly drift down her body clad in a purple bikini. Before the dive, I'd about fallen over when she revealed that, and I had continued to think about it while we were underwater. I was quickly brought back to the very intriguing present when her hands trailed down my chest, lighting my skin on fire.

"Yes. Here and now. Where should we go?"

My eyes lifted to the dive shack behind her. The clothes we'd arrived in were in there. And more importantly, so was the condom in my wallet. But it sure wouldn't be comfortable. I nodded toward the wooden structure.

"If you're serious about the here and now thing, I suggest the shack. But it'll be hotter than hell in there."

Jules laughed, a sultry sound that sent a fresh, hot wave of desire through me. I'd never heard that laugh before, and I wanted to hear it again. "The heat is perfect for how I'm feeling right now," she purred as she slowly stroked my chest.

"Couldn't agree more," I managed.

The urgency between us was electric, practically crackling in the humid air. I reached for her hand, and we stumbled toward the dive shack, drunk on desire. I fumbled with the door handle, finally wrenching it open. We tumbled inside, and I kicked it shut behind us. The dim interior hit us like a wall of heat. The sad excuse for a fan I'd left on whirred on the wall, stirring the stifling air without providing any real relief.

"God, it's like an oven in here," I muttered, sweat already beading on my skin. But as Jules pressed against me, her eyes alive with want, I couldn't have cared less about the temperature.

"Wait until we make it even hotter."

I groaned as her lips brushed my ear, my hands finding her hips. "You're killing me, Verne. In the best possible way."

As we kissed, desperate and deep, I could hardly believe this side of her. The prim, by-the-books accountant had vanished, replaced by this passionate woman who set my blood on fire. I couldn't get enough. My fingers found the strings of her bikini top, and I untied them, letting the fabric fall away.

"I can't believe you wore this today," I murmured, drinking in the sight of her as I traced my fingers over her collarbone. "Do you have any idea what it did to me during that dive?"

"I'm embracing my adventurous side, remember? Any complaints?"

"Not a single one," I growled, pushing her against the

wall. I cupped her breasts in my hands, reveling in their full softness. My thumbs brushed over her nipples, tweaking them until they hardened at my touch. She let out a breathy moan that made me twitch. I lowered my head, taking one peak into my mouth. I swirled my tongue around it before sucking gently, savoring her gasp of pleasure.

My hands kneaded her breasts as I alternated between them, licking and sucking. Her fingers slid into my hair, holding me close. The salt from the ocean lingered on her skin, mixing with her natural taste, which only inflamed my desire to taste other parts of her. As I dropped to my knees, I slid my hands down her sides. My fingers hooked into the waistband of her bikini bottoms, peeling them slowly down her legs.

"Lift your leg," I said, my voice rough with desire.

She did, resting her foot on a pile of BCDs and opening herself to me. I took my time, kissing a path up her inner thighs. My stubble rasped against her soft skin as I nipped and licked. She squirmed above me as I slowly traced the crease of her thigh with my tongue, breathing in her intoxicating scent.

Jules groaned in frustration. "Eli, please…"

I looked up, meeting her gaze. The raw need I saw there nearly undid me. This woman, always so composed, was falling apart in front of me. And God help me, I wanted to shatter her completely.

I couldn't deny her any longer. Or myself. I was damn near desperate.

I ran my tongue along her slick folds, savoring her taste. Her moans fueled the fire raging inside me. Flicking my tongue over her sensitive bud, her body arched against mine. Her nails dug into my shoulders, and I knew I was doing something right. I continued the torture, alternating between soft, gentle caresses and firmer, more insistent strokes.

"Eli!" she cried out, bucking her hips against my mouth. "Oh God… I'm…"

I redoubled my efforts, sending her hurtling over the edge with a strangled cry. The sound of it sent a primal sense of satisfaction coursing through me.

I grabbed my wallet, fingers clumsy with urgency as I withdrew the condom. But before I could rip open the package, Jules took control. She sank to her knees, tugging at my board shorts.

I closed my eyes, exhaling a groan as she took me in her mouth. Sweet mercy. The sensation was indescribable. Her tongue swirled, teasing and tasting, and I fought to maintain any semblance of control. I gritted my teeth, every muscle in my body taut as Jules worked her magic. The heat, her mouth, the lingering taste of her on my tongue—it was sensory overload in the best possible way. My hands found her hair, freeing it from its ponytail. Sopping wet raven locks spilled over my fingers as I struggled to anchor myself, guiding her movements as I struggled not to lose myself completely.

"Jules." I gasped. "You gotta stop or this'll be over way too soon."

She pulled back, a wicked gleam in her eye as she opened the condom. With deft fingers, she rolled it on.

I couldn't take it anymore. The primal need coursing through me was too intense. I lowered myself to the floor as she stretched beneath me on the wooden boards. Her skin was feverish against mine as our sweaty skin came together.

"Ready?" I breathed, searching her eyes.

She nodded, wrapping her legs around my waist. I

entered her in one powerful thrust, earning a sharp gasp from her that made me freeze.

"Don't you dare stop," she growled, digging her nails into my back.

With abandon, I drove into her, our bodies finding a frantic rhythm. The stuffy air of the dive shack clung to us. Every slide, every point of contact was slick and electric.

"God, Eli," Jules moaned, arching beneath me.

The fan whirred in the background, circulating hot air as we moved together. Jules's typically neat hair was a wild tangle, spread across the floor like spilled ink. I buried my face in the crook of her neck, inhaling the mix of salt and her natural scent.

"You feel amazing," I panted, my hips snapping forward with increased urgency. "So tight, so—"

"Less talking," Jules commanded, capturing my mouth in a hot, wet kiss.

Without warning, Jules braced her hands against my chest and rolled us over, pinning me beneath her. Her eyes blazed as she set a relentless pace that left me breathless.

"Jules." I groaned as I shut my eyes, gripping her hips. "I'm close—I can't—"

"Good," she purred, rolling her hips in a way that made stars explode behind my eyelids. "Let go for me, Eli."

Her words pushed me over the edge. My entire body tensed as waves of pleasure crashed over me, incredibly intense. I screamed something inarticulate, but I was beyond conscious thought at that point. It went on and on, the end and the beginning. Everything. Jules followed moments later, crying out as she shuddered above me.

As we caught our breaths, I gazed up at her in awe. Sweat glistened on her flushed skin, and she'd never looked more beautiful as she smiled down at me.

"Jesus," I said, still slightly breathless, "you certainly know how to keep a guy on his back. And his toes."

Jules laughed, the sound rich and uninhibited. "I aim to please."

She leaned down to kiss me. As our lips brushed, I memorized the feel—the taste—of her mouth. This wasn't just sex. This was the start of something. But right now, as I stared at the amazing woman still enveloping me, the future was the last thing on my mind.

# Chapter Sixteen

## JULES

AS I PLACED my key in the front door lock, my brain still buzzed from the wild afternoon. My skin felt tight and warm.

Alive.

The door clicked open, and a rush of cool air washed over us. Eli stepped inside behind me, his presence impossible to ignore. It was a new awareness that everything was different now. I turned and was caught up by the smile on his face—so easy, so charming, like he owned the room.

We were both sweaty and massively satiated after our encounter in the dive shack, so we'd quickly dressed and headed toward the dive shop. The building contained two private shower suites, but somehow, we both ended up in one. The result being that this time, we were not so sweaty but still satiated afterward. Part of me was shocked at my willingness—hell, it was damn near uncontrollable—to let go with Eli.

Shocked? Yes.

Regretful? Not in the slightest.

"Welcome to my humble abode," I said as I surveyed the small space. The cozy living room was filled with beachy decor, soft blues and greens that mirrored the distant ocean. Framed watercolors of sunrise skies over Driftwood Beach hung on the walls, each picture a reminder of why I loved this island.

"Nice place," Eli said, leaning against the end table near the door with a casual confidence. He looked around, taking it all in like he was assessing a dive site—eyes scanning, evaluating, appreciating. "I like it. Very organized." Smile growing, his gaze took in the neatly arranged throw pillows on the couch. Then he pointed at my bookcase in the corner. "Do you alphabetize your books or arrange them by color?"

"Alphabetize." I rolled my eyes, but I couldn't help the smile creeping onto my lips. The lightness between us was unexpected, yet so very right. "And you should be more supportive of that, considering your sister owns a bookshop."

"I am supportive. That's why I noticed it right off the bat."

"Glad to hear it. Let's cook dinner instead of chatting about my impeccable taste in decor." I led him into the kitchen, the heart of my home.

"Perfect! I do believe we've managed to work up an appetite, haven't we?" He waggled his eyebrows, which made me laugh out loud.

"I think that's a given."

"What are we making? Please tell me it involves something fried." He opened the fridge and started poking around.

"Don't know about fried, but how about fish tacos? They're tasty and simple," I suggested, nudging him aside so I could grab suitable ingredients from the fridge. I set two bell peppers on the counter next to a cutting board.

"Fish tacos? You're speaking my language!" Eli turned around to lean against the counter, his eyes lighting up. Then his smile fell, and he shook his head. "I made fish tacos a few days ago, but it didn't go well. They just swam away."

Unable to help it, I burst out laughing and bent over the counter. "Oh my God, Eli! That's the most awful joke I've ever heard."

His face was adorably smug. "Then why are you laughing so hard?"

Getting control of myself again, I bumped his shoulder with mine as I opened the white paper surrounding the fish. "I bought some nice dorado at the market yesterday, and I need to cook it. Just don't expect gourmet Michelin-star stuff."

I could feel his gaze on me, and it made my skin tingle. I reached for a knife, trying to focus on the task at hand, a light lemon herb fish, while my mind buzzed with remnants of our earlier encounter.

"All right, chef." Eli rolled up his sleeves, revealing muscular, suntanned forearms, and grabbed a knife and a second cutting board. "What do you need me to chop? Or should I just start throwing things in the pan?"

"How about you stick to the chopping?" I replied, unable to suppress a smile. "And no throwing."

"Hey, I could have been a culinary artist in another life." He picked up a pepper, inspecting it closely. "But fine, let's keep it civilized. What's next?"

"Just slice those peppers into even pieces." I glanced sideways as he brandished the knife with exaggerated flair. "And try not to lose a finger while you're at it."

"Please, the only thing I'm likely to injure is your

dinner," he shot back. As he began chopping the peppers, I couldn't help but notice how well he maneuvered the blade.

"Are you always this competitive in the kitchen?" I grabbed a bottle of pinot gris from the fridge and poured us each a glass.

"Only when I have a worthy opponent." He winked, tossing another piece of pepper into the bowl before accepting his wine.

I turned on the gas burner and laid the fish on the counter next to it, smiling at our easy familiarity. And what a change it was. I wanted to know more. "So what's your story with diving? When did you start?"

"I was a teenager." His voice shifted into something more serious and drew me in. "Learning to dive with my sister Brenna was a game changer. We were both nervous at first. The ocean can be intimidating, you know? But once we hit the water, it felt like entering another world. Just us, the fish, and the endless blue."

I watched him, riveted by the way his eyes became so expressive. "It must have built a special bond between you two."

"Yeah, it did. We spent hours exploring. But it was pivotal for me. Diving taught me to embrace the unknown, to trust myself." He stared at his wine, considering his words. "Brenna actually talked me into it—I was reluctant at first. Instead, I learned what I wanted to do with my life."

"That's so rare." His passion resonated within me, softening the edges of my own guarded heart. "Few people get to do what they love. What they were born for."

"Accounting isn't your great true love?"

I ignored the gleam in his eye. "No complaints. It suits

me very well. I love the precision of numbers, how black and white they are."

"Less messy than people, that's for sure." His eye landed on a framed picture of my parents, my sister, and me on an end table as he chopped lettuce into ribbons. "You know all about my family. What's your story?"

I took a sip of wine, considering. "I had a good childhood. Solid middle class. I had a best friend, Jessa, that I used to get into all kinds of trouble with."

Eli flashed me a deadpan look, but humor lurked in his eyes. "Really. You, trouble?"

I laughed and flipped the fish in the pan. "Probably not trouble in your definition. No police were involved." I grinned at his eye roll. "Jessa and I loved scavenger hunts. I started reading Jules Verne at the same time, and the two worked off each other so well. That's what fostered my adventurous side, I think."

"So you and your gal-pal tore around finding hidden treasures until…? I've never heard you talk about her."

My smile fell. "We grew apart by the time I left for college. Our final scavenger hunt ended in kind of a disaster during our freshman year of high school. She was sleeping over and I hid a clue in a canister of flour in the kitchen. When she tried to find it, she dropped the container, and it shattered on the floor." I shuddered at the memory. "Flour went everywhere. I mean *everywhere*. My mom completely lost it and told me to grow up. So I did. I can kind of laugh about it now, but at the time, it was a big deal. A turning point. I was mortified and felt about five years old. I cleaned up the mess and after that, the scavenger hunts were history."

"That's kind of sad," he said quietly.

I shrugged one shoulder. "Mom was right. Jessa and I

were in high school, not grade school. That incident helped set me on my way. I excelled in my math classes."

"Adventures in trigonometry?" The smile was clear in his voice as he opened the package of tortillas.

I laughed again. I liked how he always made me laugh. Eli teased a lot, but it wasn't malicious, just gentle humor. "Something like that. My future lay in spreadsheets, not treasure hunts."

"Well, I just want you to know that no police were involved with any capers Chase and I got up to as kids."

"I would imagine Chase's common sense kept some sort of tether on you."

"Yeah, he wasn't shy about saying when one of my ideas was completely out of bounds."

As we sat down to eat, I found myself musing on our talk about friends and trust. "It's kind of funny that our best friends are brother and sister. It's a wonderful thing to have someone in your life you can trust completely like that."

Eli nodded, swallowing some of his taco. "Chase is my ride or die. And even though my siblings and I fight like dogs and cats sometimes, we've got each other's backs."

"I haven't always been great at trusting people," I admitted, pushing a pepper around my plate. "Not after I left home to go to Ohio State, anyway."

Eli held my eyes, his brows rising in a silent question.

It was time to come clean with the whole story. "I told you before about Travis, my college boyfriend. What I didn't say was that he cheated on me with my college roommate and best friend at the time."

Eli set his fork down and gave me his full attention. "God, Jules. I'm so sorry."

I shrugged, but it felt unnatural, forced. "It was a long time ago. But it… it changed me. Made me build walls, you know? It took years before I could even trust another friend."

"But you did," Eli said softly. "You've got Lacey now."

I nodded, warmth blooming in my chest at the thought of her. "Yeah. Lacey's been a godsend. She bulldozed right through those walls I put up."

"Trust is tough," he agreed. "But it seems like you're doing all right now."

"Maybe." I hesitated, weighing my thoughts. "But it's hard for me to open up. You're not the only one who keeps relationships on the casual side. I don't want to get hurt again."

"Hey"—he reached for my hand, his touch warm and grounding—"you're safe with me."

"Thanks." I looked down and adjusted the napkin in my lap, uncertainty creeping in. "But being close to someone again… it scares me."

"Trust me, I get that," he said, his voice steadying. "We all have our scars, right? Just know, I'm not the cheating type."

I reached out and stroked his forearm. For all that this man had made me want to tear my hair out over the last few years, I'd never doubted his loyalty. "I know."

As we continued, serious conversation transitioned back to lighthearted banter. With Eli, that shift felt like the most natural thing in the world. And beneath it all, a fragile yet undeniable connection blossomed.

"You're so close to your brothers and sisters," I said, feeling a pang of longing for my own family moments. "It's great that you have that connection."

"Yeah." A flicker of something deeper crossed his face. "Family means everything. But it's complicated too."

"Complicated how?"

"Our parents' divorce," he admitted, his voice dropping slightly. "It was ugly. Still is, honestly. They don't speak to each other, and my dad isn't even in the country anymore. Watching them tear each other apart turned me off commitment. I guess you could say I'm not much of a *forever* kind of guy."

"Same here. My ex turned my trust into dust."

"I know the feeling," Eli agreed, his gaze steady and searching. "Yet we're both here now, right?"

My pulse quickened. We were treading into dangerous territory, but I couldn't seem to pull back. "So, um, where does that leave us? This thing between us?"

"Honestly?" Eli ran a hand through his hair. "I like you, Jules. A lot. More than I expected to."

I swallowed hard. "I like you too. But with work, and our history…"

"It's a lot," he finished.

I nodded, relieved he understood. "Exactly. But I-I don't want to stop seeing you."

My heart clenched as a sweet, boyish smile spread across Eli's face. "Good. Because I don't want to stop seeing you, either."

We sat there, smiling at each other and both of us a little… shy? Part of me wanted to pinch myself, to make sure this wasn't some surreal dream. How had we gone from workplace nemeses to… whatever this was?

The weight of my worries lifted, if only slightly. "So let's take it slow, okay?"

"Slow sounds perfect." His smile was reassuring, and I felt a surge of hope. Maybe this could work, despite the odds—and the past scars we carried. "Though one might argue what happened today doesn't qualify as slow."

I stared at his face, my pulse taking off. "Do you regret it?"

Eli stood and leaned over the table to press his lips to mine. It was a sweet, honest kiss. "Not in the slightest."

"Me neither."

I stood to clear our plates and Eli's chair scraped back. I set the dishes in the sink, my stomach fluttering as I felt his presence behind me. His arms snaked around my waist, and I leaned back into his warmth.

"You know," I murmured, "this could get messy. The resort, your family…"

Eli's breath tickled my ear as he nuzzled it. "Then we keep it our little secret. No one has to know." That familiar playful lilt wound back into his voice, yet I could sense the gravity beneath it.

"What about the rule?"

"Mom's no workplace romance rule?"

"Yeah, Eli. That one."

I could feel the movement as he shrugged behind me.

"She's got her reasons for feeling how she does, but they're old reasons. And they don't have anything to do with you and me. I've never been one to follow the rules, especially ones I don't agree with."

"But I do like to follow the rules."

"What do you want to do?"

I huffed a long sigh, not able to come up with an alternative. "I guess keeping this between us is a way to safely explore my newfound adventurous self."

"That's my girl." He squeezed my waist as our agreement settled comfortably between us, a thrilling secret laced with possibility. "What's happened between us. It feels like a weight has been lifted, you know?"

"Yeah. Like we've finally moved past all that animosity." I turned in his arms, raising an eyebrow. "You think we can pull this off?"

"Please," he scoffed, his trademark grin spreading across his face. "I'm a master of discretion."

A pure, uninhibited laugh tumbled out of my mouth. "Says the man who once wore a mankini to a staff meeting."

"Hey, that was a dare!" Eli protested, but his eyes danced with amusement. "Besides, you have to admit, I rocked it."

"Oh yes, very professional," I teased, running my hands up his chest. "I seem to recall wanting to strangle you that day."

Eli's hands slid lower, pulling me closer. "And now?"

"Now… I have other ideas." And taking his hand, I led him toward my bedroom.

As I LAY COCOONED in Eli's arms, the steady, sleeping rhythm of his breathing lulled me toward the embrace of sleep. The scent of sunshine clung to him, mingling with the fresh linen notes from my sheets. It was a comforting juxtaposition, a reminder of our day and all that had happened between us.

But then, as I relaxed against him, a whisper of unease flickered in my chest. Was keeping things light really what I wanted? My mind drifted back to the spreadsheets I'd mentioned earlier. I could almost picture the neatly organized columns of data, calculating the risk of being involved with Eli Coleridge.

I pushed the thought away. This was supposed to be fun, right? No messy entanglements. Just two people enjoying each other's company and no one else's business. That was how I'd sold it to myself. And yet, beneath that veneer of confidence, I couldn't deny a tremor of doubt.

My past echoed in my head, reminding me of betrayal

and broken trust. Reminding me how devastated I'd been at Travis's betrayal. And a friendship shattered. Those memories curled around my heart like a vice, squeezing tighter whenever I let myself think about taking a leap. But in this moment, with Eli's warmth enveloping me, it was easier to ignore the warning signs.

I shifted slightly, tucking my head into the crook of his shoulder and letting the tension drain from my body. There was comfort here, a soothing balm for my overactive mind, and I smiled slightly. He was a charmer, always managing to balance the line between playful and serious without ever tipping into danger. Yet somewhere deep down, a tiny part of me craved the exact opposite.

Then came a soft murmur, a sound that pulled me from my spiraling thoughts. Eli tensed, muscles twitching in his sleep. I paused, holding my breath, listening intently.

"Jules…" he breathed with a touch of yearning, my name drifting from his lips like a secret in his sleep.

Not Julianne anymore.

Jules.

My heart skipped a beat. The intimacy of it struck me like a wave crashing against the shore. This wasn't just a nickname. The way he'd said it felt like an invitation, a glimpse into a side of him that rarely surfaced. I snuggled closer and savored the way my name hung in the air between us, filled with unspoken layers of meaning. Was this mere sleep talk, or did it hint at something deeper?

The night wrapped around us, and with Eli's whispered name echoing in my mind, I surrendered to sleep. Caught in the delicate balance between fear and longing, I wondered if this moment was a dream or the beginning of something beautifully complicated.

# Chapter Seventeen

## ELI

THE WARM EVENING wrapped around me as I leaned back in my chair, letting the humid air settle into my bones. A gecko chirped from its perch on the wooden fence of my courtyard, casting a shadow that danced along the wood. I swirled the amber liquid in my pint glass, pretending to focus on Chase while my mind wandered off somewhere much more intriguing. Yesterday, Jules had popped into the dive shop while I was alone to ask if I wanted to go for another dive. Her voice had been sweet and inviting. But that wasn't all it promised.

"Eli, I've got a lot of ideas for the renovation." Chase's voice registered dimly. "I think we can really make the place shine."

"Uh-huh," I murmured, trying to sound engaged. "Time to get those new beach umbrellas in, right?"

"Exactly!" Chase's enthusiasm surged as he leaned forward and set his beer down next to the growler I'd brought home from Tropical Hops. "We could increase the outdoor seating, maybe even add some cabanas—"

"Chase," I interrupted, not quite able to contain my grin, "that brings up images of South Beach and the whole Miami party scene. Yuck."

"No! It's all in how you design it." I always got a kick out of how excited he could get about buildings. "Besides, imagine the Instagram potential."

"Right. It's all about the Insta." I took a long swig of Braden's latest IPA, savoring the hoppy bitterness, but couldn't stop my thoughts from slipping back to Jules and the way her hair was so silky and soft, how the glint in her eyes made my heart beat faster than any dive encounter ever could.

"Are you even listening?" Chase huffed, crossing his arms.

"Of course! Totally focused on your brilliant ideas for cabanas." I gestured dramatically, adding, "Tell me more about how you're going to revolutionize beach lounging."

"Okay, clown." He shook his head, but there was warmth in his tone. "Glad to hear it. I need your input here."

"Don't worry. I got you." I waved him off, though I felt a tug of guilt at my inability to pay attention. The gecko was still chirping, and my gaze drifted into the shadows beyond my courtyard, where the tropical plants swayed with secrets. Chase's voice faded into the background as he passionately discussed an idea he had—something about new flooring and energy-efficient lighting. But all I could hear was Jules whispering my name.

Chase paused mid-sentence, his brow furrowed. "Eli, are you okay?"

I shook my head, forcing a grin. "Yeah, just… this heat

wave we're having, man. It's like an oven out here." I lifted my beer, taking a sip that didn't do anything to cool the warmth pooling in my chest.

"Right." He raised an eyebrow. "And your dreamy smile? That's definitely a side effect of the humidity. This about Jules?"

"That's bullshit." I tried to sound dismissive, but the corners of my mouth betrayed me, twitching upward. I could almost feel the warmth of her skin against mine. Dammit.

"Seriously. You're as subtle as a brick to the face." He leaned forward, resting his elbows on the table. "What's going on?"

I sighed. My best friend was a lot of things. Stupid wasn't one of them. "Okay, fine. It's Jules."

"Ahhh. Has something changed between you guys? Lacey told me Jules was finishing her class."

"Yeah, you could say that."

"Spill. Clearly, we're not going to talk about the reno."

"We've been seeing each other… like every night since her checkout last weekend."

Going on two weeks now. Two weeks that had confirmed that our first day and night together hadn't been a fluke. We fit together like a lock and key.

"Every night? That's some serious commitment for you," he teased, but there was concern there too.

"It's more intense than I expected." I stared into my beer, swirling the golden liquid around. "I feel like I'm stuck in this whirlwind, and part of me is worried about getting swept under. But the other part? The other part wants to dive right in."

He laughed, then his expression shifted as he sensed my unease. "What's really bothering you?"

I set my glass down, but now my hands were fidgety. I twirled my thumbs. "Well, it's not just the romance. I had this nightmare last night. Mom found out about us, and she flipped out. Like, forced me to fire Jules." When I described it out loud, it sounded stupid. But I'd woken up with the blankets wrapped around my legs tight and breathing hard. The only positive was I hadn't disturbed Jules, who lay in blissful sleep beside me.

"Yikes." Chase's eyes widened slightly. "Did she at least give her a severance package?"

"Very funny." I grinned, but the humor felt thin. "It felt so real. I woke up sweating, thinking I'd lost something before I even had it. I was super relieved to see Jules next to me, oblivious and sleeping. I mean, what if Mom does find out?"

"Well, your mom isn't exactly known for her rage against the world. But doesn't she have a rule about employees hooking up?"

"Bingo. Mom's not one to rage, but worrying? That's her superpower. She likes things neat and tidy, and this… whatever this is with Jules? It's anything but." I ran a finger along the rim of my glass and watched the condensation drip onto the table. "What if it blows up in my face?"

I suppressed the urge to squirm as Chase inspected me closely. "You two have been together, what? Two weeks? Isn't it a little early to be worrying about all this?"

"Probably. I told Jules I wasn't worried. That it was a stupid, obsolete rule and I could talk to Mom if and when the time came."

"Sounds reasonable. Do you think your mom would go that far?" Chase asked, his brow lined. "I mean, firing Jules?"

I laughed at the thought now out in the world, shaking

my head. "No. If anyone got shitcanned, it would be me. Jules is too damn good at her job."

"Hardly. You're the favorite son."

I rolled my head toward him. "There's plenty of competition for that title. But you're right. It was just a dream and didn't mean anything."

"Did you tell Jules about your dream?"

I gaped at him. "Are you kidding? What am I supposed to say? 'Hey, baby, I had a nightmare where my mom turned into a monster and made me fire you?'"

I laughed, but as soon as the words left my mouth, my gut twisted. Because I also hadn't told her about that other dream. The one I'd had that first night we'd spent in her bed. That had been a wonderful dream—the complete opposite of last night's. We'd been snuggled up on the couch out here watching the stars at night. Just… together and happy.

"So who all knows about your new love connection?"

"Only you, so let's keep it that way. Besides, I'm pretty sure Lacey will pry it out of Jules soon enough."

"Exactly." He leaned forward to emphasize his point. "This is a small town. Secrets have a way of leaking."

"Relax, Sherlock. We'll be fine." I waved my hand at him. "I mean, how hard can it be to keep a romance under wraps?"

"Famous last words."

An uneasy knot tightened in my stomach. I tried to shake it off. "Besides, nobody pays attention to anything around here unless it involves drama or bad sunburns."

"And I don't need to remind you what category you and Jules fall under," Chase shot back.

"Why do you think I'm keeping this a secret? I'd rather put my head in the sand than deal with Mom's disapproval right now."

"Head in the sand? More like head in the clouds," he countered, tilting his head. "Eli, you seem… different this time. With Jules."

"Different?" I laughed, but it felt hollow. I lifted my beer in mock salute. "Seriously, Chase, we're good. I promise. Let sleeping dogs lie and all that."

"Sure, but remember that sleeping dogs sometimes wake up and bite."

"True. But if they do, I'm more than capable of dodging and smacking them on the nose for their misbehavior."

The moon hung lazily above us, casting a silvery glow over the courtyard. I straightened up in my seat, my smile falling as chagrin replaced it. "Sorry, man. I got sidetracked there with Jules, and you came over to talk about your proposal. Let's dive back into it."

He took a drink and nodded. "I know you love the place, and it represents happier days to you. But, Eli, the roofs of both room blocks are practically begging for help, and the pool area has seen better days. Like, decades ago."

I ruffled a hand through my hair and exhaled a long breath. "You're right. I know we can't keep kicking the can down the road. But it just feels…"

"Weighty?" he suggested, eyebrow raised.

"Yeah. It's hard not to think about how much is riding on all of this. Not just for me, but for everyone who depends on the place."

"And that's why these renovations are crucial. Even the budget-friendly fixes will require a financial commitment. And Band-Aid fixes aren't going to cut it. We need to arrange a meeting with the key players. I'll leave who that is up to you."

I thought about it for a moment. "Jules and Harper for sure. And any of my brothers who want to come too. But for now, I think we should keep Mom out of it. She wants to step back from resort operations, so this would be the perfect time to start." I kept quiet about the fact that she already had major reservations about the whole process.

"Sounds good to me."

"I'll set up a meeting. Just don't expect me to wear a suit or anything fancy."

That made him smile. "I think everyone would stroke out from shock."

"Fine, I'll be professional. Or at least as professional as someone can be while smelling like saltwater and sunscreen." I poured out the last of the beer into our glasses.

"Good." Chase nodded, satisfaction lighting his eyes. "We'll figure this out together, all right? Just keep your head screwed on straight."

"Thanks for the reminder, Captain Responsibility." I smirked, but deep down, I knew he was right. I had to find a way to balance everything—the resort, my family's future, and the secret romance that seemed to complicate it all. "I'm glad to have you on board, man."

I expected a smart-ass comeback, but Chase stared back evenly.

"Thanks. I am too. I'm feeling hemmed in at work lately. I always thought I'd enjoy the security of a big firm, but lately, all the corporate bullshit is driving me up the wall. A big project like this is just what I need. Who knows, maybe I'll strike out on my own someday."

I cocked my head. "Your own firm?"

Chase stared into the distance, his gaze unfocused. "I've tossed the idea around a little. It's a big risk, though, so it's not something I'm looking at near term. Let's get back to Sunset Siesta. That place is plenty of work to keep me occupied for a while."

As we resumed discussing the details, my thoughts whirled. The idea of working closely with Jules on the project was definitely enticing, but it also stirred some worries about getting in over my head. Which, as a dive instructor, was something I usually didn't worry about.

"Well, I'd better get going," Chase said after draining the last of his beer. "That will give you time to catch up with your beloved tonight."

"Shut up, asshole."

His broad grin made me smile.

"More like it'll give me some time to see how I can add Jules to the renovation team without setting off any landmines."

"Landmines? You mean like your mother finding out about your little secret?" He raised an eyebrow, clearly amused.

"Among other things."

"Look, Jules is good at what she does. Her financial expertise is necessary for this whole project." He paused, letting that sink in. "But you have to be careful, man. Keeping things quiet won't be easy."

"Yeah, I know." I held up the dregs remaining in my glass. "To keeping life interesting."

Chase left, and the silence that filled the space was thick enough to slice. My eyes landed on my phone, a rectangle I'd been trying to ignore all night. Whether I should call her.

Just to say hi.

Or to casually suggest she come over for a nightcap.

Except none of that was casual.

Neither was wanting to see her every single night. And that was a problem. The nagging, familiar fear of getting close clawed at me. This was new territory, and I hated being so unsure of myself.

"Hey, it's just a phone call," I reassured myself, settling in my chair again. I closed my eyes as the breeze brushed the hair off my forehead, but it couldn't chase away the reality that I missed her.

When I opened my eyes again, they immediately landed on my phone.

# Chapter Eighteen

## JULES

THE CORAL WALL stretched before me like a living carpet, the vibrant hues pulsing with life. I hovered, mesmerized by the delicate dance of fish darting in and out of branching corals and sponges. A gentle tap on my shoulder drew my attention. Eli pointed to a tiny crevice, his eyes crinkling behind his mask. I squinted, trying to decipher what had caught his interest, but couldn't see anything. I looked back at him and shrugged.

This time I could see his smile as he reached out a hand and rested it gently on the rock. My breath froze in my lungs momentarily as an octopus slowly emerged from the crack in the reef, its tentacles unfurling in a graceful ballet. I gasped, my exhaled bubbles racing to the surface as it reached out and gently stroked one arm across Eli's still hand. After probing for a long moment, it withdrew the leg and slid across the coral. Eli reached his hand to mine, giving it a squeeze as we watched the octopus glide over the reef, changing color and texture as it went.

I was dumfounded. Both at the octopus's display and the fact that Eli had spotted it in its hidey-hole. The animal was a smooth brown, then as the coral color changed, it instantly developed mottled white nubs all over its body. Eventually, the creature disappeared back within the reef, leaving Eli and me to drift on together, exploring this underwater world he'd shared with me.

As we finned along the coral wall, I marveled at the sheer verticality of it. I'd always imagined coral reefs as sprawling underwater gardens like the one I'd seen on my check-out dive, but this was like a living skyscraper. When I'd mentioned I wanted to go diving again, Eli had suggested taking *Sunset Diver* out to this spot, promising me a sight I'd never forget. He wasn't wrong. This dive was just the two of us, the late afternoon sun bathing the busy scene before us.

The wall stretched as far as I could see in either direction, disappearing into the misty blue depths below. Every inch was covered in a riot of coral formations—delicate fans waving in the current, bulbous brain corals nestled in narrow valleys. Eli tugged gently on my hand, guiding me along the wall. We drifted through a school of creole wrasse, their bodies flashing a brilliant blue in the diffused light.

As we ascended slowly, careful not to rise too quickly, I felt a pang of regret that our dive was coming to an end. I was saddened that Lacey hadn't finished the class and couldn't experience what I was. But then again, I didn't feel like sharing Eli right now. This special display was just for me.

After surfacing, I pulled my mask down around my neck and grinned. "That was incredible! I've never seen anything like it. That wall just went on and on."

Eli's laugh was infectious. "Just wait until you see where we're headed next."

As we climbed back into the boat, I sat next to him and patted the picnic packed inside an insulated cooler next to me. "I can't wait. I never knew diving worked up such an appetite. It seems like you're not working at all the whole time you're down there."

Eli started the engine and nodded. "It's deceiving. Though in challenging conditions, you definitely feel it."

"Guess you've earned those muscles."

"Never needed to hit the gym. Work keeps me in shape."

As we motored across the waves, I studied him. The way the saltwater beaded on his tanned skin, how his eyes lit up when he talked about the reef.

Eli shot a glance at me. "You planning on gawking at me all day, or are you ready for our next adventure?"

I laughed at getting caught. "I wasn't gawking. I was… cataloging your features. For future reference."

"Uh-huh. And how many did you find?"

"Oh, hundreds," I deadpanned. "I may need to start a spreadsheet."

His laughter carried on the wind as we sped across the waves. I closed my eyes, relishing the sun on my face and the salt spray on my skin.

The boat slowed, and I opened my eyes to a new paradise. A pristine white beach stretched before us, bordered by swaying palms. It was a tiny island that looked to be deserted. The water was so clear I could see fish darting beneath the surface.

"Welcome to Rumrunner Key," Eli announced, guiding us to a wooden dock. "What do you think?"

I drank in the view. "It's breathtaking. How did you find this place?"

"Dive shops come here sometimes for surface intervals, but it's late enough in the day that we have it to ourselves. Our own private slice of paradise."

After snugging up against the wooden dock, Eli helped me off. As we made our way down the dock, I studied the thick brush behind the palm trees. The island was flat but looked densely covered in foliage.

Eli pointed toward the tree line. "Want to see something cool?"

I squinted, following his gaze to a darker area. "Is that… a cabin?"

"Good eye, Verne." He grinned. "Rumor has it, it's got quite the history."

My curiosity piqued, I moved toward the structure. "That sounds intriguing. What kind of history?"

Eli fell into step beside me, his shoulder brushing mine. "Oh, you know. Bootleggers, hidden treasure, star-crossed lovers—take your pick."

I rolled my eyes but couldn't help smiling. "You're making that up."

"Maybe," he admitted with a laugh. "But isn't it more fun to imagine?"

As we approached the cabin, I looked more closely. The old building spoke of time and the elements, its gray cypress planks bleached silver-gray by countless days of sun and salty air. The tin roof, rusted and pitted, sagged slightly in the middle, as if bearing the weight of untold stories.

A small porch jutted out from the front, its floorboards warped and uneven. The railing had long since collapsed. The wooden planks creaked under our feet as we stepped inside. Sunlight filtered through gaps in the walls, illuminating dust motes dancing in the air.

After taking in the dry interior, I glanced up at the

beams stretching across the ceiling. "The roof is still holding."

Eli nodded as he ran a foot over a large area rug that lay in the center of the room. "It's still watertight, just a little musty."

I took in the sparse furnishings arranged around the perimeter. "It's like stepping back in time."

He ran his hand along an old table. "I always wondered about the people who sat here, what stories they might've told."

I turned to him, surprised by the wistfulness in his voice. "I didn't peg you for a history buff."

He shrugged. "There's a lot you don't know about me, Jules."

That was a fair point. "You're right. And I didn't give you enough credit for what I did know."

He shot me that adorable grin. "Well, I didn't cover myself in glory where you were concerned, either. So let's call it even."

After nodding in agreement, I inhaled the dry air of the cabin. "You're right, though. It does make you wonder who has been in this cabin and what they were trying to escape from."

Eli moved back to the entry and opened the door, gesturing to me. "Maybe that's an adventure for another day. Let's get some fresh air before we get swallowed by the mystery of the past."

"Good call. I'd prefer to avoid any ghostly encounters today." I sent him a smile as I crossed the creaky floor.

As we emerged from the cabin's shadowy interior, the brilliant sunshine momentarily dazzled my eyes. The beach stretched before us, a pristine expanse of white sand that seemed to glow in the afternoon light. A gentle breeze rustled through the palm fronds, carrying with it the salty tang of the ocean.

"You know," Eli mused as he swept his gaze across the idyllic scene, "as intriguing as that old cabin is, it'd be a crime to waste this perfect weather cooped up inside."

I nodded in agreement. "Agreed."

He gestured to the boat. "Why don't you pick out the spot while I grab the picnic stuff?"

I found a flat area near the trees that threw dappled shade over us as he quickly returned from the boat, cooler in his arms. We spread out a blanket on the sand, and I sighed in sheer happiness. The sun warmed my skin as Eli unpacked sandwiches and drinks.

"This is perfect," I said before taking a bite of my sandwich.

Eli nudged my leg with his. "Yeah, doesn't get much better than a great dive followed by a picnic on a perfect beach with my girl."

As we ate, a sense of contentment washed over me. The gentle lapping of waves, the rustling palms, the easy companionship—it was all so far removed from spreadsheets and bottom lines. All something I never knew I was missing. And all because my best friend wanted to get certified for an underwater wedding that wasn't going to happen now.

I grinned at the irony, though the whole thing was Lacey to a tee. Which reminded me. "I had breakfast with Lacey yesterday at Sweet Dreams."

"Oh yeah? How's the bride-to-be?"

"She never changes." I laughed, shaking my head fondly. "I swear, that girl could find a silver lining in a hurricane. But she was worried about me, if you can believe it."

"About you?" His hand froze as he was lifting a chip to his mouth. "Why?"

I sighed, brushing a stray strand of hair from my face. "The venue change. She was convinced I was upset about it."

"And were you?"

I leaned back, resting my hands on the blanket. "Honestly? At first, maybe. But seeing the relief on her face when I assured her it was fine… It was like this weight just lifted." I laughed, remembering the rest of our conversation. "Even when the plan was for the underwater ceremony, I never actually canceled my bridesmaid dress order."

Eli's face filled with satisfaction. "That's the Jules I know. Plan A and Plan B both in effect."

I grinned. "I had this vision of Lacey changing her mind at the last minute, and there I'd be, stuck wearing some hideous taffeta monstrosity. Fortunately, we're all still on track."

Eli's smile was warm. "You're a good friend, Jules."

I shrugged, feeling oddly vulnerable. "She's been there for me. I'm happy to be her maid of honor."

Talking about Lacey brought her brother to mind. "Any idea what Chase is cooking up for this meeting next week?"

Eli's playful expression sobered slightly. "Your guess is as good as mine. But knowing him, it'll be thorough."

I nodded, my accountant brain kicking in. "We'll need to be smart about balancing the renovations with our budget constraints. Prioritize areas that'll give us the biggest ROI."

"Look at you, all business. You're right, though. We can't go overboard."

I chewed my lip, thinking. "The dive shop could use an upgrade. Hell, so many things do."

"Yeah. There's the rub."

"Who else is coming?" I asked, curious about the family dynamics at play.

Eli ticked off names on his fingers. "Me, you, Chase, Harper, Ben, Braden. I invited Brenna and Austin, but they couldn't make it."

I nodded, noting the absences. "What about Helen?"

Eli's expression turned sheepish. "Ah, about that…" He ran a hand through his hair, mussing it further. "I may have deliberately left her off the invite list this time."

My eyebrows shot up. "Bold move, Coleridge. Any particular reason?"

He sighed. "She wants to step back from the day-to-day. But you know Mom—she's having a hard time actually doing it."

I knew Helen well and understood she had mixed feelings about updating the resort. "And is that the only reason?"

Eli shook his head. "Chase is working hard on this, and I don't want him cut off at the knees before he's even started. This is just a preliminary meeting. We won't make any decisions without her full input."

Which brought back that she would likely not be pleased about Eli and me seeing each other. I certainly felt guilty about that. So was I agreeing to keep our relationship secret so we could delay the inevitable? Or as an excuse to avoid getting close?

*Except I am getting close.*

I couldn't deny that. We'd been together nearly a month now and I still couldn't get over how two people with such different personalities and outlooks could mesh so well.

Eli picked at a loose thread on the blanket, suddenly fascinated by the worn fabric. The silence stretched between us, broken only by the gentle lapping of waves against the shore. "I almost called you the other night, but I chickened out."

I cocked my head, trying to hide how shocked I was at his admission. He was so confident! "Why?"

A flush crept up Eli's neck, but he recovered quickly, flashing me that trademark grin. "What can I say? I'm a coward when it comes to beautiful women who can eviscerate me with spreadsheets. Or rejection."

My heart did a little flip at the *beautiful* comment, but I pushed the feeling aside and smiled back. "I'd say we've moved past the rejection part."

"Ah, but how am I supposed to know that?" he replied with an arched brow. Then he placed a hand against his chest. "Can you imagine? Me, the charming beach bum, completely crushed by your indifference?"

"You are nothing if not melodramatic," I teased, matching his tone, though my heart fluttered at what he'd said. His admission lingered in the air, pulling at something deep within me. Did he care more than I thought?

"Hey, I'm serious," he continued, the casual bravado slipping just a notch. "It takes guts to reach out when you're not sure how the other person feels."

I reached out and stroked his hand, absurdly touched. "Well, for future reference, I would have answered. I would have been happy you called."

Eli's smile softened, and for a moment, vulnerability flashed in those dark-blue eyes. "Noted."

The air between us shifted. "Jules," he murmured, his voice husky. "I…"

My heart raced. "Yes?"

Instead of answering, Eli leaned in, his lips meeting mine.

His were warm and soft against mine, tasting of salt and sunshine. His hand came up to cradle my face, his calloused thumb brushing lightly across my cheekbone. I leaned into him, my fingers tracing the strong line of his jaw before sliding down to his broad shoulder. His muscles were solid beneath his sun-warmed skin, a reminder of the strength that lay beneath his easygoing exterior.

Eli deepened the kiss, his tongue teasing at the seam of my lips. I parted them willingly, a soft moan escaping as our tongues met. My fingers gripped his still damp hair. He slid his hand down to my waist, pulling me closer. I shifted to straddle his lap without breaking the kiss. His fingers dipped beneath the hem of my rash guard, tracing patterns on the sensitive skin of my lower back.

"God, woman," he breathed against my neck as his lips blazed a trail down to my collarbone. "What you do to me."

The next kiss was hungrier, more urgent. His hands gripped my hair, freeing it from its bun. I ran my palms over his skin, marveling at how good this felt.

How right.

We tumbled back onto the sand in a tangle of limbs and desire. The rhythmic crash of waves echoed the pounding of my heart. Our clothes fell away, and then it was just us—skin on skin, breath mingling with breath. Eli moved above me, inside me, and I lost myself in him.

When it was over, we lay side by side, panting. I stared up at the cloudless sky inching toward sunset, my mind blissfully, wonderfully blank. I nestled into the crook of

Eli's arm, safe and secure. A profound sense of peace settled over me, so unfamiliar it was almost unsettling.

"I can hear you thinking," Eli murmured, his fingers tracing lazy patterns on my shoulder.

I snorted softly as I snuggled closer. "That's rich, coming from you."

"Hey, I think!" He feigned offense. "Sometimes. When absolutely necessary."

I propped myself up on an elbow, studying his face. The sun caught the gold flecks in his eyes, making them glint with humor and something… deeper. My stomach did a little flip. "What are you thinking about?"

Eli's eyes dropped momentarily. "How… relaxed I feel with you. It's kinda freaking me out, actually."

I laughed, but it came out shaky. "Join the club."

His arm tightened around me, and I let myself melt back into his embrace. But as the initial euphoria faded, doubts began to creep in. This was Eli Coleridge—charming, flirtatious Eli who had probably left a string of beach flings in his wake. And me? I was the uptight accountant who color-coded her planner.

"This doesn't have to mean anything," I blurted out, immediately regretting the words.

Eli stiffened slightly. "Is that what you want?"

I bit my lip, warring with myself. "I-I don't know. You don't want a relationship."

He laughed, but there was an edge to it. "And you're the poster child for emotional availability?"

"Touché," I admitted, tracing a pattern on the blanket. "I just… I don't want to get hurt. I can't go through that again."

Eli's hand found mine, intertwining our fingers. "Jules, I may be a lot of things, but I'm not cruel. I wouldn't toy with you. Or screw around on you."

I looked up, meeting his gaze. The sincerity there made my heart stutter. "So what are we doing here?"

He smiled, that roguish expression that made my skin feel hot. "Living in the moment? Enjoying each other's company? Maybe… seeing where this goes?"

I wanted to believe him. Part of me—a growing part—wanted this to be more than a fleeting island romance. But the voice of caution, honed by past heartbreak, wouldn't be silenced so easily.

"And if it goes nowhere?" I asked, hating how small my voice sounded.

Eli cupped my cheek, his thumb brushing away sand. "Then we'll still have had this perfect afternoon. But I'm starting to get a feeling it might go somewhere pretty amazing."

# Chapter Nineteen

## ELI

I AMBLED into the conference room, my eyes immediately drawn to the dual windows framing the azure waters of the Florida Keys. Located in the same hallway that housed Jules's and Harper's offices, the aged wood floor creaked under my feet, giving the space a warm, inviting feel despite the serious nature of our gathering. We'd had to delay the meeting twice due to last-minute scheduling conflicts, but two weeks later, we were ready to hear about the future.

From my best friend, which was weird.

The long oak table dominated the center of the room, its uneven surface showing that it needed revarnishing. Worn, high-backed chairs lined either side, a contrast to the casual beach vibe that permeated the rest of Sunset Siesta. A flat-screen television hung on the wall at one end, with a collection of AV equipment below.

My eyes immediately found Jules across the table, her black hair twisted into that severe bun she favored at work.

God, how I wanted to unravel it. She glanced up, those emerald eyes flickering with our shared secret. I couldn't help the tiny smile that escaped as I slid into a chair.

"Well, well, look who decided to grace us with his presence," Braden drawled as he relaxed in his chair. His hair was darker than mine but only because he didn't work outside in the sun all day. His blue eyes lifted to the wall clock. "And a few minutes early, no less. Did you finally learn how to tell time, big brother?"

I pressed my hand to my chest in mock offense. "I'll have you know, I've always been punctual. It's just that my watch runs on island time."

Jules's lips twitched, fighting a smile. My heart did a little flip—I loved making her laugh.

The door swung open, and Chase strode in, all six-foot-two of him radiating architectural professionalism and confidence. His gray suit and yellow tie cemented the image, and I straightened instinctively, like a student called to attention.

"Afternoon, everyone," he said as he set his briefcase on the table.

A chorus of murmured greetings went around the room. As Chase unpacked his briefcase, his gaze landed on Harper. They exchanged a friendly smile. Then she fiddled with her hair as he moved to set up his presentation on the flat screen.

I leaned forward, elbows on the table. "So, Chase, what's the verdict? Are we destined for financial ruin, or is there hope for us yet?"

Chase's lips twitched as he passed around spiral-bound booklets to each of us, *Sunset Siesta Renovation Plan and Proposal* printed on the cover page. "Love your optimism, Eli. Let's get started, shall we?"

As he began his presentation, I dutifully opened my

booklet to find a detailed table of contents followed by page after page of detailed plans. I snuck another glance at Jules, who was bent over the proposal and inspecting it closely. I tore my eyes away from her mouth.

Chase's voice snapped me back to attention as he advanced to a new slide on the monitor. "Let's start with the positives. Braden, Tidal Hops has been a consistent bright spot. Revenue's up fifteen percent from last year, and you bring in tourists and locals alike."

I tried not to smirk as Braden grinned like the teacher just awarded him a gold star.

"What can I say? People like good beer."

"And, Ben," Chase continued, "your landscaping work has significantly improved the resort's curb appeal. It's making a difference in guest satisfaction scores."

Ben nodded, a rare smile tugging at his lips. A resort baseball cap perched on his head, and he smelled faintly of fresh-cut grass.

Chase turned to me. "Eli, the dive shop's numbers are solid. Your new equipment investment should start paying off quickly."

A sense of pride surged in my chest, but unease quickly followed it. This felt like the calm before the storm.

"Now," Chase's tone shifted, "for the more pressing issues."

I tensed, bracing myself. The conference room suddenly felt smaller, stuffier.

"The roofs need immediate attention." Chase pulled up a series of photos he'd taken of rooms no longer in the booking system. "There's significant water damage in several areas. The plumbing and electrical systems are outdated. They're not up to code, and you're risking major failures if you don't address them soon."

My stomach dropped as I stared at the pictures in my

presentation booklet. Moldy carpet, stains on the ceiling. You could practically smell the photos. How had we let it get this bad? I winced, imagining burst pipes flooding guest rooms, or worse, electrical fires. This was my family's legacy, our home. And it was falling apart around us.

"On to the pool area." Chase's voice seemed to come from far away as I turned the pages. "The concrete is deteriorating. The filtration system is on its last legs…"

I couldn't look at the pictures anymore and closed my booklet. But the reality looked right back at me from the wall, in vivid color. My gaze drifted to Jules, hoping for… what? Comfort? Reassurance? Her face was a mask of professionalism, but I saw the worry in her eyes.

"Now let's talk about modernization and efficiency." Chase moved to the next slide, revealing mockups of sleek, updated room designs. "Refer to chapter six. These renovations aren't just about fixing what's broken. They're about long-term savings and increased appeal."

I leaned forward, studying the images both on the screen and in my booklet. The rooms looked amazing, all coastal chic and modern amenities. But something nagged at me.

"Hold up," I said, gesturing at the television, which displayed a mockup of a new guest room. "Where's the charm? The character? We can't just turn this place into some cookie-cutter resort."

Chase nodded. "That's the challenge, Eli. We need to find that balance between preserving Sunset Siesta's soul and embracing necessary changes."

I drummed my fingers on the table, conflicted. "Yeah, but—"

"If I may," Jules's crisp voice cut in. She turned to Chase, all business. "What's the projected ROI on these renovations? And more importantly, how do you propose we finance them?"

I blinked, brought up short. Trust Jules to zero in on the most pressing issue. As she fired off questions about cash flow projections and financing options, I found myself riveted by her. Not just by her sharp mind, but by the fire in her eyes. She cared about this place.

"Substantial financial backing will be needed," Chase admitted, his tone grave. "You're looking at a very, very substantial investment."

"Not sure I like the sound of that," I said weakly as my stomach flopped like a landed fish inside me.

"Oh, boy," Harper said quietly as she rubbed a finger over her forehead.

Jules's brows drew together. "Perhaps we should phase the renovations? Starting with the most critical areas and reinvest profits as we go?"

I couldn't help but grin. "Look at you, Julianne. Playing financial Tetris with our future."

She shot me an exasperated look, but a smile lurked at the corners of her mouth, and her eyes caught mine at my use of her formal name. "Someone has to think about the bottom line, Eli."

"And thank God for that."

"I'm simply doing my job," she replied, her voice prim but with an undercurrent I recognized all too well. Warmth flooded my chest. Not heat—a warm, squishy feeling.

But as quickly as it came, it faded, leaving behind a gnawing worry. What the hell was I doing? This thing with Jules—Julianne, whoever the hell she was—it was fun, sure. But with everything going on with the resort… were we being really stupid here?

Harper's voice pulled me from my spiraling thoughts.

"Chase, what about eco-friendly upgrades? Could we integrate solar panels or other sustainable tech to offset long-term costs?"

"Excellent question," Chase replied, his tone warm. "I've actually outlined several green initiatives in the proposal. If you look at page twenty-seven…"

I watched them, the easy back-and-forth, the way Chase's eyes softened almost imperceptibly as he answered. They worked well together, these two. Weird that I'd never noticed that before. Then again, why would I? Chase got along with everyone.

My gaze drifted back to the proposal in front of me. This wasn't just some minor facelift. This was a full-blown transformation. The scope of it hit me like a wave, leaving my breath tight.

Ben leaned forward with a frown and adjusted his baseball cap. "Look, I get it. We need to make changes. But how do we preserve the soul of this place? Our family's history is in these walls."

Braden, usually quick with a sarcastic quip, nodded solemnly. "Ben's got a point. We can't just slap on a coat of paint and call it fixed. But we also can't lose what makes Sunset Siesta… well, Sunset Siesta."

For all our bickering and differences, we were united in this. I smiled fondly. "What if we focus on enhancing what we already have? Like, upgrading Driftwood Grill so it appeals to locals and not just resort guests. We keep our character but add some modern flair."

Jules's eyes met mine, a hint of approval in her gaze. "That's a solid start, Eli. But we need to address the elephant in the room." She turned to face the group, her voice taking on that no-nonsense tone that now impressed me rather than irritated me. "The renovations Chase is proposing? They're necessary, but they're also very expensive. We're looking at significant external financing."

The room went quiet. My earlier optimism deflated like a punctured beach ball.

"How significant are we talking?" Braden asked.

Jules's lips pressed into a thin line. "Based on these projections? We're looking at a multimillion-dollar investment or loan."

Chase nodded. "That's what I came up with too. It's outlined in chapter nine."

I let out a low whistle, my mind reeling. "That's a lot of beer we'd need to sell."

"Eli, this isn't a joke," Jules snapped. "We're talking about the future. Your family's future."

Her words hit me like a sucker punch. The weight of it all made me scrunch down in my chair. "So what do we do? How do we even begin to tackle this?"

Chase cleared his throat, drawing our attention. "By taking it one step at a time. Yes, it's a significant undertaking, but it's not insurmountable. And it's really necessary, guys."

Harper nodded, her eyes meeting Chase's briefly. His reassuring manner helped ease some of the tension in the room.

"Chase is right," Harper chimed in. "We've faced tough times before. Remember when that hurricane nearly took out half the resort?"

"Or when Dad thought it'd be a great idea to add a peacock exhibit?" Braden added with a wince.

Despite myself, I cracked a smile. "Yeah, that was a great idea until we realized how loud the damn things were."

"The point is," Chase interjected, "you have options. It won't be easy, but Sunset Siesta has limitless potential. The location alone is pure gold. There's plenty of land and a rare, beautiful beach. An offshore reef, activities for guests already in place… I could go on and on. You just need to tap into it all."

As the meeting wrapped up, a weird mix of hope and dread swirled in my gut. My siblings were chatting animatedly, tossing around ideas for fundraisers and marketing strategies. The weight of everything we'd just discussed pressed down on me like a physical force. But it wasn't just the daunting renovations or the astronomical costs that had my stomach in knots. It was the glaring absence that no one had dared mention.

Mom.

I rubbed my temples, trying to ease the tension building there. We couldn't move on without her input and guidance. This place was her legacy as much as it was anyone else's. And what Jules and I had going on here? It was a ticking time bomb. The thought of ending things with her made my heart feel cold inside my chest. What we shared had to qualify as being a whirlwind romance, but that didn't stop it from feeling any more intense.

Or real.

It was becoming very real.

I traced the worn grooves in the wooden top of the table, unseeing. My heart thumped like a hammer falling, each beat a reminder of the realization dawning on me like a storm rolling in from the sea.

*I'm developing feelings here. Real, live feelings.*

The thought sent a jolt of panic through me, my hand suddenly turning clammy against the smooth tabletop. Around me, I vaguely registered the ruffle of papers and murmur of voices as everyone shuffled out of the room, but it was all distant, muffled.

What if it all went wrong? What if I screwed this up like I always did? What if—

"Eli?"

I jerked my head up, startled to find the room empty save for Jules. She still sat in her chair, brows drawn, eyes searching my face.

"You okay?"

I swallowed hard, forcing a weak smile. "Yeah, just… processing." My eyes returned to the glossy proposal in front of me and I zoned out again.

"Uh, see you later?" she asked after a quick glance to make sure we were alone, her usual confidence wavering.

"Yeah, okay," I mumbled, the words tasting hollow in my mouth.

I watched in a daze as she gathered her things then stepped out the door. As it clicked shut behind her, I slumped back in my chair and dropped my head into my hands.

# Chapter Twenty

## JULES

THE WARM GLOW of candlelight danced across Eli's face, softening the angle of his jaw but doing nothing to ease the tightness around his eyes. I traced the rim of my wineglass, searching for words to bridge the distance that had opened between us at the renovation meeting yesterday. A distance I didn't think I was imagining. He'd certainly heard a lot to think about, but was that all? Hoping to get to the bottom of the mystery, I'd called him and set up a date night at Rousseau's, a local off-the-beaten-path favorite.

And now that we were here, the meeting seemed like a good place to start. I took a sip of red wine to fortify myself. "So, Chase's proposals were certainly ambitious."

Eli's gaze flickered to mine, a smile playing at the corners of his mouth. "That's one way to put it. I think astronomically expensive might be more accurate."

I smiled back. "True. But many of his ideas have merit. The updated pool area and rooms could be a real draw."

"With some real downsides." His tone was light, but his eyes contained shadows.

I leaned forward, careful to keep my voice neutral. "We'll need to crunch the numbers, of course. But with some creative financing and phased implementation, it could be feasible."

Eli's eyebrows shot up. "Creative financing? Who are you and what have you done with our by-the-book accountant?"

I rolled my eyes, fighting a smile. "I can be flexible when the situation calls for it."

"Oh really?" Eli's grin turned wicked. "I'll have to remember that."

I laughed in response, wondering if I imagined his reaction yesterday, and busied myself with a sip from my water glass. When I looked up, Eli's expression had softened.

"Jules," he said quietly, "about the meeting—"

My heart leapt. "Yes?"

Eli opened his mouth, then closed it again, shaking his head. "It's nothing. Just… a lot to process, you know?"

I nodded, forcing a smile. "Of course. It's a huge decision."

Eli's shoulders relaxed slightly, and he reached across the table to squeeze my hand. "Thanks for understanding."

The warmth of his touch reverberated up my arm, and for a moment, I let myself believe that everything would be okay. But as I met his gaze, nagging doubt lingered in the back of my mind. There was still something he wasn't telling me.

I twirled my shrimp linguine around my fork, deciding to push a little. "So which of Chase's proposals specifically do you think the resort should work on first? Any thoughts?"

Eli barked a laugh, but it was devoid of his usual levity. "Oh sure, I've got plenty of thoughts. Like, maybe we could install a money tree in the courtyard? Or train the shorebirds to work as bellhops?"

"Come on, be serious."

"Who says I'm not?" He winked, taking a sip of wine. "I hear mermaids make excellent housekeepers. Though the uniform might be an issue."

"Eli…" I sighed, recognizing his deflection tactics. Part of me wanted to push harder, to peel back those layers of humor and get to the heart of what was bothering him. But another part held back.

What if *we* were what was bothering him?

He must have sensed my internal struggle because his expression softened. "Hey, if I'm distracted, it's all your fault, not the resort's. You look beautiful. That green dress really brings out your eyes. Not to mention cleavage."

"Thank you," I murmured, not mentioning that I'd chosen this dress specifically for that reason. I tried a different subject as I swept my gaze around the inviting dining room. "It was a toss-up between here and Salty's, but I'm happy with my decision."

As I'd hoped, Eli broke out in a smile. "I'm tempted to forbid you from ever entering that joint again without me. Dangerous territory there, Jules."

"Forbid? Strong word."

He raised his glass. "That's why I said tempted. I know better than to forbid you anything."

I touched my wineglass to his with a clink. "Smart man. But my one trip to Salty's wasn't exactly my jam. Present company notwithstanding, of course."

"Of course." His smile faded, and he returned to his entrée.

As the meal continued, I was hyper-aware of every little thing—the way his fingers drummed nervously on the table, how his shoulders became tight when talk turned back to the resort. But then he'd look at me, really look at me, with such warmth and attention that my doubts would momentarily fade. Only to rush back when he'd zone out again.

When the check arrived, Eli said, "Hey, what do you say we grab a nightcap at my place? I've got a bottle of rum with your name on it."

My heart skipped. "Sounds perfect."

As we left Rousseau's, Eli's hand found the small of my back, guiding me through the door. The familiar gesture soothed me, and I leaned into his touch.

The moonlight cast long shadows across Eli's bungalow as we stepped inside. The faded lavender exterior gave way to a cozy interior, all weathered wood and nautical touches. I kicked off my heels, wiggling my toes against the cool hardwood floor.

"Make yourself comfortable," Eli called, heading for the kitchen. "I'll grab that rum."

I sank onto his well-worn but extremely comfortable couch. The sound of clinking glasses drifted from the kitchen, punctuated by Eli's absent-minded humming. And my mind returned to the distance, and the fact that I'd been too damned afraid to ask him about it directly at dinner.

*Stop being a chickenshit!*

He appeared in the doorway, two glasses in hand, a quarter full of ice and amber liquid. "Bottoms up. This is a spiced blend I get from a guy in Key West."

He sat next to me, and after clinking our glasses together, I lifted mine to my mouth. The spicy, almost sweet taste filled my senses, with a fiery satisfaction after I swallowed.

*Verne, you're stalling…*

I took a deep breath. "Can we talk about what happened at the end of the meeting yesterday?"

Eli's easy smile faltered. "What do you mean?"

"You got distant. Like you were a million miles away." I swallowed hard, hating how quiet and unsure I sounded. "And I noticed it again tonight. I just, I need to know where we stand. Is this about me?"

He brushed his knuckles down my cheek. "Jules, you have nothing to worry about. What we have is important to me."

I leaned into his touch, relief washing over me. "Then what's going on? I can tell that whatever's bothering you still is."

He sighed, his shoulders sagging slightly as he relaxed against the back of the couch. "It's the resort. Chase's proposals, the financial strain… it's all just hitting me, you know?"

"Eli," I said, my voice soft but determined. "I know there's more to it than just the resort."

A ghost of a smile flickered across his face. He ran a hand through his hair, a telltale sign of his discomfort. "Okay, you got me. This thing between us is pretty complicated. I vowed after my parents broke up never to repeat their mistakes. And you and I are getting closer… but I have to wonder if a long-term thing just isn't in my DNA."

I wasn't sure how to respond to that. Because I didn't want serious either. Did I? I opened my mouth, but he cut me off with a self-deprecating laugh.

"I should come with a built-in warning label, right? *Caution: Contents May Be Emotionally Unstable.*"

I sighed, slightly irritated. But the joking was who Eli was, though I was coming to believe his humor was more of a suit of armor than a personality quirk. Part of me wanted to push a little harder, to make him confront his fears. But I could see the vulnerability in his eyes, the way his jaw clenched. Pushing could be the worst possible thing I could do.

"You are not either of your parents," I said instead, resting my palm flat on his chest. "And for what it's worth, I think you're doing just fine in the relationship department."

I felt more than heard his soft laugh. "High praise from the resort's resident number-cruncher. And emotional avoider *par excellence*. Should I expect a performance review?"

"Quarterly evaluations at minimum," I deadpanned, then softened. "But seriously, Eli. I trust you. We'll figure this out together, okay?"

He pulled me closer and pressed a kiss to the top of my head. "Together," he echoed. "I like the sound of that."

As we stood there, wrapped in each other's arms, I pushed away the lingering doubts. Eli wasn't perfect, but neither was I. And after everything with my ex, the fact that I could trust anyone again felt like a small miracle. And for now, this moment, imperfect as it might be, was enough.

Eli leaned in, softly brushing the back of his hand down my cheek. Then his lips met mine in a tender but thorough kiss. Desire bloomed in my chest, even as a nagging voice in my head warned me this could be a distraction tactic. I pushed the thought away, surrendering to the warmth of his lips. My fingers brushed his broad shoulders as I pulled him closer, tasting the faint hint of salt on his skin.

"You're so smart, so sexy," he murmured against my lips, his voice husky. "You mean a lot to me. You know that?"

I pulled back slightly, the corner of my lips rising. "Flattery will get you everywhere, Mr. Coleridge."

He grinned, that roguish smile that made my desire go from blooming to blistering. "I'm hoping it'll at least get me to the bedroom."

I laughed, the sound quickly swallowed by another kiss. This one was deeper, hungrier, wetter. Eli's hands roamed my body with practiced ease, leaving trails of heat in their wake.

As we stumbled toward his bedroom, shedding clothing along the way, I couldn't deny how natural this felt. How right. Despite all my reservations, all my carefully constructed walls, Eli had somehow wormed his way past my defenses.

His touch was both tender and polished, focused entirely on my pleasure. Each caress, each kiss felt like a wordless promise. I mattered to him. This mattered.

"God, Jules," Eli breathed, his eyes dark with desire. "You're beautiful."

"You're not so bad yourself, beach bum."

He laughed, the sound vibrating against my skin as he trailed kisses down my neck. "I aim to please."

And please he did.

Eli's lips trailed lower, kissing along my collarbone. His hands cupped my breasts gently, thumbs dancing over the soft skin. I gasped at the sensation, arching into his touch. He lowered his head, taking one peak into his mouth. The warm, wet heat of his tongue sent arcs of pleasure through me. He concentrated on one breast, then the other, alternating between soft licks and gentle suction.

My fingers ruffled his hair, holding him close as waves of sensation washed over me. Eli's touch was reverent yet hungry, as if he couldn't get enough of me. His hands roamed lower, tracing the curves of my waist and hips. I shivered as his fingers skimmed along my inner thighs, teasing but not quite touching where I ached for him.

"Eli," I breathed, my voice thick with need.

He looked up at me, his eyes dark with desire. "Tell me what you want, Jules."

"You," I said simply. "I want you."

A slow smile spread across his face. He kissed his way back up my body, capturing my mouth as his hot, thick shaft pressed between us. When I reached to stroke the velvety length of it, he pulled his hips back with a slight shake of his head. "No. Tonight is about you."

Eli's eyes never left mine as he reached for the nightstand, grabbing a condom. Finally breaking eye contact, he rolled it on. The sight was extremely erotic, just looking at how ready he was as moonlight spilled into the room.

With gentle care, he entered me slowly, drawing a moan from my lips. The feeling of him was exquisite, a delicious stretch that sent pulses of pleasure through my body. He stilled for a moment, giving me time to adjust, his forehead resting against mine.

"You feel amazing," he murmured in a low, throaty voice.

I wrapped my legs around his waist, pulling him deeper. "So do you."

Eli began to move, setting a slow, steady rhythm that had me gasping with each thrust. His hands roamed my body, caressing and exploring as if memorizing every curve. Lifting, he pulled me up so we sat face-to-face, our bodies flush against each other. The intimacy of the position, the depth of his gaze, was different. His fingers found my most sensitive spot, stroking with exquisite precision.

I clung to him, waves of pleasure building. "Yes! I'm so close."

"I know. Me too. Let go, baby. I've got you." We climbed together, breathing ragged, until the world shattered around us in repeated explosions of sensation.

Afterward, we lay together, a comfortable silence settling over us. My eyes drifted to his nightstand, catching sight of a familiar book cover.

"You're almost done with *Journey to the Center of the Earth*?" I asked, noting the worn Sunset Siesta Dive Shop sticker he used as a bookmark.

Eli laughed quietly, his chest rumbling beneath my cheek. "I figured after finishing *Twenty Thousand Leagues*, I might as well keep the streak going. What can I say? Your namesake writes a pretty good book."

I snorted. "I'm sure Jules Verne would be thrilled to hear that ringing endorsement."

His brushed his fingers in slow sweeps down back. "Hey, from me? That's high praise. I wasn't much of a reader until I met you."

The moment, the warmth of his touch, the vulnerability still lingering in the air, made me want to open up. "There's a reason I connect with Jules Verne. Other than the name."

Eli's hand stilled. "Yeah?"

I took a deep breath. "When I was little, my dad… he wasn't around much. Always on the road for his job. But every time he came home, he'd read me a chapter. Every night until he had to leave again."

I nestled closer to Eli, drawing comfort from his steady

heartbeat. "It became our thing, you know? Even when I was too old for bedtime stories, we'd still read Jules Verne together. It was… it was the one constant I could count on."

Eli's arms tightened around me. "That sounds really special."

"It was." I swallowed the lump forming in my throat. "Until it wasn't. Until he came home one time and asked if we could skip the reading that night. Of course I said sure. I could see how beat he was. Then one night became another, and another, until we stopped reading together completely."

"Ouch. I'm sorry," Eli murmured before pressing a kiss to my temple.

I shrugged. "It's fine. Ancient history, right?"

"Maybe," he said, tilting my chin up to meet his eyes. "But it still must have hurt."

The genuine understanding in his gaze nearly undid me. I blinked rapidly, fighting back tears. "Yeah, well. Like the incident with the flour explosion and my mom, it was time to grow up."

Eli was quiet for a long moment, his fingers running through my hair. "You're one of the strongest people I know," he finally said. "And our past makes us who we are. Warts and all."

I brushed a soft kiss to his collarbone, allowing myself to bask in the warm comfort of his embrace.

As Eli's breathing evened out, I found myself caught between contentment and unease. Wrapped in his arms, I felt safer than I had in years. Yet a nagging doubt lingered at the edges of my mind.

Our relationship was still a secret, hidden away from prying eyes and wagging tongues. And with the resort's future hanging in the balance, how long could we keep this bubble intact? I wanted to believe in the connection we'd forged, but old doubts whispered.

I closed my eyes, willing myself to focus on the present —the warmth of Eli's skin, the steady rise and fall of his chest. Tomorrow would bring enough challenges on its own. For now, I'd allow myself this moment of peace, even as a part of me wondered how long it could last.

# Chapter Twenty-One

# ELI

I TOOK a long drink of Coke as I sat in a corner booth at Tidal Hops, hoping the crisp, sweet taste would snap me out of my funk. No such luck. The flavor sat flat on my tongue, a pale echo of its usual bite. I'd woken up this morning with Jules in my arms. She'd been warm and soft, her hair a mess as it tickled my nose.

And for a moment, everything felt... perfect.

Until my calm was supplanted by a gut-clenching worry that sent me scrambling from her townhouse in a flurry of excuses about forgetting I had an early BCD repair at the dive shop. Lately, I felt like my only two emotions where she was concerned were bliss and panic.

Harper slid in across the booth from me, curiosity written on her face. This meeting with her and Mom had already been on my calendar, so I asked Harper to come early. I needed a sounding board.

My sister looked me over closely as she wrapped a hand around her full glass. "Okay. Here I am. What's up?"

I eased out a long sigh. How could I explain the tangle of emotions I couldn't even sort out myself? My fingers traced condensation trails on the glass, leaving wet tracks like nervous footprints. "Well, for starters… The panic attack I damn near had this morning."

Harper's eyebrows flew up. "Laid-back Eli in a state of panic?" Her teasing tone faded as she studied my face, her eyes narrowing with concern. "What happened?"

I hesitated, unsure how the hell to explain it all. Chase knew about Jules and me, but Harper had always had a rare blend of common sense and good advice. And I needed that right now. As an added bonus, she was immune to my bullshit.

"Eli, you can tell me."

My heart thumped in my chest as I weighed my options. Finally, I let out an uneven breath and looked at her squarely. "It's Jules. Julianne."

Her surprise was genuine and immediate. "Julianne? What about her?" She left the question hanging in the air between us.

"Yeah." Heat flashed across my face as I nodded. "I haven't called her by her full name for a while now. We're together."

"What do you mean by together?"

I shot her a deadpan look. "You know what I mean, Harper. Together as in the biblical sense."

There was silence for a beat before her gaze sharpened on me. "You and Julianne are seeing each other? Wow, talk about opposites attracting. How long has this been going on?"

With the news out, the tension in my chest eased a little. "Well over a month now. Hell, closer to two. It began with, I don't know, a truce or something when we started her scuba class. It's not even… It's nothing. It happened."

"Over a month together is more than nothing, big brother. And now you're spiraling like a champ, huh?"

I shot her a warning look. "Don't dramatize it. It's just…" I hesitated, then groaned, defeated. "I'm freaking out, okay? I can't do this, Harper. I'm not built for it."

She threw out an arm in a half-shrug. "For what? Relationships? Being human? Eli, you're so good at being everything else—charming, carefree, the life of the party. But why are you so terrible at being honest about what you actually feel?"

"Because it's safer that way!" I hissed, then winced. "And this is becoming too real, Harper. Jules isn't some tourist who'll be gone in a week. She's here. Every day. Watching me. And she sees things. Too many things."

The deep line between her brows grew even deeper. "Like what?"

I glanced around to make sure we weren't being overheard. The hum of conversation filled the air, and Braden was too distracted with the afternoon rush to notice us. "She notices when I'm worried, when I pull back. Or avoid the subject. And still… she's there. Patiently waiting, like she thinks I'll come around."

"And what makes you think you won't?"

"Because I'm a disaster! Look at our family. Mom's stuck in the past, Austin's got walls bigger than a medieval city, Ben's so stuck in who he used to be that he can't become who he wants to be. Don't even get me started on Dad. Yet here I am, following right in his footsteps—superficial, incapable of sticking when it truly matters."

"Eli, stop." Her tone was firm but gentle. "You're not Dad. You're not even close. You're so afraid of failing that you've convinced yourself you're not worth the risk. But what if you're wrong? What if you're the best thing that's ever happened to someone? To her?"

The idea hit me like a gut punch, and for a second, I couldn't breathe. What if she was right? What if Jules was willing to take a chance on me, even with all my broken, terrified parts? I shook off that ridiculous thought. "That's as unlikely as snow tomorrow."

Harper leaned forward, her voice lowering. "Eli, I love you, but you're full of crap. You've been having a great time with Julianne. Now that it's getting more serious, cue the freak-out. Classic Eli avoidance tactic."

"I'm not avoiding anything," I protested, my defenses rising. "That's my whole point, Harper! This is who I am. Mr. Duct Tape and Beer, remember? I don't do serious."

"Bullshit. You're panicking because you're scared. I see right through that act of yours."

I bristled, my hand tightening around the glass. "It's not an act. Shit, now we're going around in circles."

She gave me a faint smile. "Dad leaving… it messed us all up. But at some point, it has to stop being an excuse."

I laughed, a hollow sound that was anything but funny. "An excuse? Harper, our father walked out on us over a decade ago, and we're still picking up the pieces. All of us in one way or another. Tell me how that's not a valid reason to be cautious."

Harper tilted her head and stared straight at me. "I'm not saying it isn't valid. And you deserve to be happy. But I also need to point out that you could be playing with dynamite here. And it might blow up in your face."

Sudden heat rose in my cheeks. "Dynamite? What the hell does that mean?"

"Well, for starters, if you're only telling me now, I'm thinking not too many people know about this torrid affair."

"You're right. And that's how we want it, okay?"

"Because you don't want Mom to know about it.

Secrets have a way of coming out, Eli, but that's not what I meant by dynamite."

"Go on," I prodded, though I wasn't sure I wanted to hear it.

"I mean you're falling for her," Harper said simply.

The accusation landed like a punch. I stared into my soda, watching the bubbles rise and dissipate. "I am not."

Harper's laugh was sharp. "Right. Because running is so much easier than actually feeling something."

I wanted to argue. To deflect. To crack a joke about how she sounded like a bad therapy podcast. Instead, I just sat there. Silent. Knowing she was right.

"Hey. Look at me."

I lifted my gaze, meeting her warm brown eyes. The same eyes our mom had. The same eyes that always seemed to see straight through my carefully constructed defenses.

Her lips lifted in an encouraging smile. "You two make a lot of sense in a weird way. You could stand to take things more seriously, and Julianne could stand to lighten up a little. You balance each other."

I couldn't help smiling as my eyes grew unfocused. Because it was Jules's smile I saw. "Yeah, I've noticed that too."

"Eli."

I met her serious gaze.

"I'll say it again. You're. Not. Dad. Maybe it's time to step out from his shadow."

I swallowed hard as something threatened to crack open inside my chest. I nodded, then dropped my gaze to the table again. "Thanks, but I still feel like I have no idea how to handle any of this."

My head snapped up in surprise as Harper's laugh

sounded. "You think any of us know what we're doing? You think I do?"

I scoffed. "You've got your shit together more than anyone I know. Look at Finn."

Her smile fell as she stared back at me. "Yeah, look at him. You think I don't worry every single night about whether I'm doing right by him? Whether he needs a dad in his life and not just uncles? Eli, I'm making it up as I go. Just like you."

I reached across and gave her hand a squeeze. "Well, stop worrying. He's a great kid and you're a great mom." I let go and pointed at her. "And Finn's uncles are better than any dad could ever be. He's a lucky kid to have us."

Finally, the tension broke as we both laughed and took a drink of our Cokes. I felt better having confessed to Harper, but she still hadn't convinced me anything serious could work out between Jules and me. Maybe my sister thought I could change my ways and get serious, but I knew better.

The door opening signaled Mom's arrival, and I straightened. Harper shot me a look that said our conversation wasn't over, but I pointedly ignored it.

"There are my two troublemakers," Mom said, sliding into the booth next to Harper. Her silver-streaked hair was pulled back in a barrette, and her eyes crinkled with warmth.

"Hey, Mom," I drawled, relaxing again as I leaned back. "Troublemakers? Us? I'm wounded."

Mom rolled her eyes, but there was fondness in her smile. "So what's this meeting about? Or do I even need to ask? I'm sure this is about the renovations."

I glanced at Harper, letting her take the lead. She cleared her throat, all business now. "You're right. We had our preliminary meeting with Chase, and Eli and I want to discuss his renovation proposals for the resort with you."

As Harper launched into the details, my mind drifted once again to the conversation Harper and I had just had. To how happy I was when I was with Jules. How I wanted to please her, in bed and out. I felt a pang of… something. Longing? Fear? Both?

"…which means we'd need to secure external financing," Harper was saying.

Mom's intake of breath brought me fully back to the present. "External financing? That's what I was afraid of."

"It's a significant investment," Harper continued, her tone careful. "But the potential return—"

"How much are we talking about?" Mom interrupted.

Harper hesitated, then said, "Potentially… millions."

The silence that followed was deafening. Mom's face paled, her eyes widening. This was my cue.

"Look," I jumped in, seizing the chance to redirect the conversation. "I get it. We all do. It's a lot of money, and yeah, it's risky. But we've got to do something. The resort can't keep limping along like this."

Mom focused on me, surprise evident in her expression. "You agree with this plan?"

I shrugged. "I'm just saying, we need to consider our options. The old girl needs some serious TLC if we want to keep her afloat."

"But millions in debt?" Mom shook her head, her voice rising slightly. "That's not just risky, it's… it's…"

"An investment in our future," Harper interjected softly.

I nodded, surprising myself with how much I meant it. "Yeah. I mean, change is scary, but sometimes you've gotta take the plunge, right?"

The irony of my words wasn't lost on me, and I caught

Harper's knowing look. I avoided her gaze, focusing instead on Mom's worried face. The parallels to my situation with Jules were uncomfortably clear, but I pushed that thought away. One crisis at a time.

"I don't know." Mom sighed, her shoulders sagging. "This just seems so overwhelming."

I reached out to pat her hand. "Hey, we're Coleridges. Overwhelming is our middle name, remember? We'll figure it out."

Harper frowned at me before turning to Mom. "We wanted to let you know the facts immediately—so you wouldn't feel left out of the loop. But we're in the very early stages here. We don't even know how much money we're talking about yet, or if we need a loan or can figure out a way to finance it ourselves. So deep breaths, okay? We'll tackle this together, as a family. Just like we always have."

Mom grabbed Harper's Coke glass and took a long drink, which broadcast how unsettled she was. Her hand trembled as she set it back down. "Thank you for that. I'm not trying to be difficult—this is just a lot to swallow."

I reached out and squeezed her shoulder. "Lean on us, Mom. Don't go worrying about step twenty when we're at step two. We've got your back."

As Harper gave me another long, assessing glance, I just hoped that was true.

A flash of movement caught my eye, a presence that drew me like gravity. My breath stilled as Jules glided through the pub, heading for the bar where Braden was polishing glasses. Her hair was pulled back in the usual bun, but a few rebellious strands had escaped, framing her face in a way that made my fingers itch to tuck them behind her ear.

Our eyes met, and for a heartbeat, the world narrowed

to just us. A small smile tugged at her lips. I couldn't stop myself from returning it, remembering how those same lips had felt against mine just hours ago. Turning away, she stopped next to Braden and opened a folder she carried. Their heads lowered over it.

"Eli?" Mom's voice snapped me back to reality full force. "Are you even listening?"

"Huh? Yeah, of course." I tore my gaze away from Jules, but not before catching the sharp look in Mom's eyes. Crap.

"What was that about?" She nodded toward the bar, her tone deceptively casual.

I shrugged, aiming for nonchalance but probably hitting somewhere around guilty teenager. "What was what about?"

"That… look with Julianne." Mom's eyes searched my face. "I thought you two were practically enemies. You actually smiled at each other."

"Oh, that." I forced a laugh, ignoring the way my stomach churned. "Nah, we've just come to an understanding and are getting along better. For the resort's sake, you know? See? Everyone is working together to make Sunset Siesta a crowning glory."

The lie tasted flat, like the dregs of a Coke left out too long. I risked a glance at Harper, who was staring at me with a mixture of disapproval and… was that pity?

Great.

Just great.

This whole thing was putting her in a bad spot, not just Jules and me. And we weren't teenagers, for God's sake. We shouldn't have to skulk around. Despite my fears of getting close, I had to admit that maybe it was time to move this relationship into the light a little. Not with Mom yet, but maybe a sibling gathering. We could break the news in stages, establish allies before coming clean to Mom.

Because Mom was going to be complicated.

I wasn't delaying. I was planning. I almost patted myself on the back, but there was no doubt this situation couldn't continue without something changing. If only I knew what had to give. I hated change.

"An understanding," Mom repeated as her gaze flicked between Jules and me. "Well, I suppose that's a good thing."

I nodded, perhaps a bit too enthusiastically. "Yep. Totally good. Professional. Anyway, about those renovation plans…"

As I launched into a rambling monologue about new loungers and pool tiles, I couldn't shake the feeling that I was treading water in a rip current, being pulled farther and farther from shore with each passing second.

# Chapter Twenty-Two

## JULES

I SAT AT MY DESK, surrounded by stacks of paperwork and a lingering headache. The clock on the wall read 5:00 p.m., and I was more than ready to pack up and call it a day. The cactus on my desk was looking a little droopy and thirsty. Not dissimilar to me. I rubbed my eyes, which were tired after a day spent trying to figure out how we might fund Chase's renovations. My earlier guess had proved correct—we couldn't do it on our own. We needed outside financing, and I was trying to determine how much. But I thought I'd pondered the problem enough for one day.

Before I could gather my things and head home, a soft knock on the door startled me. I straightened in my chair as Harper peered into my office, a curiously hesitant smile on her face.

"Hey, got a minute?" she asked.

My stomach fluttered. I had a feeling I already knew what this was about. A few days ago, Eli confessed that he'd told her about us, and that he wanted to tell his other siblings about us too. He made a suggestion I thought was perfect.

Ever since, I'd been wondering how to handle it from my end. The no-romance rule might have been Helen's, but I suspected Harper would back her mother on this. And Harper was my boss, which didn't fill me with confidence about the situation. I'd been trying to deny that this dithering was absolutely not my style. Was it because I knew that Eli and I hiding our relationship was wrong?

*Of course it is, you idiot. And now it's time to own up to it.*

I smiled as warmly as I could. "Of course. Everything okay?"

"Hopefully." She slipped inside, closing the door behind her, and sat on the chair in front of my desk. "I'm terrible at small talk, so let me get to the point. Eli told me. About you two."

"Oh." Even though it was what I'd expected, I stumbled for words. "I… we were going to tell you. I just—"

"It's okay," Harper interrupted, holding up a hand. "Eli beat you to it and swore me to secrecy. Figures he couldn't keep his mouth shut."

"I'm sorry," I said, straightening in my chair. "I know this puts you in a difficult position. I want you to know it won't affect my work or our professional relationship in any way."

Harper's lips quirked in a half-smile. "Relax, Julianne. I'm not here to discipline or fire you."

I sent her a smile that was only a little shaky. "I'm very glad to hear that."

She shrugged, her gaze drifting to the financial reports spread across my desk. "I'm still processing, I guess. But no, I don't mind you seeing each other."

"You don't?"

"Not as long as it doesn't affect your job performance,

which you just assured me about. Though I'm not thrilled about keeping secrets from Mom."

I winced. "Yeah, that's not ideal."

Harper's eyes met mine, a mix of amusement and exasperation in her expression. "You two picked a hell of a time to complicate things around here."

A laugh burst from me, though I didn't disagree with her. "Trust me, it wasn't exactly planned."

"With Eli? I'm shocked," she said dryly.

We shared a knowing look, and for a moment, I felt a connection with Harper that went beyond boss and employee.

"So," I ventured, "what happens now?"

Harper stood, smoothing her dress. "Now? We figure it out as we go. Just… be careful, okay? Both of you. You're going to have to come clean to Mom sooner or later."

I nodded, understanding the layers of meaning in her words. "I know. Eli and I are both uncomfortable with keeping this relationship on the down-low. I think neither of us really expected it to work out." I laughed, and it came out slightly dazed. "But it has. We'll figure out the best way to talk to Helen about it."

She opened her mouth, then hesitated as if she didn't know quite what to say. "Julianne, this place has a long history, and Mom had a bad experience with another couple who worked here and got involved with each other. I know you and Eli aren't them, and times have changed, but you two need to approach Mom carefully about this."

Guilt twisted within me, but we were on the road to full disclosure at last. "We will. Eli told me he's working on a plan."

"Oh joy. Make sure he shares it with you first, okay?"

Both of us burst out laughing.

She cocked her head to one side. "I told Eli I thought you guys were a good mix of opposites blending well."

That made warmth spread through my stomach. "Thanks, Harper. It means a lot to hear you say that."

"Well, being my brother's girlfriend gives you and me an opportunity to get to know each other better, doesn't it? You're coming to the bonfire tonight, right?"

My heart skipped a beat even as a smile broadened across my face. I'd seen the Coleridge sibling bonfires from afar, always wondering what it would be like to go. And now I was. "Absolutely. Tonight is part one of Eli's idea to bring our relationship into the daylight. He asked me to come and thought it was a good idea to start with his siblings first."

"He's probably not wrong about that. Why don't you wrap things up? We need to swing by the Kids Club so I can pick up Finn. Then we can head over there together." The resort had a children's program that Finn hung out at sometimes.

I rose to my feet, still smiling. "That sounds great. Lead on."

The western horizon was a vivid palette of orange and pink as Finn bounced over the sand, all gangly limbs and excited energy. Harper and I followed at a more sedate pace. The crackling bonfire came into view on the beach, casting a warm yellow hue over the driftwood logs and scattered blankets. The scent of woodsmoke filled the air, mingling with the salty breeze. It was... cozy. Inviting. Everything I'd imagined it would be.

My phone buzzed with a text from Eli.

Eli: On my way. Can't wait to see you.

> Jules: I'm just arriving with Harper and Finn.
> See you in a few.

A smile raised my lips as I typed the message while strolling over the sand. But as I glanced up, it faltered. The Coleridge family home stood behind the beach, a dark silhouette against the night sky, and nearly screened from view by a line of trees and brush.

The warmth in my gut turned to a knot as I sat on a soft blanket draped over a driftwood log. "Harper, is your mother joining us?"

Harper glanced up from where she was stoking the fire, the flames dancing on her cheeks. "Mom? At a bonfire? No. She's got a standing invitation, but she says she prefers her quiet solitude and letting us kids have our time."

Relief washed over me, my shoulders relaxing. That was one complication I didn't need to worry about, at least. "Oh. That's nice of her to give you guys your own space."

The crunch of sand announced new arrivals from the far side of the fire. Eli appeared with Chase trailing behind him. My breath caught as Eli's eyes found mine.

"Hey, everyone," Eli called out, his easy charm on full display. "Look who I found lurking by the parking lot."

Chase scowled. "I wasn't lurking. I was studying the air handling units."

"See what I saved you from? What would you do without me?" Eli laughed, then turned to me. His smile softened, became something just for us. "Hey, you."

As he settled beside me, his arm found its way around my shoulders. It felt right. Natural. Like we'd been doing this for years.

"So," Eli addressed the group, his voice carrying a hint

of nervous energy I wasn't used to hearing. "You all know Julianne. But tonight, I want to officially introduce you to Jules. My girlfriend."

The words hung in the air for a moment. I held my breath, waiting for… I wasn't sure what. Judgment? Disapproval?

My gaze drifted across the fire and landed on Ben, the only other family member present besides Eli, Harper, and Finn. The eldest Coleridge sibling's eyes met mine, and for a moment, I braced myself. Ben had always been the most inscrutable. Surprise was plain in his eyes, but then something shifted in his expression. It wasn't a smile, but his chin dipped in a slight nod, his eyes holding mine for a beat longer than usual. A subtle acceptance that made me feel like a lead weight had been lifted from me.

"This is a bit of a surprise."

Eli nodded. "I know. We're keeping things quiet for now, so don't blab about it, okay?"

Ben snorted. "I'm not the one with diarrhea of the mouth. That's you, remember?" Then his eyes narrowed like he wanted to say something else, but he remained silent.

As laughter rippled around the circle, I gave a little wave. "I've always gone by my full name at work, but if you guys want to call me Jules, that's fine."

A burst of laughter pulled my attention away. Chase sat on a pale driftwood log next to Harper, Finn sprawled out between them.

"No way," Chase said, his eyes wide with exaggerated disbelief. "You're telling me you can name all the dinosaurs in *Jurassic Park*?"

Finn puffed up. "Yup! There's the T-Rex, the velociraptors, the brachiosaurs, and the—"

"Whoa, slow down there, paleontologist." Chase

laughed, ruffling Finn's hair. "Save some dinosaurs for the rest of us."

I had to smile, watching the easy back-and-forth between them. Chase's smile lit up his whole face. And Harper was in full après-work mode, beer in hand. She laughed at Chase's remark.

"Who would have thought?" Eli said softly to me, following my gaze. "I think my nephew likes him as much as he likes me."

I laughed, having witnessed Finn and Eli together many times. "Oh, stop it. I highly doubt you need to worry about that. Chase is good with kids, though."

Eli and I sat on a smooth, pale log. Ben, who was staring into the fire, sat a short distance away. Harper directed a warm smile at me. "So how do you like being a certified diver at last? Worth all that classroom time and pool practice with my exasperating brother?"

I grinned, a genuine, radiant expression that felt completely natural. "I loved it. I can't wait to dive again. Lacey has no idea what she missed by not finishing the class. And I'm officially ready to admit that Eli was a fabulous instructor."

Eli's arm tightened around my shoulders, his warmth a comforting weight. "See? I told you you'd love it. Every dive is like a treasure hunt. You never know what might turn up down there. A hidden octopus, a school of shimmering fish, a long-lost Spanish galleon full of gold…"

"You're such a dork," I said, nudging him with my elbow. "But you're right. It's incredible down there, and it is kind of a treasure hunt. I used to plan epic scavenger hunts as a kid. Maybe I should try one underwater sometime. Something to really challenge your expert navigational skills."

Eli raised an eyebrow at me, eyes glinting. "Challenge *my* navigational skills? Please. I've got an internal compass calibrated to the tides, baby. You'll never stump me."

A smile played at the corners of Ben's mouth as he lifted his gaze from the fire to his brother. "That's rich, coming from the guy who once got lost on his way to his car in the parking lot. He might be a wizard under the sea, but above water, that's a different story. Eli could get lost in a closet."

"I've seen it," Chase added.

Laughter rippled through the small group, the warmth of it chasing away the slight chill of the evening.

"Yeah, yeah," Eli replied with a good-natured shrug. "But I picked the right career, didn't I?" He fished a beer from the cooler behind him and handed it to Ben. "Speaking of which, how's the security business? Still keeping Dove Key safe from rogue tourists?"

After opening the bottle, Ben returned his gaze to the flickering flames. "Not much action lately." He mumbled the words, a hint of hesitancy threading through his voice.

"Oh?" Eli tilted his head. "Slow season?"

Ben shifted, the driftwood log creaking beneath him. "Nah. I've been… looking into something else."

His cautious tone caught my attention. Eli must have heard it too. "Looking into what?" he pressed.

"An EMT program," Ben said quickly, as if the words might escape before he could stop them.

I couldn't help responding, even though I was a newcomer. "That sounds great. Emergency medical technician is a fantastic career path. You'd never run out of work." I had no idea Ben's ambitions ran in that direction, but his steady presence under pressure would be a boon.

"I don't know," Ben mumbled, picking at the label on his bottle of beer. "It's just something I'm considering."

"It wouldn't hurt to apply," Harper added from across the fire.

"Plus, you've had plenty of practice patching up this knucklehead," Eli added, jerking a thumb at himself.

Ben actually laughed at that, a rare, rich sound. "True. Though most of your injuries were self-inflicted stupidity."

As they chattered back and forth, warmth spread through me. I looked around the circle of faces, illuminated by the flickering flames, and felt a sense of belonging I'd never expected to find here. And all because of Eli.

Because I was falling in love with him.

I was falling hard for this gorgeous, goofy, never-serious opposite to me. And none of that mattered. Only we mattered.

Then my gaze met Eli's. His eyes turned sultry, and my body responded automatically. He tilted his head slightly toward the screened foliage, a silent question in his eyes. I nodded, almost imperceptibly.

"Hey, I'm gonna grab another drink," Eli announced, his voice casual. "Jules, wanna join me?"

My blood sang as I stood and shook my half-full beer. "Sure, I could use a refill."

As I rose, I was grateful the rest ignored both us and the cooler behind Eli. We walked away from the fire, the voices of the others fading as we headed toward the tree line and privacy. Eli led me to a small glade, the sand ringed three-quarters of the way around by scrubby trees. The moment we were out of sight, he pulled me close.

"God, I've been wanting to do this all night," he murmured, his lips brushing my ear. "And more."

I tilted my face up to his. "Seems like a private spot."

His mouth lowered to mine. I melted into him, my fingers dragging through his hair as he pressed me against a nearby tree. The rough bark at my back was a stark contrast to the warmth of his body.

"Eli." I gasped between kisses. "This is…"

"Crazy?" he finished, trailing kisses down my neck.

"Dangerous," I corrected, my eyes fluttering closed as I thought of the house not far away.

His hands roamed my body, igniting my skin everywhere they touched. I'd never felt so alive, so wanted. And it wasn't just the physical connection—it was everything. The way he'd introduced me to his family, included me in their traditions. Like I was part of them. Maybe now was the right time to tell him how I felt. To finally find the courage to fly.

"Eli, I—"

A wry, tolerant laugh sounded from the opening behind us. "I guess this is why I never show up to these things." Helen's voice carried clearly as she stepped out of the shadows.

Eli and I sprang apart, startled.

Her amused, indulgent expression morphed when her eyes shifted from Eli to me. When she recognized me, they flew open wide. Shock filled her face, then transitioned to unmistakable disapproval as she stood ramrod straight.

Her head whipped back to her son. "Elias Coleridge, what in God's name is going on here?"

Eli's hand dropped from my waist, leaving me cold. "Mom, I can explain—"

"Explain?" Helen's eyes flashed. "Do I look stupid to you?"

"Of course not." His face visibly paled and I couldn't string two words together.

Her scowl deepened. "I knew I hadn't misread what I saw between you two at the pub. You lied to me, Eli!"

I shrank back against the tree, wishing I could disappear into its bark. Shame slithered through me, winding through my guts like a serpent. Eli stepped forward, his stance protective.

"It's not like that," he insisted, but his usual charm faltered. "Jules and I, we—"

"I don't want to hear it. I have only asked one thing from my kids regarding this resort. One rule—no getting involved with other employees." Helen's gaze swept over me, disappointment etched in every line of her face. "I expected better from both of you."

My throat constricted. "Mrs. Coleridge, I'm so sorry. We never—"

"Save it, Julianne. I thought you, of all people, understood the importance of professionalism."

The serpent grew, becoming a dragon trying to eat me from the inside out. I'd worked so hard to prove myself, and now…

"This ends right now," Helen said, her voice dripping with ice.

Panic clawed at me. How could I have been so stupid? This wasn't just about our relationship. My career could very well be at stake.

"Mom, please," Eli tried again, but Helen held up a hand.

"You and I will discuss this later. Privately."

And that was clear as glass.

"I'll go," I mumbled, edging away.

Eli reached for me. "Jules, wait—"

But I was already retreating, my vision blurring with tears. Behind me, Eli called out, "I'll fix this, I promise!"

His words echoed in my head as I stumbled down the beach toward the parking lot. The sand shifted beneath my feet, but the image of Helen's face, her furious disappoint-ment, was all I could see. Shame was all I could feel.

That earlier sense of belonging mocked me, leaving me cold and alone in the dark as I trudged to my car. And I had no one to blame but myself.

# Chapter Twenty-Three

## ELI

JULES DISAPPEARED INTO THE DARKNESS, her silhouette fading against the inky blackness. My gut twisted, the taste of our interrupted kiss still lingering on my lips. I wanted to run after her, to explain, to make things right. But Mom's laser-focused glare pinned me in place.

"Elias James Coleridge," Mom's voice cut through the night air like a blade. "I can't believe you lied right to my face!"

I plastered on my brightest smile, the one that usually got me out of trouble. "Come on, Mom. It's not—"

"Don't you dare try to charm your way out of this," she snapped. "Do I ask that much of you? I only ask one thing of everyone who works here. And not only did you break that trust, you went behind my back. That's what really hurts."

My smile faltered. "Mom, I—"

"No excuses. I want an explanation. Now."

I rubbed the back of my neck, buying time. How could I explain something I barely understood myself? "Look, it just happened, okay? We didn't plan it."

Mom's eyes narrowed. "And that justifies it? Lying? Sneaking around like this? Eli, after everything we went through, don't you understand the kind of chaos this invites?"

"It's not that serious," I insisted, my voice rising. "We're just having fun."

The moment the words left my mouth, I knew I'd made a mistake. Mom's expression hardened, her lips pressing into a thin line. "Then it should be easy to end it." Her tone left no room for argument.

My stomach dropped. "What?"

"You heard me. End it." Mom's voice softened slightly, but her words still hit like a physical force. "Julianne is a vital part of our team. Do you realize you've put her job at risk?"

I felt like I was drowning, gasping for air. "Mom, please—"

"No. My God, Eli. You two aren't teenagers. So stop acting like it! There's no more to discuss—this ends tonight." And with that final proclamation, she whirled and went back toward the house.

It was on the tip of my tongue to yell at her to stop treating me like a kid, except for one thing. She was right. Jules and I had been acting like stupid teenyboppers. And I'd been avoiding telling her simply because I didn't want to face a scene like we'd just had.

The finality in her voice shocked me to my core. I'd seen Mom angry before, but this was different. This was the voice of the woman who'd kept our family together through Dad's betrayal, who'd fought tooth and nail to keep the resort afloat despite the betrayal of people she trusted. And now, that same determination was aimed squarely at me.

I opened my mouth, searching for words, but found none. The weight of her disappointment crushed me, coming squarely from the woman who'd always been my biggest supporter.

For the first time in my life, I had no idea how to fix this.

Chase stepped into the glade, his hazel eyes filled with concern. "Hey. We all heard that. Everything okay?"

"No. Not even a little." I hissed a breath out through my teeth. "She never shows at these things! Why tonight, of all nights?"

"Uh, well, she does live fifty feet away, you know. What are you going to do now?"

I paced the sand, my bare feet kicking up tiny arcs of moonlit granules. Mom's words echoed in my head like a goddamn broken record. The resort was everything to her, her life's work. One rule. Just one stupid rule about workplace relationships, and I'd blown it spectacularly with my inability to keep my hands off Jules.

"Mom's pissed at me," I muttered. My hands were shaking—actually trembling—which never happened. I wasn't the guy who got nervous. I was the guy who could talk his way out of everything.

But not this time.

Jules was different. Smart. Complicated. The exact opposite of every woman I'd ever dated. And I needed to talk to her. Fix this.

"Yeah, Helen was pretty angry. That came through loud and clear."

I shot a glare at Chase. "Workplace romances happen all the time! I'm not sure her stupid rule is even legal."

"So what? What are you going to do? File an official grievance against your own mother?"

"I need to convince Mom that times have changed. And I'm not some random employee she hired. I'm her son, for God's sake!"

"Hey, maybe we should take a breath here," he said, his voice calm and measured. "Helen's rule about employee relationships is there to protect the resort and everyone who works here."

I whirled to him, betrayal burning in my chest. "Seriously? You're taking her side?"

Chase held up his hands. "I'm not taking sides. I'm just trying to provide some perspective, okay?"

I slumped, all the air going out of me like a balloon. "I need to call Jules and tell her we need to be super careful for a couple of weeks. Let this blow over, then things will be fine."

He stared at me evenly. "Isn't that what got you into this mess? And how do you think Jules would feel about that idea?"

My anger flared back up as I resumed pacing. "She'll agree with me. This isn't a big deal."

Chase's brow smoothed, incredulity washing over his face. "This is a pretty goddamn big deal, Eli."

"You're saying I should give up on something good because it scares Mom?"

"No. That's not what I meant." Chase grabbed my arm to stop my pacing. "Look, man, I know you. When things get tough, you tend to... well, you sabotage yourself. I'm worried you might be doing that now."

"What the hell are you talking about?"

The tension between us crackled like a live current. Chase knew me too well—knew exactly how to push my buttons. And right now, he was dangerously close to striking a nerve.

"You always do this," he said softly. "When something matters, you act like it's a not big deal. That way you don't have to take responsibility."

His words hit me like a slap. The accusation stung because deep down, I knew it was true. But admitting that felt like admitting defeat.

"You don't know what you're talking about," I growled, pulling my arm away. "None of you do."

Without another word, I stormed down the beach, sand kicking up behind me. The sound of the waves against the shore matched the roaring in my ears. My chest felt tight, panic clawing at my insides as the reality of the situation sank in. I could meet with Mom after we'd both had a chance to cool off.

Jules? I needed to talk to her.

But as I reached for my phone, I had no idea what to say. How could I explain this mess? For the first time in years, I felt completely and utterly lost. My trademark charm and easy humor had deserted me, leaving nothing but raw, aching vulnerability in their wake.

I fumbled with my phone, my hands shaking as I pulled up her number. The first ring felt like an eternity. By the third, my heart was pounding against my ribs.

"Come on, Jules," I muttered, pacing along the shoreline. "Pick up, pick up…"

Voicemail. Damn it.

I hung up and immediately redialed, desperation clawing at my throat. When it went to voicemail again, I called back. Again.

"Please, baby," I whispered, squeezing my eyes shut.

On the fourth ring of my third attempt, she answered. My breath caught. "Jules? Thank God, I—"

"What do you want, Eli?" Her voice was ice, sharp enough to slice through my momentary reprieve.

I faltered, thrown by her tone. "I… I wanted to explain. About what happened with my mom—"

"There's nothing to explain," Jules cut in, her words clipped and professional. "It's clear where things stand."

My stomach dropped. "No, listen. We can figure this out. We just need to—"

"We don't need to do anything," she interrupted again. "Your mother made her position quite clear. And after thinking about it, I agree with her."

I stumbled to a halt. I gripped my phone tighter, a horrible tightness clenching in my gut. "You agree? Jules, please. We don't have to end anything. We can keep this quiet for a while, only until things settle down. Just for a while longer."

"No." Her voice was firm, unyielding. "I'm not interested in a relationship I have to hide, Eli. That's not who I am."

My heart hammered against my ribs. This was all falling apart too fast. "But we're not hiding, not really. We're just being discreet until Mom cools off. There's a difference."

"Is there?" Jules's tone was cool, detached. "Because from where I'm standing, it looks a lot like sneaking around and lying. And I've had enough of that. It doesn't matter anyway—your mom knows now. And she's not happy about us, in case you didn't notice. It's over, Eli. Somehow, over the past couple of months, I seem to have forgotten who I was. Maybe I should thank your mom for reminding me."

Something inside me snapped. Fear turned to anger, hot and desperate. "So that's it? You're going to throw away everything because my mom freaked out? Real mature, Jules."

"Don't put this on me," she shot back. "This is exactly why workplace relationships are a bad idea. The complications, the drama—"

"Oh, spare me the HR handbook," I spat, pacing on the beach, panic gnawing a hole in my stomach. "We can make this work. We just need time—after Lacey's wedding, after we sort out the resort improvements…"

"And how long will that take?" Jules interrupted. "A month? Six? A year? No! I won't live like that."

The fight drained out of me, replaced by a cold, sinking feeling in my gut. Jules's calm logic was like a bucket of ice water, dousing the flames of my anger and leaving me shivering.

"Jules, please," I said, my voice quiet and pleading. "We can figure this out."

"Let's look at the facts, Eli." She sighed, and I could picture her pinching the bridge of her nose, the way she did when reconciling particularly tricky accounts. "Your mother, who ran this resort for years, explicitly forbids relationships between employees. And she has good reason for that—which you and I have both been ignoring. The resort is facing major financial decisions that require our full, unbiased attention. And Lacey's wedding is in two weeks, and I'm her goddamned maid of honor!"

My mouth opened and closed, but no sound came out.

"I'm not trying to hurt you," Jules continued, her voice softening slightly. "But these are the realities we're facing. Continuing this relationship would be irresponsible and potentially disastrous. Especially for me. I like working at the resort, Eli."

I closed my eyes, feeling the weight of her words. "So that's it? We're just… done?"

There was a long pause before Jules spoke again. "It's for the best, Eli. We both need to focus on what's important right now."

"You were important to me," I murmured, hating how small my voice sounded.

"I know," Jules replied, and for a moment, I thought I heard a crack in her composure. "And I was fall—never mind. That doesn't matter. This isn't going to work. Good night, Eli."

"Jules, wait," I said, but the line went dead.

I stared at my phone, my mind struggling to process what had just happened. The screen dimmed, then went dark, mirroring the hollow void spreading through my chest.

# Chapter Twenty-Four

# JULES

THE SUN DAPPLED through the lush canopy of Memorial Park, casting flickering shadows across the vibrant green grass. Located in the northeastern quadrant of Dove Key, the park had a lovely open area along with a baseball diamond and a sandy beach. The diamond was empty, and we were well away from the beach revelers, making for a serene, blissful atmosphere. Or it should have been. I plastered on a smile, willing my face muscles to cooperate as I helped Lacey spread out a red-and-white checkered picnic blanket.

"Jules, you're a lifesaver," Lacey said, arranging platters of sandwiches and fruit. "I don't know how I'd get through this wedding chaos without you."

I forced out a laugh that I prayed sounded heartfelt. "What are best friends for? I live to serve as your personal wedding planner, slash therapist, slash punching bag."

Daniel plopped down beside Lacey, grinning. "Don't

forget *voice of reason* when she threatens to elope every other day."

"Two times!" Lacey protested, swatting his arm playfully. "I threatened to elope twice, darling."

Their easy banter twisted something painful inside me. I busied myself with straightening the napkins, trying to keep my carefully constructed mask from crumbling.

Randy passed a sandwich to each of us. "Well, we can officially check off the rehearsal now. Hopefully, the weather will be this nice for the real deal."

I glanced at the vivid blue sky with its soft, puffy clouds and nodded. "I'll second that."

"Hey, gang!" Chase's cheerful voice rang out as he approached, carrying a cooler. "As requested, I come bearing liquid refreshment."

I looked up, meeting his eyes. A complicated mix of gratitude and unease washed over me. Chase's presence was a welcome buffer but also a reminder of the tangled web of relationships at Sunset Siesta.

"My brotherly hero," Lacey declared, making grabby hands at the cooler. "Please tell me there's something stronger than lemonade in there."

Chase winked conspiratorially. "I may have snuck in a bottle of wine. For toasting purposes only, of course."

After Chase uncorked the wine and we drank it out of red Solo cups, we discussed the upcoming ceremony, only a week away now.

And a week since Eli and I had ended…

Both Lacey's and my dresses were ready and gorgeous, and we'd just finished the official rehearsal here at Memorial Park. My best friend was on top of the world, and I was miserable. But I laughed merrily as we made a plastic toast with our cups to love and marriage.

As we settled into lunch, the conversation turned to a commercial strip mall Chase was designing, a reminder that the resort wasn't the only slice of the architect's pie. Of course thoughts of the resort inevitably brought back Eli.

Lacey's gaze flickered to me, her sunny smile faltering. "You hanging in there, sweetie?"

My fingers clenched around a napkin. "I'm fine. Today's about you and Daniel, not me."

Lacey shook her head. "Jules, you don't have to pretend. We're your friends. We care about you."

The gentleness in her voice threatened to undo me. I blinked rapidly, fighting back the sting of tears. "I appreciate that, but really, I'm okay. Let's focus on the important stuff, like making sure Daniel doesn't trip walking down the aisle."

"Hey!" Daniel protested with a laugh.

Chase cleared his throat, looking uncomfortable. "Listen, Jules… I just wanted to say I'm sorry about how you and Eli ended up. I thought you two made a good couple. Your differences complemented each other, but maybe it just wasn't meant to be."

His words, clearly meant to be kind, were like a knife twisting in my gut. I sucked in a sharp breath, the loss of what could have been hitting me with fresh intensity. "Thanks. But sometimes good isn't enough, is it?"

Lacey's hazel eyes met mine, filled with sympathy and something deeper—understanding. She'd known Eli for years, long before I'd arrived on Dove Key.

"You deserve to be happy, Jules. If not with Eli, there's someone out there for you."

I swallowed hard. Because that was the problem. We'd broken up a week ago, but I didn't want to be with anyone else. And I still couldn't figure out how that had happened. How I'd managed to fall head over heels for Eli Coleridge.

The weight of regret settled over me like a heavy blanket. I'd known from the start that getting involved with Eli was a risk. Hell, it was practically a textbook example of *conflict of interest*. But I'd ignored every red flag, every warning bell.

"God, I was so stupid," I said, more to myself than anyone else. "I let myself believe in this… this fantasy. As if duct tape and beer could ever truly mesh with spreadsheets and profit margins."

Lacey squeezed my hand. "Jules, you can't beat yourself up—"

"Can't I?" I interrupted, a bitter laugh escaping me. "I knew better, Lace. I knew the score from day one, but I jumped in anyway. I let myself believe it could really work out. And now look where we are."

I glanced around the picturesque park with its swaying plumerias and laughing families. How many times had I lectured clients about calculated risks? And here I was, the supposed expert, having taken the most reckless gamble of all with my heart. I took a deep breath, trying to regain my composure. But it didn't work. The frustration that had been simmering since that awful confrontation with Helen and Eli's phone call after finally bubbled over.

"You know what really gets me?" I said, my voice low and tight. "He didn't even try to fight for us. Not one bit. He just told Helen we weren't serious and it was no big deal."

Lacey's brow furrowed. "Oh, Jules…"

"I mean, I get it. I do. Eli's always been the guy who drifts in and out like the tide. It's part of his whole… thing." I waved my hand vaguely as if I could conjure his easygoing charm out of thin air. "But part of me thought… I don't know. That maybe this time would be different."

The realization hit me like a punch to the gut. "God, I'm such a cliché. Thinking I could change the commitment-phobic guy." Lacey opened her mouth to speak, but I shook my head. "No, you know what? It's fine. Really. This is exactly who Eli is. I knew that going in, and I can't blame him for being true to form. At least now I have clarity, right? No more wondering *what if.*"

Chase shifted, his gaze thoughtful and measured. "To be honest, I wondered, too. About whether Eli was changing this time."

His words hung in the warm, tropical air, weighted with possibility. I looked up, surprised. Chase wasn't one for casual observations, and his carefully chosen words carried more significance than a simple throwaway comment.

"What do you mean?" I asked, my fingers absently tracing the edge of my Solo cup.

"He was different with you," Chase continued, his eyes distant. "More focused, even serious. When we'd grab beers together, he'd talk about you in a totally new way. Not just as another casual relationship, but like you were something substantial. Something real."

A complicated knot formed in my throat. The last thing I wanted was false hope, and I couldn't see any light at the end of this dark tunnel. "I did too. Looks like we were both wrong."

"Helen finding out about you two—that wasn't a small thing," he continued. "For Eli, family dynamics are complicated. Always have been."

I bristled, my armor sliding back into place. "Helen's

disapproval isn't exactly a new concept for Eli. He's been navigating her expectations his entire life."

Daniel gave an awkward little shrug. "Family expectations are rough. And the Coleridges aren't exactly known for their boring, easygoing lives."

Chase nodded. "True. Helen's always been protective of the resort, of the family legacy. And I'm sure he was pretty crushed at her reaction. Maybe he just needs a little time to process what happened."

Sitting up straighter, I shook my head. "I'm not going to be his secret. If Eli can't work this out with Helen, there's no way forward for us."

Chase held out a hand. "And you're completely right to feel like that. All I'm saying is if you give Eli enough time to stew, maybe he'll see that too."

We'd avoided each other this past week, not speaking at all. Harper had been sympathetic, but I hadn't seen Helen at all. "Well, as of now, he's not even trying. So that's where it stands. Nowhere."

Lacey's eyes were full of sympathy, and I couldn't bear to see it. Not now. I straightened my shoulders, plastering on a smile that felt more like a grimace. "Enough about my disaster of a love life. We're here for you, remember? Your wedding is the priority."

"Jules, you don't have to—"

I cut her off with a hug, squeezing perhaps a little too tightly. "I want to. Your happiness means everything to me, Lace. And you too, Daniel. I'm not going to let my drama overshadow your big day."

As I pulled back, doubt flickered in Lacey's eyes. I doubled down on my false bravado. "As maid of honor, it's my job to head off trouble at the pass. Now, tell me all about the seating arrangements. Any last-minute family feuds I should know about?"

MONDAY MORNING HIT me like a hangover, minus the fun of actually drinking. I shuffled into the resort's lobby building, the familiar scent of coconut-vanilla air freshener offering little comfort. My heels clicked against the polished floor, each step a reminder of the professional mask I needed to don.

As I approached my office, voices drifted from Harper's open door. I froze, recognizing Helen's authoritative tone.

"You're right, Harper. We need to move forward. It terrifies me, thinking about that kind of loan… But seeing the state of those roofs, hearing Chase's plan, I need to face that controlled risk is better than guaranteed decline."

My breath caught. Helen agreeing to renovations?

Harper's voice followed, softer but equally determined. "I'm glad to hear you say that, Mom. We need to move forward, for the resort's sake. And for the family too."

I inched closer, guilt twisting my stomach. This was the very thing Eli and I had pushed for, but now it felt tainted by our ill-fated relationship.

Helen sighed. "I just hope this whole situation with Eli and Jules hasn't complicated things further."

My cheeks burned. Of course it had complicated things.

"It's all tied together in my head," Helen continued. "I can't help it. But maybe I'll be able to handle this financial risk better now that they aren't together anymore."

"Speaking of," Harper said, "we should talk to Jules about—"

I jerked away from the door, nearly tripping over my own feet. My heart raced as I ducked into my office, closing the door with trembling hands.

What now? Would they fire me? Demote me? The

thought of losing my place at Sunset Siesta, my home away from home, sent a wave of panic through me. I paced my small office, fingers twisting anxiously. No. I couldn't let it end like this. I had to face the music, explain myself, do… something.

Taking a deep breath, I smoothed my skirt and retwisted my bun, armor against the uncomfortable conversation ahead. Then, squaring my shoulders, I marched back out and knocked on Harper's door.

"Come in," Harper called.

I stepped inside, taking in the familiar warmth of Harper's office. A bleached wood desk with two armchairs in front, one currently occupied by Helen. Soft, earthy tones and driftwood accents created a soothing atmosphere that usually put me at ease. Not today.

Harper sat behind the large desk, and both women stared at me, their expressions unreadable. My throat went dry.

"Julianne," Harper said, surprise coloring her voice. "We were just about to call you in."

I clasped my hands to stop them from shaking. I was back to Julianne now. "I, uh, I actually wanted to talk to you both."

Helen's eyebrow arched. "Oh?"

I took a deep breath and gazed straight at Helen. "I want to apologize—for the disruption my relationship with Eli has caused. And I regret that it's taken me a week to do so formally. The situation was unprofessional, and I never meant for it to affect the resort or your family. I know things have been tense, and I take full responsibility for my part. I just want you to know that it's over now. Eli and I… we're done." I swallowed hard, fighting to keep my voice steady. "I hope we can move past this and focus on what's best for Sunset Siesta."

The silence that followed felt endless. I resisted the urge to fidget, to fill the quiet with more rambling apologies. Instead, I met their gazes, hoping they could see my sincerity.

Harper's response caught me off guard. Instead of the anger I'd braced for, her eyes filled with sadness. "Oh, Julianne." She sighed the words, her voice soft. "I'm sorry it didn't work out. For what it's worth, Eli's been really happy since you two got together."

My chest tightened. I hadn't expected sympathy, and it threatened to crack my carefully constructed façade.

Helen, however, remained a picture of cool professionalism. "Thank you for following through with my wishes, Julianne. It's for the best. We had a very bad experience with a workplace romance in the past, which is what caused my edict."

I nodded, not trusting my voice. The contrast between the women was stark—Harper's empathy versus Helen's detachment. But as I glanced back at Harper, I caught a flicker of something in her eyes. Understanding, maybe? A silent acknowledgment of the messy tangle of emotions we were all caught in?

"I'm sorry for the pain both you and my son are going through." Helen cleared her throat and let a faint smile show. "We do appreciate what you do here, Julianne, and I want to assure you that your position here is not in jeopardy. You're a valuable asset to Sunset Siesta."

A thousand pounds lifted from my shoulders, but the feeling was tempered by the underlying tension still crackling in the air. "Thank you. I'm relieved to hear that."

"The unfortunate incident with Eli aside, your work has been exemplary," Helen continued. "We're counting on you to help guide us through these renovations."

I straightened my shoulders, grasping at the lifeline of

professionalism she'd thrown me. "Of course. I'm committed to seeing Sunset Siesta thrive."

Harper leaned forward, a smile on her face. "We know you are. That's never been in doubt. Would you prefer we call you Jules?"

I straightened, not about to rock the boat now. "I've always been Julianne as a professional. No need to change that. Thank you very much for your support. Both of you."

I took a deep breath, resisting the compulsion to smooth my skirt. I focused on Eli's mother, seeing the echoes of him in her. I couldn't deny the man Eli was, and I couldn't regret that I'd gotten to know him. Maybe regret falling in love with him, but God knew I wasn't without my own faults, either. "Helen, I wanted to let you know you raised a wonderful son. Eli and I didn't see eye to eye for a very long time, and that blinded me to his positive qualities."

Helen's mouth formed an *O*, surprise flickering across her face.

I plowed on, the words tumbling out before I could second-guess myself. "It's not just his charm, though that's part of it. He genuinely cares about people, makes them feel seen. I've watched him turn even the grumpiest guest's day around with just a joke and that ridiculous smile of his."

A smile touched Helen's lips, easing the years from her face. "He's always been like that. Even as a little boy, he could charm the birds out of the trees."

I nodded, a lump forming in my throat. "He still can."

Helen's gaze softened, something vulnerable in her expression. "For all his faults—and Lord knows that boy has plenty—I love him fiercely."

The pride in her voice hit me like a punch to the gut. I

blinked rapidly, fighting back the sudden sting of tears. This wasn't the cool, collected Helen I was used to. This was a mother who was proud of her son.

For a moment, we just looked at each other, a newfound understanding settling between us. I saw past the stern matron to the strong, resilient woman who'd shaped Eli into the person he was. The resentment I'd been harboring toward her began to crumble, replaced by a grudging respect.

Helen cleared her throat, composure settling back over her like a familiar cloak. But there was a softness in her eyes that hadn't been there before. "Thank you, dear. For seeing the good in him, even now."

I managed a small smile, feeling oddly lighter. "It's not hard to see once you know where to look."

As I left Harper's office, my mind reeled. Our fragile truce had somehow transformed into something new by the end of the conversation. A shared understanding. A bridge, however tenuous, across the chasm that had separated us.

I closed the door to my office, the familiar click of the latch echoing in the sudden silence. The meticulously organized space that had always been my sanctuary now felt suffocating. I slumped into my ergonomic chair, its usual comfort doing nothing to ease the ache in my chest.

Eli's handsome face flashed in my mind, so I catalogued every difference between us. How Eli was everything I wasn't—carefree, spontaneous, allergic to responsibility. But even as I listed our differences, the spark they'd ignited couldn't be extinguished so easily. The way his laid-back attitude had challenged my rigid worldview. The exhilarating feeling of letting go in his presence.

"And now it's over," I whispered, the words tasting like

ash in my mouth. "Because I won't bend, and he can't commit. And neither of us is brave enough to fight for it. Dammit, Eli." A tear slipped down my cheek. I rubbed it away in irritation. "How am I supposed to move on from this?"

# Chapter Twenty-Five

## ELI

THE EARLY MORNING sun peeked over Mom's back patio in soft golden hues, painting the sky with strokes of pink and orange as I approached the sliding glass door, two steaming lattes clutched like fragile offerings in my hands. My heart hammered a nervous rhythm against my ribs. After a night spent staring at the ceiling fan, replaying every moment with Jules, every argument with Mom, every fear I'd ever buried, I knew I couldn't put this off any longer.

I knocked lightly, then slid the door open a crack. "Morning, Mom," I called out, injecting a cheerfulness I didn't feel into my voice. "Brought you a freshly brewed latte. Hope I didn't wake you."

Mom appeared in the kitchen doorway, tying the sash of her familiar floral bathrobe. Her hair was loose, cascading around her shoulders, and making her look younger, softer. A warm smile touched her lips, but her eyes held a familiar wariness that did little to soothe the anxious fluttering in my gut. "Eli, sweetheart. How thoughtful. You're up bright and early. Looks like a lovely morning. Let's go outside."

I followed her onto the patio, the gentle rhythm of waves a contrast to the turmoil churning inside me. The air was cool, carrying the clean scent of salt and damp sand. I handed her a latte, the warmth of the cup a small anchor in the sea of my uncertainty.

"So," Mom said, settling into one of the cushioned wicker chairs, her gaze calm as she watched me. "To what do I owe this early morning visit?"

I sank into the chair opposite hers, trying to mirror her relaxed posture. I flashed what I hoped was a winning smile, the one that usually got to her. "Can't a son just want to spend some quality time with his favorite mother?"

She arched an eyebrow as she took a slow sip of her latte. "At six-thirty a.m.? With artisanal lattes you clearly went out of your way for? Try again, Elias."

Caught. I let out a sigh, scrubbing a hand over my face. The charm offensive wasn't going to cut it today. "Okay, you got me." I leaned forward, elbows resting on my knees, the warmth from my own cup doing little to penetrate the chill of my nerves. "I wanted to talk. About... you know. The situation."

"Julianne," Mom supplied softly, giving nothing away.

The name hung in the air between us. I nodded, my throat dry despite the coffee. "Yeah. Jules."

Mom sipped her latte, her eyes never leaving my face. "I assume you're here to change my mind."

"I'm here to have a conversation." I made sure to keep my voice level and calm. "To explain why she is important to me."

She nodded, her expression softening. "I'm listening."

I leaned forward, elbows on my knees. "Jules isn't just some fling, Mom. She's… well, different."

"I know she is," Mom said gently. "That's part of the problem."

I frowned, confused. "What do you mean?"

Mom sighed, setting down her latte. "Eli, you've always had a way with women. You have a way with everyone. Frankly, I'm astonished you weren't pounding on my door the morning after the bonfire assuring me this relationship was nothing special and therefore I should just ignore that it was going on. Instead, you've spent nearly a week acting very differently and therefore demonstrating that Julianne is different. This is the first time I've seen you truly care about someone. It makes the situation even more complicated."

"I know it's complicated, but that doesn't mean it's not worth it," I argued.

"Let's forget the resort policy for a moment, forget the complications." She leaned forward, the lines in her brow displaying a maternal concern that disarmed me more effectively than any anger could have. "I've known you since you emerged from my own body. Watched you navigate friendships, heartbreaks. Everything. I can see that you're more serious, more… invested. I want to ask you a question, and I'd like an honest answer." Her eyes held mine, demanding truth. "Are you in love with her?"

The question knocked the air from my lungs. Sharp, freezing panic seized me. Love. The word echoed in the chambers of my heart, a truth I'd been circling warily. Because naming it made it real. Saying it out loud, especially to Mom, was like stepping off a cliff into an unknown abyss. All my old fears surged—the ghost of my father's abandonment, the messy, painful wreckage of my parents' marriage, the deep-seated belief that I was incapable of the kind of lasting commitment love required.

My mouth went dry. I could feel the *yes* deep in my throat, wanting to be released. But the fear clamped down and silenced it. I tore my gaze away, fixing it on a distant sailboat gliding across the horizon. I fidgeted with my cup, spinning the cardboard around in my hands.

"Mom, I… I care about her. A lot. More than I can even say." The words were inadequate, flimsy shields against the enormity of what I felt. I hated how my normally silver tongue was abandoning me. "She's incredible. Smart, funny, beautiful. She challenges me in ways no one else ever has. Things are… they're serious between us." I forced myself to meet her eyes again, pleading for her to understand the unspoken. "She's important to me. Really important."

Mom watched me, her expression shifting from searching to something akin to gentle sorrow. A soft sigh escaped her lips. "You care deeply. She's important. You said all of that." She paused, letting the observation settle between us. "But you couldn't say the word, could you? Even now. You can't say you love her."

It wasn't an accusation, more a statement of fact, delivered with a quiet sadness that pierced every defense I owned.

"That's not fair," I mumbled, bristling. "It's just a word."

"Honey," she said, her voice filled with understanding, "*that's* what worries me more than any silly resort policy. It's not whether you can have a relationship in this environment, but whether you're truly ready for one. Especially with someone like Julianne, someone so grounded. You two are very different personalities."

"So what? Maybe that means we work even better as a couple."

She gently held up a hand. "Does it? Sweetheart, real love means not running from deep feelings, protecting that bruised heart after your father left." Her eyes held a profound empathy. "I understand *why* you do it. So you don't get hurt. You push people away, or worse, you hold them close enough to feel the warmth but never let them fully in, until you inevitably bolt when things get too real, too demanding."

"That's not fair," I mumbled, feeling like that heart-broken teenager again.

"I don't want to see you get hurt, Eli. And frankly," her gaze sharpened slightly, "I don't want to see *her* hurt either. Julianne strikes me as someone who values stability, loyalty. Getting deeply involved with someone who isn't sure, who can't even voice the depth of his feelings… Eli, that's a recipe for pain. For both of you."

"So I should just walk away because I'm scared?" My voice rose, frustration breaking through the cracks. "Because *you're* scared for me?"

"That's not what I'm saying at all." She sighed again, the sound heavy with past experience. "Honesty is crucial, Eli, but it wasn't enough back then either. You have to see the parallels between you two and Russell and Lucia."

I nodded grimly, the familiar story settling like acid in my stomach. "Yeah, Mom. I remember."

"Everyone thought they were perfect," she continued, her voice taking on a distant quality as she recounted the painful history, framing it not as news to me, but as context for her fear. "A passionate couple who found each other here at this resort. Our bookkeeper and a dive shop clerk. But that closeness, that trust we all placed in them partly because they seemed devoted to each other? Russell used it. He cooked the books for months, systematically bleeding us dry. And Lucia wasn't just turning a blind eye. She was his accomplice, covering his tracks, using the trust we had in her at the dive shop. Together, they used us to finance their new life together."

She paused, letting the mechanism of their betrayal hang in the air. "By the time we discovered the discrepancies, they were gone. Vanished. And they took… well, you know what they took." She didn't need to state the near-crippling amount. The impact was etched on her face. "It wasn't just the money, Eli. It was the violation. Their relationship nearly destroyed this resort. We were leveraged to the hilt trying to cover the losses, days from foreclosure."

I FLINCHED AT HER WORDS. I'd been a senior in high school when this went on, so it was living history to me. But hearing it now, seeing the ghost of that old terror flicker in her eyes, made it visceral in a new way. I was dealing with my own reactions to those events at the time, but I didn't realize exactly how close we'd come to going under. And the woman across the table from me was the reason why we'd made it. As a resort and a family. A chill traced its way down my spine despite the warm morning air, and I had to consciously force my shoulders to unclench.

As she continued, her voice trembled slightly. "And that pressure, that financial terror, it poisons everything, you know? Your father and I were already struggling." She glanced down and separated her wringing hands, placing them flat on her thighs before meeting my gaze again. "Things hadn't been right between us for a while, small cracks forming. But the stress of the embezzlement, the sheer panic of potentially losing everything we'd built together magnified every fault line. The arguments became constant, bitter. The trust wasn't just broken by Russell and Lucia. It shattered between Archie and me too. We blamed each other, we withdrew. That betrayal, the financial ruin looming over us, took whatever was left of our marriage and just... blew it to cinders. He walked out not long after. That whole period cost me my savings, nearly my home, and ultimately, my husband."

She looked at me pointedly. "So when I saw you and Julianne in each other's arms, right there by the bonfire... For a split second, it wasn't you I saw. It was the memory of that time—the secrecy, the passion mixed up with the business, the potential for everything to just implode. It brought back that awful feeling of vulnerability, of things spiraling out of control right under my nose."

I tried not to squirm as guilt twisted inside me. "I didn't think about that. I'm sorry. We never meant for you to feel like that."

"Of course you didn't." Her voice finally took on some warmth again. "I know that. But I hope you understand better where I'm coming from now. That when I see another workplace romance, especially involving someone in a position of financial trust like Julianne, my alarm bells ring loudly. It's not that I don't trust her, Eli. It's that I know firsthand how devastating the consequences can be when personal feelings and professional responsibilities get tangled in the heart of *our* family business. And how easily it can destroy more than just the balance sheet."

Her gaze became almost pleading. "Sweetheart, my greatest joy is seeing my children happy. Truly settled, confident, and content. If you had come to me right now, looked me square in the eye, and said with absolute certainty, without a flicker of doubt, 'Mom, I love Julianne Verne, and I am all in, ready for whatever comes,' then perhaps we'd be having a different conversation."

My heart took off again, thumping out of my chest as I parted my lips. The opening was there. All I had to do was say it. My chest froze, the words sticking in my lungs. Nothing came out, and I closed my mouth again and took a sip of coffee I didn't even taste.

She leaned forward again, her hand covering mine on the table. "Right now? Your hesitation, the panic in your eyes this very moment… it tells me *you're* not there yet. You're still battling those old fears, Eli. And jumping deeper into this relationship, especially keeping it hidden while you're still fighting those demons is reckless. It's unfair—to you, to her, and yes, to the stability this family and this resort desperately need right now."

Her grip tightened slightly. "Maybe what you need isn't diving into this even deeper, but some space. Time for *you* to really confront those fears, Eli. To be absolutely sure of what you want, of what you're capable of offering. Because Julianne deserves someone who is committed, without reservation. And so do you. You deserve to be free of that fear."

Her words landed like body blows. She wasn't just enforcing an arbitrary, outdated rule. She was calling out my deepest insecurities, my years-long pattern of emotional evasion. And damn her, she wasn't entirely wrong. I *was* scared. I *had* hesitated.

Frustration warred with a sickening wave of self-awareness. I felt trapped, misunderstood, yet simultaneously exposed. She thought I wasn't ready? Maybe she was right. But it didn't feel like protective concern. Her opinion felt like judgment, like she was using my own internal struggle against me, perhaps even prioritizing the resort's smooth operation over my messy, complicated heart. It was almost a relief when a hard knot of anger formed in my gut. That gave me something to focus on other than the clawing panic that had lodged in my heart.

"So that's it?" My voice was rough, tight with resentment. "You're saying I have to choose? Walk away from something… something really good because I'm not fitting into your perfect picture of commitment right now?"

"I'm saying," Helen replied, her voice gentle but unwavering, "that maybe this painful situation is forcing you to confront things you've avoided for a long time. Maybe this pause is exactly what *you* need, Eli."

I pulled my hand away, standing abruptly. The carefully controlled conversation had imploded. I felt raw, angry, and utterly lost. I turned away from her and stalked toward the edge of the patio, needing distance. The vast ocean offered no answers, only mirrored the turbulent chaos inside me.

She hadn't forbidden it. She'd just made it impossible. Mom had put the ball entirely in my court, knowing damn well I was terrified to pick it up and run with it. And it left me stranded, caught between the woman I was undeniably falling for and the lifelong fears I still hadn't conquered.

# Chapter Twenty-Six

## JULES

THE EARLY EVENING sky above Memorial Park was alive in shades of gold and pink as I sat at the table next to Lacey, who looked radiant in her white lace wedding dress. Adorned with pearls and sequins, she sparkled like a diamond under the evening light. Even I had to admit my fitted navy dress made me feel uncharacteristically glamorous. The fabric hugged my body just right, or maybe her joy radiated so fiercely that I couldn't help but catch some of the glow.

"Can you believe we're actually here?" Lacey murmured to me before taking a healthy swig of champagne. The long table was covered in a white cloth, with floating candles inside clear vases placed strategically to illuminate the gardenias and pink roses surrounding them. Daniel sat on her other side, with Randy next to him. Randy wore an unmistakable expression of relief, having just given his speech. My time was coming up.

"Believe it," I replied with a grin, nudging her playfully.

"You're officially off the market, Ashworth. Fully Lacey Greene now. We signed the marriage certificate and everything."

She laughed, a sound so pure it made my heart swell.

"Guess it's time. Wish me luck." I stood and raised my glass, the weight of everyone's gazes on me. "When Lacey and I first met, I never imagined I'd be standing here today, watching her marry the love of her life. Lacey, you've grown so much, becoming this incredible woman who's ready to build a beautiful life with Daniel."

The words felt empty in my mouth. I swallowed hard, pushing down the lump in my throat as I continued my rehearsed speech. Comforting and uplifting, it was the opposite of how I felt. Lifting my chin, I scanned the crowd with a warm smile.

"I remember when Lacey first told me about Daniel. She was so nervous, fumbling over her words like she'd just downed a triple shot of espresso. But then she said something that stuck with me: 'I feel like I can finally breathe when I'm with him.' That's what love should be, right? That effortless and inevitable, like the tide rolling in."

I glanced at Daniel, who was watching Lacey with sheer adoration. "Daniel, you've become more than just a husband to Lacey. You've become her partner in every sense of the word. You've seen her at her worst, like when she eats an entire pizza by herself and insists it's *just a snack*"—I paused to let the audience laugh—"and still you love her more for it."

Lacey's cheeks flushed with embarrassment and not a little delight. I continued, my voice softening. "Lacey, you've always been the sunshine in my life, the one who reminds me to laugh when I'm too busy being serious. You've taught me that love isn't about perfection—it's about navigating life's messy moments together. And,

Daniel, you've clearly mastered the art of putting up with Lacey's… *unique* brand of chaos. Anyone who can handle a glitter explosion and a last-minute wedding venue change deserves a medal. But seriously, you two complement each other perfectly, and that's what makes your love story so special."

My lips curled into a wide smile, and I raised my glass higher, the champagne catching the light. "So here's to Lacey and Daniel. May your love continue to be the kind that makes us all a little hopeful and a lot happy. Cheers to a lifetime of adventures, laughter, and maybe a few more pizzas."

Still smiling as I watched them share a tender kiss, the weight of my own solitude pressed against my ribs. Eli and I had finally faced our inevitable crisis. But instead of facing it together, he'd run. He'd hidden behind his familiar brand of lying low to avoid the consequences. He wasn't willing to fight for us, not really. And the realization stung.

Lacey was glowing, utterly enveloped in her newfound joy. A pang of longing shot through me. Would I ever find someone to look at me like that? Someone who could see past my meticulous nature and into the messier parts of my heart? It felt a million miles away, an impossible dream scattered along the sandy shores of Dove Key.

As I took my seat again and swigged a long drink of champagne, I studied the hazy horizon. Should I leave Sunset Siesta? I could forge a fresh start, somewhere Eli's ghost wouldn't haunt every corner. But the thought of abandoning the resort, my home for so long, filled me with bitter resentment. I was trapped, torn between my broken heart and the career I'd worked so hard to build.

MONDAY MORNING, the rain pelted against my office window as I stared at the spreadsheet before me. Numbers were my shield against emotional turmoil. I threw myself into the renovation budget with renewed vigor, determined to focus on the task at hand and the meeting I had with Harper shortly.

"Deficit… liability… projected income," I muttered, the familiar financial jargon a soothing balm to my frayed nerves. And work became my refuge, allowing me to disappear into the figures, my ugly love life fading into the background.

A knock at the door jolted me from my concentration. I quickly smoothed my hair and straightened my blouse as I called out, "Come in."

Harper entered, her usual bright energy tempered by something I couldn't quite place. Concern, maybe?

"Good morning, Jules," she said warmly, then caught herself. "Oh, I'm sorry. I mean, Julianne."

A small smile raised my lips. "It's okay, Harper. You can call me Jules if you'd rather. I think we've earned that level of familiarity by now, don't you?"

An unexpected warmth bloomed in my chest when Harper's smile reappeared as she settled into the chair across from me.

"I agree, and I'd like that." Then her expression grew thoughtful. "How are you doing? Really?"

I hesitated, torn between my instinct to maintain professional distance and the genuine care I saw in Harper's eyes. "I'm… managing. Focusing on work helps."

"It always does. For me too." She shifted, leaning forward slightly. "So what's the financial situation looking like with regard to renovations?"

I exhaled slowly. "I wish I had better news, Harper. I've gone over everything with a fine-tooth comb, explored every possible cost-cutting measure—including potential staff reductions, which I hate to even consider. But the hard truth is, we need a loan, and it's not going to be a small one."

Harper's shoulders sagged slightly, but she nodded, her expression resolute. "That's nothing we weren't expecting, huh? Thanks for running the figures anyway. What do you recommend as our next step?"

I turned the screen so Harper could see the spreadsheet, sending a small thank you to the universe that the thing didn't short out and go dark. "Based on Chase's assessment, our top priorities have to be the roofs and the HVAC system. They're not sexy upgrades, they won't directly boost bookings or guest satisfaction, but they're absolutely critical for the resort's long-term viability."

As I spoke, I pictured the charming, slightly ramshackle buildings of Sunset Siesta. The place had wormed its way into my heart, becoming more than just a job. "I know it's not ideal, but if we secure a loan for these essential repairs, we can at least ensure the resort stays operational while we work on more guest-facing improvements."

Harper's brow lowered. "I hear you. But balancing these immediate needs with our long-term goals isn't an easy decision."

"Of course not."

"I'll need to discuss this with the family," Harper said as she rubbed a hand over the back of her neck. "There are so many factors to consider."

"There certainly are. Let me know what you decide." My words sounded so formal, so distant.

Harper's eyes softened as she looked at me. "Jules, I can't tell you how much I appreciate your work on this. Your dedication to Sunset Siesta… it's truly invaluable."

Her words hit me unexpectedly, stirring something

deep inside. My professional mask slipped as I glanced at my bookcase with its battered Verne books and my scrappy little cactus on the desk. "This place isn't just a job for me anymore. It's home. I want to do everything I can to secure its future."

"That's exactly why we're lucky to have you. I'll set up another formal meeting with Chase next week sometime after the family meeting. Be on the lookout for a calendar invite."

"I will. Let me know if you need any figures beforehand. I'll have them prepared."

"Thanks, Jules. See you later."

As she left, a sense of connection lingered between us —something deeper than mere professional respect. At least some good was coming from this disaster.

The dreary Monday afternoon dragged on. I worked on payroll, fingers flying over the keyboard as I entered numbers and checked calculations. Something was missing. With a groan, I realized Eli hadn't sent over the dive op payroll files. My heart sank as I glanced at the clock. If I didn't get those soon, I'd be in trouble. I thought about a phone call or email request, but I didn't want to give him any reason to keep ignoring me.

I rose and made my way down the weathered wooden pier toward Eli's domain. The rain had stopped, but the sky still hung low, casting a gray pallor over everything. As I entered the shop, I caught snippets of laughter from the classroom. Eli's voice carried to me, warm and animated, cutting through the humid air like a knife. I paused outside the classroom door, just out of sight.

"Okay, folks! When you dive deep, remember—the air in your tank is compressed even more, right?" His tone was playful, filled with that familiar humor. "So if you think you're going to breathe the same amount of air down there as you do at thirty feet, think again! You gotta manage your air like it's the last slice of pizza!"

The students laughed, and my heart twisted. I leaned against the wall, listening as he continued, his passion for diving evident in every word. He had a gift for making complex concepts feel accessible, even fun. I could picture him in the water—confident, magnetic, alive.

"Now, when we reach depth, we'll also need to watch for narcosis." His voice dropped slightly, becoming serious yet still engaging. "Just like how you might make question-able life choices at a party, you can make some… inter-esting decisions at depth if you're not careful."

Another round of laughter erupted, and an aching nostalgia washed over me. I realized I was smiling without even knowing it. God, I missed this. I missed him—the Eli who made me laugh until my sides hurt, who lit up every room he entered.

"Seriously, though, nitrogen narcosis is no joke. Not everyone experiences it, but if you find yourself feeling loopy or euphoric, let your buddy and dive leader know. That's all for the classroom session. See you guys bright and early tomorrow."

As the students filed out, I stepped into the dive shop, my heart humming despite my efforts to remain calm. The bright aquamarine walls of the dive shop surrounded me, still echoing with Eli's enthusiasm. He glanced up, his eyes widening slightly at the sight of me. He looked breathtak-ingly good—tousled blond hair, sun-kissed skin, a faded Dive Sunset Siesta T-shirt clinging to his athletic frame.

"Hi, Eli." My simple sentence pleased me. It sounded friendly, professional. Not the tone of a woman who was trying to refrain from jumping into a man's arms. Right this second.

"Jules." His voice was more cautious as he closed a file

folder and placed it in his backpack. "What brings you by?"

"Just checking on those payroll files. You haven't sent them over yet."

He winced. "Damn. I'm sorry. I had to lead an unexpected dive trip this morning and it slipped my mind. I've got them ready, though—give me just a sec."

I nodded stiffly as he moved to the computer. My eyes traced the familiar lines of his back, remembering how it felt to wrap my arms around him. This man was similar to the Eli I'd once battled with, but different too. That Eli would have never spared a second thought for the payroll report.

"Should be right here…" He clicked a few buttons, and I shifted my weight, fighting against the swirl of emotions rising inside me. "There," he said, turning back to me. "Just emailed them to you."

"Thanks." I kept my tone light and friendly. "Here we are, two coworkers getting along famously. I didn't even have to nag. Quite a change from how we started out, huh?"

I'd meant it as a light-hearted quip, but Eli's face crumpled, pain flashing in his eyes. "Yeah. Not how I wanted things to change, though."

My breath caught in my throat. "What do you mean?"

"This. Us." Eli's voice was raw, filled with regret. "Being forced to choose between my family and you. I hate it, Jules. I talked to my mom, but she still won't budge."

I got it. Truly. Family loyalty ran deep. Especially for Eli, who'd watched his parents' bitter divorce transform familial love into a minefield of betrayal and pain. He'd had no choice.

But understanding didn't make the ache any less devastating.

I couldn't ask him to choose me over his family, for God's sake. And how would that solve anything if we were together, but the rest of the resort was united against us?

I raised my chin, refusing to show how I felt. "It's a complicated situation. People say that what's meant to be finds a way. Guess we're just not meant to be." I nodded with my head at his computer. "Thanks for sending over the file."

I headed toward the exit, the weight of unsaid words filling the air between us.

"Jules, please…"

I couldn't bear to look back. The pain in my chest was suffocating, and as I walked down the pier, each step felt heavier. The beauty of the ocean shimmered around me, but all I could think about was the chasm between what I wanted and what reality offered.

The thought of leaving Dove Key flitted once more through my head. But I disregarded it for one simple reason. I had a feeling that no matter where I went, Eli would always be a part of my story—a bittersweet reminder of what could have been.

# Chapter Twenty-Seven

## ELI

THE CONFERENCE ROOM hadn't changed much. I thought back to all those meetings when Jules and I sniped and sparred with each other in this room. Back when we had been enemies instead of whatever we were now. Same scratched oak table, same faded nautical prints on the walls. Yet we had gone from adversaries to lovers to… ex-lovers?

I shifted in my seat, trying to channel my usual easy-going vibe, but my leg wouldn't stop bouncing under the table. The air crackled with a mix of hope and nerves as my family filed in. Harper's lips were pressed into a thin line, all business. Braden's eyes held that familiar glint of hopeful ambition. And Mom looked… wary.

When Jules walked in, my heart did its usual flip-flop. Her bun was extra severe today, not a hair out of place. Desperate for some connection with her, I caught her eye and winked. "Looking sharp, Verne. Did you iron your pencil this morning too?" Yeah, that damn mouth of mine.

But I caught the hint of a smile as she slapped back without missing a beat. "I see you've combed your hair for once, Coleridge. Special occasion?"

Since my heartfelt confession last week about my misery, we hadn't talked again. I knew how she felt—the only way forward was for us to be accepted as a couple. Except I couldn't figure out how to make that happen. So I played the part that was expected of me, clutching my chest in mock offense. "You wound me. I'll have you know I run my fingers through it at least twice a day."

Chase was the last to arrive, dropping into the seat next to me with a nod, and once again dressed in a suit and tie. The room fell silent, that moment before the plunge.

I cleared my throat. "Well, gang's all here. Shall we get this party started?"

Harper shot me a look from Chase's other side. "This isn't a party, Eli."

I pointed to the sheet cake in the middle of the table. I hadn't liked that idea, afraid of jinxing our decision, but Harper had overruled me. We'd met as a family two days ago and come to our decision. Very democratically, very un-Coleridge-like. I smirked back at her, indicating the cake. "Could've fooled me. We've got cake, right?"

Braden snorted. "I could get beer if anyone's thirsty."

Mom sighed. "Children, please. This is serious."

The laughter died away, leaving that prickly anticipation. My stomach churned. We'd made our decision but now came the hard part—actually following through. I glanced around the table, taking in the familiar faces. My tribe. The people I'd do anything for, even if it meant embracing change that scared the hell out of me.

Chase cleared his throat, his eyes scanning the room. "Well, I suppose we should get down to business. What's the verdict on the renovations?" In keeping with family solidarity, I hadn't said anything to him about what we'd come up with, but I hoped he'd be pleased.

The air in the conference room seemed to thicken. I held my breath, waiting for Harper to speak. As general manager, it was on her to make the announcement. She straightened in her chair, her usually warm eyes now reflecting determination and caution. "After careful consideration, we've decided to proceed with a limited renovation through your firm, Chase. We'll focus on essential repairs and upgrades—the roofs, HVAC systems, and guest room beds and linens. To finance this, we'll secure the necessary loan."

Chase nodded, his expression professional. "That's a solid plan. It addresses the most pressing issues while keeping costs manageable."

"Exactly," Harper agreed. "We're balancing the need for improvements with our financial constraints."

I caught Braden shifting in his seat, his blue eyes sparking with that familiar determination.

*Here we go.*

"I hear you," Braden started, his voice casual but firm. "But I just want to reiterate what I said before. Sometimes, a bigger risk can lead to bigger rewards."

I couldn't help but nod. He had a point.

Braden continued, gesturing animatedly. "Look at Tidal Hops. When I started, everyone thought I was crazy to take out such a big loan. But now? We're thriving and I've already paid it back. If I'd played it safe, who knows where we'd be."

The room fell silent, considering his words. I found myself torn, caught between our cautious plan and the allure of a bolder strategy.

"Braden's got a point," I heard myself say. "A more comprehensive renovation could really put us on the map. Give us that competitive edge we've been talking about."

Mom's eyes narrowed slightly, and the worry lines deepened around her mouth. But before she could speak, Harper jumped in. "I understand where you're coming from, guys. Really, I do. But we have to consider the financial implications first. This isn't just about the next few months. We need to think long-term stability. We already made the decision, remember?"

Mom leaned forward, her silver-brown braid falling over her shoulder. "Braden, honey, I'm so proud of what you've accomplished with Tidal Hops." Her smile was warm and proud, but I noticed a slight tremor in her hand as she reached for her glass of water.

"But?" Braden prompted gently.

Mom cleared her throat and set her glass back down firmly. "No more buts, just a push for caution. I know you've all wanted to strangle me at points for the last few months, but I've come around. I'm still not thrilled with getting a loan, but… I'm sure I'll get used to the idea. As long as the loan is for the smallest amount possible."

My chest tightened. I'd never seen Mom look so vulnerable, so unsure. She'd always been our rock, the one with all the answers. Now, seeing her struggle, I felt a rush of empathy. This wasn't just about business for her. It was about protecting the very heart of who we were.

"Mom," Ben said softly. "We understand. Really."

"Julianne, what are your thoughts on the financial impact?" Harper asked, tactfully steering the conversation. "Is there a way we can mitigate some of the risk?"

Jules straightened in her chair, all business. But I caught the softness in her eyes as she glanced at Mom. "Based on my projections, we could offset a portion of the loan costs with a modest room rate increase. Given that guests will directly benefit from the upgrades to beds and linens, I believe we can justify a five to seven percent increase without significant pushback."

"That's not too much," Austin mused, stroking the dark stubble on his chin. "We could market it as part of an Enhanced Guest Experience package or something. Pair it with my fishing charters or Eli's dive trips."

Mom nodded slowly, some of the tension easing from her shoulders. "And you believe this increase would be enough to cover the additional costs, Julianne?"

"Oh, no," Jules replied crisply. "We're still talking about a loan in excess of a million dollars. But rate increases are necessary to ease the burden. Combined with the projected increase in bookings from the renovations and more advertising, I believe we can manage the loan responsibly."

My siblings exchanged glances, a mix of relief and cautious optimism on their faces. It wasn't the grand, sweeping change some had hoped for, but it was a step forward. A compromise that respected both our dreams and our very real financial constraints.

Harper leaned forward, her eyes scanning the room. "I know we all wish we could do more. But this is a solid start. We're addressing the most critical issues, and we can always reassess down the line."

Brenna nodded, a lock of her auburn hair falling across her face. "Exactly. My bookshop didn't become a success overnight. I started small, built gradually. Now look at it."

"Same goes for Calypso Key," Hunter chimed in from her side, his deep voice carrying easily through the room. "We've had our share of financial hurdles too. It's part of the game when you're running a resort."

I couldn't help but smile at the solidarity. And Hunter

was one of us now, nearly as much a Coleridge as he was a Markham.

Mom's eyes glistened as she looked around the table. "I can't tell you how much your support means to me and how *proud* I am of all of you. I just wish there were a less risky way." She straightened in her chair. "But enough of my fretting. We've made our decision, and I stand by it. Sunset Siesta has weathered tougher storms than this."

Chase loudly cleared his throat, drawing all eyes to him. He actually *fidgeted* in his seat. Finally taking a deep breath, he swept his eyes around the table. "What if there was another way?"

I turned to give him my full attention. What was he up to?

"Helen," Chase continued, his tone careful but confident, "have you ever considered bringing on a partner? Someone to invest the funds needed for a full renovation in exchange for a share of the profits? Uh, someone like me, for example."

The room fell silent. I gaped at my best friend, a searing hope igniting in my chest. This was the first I'd heard of this idea. How long had he been sitting on it?

"I…" Mom looked stunned, her eyes wide. "We've never had anyone but family involved in ownership."

Before I could stop myself, I blurted out, "But Chase is practically family, isn't he? I mean, he's been part of our lives forever. This could be the perfect solution!"

Jules raised an eyebrow at me, her lips lifting in that adorable way that meant she was both amused and exasperated. I flashed her a grin, riding the wave of sudden possibility. I turned to Mom, whose eyes were the size of saucers. She looked like she was about to keel over on the spot.

Chase must have seen the same thing because he held a hand out in a placating gesture. "I'm not talking about an equal partnership here. More like twenty-five percent. Enough to make the renovations happen without you all taking on debt."

I leaned back, mind racing. This was genius. It solved our financial issues and gave Chase—someone we all trusted—something too. Plus, if Mom was willing to consider this kind of change… I forced my eyes not to swerve to Jules.

Ben sat up straight in his seat. "That's a hell of an idea, Chase." His eyes shifted to me. "Did you two cook this up together?"

I laughed. "This is the first I've heard of it. Dude can keep his cards tight to his chest."

Now Chase was positively blushing. "Being a bachelor, I don't have any expensive needs. I've saved a lot over the years. And… I've felt stifled at work lately. I've been thinking about starting my own architectural firm. Sunset Siesta would be a great way to start."

"It's an intriguing proposal," Mom said slowly, her brow furrowed in thought. She turned to Jules. "Julianne, what do you think? From a financial standpoint?"

"It could work beautifully," she replied, her voice steady and assured. "The injection of capital would allow for comprehensive renovations without over-leveraging the resort. And Chase's expertise would be invaluable moving forward."

We discussed it a while longer, with Chase making sure we would be okay with partnering with a new firm. Austin pointed out that Chase was the one taking the biggest risk and no one brought up any objections.

"Let's vote on it," I said. "I say yes. Harper?"

Around the table, one by one, *yeses* rang out. Then we all turned to Mom. This was it—the moment that could change everything.

# Chapter Twenty-Eight

# ELI

I HELD my breath as Mom's gaze swept around the table, a lifetime of shared history evident in her softening expression. "This whole process has forced me to face a lot of fears I preferred to bury. It brought up a lot of old trauma, but the last few months have shown me other things too. That my kids are all adults now. How trust can be rebuilt, even in unexpected ways. And most of all, that maybe clinging to old fears is hurting us more than taking a calculated risk with someone who is nearly a son to me too."

A smile rose on her face as her gaze settled on Chase. "We'll need to hash out the details, of course. But... welcome to Sunset Siesta, partner."

The room erupted in cheers and laughter. I whooped, pulling Chase into a seated bear hug. "You sneaky bastard. Why didn't you tell me?"

He grinned, clapping me on the back. "And ruin the surprise? Where's the fun in that?" Then he flushed, that shy look coming over him again. "I told you I've been getting itchy feet at my current job. The more I thought about it, investing in Sunset Siesta seemed like a perfect first job for Ashworth Architectural."

I nodded. "Nice name."

He laughed. "That just popped into my head. I'll probably change it three times before I actually hang out my shingle. God, now I sound like Lacey."

Harper had reached over and touched Chase's hand. Just a gentle touch, fingers barely brushing the back of his hand, but Chase's head whipped around, his entire focus suddenly laser-locked on her. Just like that, I might as well have been wallpaper.

"Thank you," Harper said softly. "I hope you know what you're getting into."

His cheeks took on a tinge of pink. "All kidding aside, I've been thinking about it for a while. I've got money to invest, and a big project would really help get my new firm off the ground. I know all of you, not just Helen, were reluctant to go into debt. This arrangement works for all of us."

Harper's eyes swept around the happy room, and she barked a laugh. "I have a feeling something new is starting in this room."

Chase continued his now very credible imitation of a ripe tomato. "So do I. I can't wait to get started."

After darting my eyes to Jules, I drummed both hands on the table until everyone quieted and looked at me. "One other thing. Once we're established and the bottom line is looking less crimson, our accountant here is more than overdue for a new computer. The museum called and wants that one back."

Still smiling, Jules cocked her head at me as Harper nodded firmly. "Absolutely. You've been more than patient, Jules. We'll make sure it happens."

The conference room buzzed with energy as Brenna handed me a piece of cake, then passed out more to the rest of us. We broke into smaller groups to chat. Braden was already pitching potential craft beer collaborations to Chase, while Austin and Ben quietly conferred with Mom, probably discussing logistics. I made my way over to Harper, who was positively glowing.

"So," I drawled, "how long have you and our new business partner been cooking this up?"

Harper's eyes widened. "What? No, I had no idea—"

I cocked my head to one side. "Really? You two looked chummy. Let me remind you that he's my friend, not yours."

She rolled her eyes. "Oh, keep your fat mouth shut or you'll chase him away and he'll change his mind."

"Not a chance," I said with a wide grin. "Chase is one of those guys who means what he says. He's kind of like a dull, boring rock like that."

She just stared at me. "It is an absolute mystery to me how you have any friends at all."

"Aw, you're just jealous." I laughed, relief from the meeting coursing through me. "Besides, I don't need to worry about you poaching him from me. I told him years ago that I'd kill him if he went near either of my sisters. He's a man of his word, my Chase."

I went to grab a glass of sparkling cider from the bottles that had appeared out of nowhere and caught Jules's eye across the room. She was beaming, her eyes sparkling with a mix of professional satisfaction and personal joy. I wanted nothing more than to sweep her into my arms and kiss her senseless.

Instead, I mouthed *thank you* to her. She gave me a small nod, her smile softening. For the first time in weeks, I felt like we were on the same page, moving forward together.

I made my way over to her, weaving through my celebratory family members, and handed her a glass of cider. "So, accountant extraordinaire, think we might actually pull this off?"

Jules lifted her glass, her eyes dancing. "Well, Mr. Coleridge, I'd say the odds are looking better than they were a month ago."

I bowed. "High praise indeed."

"Chase coming on board is a great idea."

"The old boy is full of surprises, isn't he?"

She laughed and nodded as everyone else slowly filed out of the room. Mom and Chase walked out side by side, and she touched his arm as she laughed at some remark he made.

"Thank you for asking about a new computer for me. That will be heaven when it happens."

My eyes snapped back to Jules. "Of course. I have to say these things publicly, so you don't get out your red pen and axe yourself again."

Our eyes held for a moment that stretched into eternity. Until Jules blinked and said, "Thanks again. I'd better get back to work. See you later."

Then she was gone.

The door clicked shut, leaving me alone in the sudden, echoing quiet. A ghost of Jules's smile lingered in the air, the brief spark of connection we'd shared still warming my chest. For that instant, seeing the approval and maybe something more in her eyes, everything had felt right. Possible. Like we were a team again, even without saying a word.

I sank back into my chair, thoughtful. The successful outcome of the meeting should have left me elated. Chase onboard as a partner, a viable path forward for the resort, Mom actually embracing change… it was everything we'd hoped for. There was cake, for crying out loud. I *should* have been popping champagne or at least cracking open one of Braden's celebratory IPAs.

Instead, the silence pressed in, amplifying the contrast. The resort's future looked brighter, but mine? It was shrouded in the fog of my own making. That brief moment with Jules just highlighted the chasm between the progress we'd made professionally and the stalemate we were trapped in personally.

My thoughts drifted back, inevitably, to that morning on Mom's patio. The sun on the water, the scent of coffee, the weight of her question hanging between us. *Are you in love with her?*

The memory wasn't just painful now. It was clarifying. Today Mom had accepted Chase and taken that leap of faith despite her deep-seated fears about finances and outsiders. It threw my own failure into sharp relief. She *could* overcome her past pain when faced with solid commitment and a clear path forward. Chase offered that for the resort.

And what had I offered when asked flat out about my feelings? Hesitation. Deflection.

*Your hesitation tells me you're not there yet, Eli.*

The realization washed over me and left me numb. It wasn't just about a rule. It wasn't just about Mom's fears, valid as they might be. It was about *me.*

A sickening certainty washed over me and left me numb. Suddenly, all this dancing around the damn resort policy looked like nothing more than a smokescreen. And Mom's fears? Deep as they ran, rooted in real pain I couldn't deny, even *they* weren't the ultimate roadblock. No. The real problem, the anchor dragging us down, the reason Jules and I were stuck in this miserable limbo... stared right back at me if I only had the courage to see it.

Me.

My inability to stand tall and claim the most important feeling of my life because I was still chained to the ghosts of my parents' failed marriage, still terrified I was doomed to repeat it. The fault wasn't a rule, or a ghost from the past. It landed squarely in my lap.

I dropped my head into my hands, the smooth wood of the table cool against my forehead. The warmth from Jules's smile moments ago evaporated, replaced by a chilling self-awareness. Mom hadn't blocked us. I had. And only I could fix this.

*I love her.*

The truth screamed silently in the empty room. I loved Julianne Verne. I loved her intelligence, her ridiculous organizational skills, her hidden adventurous spirit, the way she made me laugh, the way she made me *better*. Loved the way she looked at me, like she saw something worth holding onto beneath the jokes and the laid-back facade.

And I had failed her. Failed myself. I hadn't been able to give Mom the certainty she needed because I hadn't fully embraced it myself, hadn't trusted myself not to screw it up.

A surge of something hot and sharp—anger mixed with shame—flooded me. Anger at my own cowardice. Anger at the past that still held me hostage. Anger that the one time something truly real came along, I fumbled it because I couldn't conquer my own demons.

I pushed back from the table abruptly, the chair scraping loudly against the floor. I stalked to the window, staring out at the familiar vista—the pier, the dive shop, the endless blue horizon. My world. My cage.

If I couldn't prove my commitment *here*, within the tangled web of family history and resort expectations, maybe the only way was to break free entirely. It felt drastic, terrifying, like cutting off a limb. But if I needed to make a display of my feelings, I couldn't think of a stronger one.

I could get a job anywhere. Calypso Key, maybe. Start fresh. Prove to Jules, prove to myself, prove to the goddamn universe that I *was* all in. That my love for her was bigger than my fear, bigger than this place, bigger than the ghosts of the past. It wouldn't be easy, leaving behind everything I'd ever known. But I didn't have a choice if I wanted to be with Jules. And I wanted that more than anything.

"If this is how it has to be," I said to my reflection in the window, "so be it."

# Chapter Twenty-Nine

## JULES

I SWIRLED the red wine in my glass idly, my gaze fixed on some indistinct point beyond the droning television. As I sat on the couch, my living room felt oddly claustrophobic tonight, the coastal-themed décor anything but relaxing. I took another sip, hoping the earthy Cabernet might dull the riot of thoughts ricocheting through my mind.

No such luck.

The renovation meeting, Chase's surprise partnership offer, that charming grin Eli had flashed my way—it was all tangled up. What had started as elation after the meeting had gradually transformed into a jumble of mixed emotions at home.

I grabbed the remote and flipped aimlessly through channels. Nothing caught my attention. My finger paused over the button as a familiar face appeared on screen—a tanned, rugged diver exploring some impossibly gorgeous reef. For a moment, all I could see was Eli, his eyes sparkling with the same infectious enthusiasm anytime he talked about the ocean.

"Nope. Absolutely not."

I clicked off the TV with a huff and tossed the remote aside. But in the sudden silence, the memories rushed in. Shared laughter over his terrible puns. The warmth of his hand on the small of my back. The way his eyes had locked with mine across the conference table, a flicker of emotion passing between us. That humorous, casual conversation we'd had at the end of the meeting only cemented in my mind how much I missed him. Us.

The thought of working beside him day after day was almost too much to bear. And resenting Helen for her position was futile. She had her reasons, and I didn't even disagree with them. I just wanted her to make an exception for us. But was that fair?

I stood abruptly, pacing the length of my living room as my analytical mind kicked into overdrive. The resort's future was looking up at last. I should have been thrilled. Instead, I felt lost. All that time I'd spent working on how to fund the renovations, obsolete. Of course I was thrilled with how it had all worked out… but what now?

"Okay, I need to approach this logically. Pro-con list. That always helps."

I snatched a notepad from the coffee table, scribbling furiously as I spoke out loud to the empty room. "Pro: The resort's future is looking much rosier. Con: My months of financial projections are basically useless now. Pro: My job is secure. Con: Said job involves watching the man I lo—the man I used to—Eli, move on with his life."

I couldn't write that last sentence down. I couldn't even say it coherently! I stared at the list, willing it to make sense. But the neat columns of pros and cons couldn't capture the ache in my chest or the way my stomach fluttered every time Eli's name crossed my mind.

I had to find a way to move on. It was best for everyone, especially me.

When my gaze landed on my laptop on the couch, I marched over and sat to open the lid. My fingers hesitated over the keys before typing *accounting jobs Florida*. The search results populated, a sea of possibilities that felt more like a cage. As I scrolled through job listings, each one felt like a step farther from everything I'd built here. A corporate gig in Jacksonville. Non-profit work in Orlando. All so sterile. No ocean breeze. No sand between my toes. Or worse—exactly like what I already had, just… not here.

Not on Dove Key.

Not near him.

I slammed the laptop shut, my pragmatic facade crumbling with a long groan. "Who am I kidding? I can't leave Dove Key. It's home."

A sharp knock at the door made me jump. I set my laptop aside and padded across the hardwood, curious. When I swung the door open, my heart studded to a halt.

Eli stood on my porch, eyes blazing with an intensity I'd never seen before. His usual easy grin was nowhere to be found. He wore a fitted polo shirt and dressy shorts, and he looked good enough to eat with a spoon.

"Eli?" I squeaked, acutely aware of my ratty sweatpants and messy bun. "What are you—"

"Can I come in?" he asked, already stepping over the threshold.

I gestured weakly. "Sure, make yourself at home."

He paced my living room like a caged tiger while I poured him a glass of wine and refilled mine. When I offered him one, he waved it off, which was beyond weird. "No, thanks, I'm good."

I set both glasses down, studying his flushed face. "You seem excited. Is this about the meeting?"

Eli ran a hand through his hair, messing it up in that endearing way that always made my heart clench. "Jules, I..." He stopped, seeming to struggle for words.

I waited, my heart in my throat. What could have him so worked up?

"Look," he finally said, his gaze locking onto mine. "I know things have been complicated between us. But today I realized something important."

I swallowed hard. "Oh?"

I watched Eli's face transform as he spoke, a tableau of emotions playing across his features. Something raw and vulnerable had replaced his usual carefree demeanor. Something that made my heart gallop in my chest.

"You're right about this having to do with the meeting. I was so... *proud* of how Mom jumped into the unknown and agreed to Chase's partnership. And I thought, I hoped, maybe it meant she was coming around, you know? About us."

My breath caught. I'd been trying so hard not to love him, but hearing him say *us* sent a thrill through me.

"What happened?" I asked softly, afraid of the answer.

Eli's shoulders sagged. "I talked to her after the meeting. She's still... she doesn't want us together, Jules."

The hope that had begun to bloom in my chest withered. "Oh."

"But I don't care," Eli said fiercely, crossing the room to me in three quick strides. He took my hands in his, his touch sending sparks up my arms. "That was the realization. I love you. I'm not letting anyone come between us, not even my mother."

My heart stopped, then started racing double time. "Eli, I—"

"I've found a solution," he continued, his eyes boring into mine. "We can be together."

The words I'd been holding back for so long came rushing out. "I love you too, Eli. God, I've been trying so hard not to, but I can't help it."

His face lit up with transcendent joy, and for a moment, everything else faded away.

"What's your solution?" I asked. "How can we possibly make this work?"

Eli's eyes were filled with determination, but there was a flicker of something else—uncertainty, maybe even fear. "Simple. I'm leaving Sunset Siesta. I've already reached out to other dive operations, including Calypso Key."

I jerked my hands back as if I'd been scalded, my heart hammering against my chest. My skin broke out in goose bumps, and needing to be in motion, I started pacing. "What? This is too much. Too drastic."

"No, it's not." His voice followed me as I moved. "You need to stay where you are, Jules. The resort needs your skills, especially now. But me? I'm just the guy who takes people diving."

I whirled to face him, frustration rushing out. "Don't you dare downplay your importance! The dive shop is integral to Sunset Siesta's identity. And it's your home, Eli. It's who you are. I never asked you to give that up for me."

A wry smile played at the corners of his mouth. "Home is where the heart is, right? And my heart's with you."

"Eli, Sunset Siesta is your home, your family's legacy. You can't walk away from that!"

Eli nodded. "But things change, don't they? Look at Brenna—she's made her own path with the bookshop. And Ben wants to be a paramedic, if he'd only admit it."

I shook my head, struggling to process his words. "That's different. This is… it's too much."

He rose and stepped closer, his eyes pleading. "Is it? If it means we can be together?"

My thoughts whirled, a massive knot I couldn't begin to untangle. How could I let him give up everything for me? But how could I bear to lose him again? I stared at Eli, really looked at him. The determination in those indigo eyes, the set of his jaw—it hit me like a tidal wave. This wasn't some impulsive, beach-bum decision. He'd thought this through, weighed the consequences.

For me. For us.

"Eli," I murmured, my voice cracking. "You can't just throw everything away. Not for me."

He cupped my face, his calloused hands surprisingly gentle. "Don't you get it? You're not just some number in my, uh, ledger. You're the whole damn balance sheet."

I couldn't help but smile, even as tears pricked at my eyes. "Did you just use an accounting metaphor?"

"See? You're rubbing off on me." He grinned, but it faded quickly. "I mean it, though. I love you. And if leaving Sunset Siesta is what it takes—"

"No," I cut him off, placing my hand over his. "God, Eli, I love you too. So much. But that's exactly why I can't let you do this."

His brow furrowed. "What are you talking about?"

I took a deep breath, steeling myself as I took a step back. I fought back the tide of emotion swelling within me. I had no choice, even though my heart was rending itself half inside my chest. "If you give everything up, even for me, you'll resent it. Resent me. And I couldn't bear that."

"Jules, I would never—"

"Maybe not at first," I said, gently caressing his face.

"But eventually? Sunset Siesta is literally in your blood. I can't be the one to take you away from it."

The pain on his face damn near killed me. "That's not true."

"It is." I pressed my forehead to his cheek, breathing in the scent that clung to him. "I know you, remember? Better than you think."

Eli's hands settled on my waist. "Then you know I love you."

"I do." The words caught in my throat. My inhale was shaky, but I had to get through this. "Which is why I can't let you make this sacrifice. You belong here. At the resort. With your family."

He pulled back, searching my face. "And where do you belong?"

I blinked back tears as I forced a trembling smile. "I'm still figuring that out." Straightening my shoulders, I steeled myself for what I was about to say. "Maybe, maybe I should be the one to leave."

Eli's eyes widened. "Jules, no—"

"Hear me out," I said, holding up a hand. "I could look for a job in Miami. It's not that far. We could make it work, see each other on weekends."

He shook his head, his jaw clenched. "That's not the answer."

"Why not?" I challenged, even as my heart ached at the thought of leaving Dove Key. Of leaving him.

He paced my small living room. "Because Dove Key isn't just my home anymore. It's yours too. I know how much you love it here."

I swallowed hard. He wasn't wrong. "But if it means we can be together—"

"At what cost?" Eli turned to face me, frustration clear in the lines on his forehead. "You'd be miserable in Miami, stuck in some corporate hellhole. And I'd be miserable knowing you gave up everything for me. It's exactly the same thing you brought up about me leaving. And I can't stand the thought of you so far away."

"So what do we do?" I asked, my voice cracking.

Eli's expression softened. He crossed the room to capture my face between his warm hands again. My breath caught as he leaned in. Then his lips were on mine, and the world fell away.

The kiss was deep, passionate, a promise sealed without words. My hands found their way to his sun-bleached hair, fingers gripping the soft strands as I pulled him closer. When we finally broke apart, both breathless, Eli rested his forehead against mine.

"I swear to you," he murmured, his voice rough with emotion. "I'll find a way for us to be together. Here, on Dove Key."

I barked a shaky laugh. "And how exactly are you going to pull off that miracle?"

He lifted his head, a familiar glint of mischief in his eyes. "Hey, I once convinced a stuck-up accountant I was the best person to teach her how to dive. Anything's possible."

"I was not stuck-up," I protested, unable to resist his humor even as my lips tingled from his kiss. "Just... professional."

"Potato, po-tah-to." His grin faded into something utterly and completely serious. "Have faith in me, Jules. In us. Right now. I don't know how I'm going to make this happen, but I will."

I hesitated, years of pragmatism warring with the wild hope—the desire to just believe—blooming in my chest. I studied his face. The determination etched there, the unwavering belief that we could overcome this. And looking at him, I understood something fundamental inside me had shifted. It had shifted a while ago. I gripped his shoulders tighter. "I've come to realize you're capable of accomplishing whatever you set your mind to. I do trust you. And for you, I'll take a leap of faith. I believe you'll find a way."

A slow, brilliant smile spread across his face that filled my weary soul. He nodded once, firmly, then spun on his heel and strode out the door.

# Chapter Thirty

## ELI

I UNCLIPPED my helmet and set it on the handlebars of my bike. The afternoon was hot and still today, with little breeze to soften the punishing sun. The little bell above the door of Bookshop in Paradise jingled as I stepped inside, the familiar scent of old paper and fresh coffee wrapping around me like a warm hug. And I needed a hug after a nearly sleepless night followed by a challenging morning with students.

Hours of tossing and turning hadn't made me any surer of how to approach Mom, but Jules's trusting face when I'd left her place only made me more determined. So here I was now, seeking Brenna's advice. And hoping her insight could help me navigate the minefield of convincing Mom that Jules and I weren't going to be neatly swept away just because she wanted it.

And who better to give me advice than Brenna? After all, she got this whole thing rolling in the first place by helping me figure out what Jules's nickname meant.

But the sight that greeted me stopped me in my tracks. Brenna, Hunter, and *Mom* were huddled together by the checkout counter, their laughter floating through the air like music. Mom held a Nora Roberts novel in one hand.

"I swear, Helen, if you keep buying every book that comes out, we'll have to expand the shop just for you," Hunter teased, his arm draped casually around Brenna's shoulders. Dressed in black jeans and a gray shirt, he towered over her. His smile and relaxed posture couldn't hide those muscles. I still wasn't sure whether to believe the stories that he'd been a covert assassin in his former career.

Mom grinned as she patted his giant arm, tattoos and all. "Well, someone has to keep this place prosperous, right?"

My gut tightened with an uneasy mix of hope and fear. The easy camaraderie between them, the warmth, was a far cry from the tension that used to crackle whenever the Coleridges and Markhams crossed paths. If Mom could let go of decades of rivalry with the Markhams, maybe there was hope for me and Jules. There had to be. But my idea of discussing the subject with Brenna just went out the window. So what now?

My sister spotted me first, her face lighting up. "Eli! What brings you to my humble abode of literary wonders? Did you actually interrupt your siesta for this?"

Nerves or not, my smile naturally appeared as I approached the trio. "I get plenty of beauty sleep at night, drama queen." Hopefully, the bags under my eyes didn't give the lie to that statement.

Mom turned to give me a side hug. "Sweetheart. What's up?"

The words stuck in my throat. After hours of agonizing over how to approach her, she was right in front of me. So

I did what I always did—deflected. "Oh, you know. Just… browsing for a new read."

Brenna's gaze sharpened, and I knew she'd seen right through me. Sometimes having a perceptive sister was a real pain.

"Well, don't let us keep you," Mom said, nodding to her book with a smile. "Although if you're looking for recommendations, I hear this new Nora Roberts is quite good."

A laugh tumbled out of my mouth. "Thanks, Mom, but I think I'll stick to my adventure stories." I couldn't help but grin as I took in Mom with my brother-in-law, her hand still on his arm. "Well, well, well," I drawled, leaning against the counter. "If someone had told me a year ago that I'd see Helen Coleridge giggling with a Markham in a bookstore, I'd have told them to lay off the rum punch."

Mom huffed, but there was no heat in it. "Very funny, Elias."

"No, seriously," I continued, warming to my theme. "Next thing you know, we'll be serving craft beer at the resort and hosting underwater weddings. Oh, wait…"

Hunter grinned. "He's got a point, Helen. Times are changing around here."

I watched Mom's face carefully, searching for any sign of disapproval. But instead of the frown I half-expected, a softness filled her eyes that made my heart skip a beat.

"You're right," she said quietly. "Things are changing. And maybe… maybe that's not such a bad thing."

Brenna, bless her, seized the moment. "Not a bad thing at all. And that's what I love about us Coleridges. We're stubborn as hell, but when it comes down to it, we're all about family. We adapt, we grow. Just look at how we're turning the resort around."

Pride mixed with a hint of wistfulness in Mom's eyes.

"You're right. I'm proud of all of you. The way you've stepped up, the fresh ideas you've brought… it's exactly what we needed. It's made me realize that my kids are more than ready to take the reins of the resort. I only get in the way."

We all spoke all over each other to argue about that, but Mom held a hand up, laughing. "I'm not going out to pasture just yet, but I've been saying for a few years now that I wanted to step back. All this change is a sign that it's the right time. And I'm happy about that."

"Change can be beautiful," Brenna said, squeezing Hunter's hand. "Look at us. Who would have thought a Coleridge and a Markham could find happiness together?"

"Certainly not me," Hunter admitted with a half smile. "But I've never been so glad to be wrong."

Mom's gaze flickered between them, and something shifted in her expression. "You two have shown me that sometimes, the most unexpected pairings can bring out the best in each other."

My throat tightened. Was she talking about just Brenna and Hunter, or…?

Hunter's phone pinged with a text, and he lifted it. "It's from Ben. I'm supposed to be helping him with a case, so I'd better head out. Good seeing you guys. Love you, sweetness." After giving Brenna a quick kiss, he moved toward the back door with nearly silent strides.

Still smiling, Brenna swept her eyes over Mom and me. "That's what love does. It breaks down walls and bridges divides. It makes us stronger, as individuals and as a family."

I felt a surge of gratitude for my sister. She was handing me the perfect opening on a silver platter. Mom's eyes met mine, and suddenly, I knew. This was my moment.

"Hey, Mom?" I said, my voice reassuringly steady. "Can we talk for a minute? Just us?"

Mom's eyebrows arched slightly, but she nodded. "Of course."

Curiosity flickered in Brenna's eyes, but she pointed to her computer. "There's a great little nook in the far corner. I need to place my order, so take your time."

I led Mom to two faded but incredibly comfortable wingback chairs with a circular table between them. She set her novel on the table as we sat. My heart hammered against my ribs. I wiped my suddenly clammy palms on my shorts, buying time as I searched for the right words.

"Mom, I know you've been worried about the resort," I began, meeting her eyes. "And I get it. The finances, Jules and my whole workplace-romance thing… it's been a lot."

She tilted her head, curiosity mingling with concern on her face. "Eli, what's this about?"

I took a deep breath. "It's about Jules. And me. Us."

Mom's shoulders stiffened, but I plowed on before she could say anything. "You said something when we talked that morning on your patio that hit me like a ton of bricks."

That made her curious. "What?"

"You asked me if I loved her." The memory of my painful silence, my fumbling non-answer, burned with fresh shame. "And I couldn't say it. I choked. You were right. I hesitated. I was scared. I've always been afraid to fall in love. I admit that your divorce from Dad messed with my head pretty bad. I've always been afraid to get close."

Her eyes clouded. "I feel terrible that it had such an effect on you kids."

I gave her a little shrug. "How could it not? He walked out on all of us, not just you. But that's not my point. I've been doing a lot of thinking since then. About Dad, about

Russell and Lucia, about why I run when things get real. About why that word felt like jumping off a cliff."

Then I looked her straight in the eye, forcing the fear down. "But Mom… I do. I love her. Julianne Verne. I am completely, terrifyingly, head-over-heels in love with her. I told her so last night."

The words hung in the air, finally spoken, finally real. It felt like shedding a skin I'd worn for far too long.

Surprise rippled across Mom's face, quickly followed by a complex mix of emotions—relief, lingering worry, and finally, unmistakable pride.

"And I know," I pressed on before she could speak, "I know that probably scares you. Given the resort, the history, everything you went through. I get why you're worried. And I understand why the idea of a workplace romance, especially when the resort is financially precarious, brings back awful memories. What happened with Russell and Lucia, how it poisoned everything, nearly ruined us, even pushed you and Dad further apart… that's a heavy weight to carry. I finally understood that better when you told me."

"Sometimes it felt like a piano on my back," Mom agreed quietly, her fingers tracing the pattern on the armrest.

"But Jules isn't Lucia." I punctuated each work by tapping the side of my hand against my other palm. "And I'm not Russell. More importantly, Mom, *I'm not Dad*. I'm not going to walk away when things get tough. This relationship… Jules… she doesn't make me want to run. She makes me want to *stay*. To build something real. For the first time, I actually care about budgets and profits and all that stuff I used to blow off."

A tiny smile tugged at Mom's lips as if she couldn't help it. "I had noticed a change in you lately." Then her expression grew serious, her gaze softening. "But since the bonfire, that easy grin hasn't reached your eyes nearly as often. There have been times, when you thought no one was watching… I saw it. Honestly, sweetheart, I've been worried. Seeing you so unhappy while trying to pretend everything was fine… it forced me to take a hard look at my own part in it. It made me reconsider if my hard line was truly about protecting you, or just about protecting myself."

I smiled faintly at her. "You saw that, huh? Yeah, things have been rough. I understand your fears, Mom. I really do. You have every right to want to protect this family, this legacy, after everything. But Jules and I aren't a threat to that. We're part of its future."

I paused, gathering courage for the next part. "I need you to know something. I was so convinced there was no way forward for us *here*, that I decided to leave. Quit my job at the resort. Find work somewhere else, maybe Calypso Key. I thought it was the only way to prove I was serious, the only way we could be together without defying you or putting the resort at risk."

Mom's hand flew to her chest, her eyes wide with shock. "Eli! You wouldn't…"

"I was going to," I confirmed grimly. "I went straight to Jules last night and told her my plan. I thought she'd be relieved, happy even." I shook my head at the memory. "But I was very wrong. She flat-out refused. *She* was the one who reminded me what Sunset Siesta means, what *family* means. She told me I belonged here, that walking away wasn't the answer. She believes in this place, Mom. Believes in *us*, all of us, enough to stop me from making a huge mistake, even when it might have made her own life easier."

I met Mom's gaze again, laying my heart bare. "So I

told her I'd find a way. I love her. And I want to build a life with her, *here*. With our family."

Mom was quiet for a long, stretching moment. Tears welled in her eyes, shimmering in the soft bookshop light. She reached out, not just taking my hand, but gripping it tightly.

My voice cracked as I added, "I'm asking for your blessing. Not just because I respect you and I love you, but because I want you to be part of this. Part of Jules and me. Because I'm pretty damn sure she's the one for me."

Mom was quiet for a long moment, her eyes becoming wet and teary. I held my breath, my heart pounding so loud I was sure Brenna could hear it from twenty feet away.

She squeezed my hand hard, then finally spoke. "Oh, son. I've been so afraid of what might happen, I didn't see what was right in front of me." Pausing, she smiled and swept her gaze over me. "I can hardly believe I'm talking to my son Eli right now. And the situation with Chase showed me that being afraid of possibilities isn't helpful. In the process, I learned a thing or two about letting go of fear."

I blinked, surprised. "What do you mean?"

"I was so afraid of change, of losing control," she admitted, squeezing my hand before letting go and settling back in her chair. "But I've known Chase since he was a boy, and I know the man he is now. And seeing how happy Brenna is, how well she and Hunter work together, it made me realize that sometimes, taking a chance is worth it."

Her smile, when it came, was tremulous but genuine. "All I've ever truly wanted is for my children to be happy, truly happy. And I see it now, Eli. I see it in your eyes." She released my hand and gently patted my cheek. "Of course you have my blessing. Both of you."

Relief washed over me, so potent my head swam. I surged forward, pulling her into a fierce, tight hug, burying my face briefly in her shoulder. "Thank you, Mom," I choked out, the words thick. "Thank you."

She held me tight for a moment, then pulled back, smoothing my undoubtedly messy hair with a mother's familiar touch. "I'm sorry if I made things harder than they needed to be. My past casts long shadows sometimes."

I nodded, blinking rapidly, managing a shaky laugh. "I know, Mom. Me too. But maybe we're finally stepping into the sun."

"Who knew you were such a poet?" She smiled, all traces of tension around her eyes gone now. "I hope you understand my reservations came from fear, not a lack of faith in your judgment."

I nodded, blinking back tears. "I know, Mom. Though my judgment has been pretty crappy in the past, so you weren't totally off base."

We both laughed, and as we embraced again, I felt lighter than I had in weeks.

I pulled back from her, my chest swelling with relief and gratitude. "You have no idea how much this means to me." My voice was still rough with emotion. "Not just for Jules and me, but for all of us."

Mom's eyes crinkled at the corners as she smiled. "I think I'm starting to understand, sweetheart." She patted my cheek gently. "Now, go on. I'm sure you're eager to share the news with… Jules. I think her formal name is a thing of the past now. Plus, I've got a new book I'm dying to get into!" Waggling her brows, she picked up the Nora Roberts from the table.

We both stood and I held her tight. "I love you, you know."

"I do. And you'll never know how much I love you."

"Even though I accidentally set fire to the fishing shed when I was eight? It really was an accident, I promise."

With a wry expression, she held out a lock of particularly gray hair. "See this one? You own it."

Laughing again, I walked her to the door of the shop. As she walked away, a big grin remained on my face.

"Okay, big brother. What the hell was that about?"

Whirling, I bounded over to where Brenna was arranging a display of new releases and gave her a big hug. "Jules and I are officially a thing now! Mom gave me her blessing."

Brenna's comically shocked expression was priceless. "Get out! How did you make that miracle happen?"

I told her, itching to get to Jules, when Brenna asked what I was going to say to her. I frowned. "What do you mean? I'll probably just blurt it out. I blurt everything out."

Brenna rolled her eyes. "God, Eli. Mom coming around is a pretty huge deal. So plan out what you're going to say to Jules!"

"Huh. Maybe that's not such a bad idea. I came in here in the first place to get your input on how to talk to Mom. So how about helping with this instead?"

"Now you're talking!" Brenna's face morphed into excitement as she rubbed her hands together. "You need to show her what she means to you. What would be special to her?"

I glanced around the bookshop, drawing inspiration from the shelves upon shelves of stories surrounding us. "Well, what about something Jules Verne themed?"

Brenna gasped and clapped her hands, her creative mind already whirring with possibilities. "Oh, that's perfect! You said you really liked *Twenty Thousand Leagues Under the Sea*. And that theme is perfect for you two."

I nodded, tapping my cheek. "I tore right through that one. We could do something with that. It's not just the adventure, though. For Jules, these stories represent something more. A chance to break free from the spreadsheets and numbers, you know?"

Brenna nodded, her expression softening. "A glimpse into a world of possibility."

"Exactly!" I snapped my fingers, the pieces falling into place. "She's told me how she used to love exploring and stuff like that. That's what I want to give her. Not just the news about Mom, but…"

Suddenly, it hit me. The perfect way to bring it all together. I sucked in a huge breath, a wave of goose bumps rolling over me. "Oh my God, Brenna. I've got it!"

She raised an eyebrow, intrigued. "Well, don't keep me in suspense. What's this brilliant idea?"

I leaned in close, my voice dropping to a conspiratorial whisper as I shared my plan. With each detail, Brenna's smile grew wider.

When I finished, she raised both hands to her mouth. "Eli, that's… that's absolutely perfect! Hmmm, maybe we should add a romantic touch to it too."

I scowled. "Ugh. That's not exactly my wheelhouse, sis."

Brenna positively beamed at me. "Oh, you big idiot. This entire idea is the embodiment of romance. Give yourself more credit. Jules is going to love it."

"I hope so because it's the best I can come up with."

"I know so," Brenna assured me. "Now let's get started…"

# Chapter Thirty-One

## JULES

GOLDEN SUNBEAMS POURED through my kitchen window, brightening the space and illuminating the specks of dust dancing in the air. I sat at my dining table, a warm cup of coffee cradled in my hands. It was creeping close to noon, but Sunday mornings were made for extra coffee and good books. I picked up my well-loved copy of *Around the World in Eighty Days,* willing myself to get lost in Phileas Fogg's grand adventure.

I'd had breakfast yesterday with Lacey at Sweet Dreams. The memory of her excited chatter about newly wedded happiness collided with my own hesitant confessions.

"So you and Eli are…?" Lacey had prompted, stirring her latte.

I'd shrugged, trying to keep my voice casual. "In limbo now, I guess. Sort of together but not. We've texted but haven't really seen each other since he came over. He promised to talk to Helen, but…"

"But you're not sure he will?" Lacey's brow creased in concern.

"No, it's not that." I paused, searching for the right words. "I trust him, Lace. It's just… I don't see how this is going to work out. Helen has made her feelings crystal clear."

Lacey gave me a sympathetic half smile. "Hey, if anyone can charm his way out of this mess, it's Eli. That man could sweet-talk a shark out of its teeth."

I laughed despite myself. "True. But this isn't just some random obstacle. It's his mother."

"All the more reason for him to fight," Lacey insisted.

Now, sitting alone at my dining table, I clung to that memory of hope. Eli had worked all day yesterday, then sent me an apologetic text saying he was beat and headed straight to sleep. Had he even had a chance to talk to Helen? Was he having second thoughts?

I set my mug down with a little too much force, sloshing coffee onto the pristine white tablecloth. Great. Another mess to clean up. With a deep breath, I picked up *Around the World in Eighty Days* once more. I'd lose myself in Fogg's journey, I decided. Let the familiar prose wash away my worries, if only for a little while.

When I lifted my coffee cup to my lips, I discovered it was cold, and I'd been reading the same page for five minutes. I set the book down with a sigh. Who was I kidding? My gaze drifted to my phone, silent and unhelpful. I could text him, couldn't I? Just a quick check-in. Nothing desperate or needy.

Before I could second-guess myself, I grabbed my phone and fired off a text to Eli.

> Jules: Morning, Coleridge. You alive? The sea monsters haven't dragged you down to their lair, have they?

I chewed my lip, waiting. The typing bubble appeared almost instantly, which made me smile.

> Eli: Barely. Slaving away over dive class plans. Turns out teaching newbies how not to drown is more exhausting than it looks. Send coffee. And a massage. Maybe a naked massage?

> Jules: You and your gutter mind. Don't we have other pressing issues? Such as a certain discussion with your mom?

My heart skipped. I took a steadying breath, fingers hovering over the keys as I waited.

> Eli: Patience, my dear Verne. Good things come to those who wait. And those who wear little red bikinis you might be hiding from me.

That made me laugh out loud.

> Jules: You'll have to earn a glimpse of that. Though after spending weeks pretending we hardly know each other, I might just rip your clothes off the next time I see you.

> Eli: Challenge accepted.

"I don't want to get too off track here. Focus." Frowning, my thumbs flew over the screen.

> Jules: Only if this on-again, off-again thing is settled.

> Eli: I think you underestimate my powers of persuasion. And my appreciation for red bikinis. 🔥 So… are we a couple again or what? It's kind of important for future planning purposes. And bikini-related activities.

> Jules: That depends entirely on your conversation with your mother.

> Eli: Let's just say you might have an answer to that sooner than you think. 😌 Some treasures are worth waiting for.

I huffed, frown deepening. "What the hell is that supposed to mean?"

> Jules: Then I guess I sit here and twiddle my thumbs.

> Eli: I can think of much better uses for those thumbs. And your fingers. And my God, your tongue!

"Oh, Eli. You are priceless." I typed my next two words and sent them with hardly a thought.

> Jules: Love you

For a moment, my stomach twisted. Should I have said that?

> Eli: Wow. We did say that, didn't we? No going back now. Love you too, boo. Talk to you soon.

Laughing and much more relieved than I wanted to admit to myself, I set my phone down. I felt lighter, yet incredibly curious as to what might be brewing beneath Eli's teasing words. With a sigh, I returned to my book, attempting to immerse myself in another world. But just as I settled into the rhythm of Verne's prose, the doorbell rang, jolting me from my thoughts.

A courier stood on my doorstep, package in hand. "Delivery for Julianne Verne?"

"That's me," I said, puzzled. I wasn't expecting anything.

I signed for the package and retreated inside, turning the small, brown-paper-wrapped parcel over in my hands. No return address, and my name and address were typed on a generic label.

I tore open the wrapping and opened the cardboard box.

My breath caught as I recognized the contents immediately—Eli's magnetic dive slate. It was battered and framed in blue plastic, an integral part of him. And I glimpsed a scrawled hand forming an okay signal with the thumb and first finger. "What the…?"

I lifted the slate out, my eyes widening as I read the message written next to the cartoon hand.

*Mom gave me the official okay signal. I'm not kidding. Smooth seas ahead! To find out how, head to where I first helped you jump into the unknown. Also where you learned walls are better underwater than in offices.*

My heart raced. What did this mean? And where was I supposed to go?

Without wasting another moment, I set the slate down and picked up my phone, grinning widely. My fingers flew across my phone screen as I fired off a text to Eli.

> Jules: Care to explain the mysterious package that just arrived at my door? 😕

His reply came moments later.

> Eli: Package? What package?

I snorted.

> Jules: Nice try, beach boy. I know your handwriting. And your dive slate.

> Eli: Ooh, intriguing! Maybe you should follow the instructions and see where they lead.

I could practically hear the playful lilt in his voice.

> Jules: You're really going to play dumb?

> Eli: Who, me? Never. 😇 But if strange packages containing puzzles are arriving at your doorstep, it might be worth investigating, don't you think?

My smile widened.

> Jules: You're impossible.

> Eli: Impossibly charming, you mean. Now go on, Ms. Verne. Sounds like an adventure awaits!

I shook my head, intrigued. It was clear what he was up to. Eli was sending me on a scavenger hunt. And the first clue indicated he had already talked to his mother and secured her blessing for us. But what now?

I read the clue again. "…where I first helped you jump into the unknown."

It hit me suddenly—it had to be *Sunset Diver*, where I'd jumped into the ocean, and we'd done our wall dive.

I grabbed my keys and the slate, then bolted out the door. As I drove to the resort, possibilities collided in my head. What did Eli mean about his mom giving the okay? How could that possibly be true?

I parked haphazardly and jogged toward the pier, the dive slate clutched tightly in my hand. I scanned the area, searching for any sign of Eli. *Sunset Diver* bobbed gently in its slip, but he was nowhere to be seen. The whole area looked deserted, guests and employees off to other things now.

Stepping aboard, my gaze landed on a wooden tray on the fiberglass bench across from me. A fabric-covered square box sat on top of the tray. The fabric was abstract swirls of blue and lovely. Picking it up, the box was warm, velvety against my hands. I opened it and spied a clear glass bottle with a rolled-up piece of paper inside the neck.

Biting my lip to keep my smile from reaching ridiculous proportions, I lifted the bottle and extracted a rolled parchment of beautiful quality from the bottle's neck. When I unrolled it, Eli's familiar handwriting greeted me.

*"Put two ships in the open sea, without wind or tide, and, at last, they will come together."*

A gasp escaped my lips and my smile turned tender. The quote from *Twenty Thousand Leagues Under the Sea* hit me like a wave. "Oh, Eli."

Then I noticed something else on the tray, a folded

piece of resort stationery. After opening it, another message awaited.

> *I asked you to have faith in me. You helped me see that we could navigate the rough seas and find our way back to each other. Our journey is just beginning, but I promise you, I'm not letting go. Your next clue awaits where our passion first exploded (Don't get overheated!).*

A laugh burst from my lungs, and I had to blink several times to clear my blurred vision. "I can't believe you did this."

As I traced his words with my fingertip, the realization of what he'd done, this elaborate scavenger hunt, overwhelmed me. Each clue was proof of our connection, as well as the depth of his feelings. I held the bottle to my chest, overcome by emotion.

"You ridiculous, wonderful man," I said with a mingled sob and laugh. "You actually understand me."

My mind raced, piecing together the fragments of our story. The obstacles we'd faced, the doubts we'd harbored… all of it faded away in the face of this gesture. Eli wasn't just reassuring me. He was laying his heart bare, proclaiming his commitment in a way that spoke directly to my soul.

I took a deep breath, composing myself. "Okay. Where did our passion first explode?"

Then I laughed out loud as my head turned of its own volition to the black-and-white sand beach.

And the dive shack.

With a grin, I carefully rolled up the parchment and replaced it inside the neck of the bottle. I placed it and the note, along with the slate, in the fabric-covered box before setting off toward the next stage of Eli's romantic treasure hunt, my heart lighter than it had been in weeks. Maybe ever.

The sand shifted beneath my feet as I hurried to the yellow shack, the box of treasures cradled against my chest. My heart raced, not just from the brisk pace, but from the anticipation of what I might find next.

I paused at the door, my fingers tracing the peeling paint. When I opened the door, the familiar scent of neoprene and salt washed over me, with the accompanying blast of heat. But my eyes were immediately drawn to the center of the room.

There, on the floor where we'd collapsed in a tangle of arms and legs, sat a beautiful antique silver platter. And on it…

"Oh, sweetie," I breathed, sinking to my knees in front of it.

Eli's battered copy of *Twenty Thousand Leagues Under the Sea* lay before me. I reached out, my fingers trembling slightly as I lifted it.

A folded note slipped from between the pages and fluttered to the worn wooden planks. I set the book aside and carefully unfolded the paper to reveal another written note.

*I used to tease you about your nickname, but now I realize it perfectly reflects your adventurous spirit and your deep love for the ocean. I should have seen it sooner. Your final clue is in the place where I couldn't resist you any longer and finally kissed you.*

I pressed the note to my lips, closing my eyes as memories washed over me. Memories from this very building, memories of the heated arguments we used to get into, which seemed so silly now. Then the memory of where we'd kissed for the first time. My eyes flew open.

The dive classroom.

Eli's intense gaze as we'd argued about replacing the scuba kit flashed before me. Along with the electric moment when he'd marched over to give me that devastating, irresistible kiss.

I gently placed the note inside the book, adding them to my growing collection of mementos. As I stood, I caught sight of my reflection in a dusty mirror. My cheeks were flushed, eyes bright with unshed tears, and a smile I couldn't suppress raised my lips.

"Well," I said to my reflection. "I guess I'm going back to school."

I couldn't maintain a professional pace, finally breaking into a run as I rushed toward the dive shop, the box of treasures held tightly. The pale wooden boards of the pier creaked beneath my feet, but I barely heard them.

*Your final clue…*

The sign on the glass door had been flipped to *Closed*, though it was several hours before the usual closing time. I had a feeling that was intentional, and I couldn't wait to see Eli. I yanked open the door, anticipation thrumming through my veins. My stupid, broad smile froze at the empty shop before me.

"Eli?" I called out, my voice echoing in the silence.

No response.

I made my way down the short hallway, pausing briefly to peek inside the employee break room. Empty. Finally, I reached the dive classroom.

The room, silent except for the hum of the air conditioner, was bathed in the soft light streaming through the large window. My eyes were immediately drawn to the white table at the front, where a blue rectangular placemat stood out starkly against the pale surface.

As I approached, my breath froze in my throat. There,

nestled on the placemat, was a stunning piece of multicolored coral, shaped by nature to suggest a heart. The stone-like coral was a blend of colors, from pale blues and purples to vibrant pinks and oranges. I'd never seen it before but could instantly see why Eli had been drawn to it.

"Oh my," I whispered, gently setting down my box of clues on the table.

My fingers hovered over the coral heart, almost afraid to touch such a thing of beauty. Beneath it, I spotted another folded note. With trembling hands, I lifted the delicate heart and unfolded the paper. Eli's words leapt off the page.

*I found this years ago and thought it represented my one true love. The ocean. I was wrong. Diving is my passion, but you're my heart. We were meant to be together.*

I pressed the note to my chest, overwhelmed by the depth of emotion behind his words. My tears finally spilled over as I stood there, holding the coral heart and reading Eli's words over and over. My heart felt like it was bursting, and it was the sweetest ache I'd ever experienced.

But as the wave of feeling subsided, a new confusion crept in as I scanned the room. What now?

I flipped the note over—blank. Lifted the placemat to find nothing underneath. My eyes darted around the classroom, searching for any hint, any clue about what came next.

"Come on, Coleridge," I said, a nervous laugh escaping me. "Don't leave me hanging here."

The silence of the empty classroom felt deafening. I circled the table, scrutinizing every inch until I stood in front again. My analytical mind, usually so reliable, felt scrambled.

I wiped my face dry and picked up the coral heart again, marveling at its subtle patterns. My gaze drifted to the box of collected treasures. Each item represented a piece of our journey from antagonistic coworkers fighting at every opportunity to lovers who couldn't be apart. For weeks, maybe months, I'd known I was in love with Eli. But this sweet, thoughtful hunt showed me exactly how deep that emotion ran. To my soul.

Because he'd asked me to have faith in him.

Setting the heart down, I scanned the note yet again. What was I missing? Where was I supposed to go from here? Just as I began to worry I'd gotten something wrong, that deep, teasing voice drifted through the air.

"Looking for something? Or maybe someone?"

# Chapter Thirty-Two

## ELI

JULES WHIRLED around with her eyes wide and filled with awe. My heart did something ridiculous as I took in her flushed cheeks and the wisps of dark hair escaping her silver clip. Lurched. Soared. She looked like sunlight breaking through the clouds, alive and radiant.

I wanted to capture this moment, etch it into my mind forever. God, she was beautiful. I crossed the room, each step deliberate. Not my usual lazy, easy saunter, but something more purposeful. Something that said *this matters*.

"Eli," she breathed, a smile blooming across her face.

My hand found her cheek of its own accord, thumb brushing over her soft skin. "Hey there, green eyes."

I'd watched from the front door of the dive shop as she found the message in a bottle I'd placed on the dive boat, then hurried to the dive shack. When she'd reappeared to race toward the dive shop, I'd tiptoed to hide in a storage closet. Finally confident she was in the classroom, I'd moved to watch from the shadows, delighted beyond measure as she read my note before looking everywhere for the next clue.

"What? When? How…" I smiled as she glanced at the box on the table, then turned back to me. "You talked to Helen?"

I nodded, unable to keep the grin off my face. "I did. Yesterday. And we've got her full approval now."

Jules's mouth dropped open. I wanted nothing more than to kiss those perfect lips, to show her exactly how much this moment meant to me. But I held back, savoring the way her eyes searched mine.

"Really?" Jules clutched the coral heart like a precious jewel, her eyes shimmering with unshed tears. "How did you… I mean, she was so adamant before. What changed her mind?"

I shrugged, but my trademark casual gesture couldn't hide the emotion I was feeling. "I just told her the truth. That I couldn't live without you." The words hung between us, stripped bare and honest.

My fingers brushed her wrist, tracing the line where professional Jules—the buttoned-up accountant who'd challenged me at every resort budget meeting—gave way to something more vulnerable. Something real.

"I poured my heart out," I continued, my voice low. "Told her how you challenge me. How you make the resort better. How you make me better. Mom realized pretty quickly how much you mean to me."

Jules blinked. Once. Twice. And then she laughed— that rich, unexpected sound that so few people heard. The laugh that said she was more than spreadsheets and careful calculations. The laugh that said she was alive. "This is the most amazing thing that's ever happened to me."

I grinned, the kind of smile that had to show every

complicated, joyful thing I was feeling. "I have to confess that Brenna helped me plan the scavenger hunt."

Jules swatted my arm. "Please. This is pure you. Completely, ridiculously you."

I raised an eyebrow. "Ridiculous, huh? I'll have you know, a lot of thought went into this little adventure."

"I know it did," she said quietly, her smile fading as she dropped her eyes to the heart still held in both hands. "I still can't believe it's all real."

I gently lifted her face with my knuckle. "Believe it. All of it."

Taking her hand, I led Jules back to the table. The remnants of the scavenger hunt lay tucked inside the box —my dive slate, the bottled message, my dog-eared copy of *Twenty Thousand Leagues Under the Sea*, and, of course, the coral heart, which she placed on the table.

"So," Jules said, her voice soft with wonder as she removed the other items and lined them up next to the heart, "walk me through this masterpiece of yours. I can't tell you how incredible this all is."

I picked up the worn novel, running my thumb along its cracked spine. "Well, I wanted the whole thing to be Jules Verne–themed. Seemed fitting, given your nickname and all." I winked at her. "And this book? The adventure, the mystery... kind of reminded me of you from the start."

Jules grinned in pure delight. "Smooth talker."

I laughed, setting the book down and reaching for the bottled message. "I got this parchment from Brenna's shop. Thought it'd add a nice touch of authenticity to the whole message in a bottle thing."

"And the dive slate?" Jules asked, running her fingers over the plastic surface.

"Ah, well, that was just practical—I had to start somewhere. Though I'm glad to get it back. Can't imagine teaching without it."

She laughed, the sound warming me from the inside out. "Heaven forbid."

I grinned and lifted the coral heart. Its familiar weight settled in my palm, but now it felt different. Charged with new meaning. I pointed with my chin at the tall oak bookcase at the front of the classroom. "I found this years ago on a dive in the middle of a sand patch. Don't worry—I'd never take anything live out of the ocean." My chest swelled a little at the pride in her eyes as she smiled. "I kept it in the bookcase there in the corner. Always thought it represented my love for the ocean."

Jules's eyes softened as she looked at me. "And now?"

I swallowed hard, tamping down the emotion. "Now I realize it was always meant for you. A treasure I'd been holding onto without even knowing why."

"I love it," she whispered. For a second, I thought she might cry. Then she laughed, a soft, melodic sound that touched something deep within me. "So my love is tied to a rock?"

"Hey, it's a beautiful rock!" I protested. "It's coral, and it's special. Just like you."

"Flattery will get you everywhere, Eli Coleridge."

"Good, because I'm just getting started. We are." I gently returned the coral and stepped closer.

Her breath caught, and I saw tears shimmering in her eyes. "Thank you."

I took a deep breath, examining the way my heart pounded. And discovering I was fine with that. "I need to be honest with you. These feelings, they scared the hell out of me at first."

She lifted her head, acceptance flitting through her eyes. "I know they did."

I ran a hand through my hair, struggling to find the right words. "For years, I thought all relationships led to pain and resentment. And I was determined not to follow in my parents' footsteps."

"So you kept everyone at arm's length."

"Yeah," I admitted. "I was terrified of repeating their mistakes. It almost drove me away from you."

She reached out, intertwining her fingers with mine. "And now? How do you feel?"

I gazed into her eyes, marveling at the depth of emotion I saw there. "Now? Loving you feels like the most natural thing in the world. I spent my whole life running from anything that felt real. You make me want to stop running. Because it's not fear anymore. It's strength."

Jules's lips curved into a soft smile. "I understand that fear, Eli. After what happened with Travis… I was so afraid to trust again, to open myself up to that kind of pain."

"Hey," I said gently, stepping closer, bridging the distance between us again. "I get it. I really do. You've got your walls, and I've got mine. But when I'm with you, those walls don't seem so solid anymore."

"Because they're not, yours or mine. Trust changes everything. *We're* different."

I nodded. "Completely different. I trust you. Implicitly."

"And us?" The question hung between us, weighted with possibility.

"Us," I replied quietly, "is the best thing that's ever happened to me."

The classroom around us, with its marine life posters and whiteboards, became smaller. Peripheral. Her fingers traced the edge of my T-shirt, a deliberate touch that sent electricity skating across my skin.

She wrapped her arms around my neck as she pressed herself tightly to me. "Your passion for life is infectious. You made me remember what it feels like to truly live, not just go through the motions and call it a life. I've missed you every day."

Taking a step back, I cupped her face and stroked the warmth of her skin. Saw everything I'd been afraid of—and everything I now wanted—reflected in her eyes.

"I love you," I said. Not a declaration. A promise.

Then I kissed her.

Deep. Consuming. No holding back.

"I love you too. So much." She pressed the words into my mouth.

The kiss deepened, becoming raw and urgent. I slid my hands down her back, tracing the line of her spine through her thin shirt. Jules gasped against my mouth, then followed that up with her tongue. I moaned as it skated over the roof of my mouth.

When we finally broke apart, both breathless, Jules's eyes were dark with desire. She glanced around the empty classroom, a mischievous smile playing at her lips. "You know, I noticed when I came in that the dive shop is closed. We're all alone here."

My pulse skipped at the implication in her words. "Why, Ms. Verne, are you suggesting what I think you're suggesting?"

She bit her lower lip and gave me a scorching look through lowered lashes, which only made me throb harder. "Maybe. What are you going to do about it?"

A half smile spread across my face as that delicious, familiar heat pooled in my belly. "Well, that depends. What exactly did you have in mind?"

Her fingers trailed down my chest, her touch inflaming me even through the fabric of my shirt. When she reached the waistband of my shorts, her hand dipped lower, palm pressing against my rock-hard shaft.

"Oh, I have all sorts of ideas," she murmured, her voice husky.

My breath caught in my throat. This was my by-the-book, spreadsheet-loving Jules. And she was so much more.

"Care to share some of those ideas?" I managed to choke out, my voice embarrassingly strained.

Instead of answering, Jules sank to her knees, her hands working at the button of my shorts. My heart thundered in my chest as she took me into her mouth. Our eyes stayed locked.

Holy shit.

Her tongue swirled around me, achingly slow, and I couldn't hold back the groan that escaped. My hands found their way into her hair, not guiding, just needing something to hold onto as waves of pleasure washed over me.

"God," I breathed, my eyes screwing shut as she continued her torturously slow pace. "You're killing me here."

I felt more than heard her laugh, a vibration that made me grit my teeth to hang on. I forced my eyes open, needing to see her. The sight of her looking up at me, those bright eyes filled with desire, nearly undid me right there.

I took a shuddering breath, summoning every ounce of willpower I possessed, and took a step back. With a gentle tug on her arm, I urged Jules to her feet.

Her eyes widened in surprise when I picked her up and set her on the table, gently brushing the scavenger hunt items to the side. I lifted her shirt off and unhooked her bra, then removed my own shirt. When I hooked my fingers into the waistband of her shorts, she raised her hips, helping me slide them off.

I paused, drinking in the sight of her. My hands trailed up her thighs, savoring the softness of her skin.

"You're so beautiful."

Her chest moved with the force of her breathing. "Eli, I want you so bad."

I silenced her with a deep, ravenous kiss. Then I trailed my lips down her neck, her collarbone, one beautiful, perfect breast and the other. Then lower still.

Her breath hitched as I settled between her legs. Her taste was intoxicating, and I lost myself, my tongue exploring every inch of her. Jules's cries filled the room, her hips bucking wildly as I brought her closer and closer to the edge, committing every gasp and shudder to memory. Her fingers gripped my hair, urging me closer.

"Oh God," she whimpered. "Right there."

She was usually so controlled, so measured. But not now. Now she unraveled beneath my touch. And only I knew this other side of her. I mapped her with the same precision she used at work. Every response. Every breath and gasp. Cataloging. Analyzing. Destroying her composure inch by deliberate inch.

Her fingers gripped me tight. Her breath came in short, ragged bursts that echoed through the empty classroom.

"Yes…" she moaned.

And I was relentless. Determined to make her cry out. To shatter every professional wall she'd ever constructed. Her thighs trembled against my shoulders as I built her up higher and higher. And then, with a final flick of my tongue, she shattered, her climax pulsing through her. I held her steady as she came apart, my name a breathless chant on her lips.

I fumbled for the condom in my wallet, nearly dropping it in my haste. Still on the table, Jules watched me with hooded eyes, her chest heaving. "Come here." She pulled me close.

I slid into her with a groan, overwhelmed by the sensation. She was so warm and ready. We moved together urgently, the pent-up desire and frustration finally unleashed. The table creaked beneath us, but I couldn't have cared less.

"Jules," I panted, "you feel amazing."

She responded by wrapping her legs tighter around my waist, drawing me deeper. My world narrowed to this woman beneath me, around me—her heat, her rhythm, the way she arched her back. Every thrust felt like a revelation, like coming home. She was liquid fire around me, tight and soft and impossibly responsive. Her fingers dug into my back, making me hiss with pleasure and pain in equal measure.

The tension built, coiling tighter and tighter until it snapped. We cried out, clinging to each other as waves washed over us. Nothing else existed but this connection.

As our breathing slowed, I gazed into her eyes.

"You're the one for me," I said softly, hoping she understood the weight of those words. "I hope you know that."

She nodded, a smile rising on her face as she brushed away a bead of sweat from my cheek. "I do, because you're the one for me." She barked a laugh, and it sounded slightly bewildered. "Never thought a philosophy of duct tape and beer would rub off on me. But turns out? It was exactly what I needed."

We both started laughing.

Loud.

Uninhibited.
Completely, perfectly us.

# Chapter Thirty-Three

## JULES

THE DRIFTWOOD LOG beneath me creaked, its worn surface smooth and comfortable. Firelight danced across Eli's profile, catching the golden undertones of his skin. Two weeks since Helen's blessing, and the beach that had once felt like a battlefield now hummed with comfortable intimacy. He wrapped an arm around me, his body a welcome shield against the unseasonably cool night air. I snuggled closer.

"You okay there?" Eli's voice was low, meant only for me. "Getting cold?"

I shook my head, smiling up at him. "I'm perfect right where I am."

The beach stretched out before us, bathed in oranges and yellows from the bonfire. It was strange how a place that had once felt so foreign now felt like home. Then again, a lot had changed in the past few months.

On Eli's other side, Chase shifted on his log to toss a good-sized piece of driftwood on the fire. A cascade of sparks lifted and snapped into the night, and I smiled as they winked out one by one.

"Sure you want to sit next to me, Chase?" Eli's voice rang out, loud enough for everyone to hear. "We wouldn't want to tarnish your impeccable reputation."

Amusement broke through Chase's composed exterior. "You haven't managed to wreck it yet. At least I'm not the one who thinks Casual Friday means board shorts and a surfing sweatshirt." He gestured at Eli's laid-back attire.

"Hey, I'm just keeping it real."

"Don't mind him, Chase," I reassured, casting a sidelong glance at Eli. "He always dresses like he's about to meet the ocean rather than a group of friends and family."

"Well, if we're being honest, I actually think he pulls it off," Harper chimed in next to me, her laughter mingling with the crackle of the fire.

"Thank you, Harper. At least someone appreciates my fashion sense," Eli said, puffing out his chest in mock pride.

"Fashion sense? More like nonsense." I couldn't help but laugh, shaking my head. The banter felt so easy, so right.

"At least I'm not overdressed for the occasion," Eli added with a wave at Chase in his button-down shirt and slacks.

"Hey," Chase replied. "I came straight from work. Didn't realize there was a dress code for Coleridge bonfires. Should I have worn something more casual?"

"I'll let it slide this time. Fortunately for you, we don't bite—unless you're a s'more," Eli quipped as he roasted a marshmallow that was looking alarmingly incendiary. "Finn, tell him we only chew on marshmallows and chocolate here."

Grinning, the boy placed his marshmallow-filled skewer into the flames. "Yep. Lots of it."

Harper leaned in to look at Chase. "I imagine you'll be coming to more bonfires now. Despite having been friends with Eli for ages, you haven't joined us much until recently."

He shrugged. "I guess I never wanted to intrude on family time. Plus, Eli is an ass."

A murmur of agreement swept around the bonfire. Eli scowled at everyone.

A few moments later, Finn's excited shout pierced the night as he triumphantly held up the perfectly toasted marshmallow, its golden-brown surface glistening in the firelight. "Look, Mom! I did it!"

Chase laughed, inspecting it from across the fire. "Now that's what I call precision roasting. You could teach your uncle Eli a thing or two."

Eli scoffed as he blew the flames out on his. "Hey now, some of us prefer our marshmallows with a bit of char. Adds character."

"Is that what you're calling those blackened lumps you've been eating?" Chase indicated Eli's s'more, which I had to agree looked disgusting.

"You know," Chase said, his tone shifting slightly, "I used to think having everything planned out was the key to success. But life has a way of throwing curveballs, doesn't it?"

Eli leaned forward, interest piqued. "Oh? Is Mr. Perfectly Planned admitting to some spontaneity in his life?"

Chase's lips lifted in a small smile. "Let's just say my new business venture wasn't exactly part of my five-year plan. But sometimes, the best opportunities come when you least expect them."

I watched the dynamic between them—lifelong friends who spoke in a language of playful jabs and unspoken understanding. Eli's world had always been about spontaneity, while Chase represented methodical precision. Yet here they were, comfortable in their differences.

I bumped his shoulder. "You're definitely turning over a new leaf, Coleridge."

His laugh was low, intimate. "Maybe. But some things never change."

"I don't know," I said. "Should I be worried you'll start color-coding your dive schedules next?"

Eli's eyes met mine, and in that moment, I saw a depth of emotion that took my breath away. It was as if all our shared history, all the battles and misunderstandings and eventual understanding, were reflected in that single look.

"Nah," he murmured. "I think I'll leave the spreadsheets to you. But maybe I'm starting to see the appeal of looking ahead a bit more."

My heart swelled, and my eyes grew misty as I scooted closer. "Well, as long as that future includes plenty of poorly roasted marshmallows and private classroom sessions, I think we'll be just fine."

From the far side, Braden picked up a log and tossed it into the flames. The fire sent up an explosion of sparks, making me jump and ending the moment between Eli and me.

Lacing his fingers between his knees, Braden focused on Chase. "So when are you planning to start waving that magic wand of yours over our beloved resort?"

The architect laughed. "Magic wand? I think you're confusing me with Harry Potter."

"You know what I mean. The renovations."

Helen, who'd been quietly observing our banter, leaned forward. "I have to admit, I'm rather eager to see what you have in store for us, Chase."

My heart warmed at Helen's words. Her presence as

she sat between Finn and Braden, her genuine interest in the project, showed exactly how far we'd all come.

Chase straightened, his posture a perfect blend of confidence and professional precision. "I'm still looking at places to set up shop, but the Sunset Siesta renovation plans are already in development."

"So what's the timeline?" Austin asked from Chase's other side. Always watchful and quiet, if not a little grumpy, the fishing captain doled out words like carefully tended lines, casting them only when the moment was right.

"Measured," Chase emphasized, a hint of playful sarcasm threading through his professional demeanor. "Let's not rush anything. We want to preserve the resort's character while bringing it into the twenty-first century. It's a delicate balance. But I promise we'll be starting soon."

I appreciated his deliberate approach. Numbers and strategy were my love language, after all.

"Look at you, all grown up and responsible," Eli teased, but the respect in his voice came through clearly.

"I think that sounds perfectly reasonable, Chase," Helen added. We've waited this long. A bit more patience won't hurt us."

Harper finished her s'more, then her gaze drifted to Chase. "We're all looking forward to seeing you around more often. Just like old times, except you and Eli are all grown up now."

Their eyes met—a lingering moment that made the firelight seem to shimmer differently. Curiosity pricked at the edges of my awareness, but I'd learned enough about family dynamics to know when not to pry.

Austin turned his attention to Eli and me, and a mischievous smile broke through his serious expression.

"So, looks like the workplace romance thing is working out pretty well."

Eli took a seated bow. "Remarkably well with the new policy in effect."

Helen's laugh was knowing, a sound that suggested she was several steps ahead of everyone else. "A new policy for a new age. Department heads now have full discretion in these matters."

Eli's chest rumbled with laughter. "The only problem is that I'm one of those department heads in question."

"Don't let it go to your head," I said as I bumped him with my elbow.

Helen raised a finger. "Now, Eli, I think you're forgetting something important here."

Eli cocked an eyebrow. "Oh? And what's that?"

"Your authority extends to the dive operation." Helen paused, her amused eyes darting between us. "You might be in charge there, but in personal matters, I have a feeling that might not be the case."

Bursting into laughter, I held up my can of beer to her. "I'll drink to that!"

As the conversation drifted to other topics, I soaked in the comfort of Eli's presence. The crackling fire, the laughter of his family—our family—all faded into a pleasant background hum.

I leaned in close, my lips brushing his ear. "So your place or mine tonight?"

Eli's arm tightened around me, a sly smile rising. "Wherever you want. I've just been reminded in no uncertain terms that I'm not the one in charge here."

Ignoring that remark, I gazed up at him with warmth blooming in my chest. "Your bungalow. I'm starting to prefer it."

His eyebrows shot up. "Really? I thought you said it was… What was it? A chaotic bachelor pad?"

I smiled, remembering my initial reaction to his laid-back living space. "Your bungalow has grown on me. It has more privacy than my townhouse and loads more character. It feels…" I paused, searching for the right word. "It feels like you."

Eli's eyes softened, and he pulled me closer. "Well, I gotta admit, it feels a whole lot brighter with you in it. Maybe we can make it feel more like us. I want you there as often as possible, Jules."

My heart skipped a beat. We'd come so far from where we started, and every day seemed to bring us closer. I leaned in, pressing a quick kiss to his cheek, mindful of our family around us.

"Then take me home, Coleridge."

---

SUNLIGHT FILTERED through the gauzy curtains of Eli's bedroom, painting patterns across the rumpled sheets. I blinked awake, feeling Eli's warmth against my back, his arm draped over my waist. I rolled over to face him, drinking in the sight of his messy hair and sleepy smile.

"Morning, beautiful," he mumbled, his voice rough with sleep.

"Morning yourself, handsome. What's on your schedule today?"

Eli stretched, his stomach muscles rippling in a way that momentarily distracted me. "Leading a morning dive trip. Should be a nice change of pace. I've been teaching a lot lately."

"But you're such a good teacher," I said, tracing

patterns on his chest. "Your students are lucky to have you."

He caught my hand, pressing a kiss to my palm. "You're biased."

"Doesn't mean I'm wrong."

Eli laughed, pulling me closer. "I love both, honestly. Teaching newbies, seeing that moment when it all clicks for them, is the best. But there's something special about leading experienced divers too. Sharing the beauty down there with people who really get it."

I nodded, understanding the passion in his voice. It was one of the things I loved most about him—his ability to find joy in his work, whether he was teaching or exploring.

"What about you?" His fingers played with a strand of my hair. "Big plans for the day?"

I propped myself up on one elbow, my tresses falling in a tumbled cascade over my shoulder. "Actually, I'm kind of excited about today's workload. I know, I know"—I held up a hand as Eli's eyebrows shot up—"but hear me out. I'm starting the new fiscal year quarterly budget projections, and for once, I get to incorporate some exciting figures."

"Exciting figures?" Eli's lips rose in a teasing smile. "Hon, your idea of excitement never ceases to amaze me."

"I'm serious! Chase's renovation plans are going to breathe new life into the place. The potential change in the figures, not to mention the ROI..." I trailed off, catching the amused glint in Eli's eye. "And I've lost you, haven't I?"

Eli laughed, pulling me back down beside him. "Not at all. I love seeing you all fired up about spreadsheets and ROIs. It's adorable."

"Adorable?"

"Yes, and impressive too," Eli said, his tone softening. "I don't know what we'd do without you."

Warmth spread through my chest at his words. "We make a good team, you and I. Your charm and my practicality."

"More like your brilliance and my bumbling attempts to keep up."

I tilted my head to look at him. "Hey. We complement each other perfectly. Our differences aren't weaknesses, Eli. They're what make us strong together."

"Wow, now I'm getting all flustered over here." He scratched the back of his neck, a sheepish smile breaking through. "I guess I just can't wrap my head around the fact that you love me. You're so far above my pay grade it's not even funny."

"Stop saying that and believe it," I replied firmly. "You showed me how to embrace life instead of analyzing every little detail. That means more than you'll ever know. I love you, board shorts, scuba tanks, and all."

Eli's lips curved into that devastating smile of his, the one that made my stomach flutter wildly. "Well, if you love my scuba tanks so much," he murmured, his voice dropping to a husky whisper, "how about we explore some… deeper waters?"

I screwed my eyes shut and groaned as I bit back a grin. "That was terrible, even for you."

"Got you to smile, though, didn't it?" His fingers trailed up my arm, leaving goose bumps in their wake. "Come on. Let me distract you from all those numbers swirling in that beautiful head of yours."

His touch ignited an ember that had become beautifully familiar. I leaned into him, my body already responding. "Hmm, and how do you propose to do that?"

Eli's answer came not in words, but in the gentle press of his lips against my neck, just below my ear. I shivered, my eyes fluttering closed.

"Like this," he murmured against my skin. "And this."

His lips traced a path down to my collarbone, and I found myself melting into his embrace. I turned in his arms, capturing his lips with mine. To hell with morning breath. As we lost ourselves in each other, I caught a glimpse of our future—mornings filled with laughter, evenings spent by the water, a lifetime of adventures both big and small. And at the center of it all was this man who had stolen my heart and given me his in return.

# Epilogue

## ELI

ONE YEAR LATER

I clutched the thick, messy file folder tight against my chest as I strode across the sun-drenched grounds of Sunset Siesta, my steps light and damn near bouncy. The folder was a chaotic mess of papers—colorful doodles of fish on the cover and many faint coffee rings adding character to the otherwise boring documents inside—but it made me smile. Around me, the resort thrummed with life, happy guests lounging by the pool, the distant buzz of saws from ongoing renovations, and the salty breeze carrying promises of hamburgers from Tidal Hops.

I caught sight of Dave, a regular on the dive boat this week, emerging from the pool. His enthusiasm for the ocean rivaled my own.

"Hey, Dave!" I called out, grinning. "See you on the boat tomorrow?"

He gave me a two-finger salute. "You know it, Eli."

"That's what I like to hear. Enjoy the rays, man."

I took in the peaceful scene. It was clean and lushly tropical, the result of some added landscaping that Ben had found in a liquidation sale. Renovations were progressing around the resort but not in the pool area yet.

As Dave settled onto his lounger, pride surged within me. This place was thriving, and I was no longer just the carefree dive instructor wandering aimlessly. I was part of something bigger now—a family business that carried the legacy of the Coleridge name. A year ago, I might have balked at the thought, but now? Now it felt right.

And that was only part of it.

With flurries building in my stomach, I continued toward the lobby building. The sound of laughter and splashing water faded as I pushed open the double glass doors, replaced by the soft hum of air conditioning and the faint melody of some soft reggae playing over hidden speakers. The interior was cool and inviting, with a light citrus scent in the air.

I strolled past the check-in desk where our receptionist, Dana, was busy fielding a call with her usual grace. She flashed me a quick smile before returning to her conversation about room rates and dolphin tours. Continuing down the hall lined with glossy photos of underwater scenes from around Dove Key, courtesy of me, I passed by Harper's office, empty at the moment.

When I paused outside Jules's office, a grin spread across my face at the sight before me. She sat behind her desk with both hands buried in her long raven hair, face scrunched up in frustration as she stared at her sleek monitor. With a huff, she started typing furiously, leaving her locks in complete disarray.

"Looks like someone forgot her bun today!" I called

out, leaning against the doorframe. "Bird's nest chic really suits you, hon."

Her eyes flicked up, surprise morphing into a reluctant smile. "Very funny, Eli." She lifted both hands to her hair, taming the mess. "I learned a long time ago that some days I need to keep my hair down or I'll pull it all out. At least I've got my new computer. Financial audits are one of the few things I truly loathe, but they're necessary. Unlike your jokes."

"Hey! My jokes are essential for the well-being of this place." I sauntered in, the flurries turning into a full-grown storm inside my stomach. "Well, I hate to add to your workload, but…" I held up the huge, disheveled folder. I'd stuffed it with every stray financial piece of paper I could come up with. "I forgot to give you this one. Hope it doesn't set you back too much."

Jules's eyes widened, a mix of exasperation and amusement dancing across her features as she reached for the folder. "You're killing me, Eli. Really? Fish cartoons?"

"You never appreciate my artistic talent."

Jules flipped through the papers, her brow lowering more with each page. I could practically see the gears turning in her head as she flipped through the disarray, trying to restore order in her mind and her workspace. It was tough, but I managed to keep the smile off my face.

"Honey, this is a disaster. It looks like a hurricane hit it." She paused, shooting me a pointed look. "You have duplicate invoices here, I'll have you know."

"Duplicate? You mean I'm double the fun?" I shot back, trying to suppress the urge to laugh. Watching her wrestle with my mess was immensely satisfying.

"Fun doesn't exactly cover your complete lack of organization." She sighed dramatically, but I could see her fighting a smile. Then she peered closer. "Wait… is that a ketchup stain?"

I shrugged nonchalantly. "What can I say? I'm a multi-tasker. Paperwork and lunch, all in one go."

She gave me a deadpan stare. "At least it's not blood. How you manage to run the dive shop without drowning in chaos is beyond me."

"Ah, it's all part of my charm." I winked, and she returned to sorting through the mess.

Suddenly, Jules froze. Her eyes widened, fixed on something nestled against the spine. The papers in one hand slipped from her fingers, forgotten as they landed on the desk.

Time stopped.

The only sound in the room was the thundering of my own heartbeat. I drank in every nuance of her reaction. The slight parting of her lips, the catch in her breath, the way her fingers shook as they hovered over the diamond ring.

"You know," I said softly, my joking tone gone, "it's funny how easy it is to miss what really matters when you're buried in the numbers."

Jules snapped her head up, her eyes enormous. She opened her mouth to speak, but no words came out.

I stepped around the desk, my heart now threatening to pound right out of my chest. "The things that used to drive me crazy about you? Your laser focus, that stubborn determination, how passionate you get about work? They're the things I love most now. Some of the things, anyway. If I list everything, we'll be here all day."

Jules's fingers closed around the ring, lifting it from the folder. She stared at it, spellbound.

My legs felt like jelly as I gently took the ring from her.

Swallowing hard, I dropped to one knee. "Julianne, you've changed everything for me. You've helped me face the stuff I've been running from my whole life. Helped me see a future I never thought was possible.

"I used to think commitment was a dirty word. But with you? It feels like the most natural thing in the world. You might have moved into my place six months ago, but I guess that's not enough for me. I know I'm not exactly the poster boy for seriousness. But, Jules, I'm dead serious about you. About us."

I strove to memorize every moment of this. The way her raven hair framed her cheeks, the slight tremble of her lower lip. Her eyes widened, and her mouth hinged open.

I pressed on, my voice growing stronger with each word. "You've had faith in me when I didn't have it in myself. You've pushed me to be better. And along the way, you've become my anchor."

My hands were slightly unsteady as I took the ring from her and held it up. "I want to build a future with you. Here and wherever else life takes us. Will you marry me?"

"Eli, I…" she began, her voice thick with emotion. As she cleared her throat, a smile broke across her face, brilliant and genuine. She vaulted to her feet. "Yes. Yes, I'll marry you!"

My heart took flight. I rose and slid the ring onto her finger. She let out a watery laugh, flexing her hand to admire the sparkle. When I wrapped my arms around her, I marveled at how perfectly she fit against me. Her body trembled slightly, and I realized she was laughing, a sound I'd grown to love more than the sound of waves on the shore.

"What's so funny?" I murmured into her hair, breathing in the faint scent of her shampoo.

"Us," she replied, her voice muffled against my chest. "Getting engaged in my office. Two years ago, I would've bet my entire savings account that this moment was beyond impossible."

I laughed, tightening my hold on her. "Good thing you didn't. I'd hate to start our engagement broke."

With a surge of joy, I lifted her off her feet and spun her in a circle. Her startled yelp turned into peals of laughter, echoing off the walls of her office. After she returned to earth, her gaze drifted to the scattered papers on her desk—and now on the floor too—a familiar, calculating look crossing her face. Her fingers traced the edge of an invoice, then she looked up at me with that trademark arch of her eyebrow. "So… do I still need to worry about this file?"

I threw my head back and laughed, a sound that emanated from somewhere between my chest and my soul. "That file is pure junk. Total prop. I've been stuffing it with every piece of paper I could find for the last two weeks, after I bought the ring and came up with the idea." I glanced at my fingers intertwining with hers as her ring glittered. "I've already given you everything that actually matters."

"Yes, you certainly have." Then she laughed and shook her head. "Only you would turn a marriage proposal into an elaborate paperwork joke."

"Hey, I know my audience." I tapped the side of my nose. "Accountant's weakness—messy file management."

Jules groaned, but her eyes were sparkling. The diamond caught the light, casting tiny rainbows across her fancy new computer screen, a splash of unexpected color amid the neat columns of numbers.

I laughed again as my gaze took in the utter chaos and

mess on her blotter. "You know, I think I'm finally rubbing off on you. Your desk looks suspiciously like mine."

Jules playfully swatted my arm. "Don't get any ideas, Coleridge."

I raised an eyebrow, fighting back a grin. "Sure, sure. Keep telling yourself that."

The current state of her desk was just like us. Unexpected. Perfectly imperfect.

---

THANK you for reading BETTER THAN NEVER! I hope you loved Eli and Jules and getting to know the whole Coleridge gang. Enemies to lovers/opposites attract is such a fun dynamic, and these two were so fun to write about!

If you'd like a glimpse into **Eli and Jules's happily ever after**, scan or click below to sign up for my newsletter:

Beach Read Update
(www.erinbrockus.com/never)

As a THANK YOU, I'll send you a **bonus scene** which peeks into their lives several years in the future.

If you're already on my list, I've got you covered! At

the bottom of each newsletter is a link to all my free content for subscribers. Just find your last email from me to read this bonus, as well as any others you might have missed. Or you can simply sign up again—you'll have your bonus in a flash.

*KEEP READING for a peek at what's next in the Sunset Siesta series…*

## Second Epilogue

# HARPER

## ONE MONTH AFTER CHASE'S PARTNERSHIP

I leaned back in my chair, the protesting groan of its ancient springs a perfect harmony to the sigh that escaped my own lips. It had been that kind of week. Another Sunset Siesta workday was drawing to a close, or at least, my official involvement in it was. The resort itself, of course, never truly slept. A scribbled note lying on the corner of my desk—*Pick up Finn @ Kids Club 5:00 p.m. SHARP!*—served as my primary directive for the next hour.

The week had been packed with decisions that irrevocably altered the landscape of our family and the future of this resort. Eli, my wild, wonderful, exasperating brother, was solidly in a genuine, for-real relationship. I barked a laugh that it was with none other than our brilliant, formidable accountant who now possessed a smile that could melt glaciers. Their joy was a bright, infectious thing.

A reminder that sometimes, against all odds, things did work out.

And then there was Chase Ashworth.

My gaze drifted to the large roll of architectural paper dominating my small conference table. It had been unfurled there this morning by Chase himself, a bare canvas upon which he'd already begun to sketch the audacious, exhilarating, and frankly terrifying future of Sunset Siesta. His partnership, his investment, was the miracle we hadn't dared to hope for, the lifeline that might just pull us back from the brink.

My practical, budget-conscious, general-manager brain was still doing frantic, slightly panicked calculations about the sheer scope of his vision. But the part of me that had grown up within these sun-bleached, salt-kissed walls, the part that loved this place with a fierce, protective loyalty, couldn't deny a thrill of anticipation.

A light knock on my open door pulled me from my thoughts. Chase stood there, looking less like the high-powered architect who had calmly presented a multi-million-dollar renovation strategy and more like someone who'd forgotten what time it was. His dark hair had that slightly disheveled look it only got when he was deep in a design problem, and he was holding a drafting pencil like it was an extension of his own hand.

"Harper, got a minute before you head out?" He didn't wait for an answer, already stepping inside, his energy immediately filling the small space. "I was just looking at the lobby footprint again, and an idea hit me about the flow toward the ocean view. Mind if I sketch it out quickly while it's fresh?"

I glanced at the clock on my computer screen. 4:40 p.m. My date with a five-year-old loomed. "Just a quick one, Chase." I wanted to get that up front, knowing from experience that Chase's *quick sketch* could easily morph into a full-blown design symposium. "I'm picking up Finn at five."

A flicker—amusement? Understanding?—crossed his face. "Noted. This won't take long. Promise."

He'd always been wonderful with Finn, and my son was slightly awestruck that he designed huge buildings for a living. I'd always been slightly apologetic about Finn's persistent and verbal interest in Chase's work, but he would just give me that slightly shy smile and say it was nice to be noticed.

He joined me at the conference table, unrolling more of the paper with an impatient flick of his wrist. Then he removed some clips out of his pocket to attach the huge sheet of paper to the table surface.

I bit my lip, but a laugh still escaped. "You keep clips in your pocket?"

He smiled without removing his attention from what he was doing. "Occupational necessity."

The man was a study in focused intensity when a design problem had its hooks in him. It was impressive. He retrieved the drafting pencil from behind his ear, and suddenly, he wasn't just Chase, Eli's lifelong friend. He was Architect Ashworth, a creator, his hand moving with a swift, sure precision that was almost mesmerizing to watch. I couldn't stop staring at his hands, at how they were sure, confident, and... sexy.

*Shit.*

"See, if we re-angle this existing load-bearing wall here, even by just a few degrees..." He was completely absorbed as lines and shapes began to appear on the paper. "And yes, I know, structural engineer consultation required, budget implications, the works... But if we do that and use a lighter, more reflective material for this soffit detail, it will completely transform the entryway. It will draw the eye directly through the main space, past the new reception area, straight out to the terrace and the beach the moment someone walks through those front doors."

He paused, tapping the paper with his pencil, his hazel eyes, flecked with gold in the afternoon light, fixed on his emerging vision. "It's about the initial impact, Harper. That immediate sense of stepping into paradise. It sets the tone for their entire stay."

I leaned closer, trying to follow his logic, to see what he was seeing in those bold, confident strokes. And I did. Chase had a way of articulating potential, of making you believe in the transformative power of space and light, that was undeniably compelling. Even as my internal calculator was screaming about demolition costs and the price of custom-milled, hurricane-rated, unicorn-hair-woven soffit material.

"That sounds beautiful, Chase," I conceded, my own pen tapping against a notepad where I was mentally itemizing the new line items he was casually creating. "But what does re-angling a load-bearing wall actually do to our meticulously crafted budget? And that reflective soffit material. Is it sourced from a rare, extinct Keys tree and priced accordingly by the square inch?" My tone was light, teasing, but the underlying concern was real. My job was to keep his magnificent vision tethered, however loosely, to the planet Earth and our current financial stratosphere.

He shot me a quick smile and dipped his head, acknowledging my point but not remotely deterred by it. "There are always options. But the core idea of that unobstructed sightline is non-negotiable if we want to create something truly special. It's about the promise of what Sunset Siesta offers, delivered the second guests arrive."

He was right.

Annoyingly, breathtakingly right.

He saw things I didn't, possibilities I hadn't dared to imagine for this place I loved so fiercely. He wasn't just talking about moving walls. He was talking about shifting perceptions, about elevating the entire guest experience while staying true to our roots. He painted pictures with architectural jargon and charcoal lines, and damn him, they were beautiful, intoxicating pictures. And I was the one who focused on figuring out how to pay for all that five-star paint.

We were both hunched over the blueprint now, heads close as he pointed out a specific angle for the new, more discreet reception island to improve guest flow and create a more personal check-in experience. His shoulder brushed mine as he reached across me to indicate a potential spot for a stunning piece of local art he envisioned as a focal point.

The contact was fleeting, purely accidental, the kind of incidental brush that happens half a dozen times a day in a busy office. But my skin registered it with an unexpected, entirely unprofessional zing. Heat. A ridiculous little jolt that shot straight up my arm and settled somewhere in my chest, making my breath catch for a split second. I looked up, startled, and he was already turning back to the plan, probably oblivious to my minor internal combustion.

Or was he?

It was hard to tell with him, but our eyes met often over blueprints and meetings. The faint, clean scent of his after-shave, something woodsy and understated that I hadn't consciously registered before, hung in the small space between us. Chase straightened up and ran a hand through his dark hair, leaving it slightly rumpled in a way that was far too endearing for a man who was about to add at least another fifty thousand dollars to my renovation headache.

He blinked, as if just surfacing from whatever deep architectural waters he'd been swimming in.

"It's a beautiful design, Chase." And we're looking at renovating the lobby in the second phase, so maybe we can save up for your extinct-wood floors."

He burst into a full, dazzling smile and I couldn't stop myself from blinking several times.

He glanced at the clock on my wall, then back at me, a flicker of apology in his eyes. "I'll let you go pick up Finn. Sorry, I get carried away when I'm hashing out these initial concepts. But I think we're onto something exciting here, Harper. This lobby could be the heart of the new Sunset Siesta."

I nodded before gathering my purse. My mind was a jumble of demolition plans, budget lines, and the lingering, unsettling warmth where his shoulder had brushed mine. My office even smelled like him now. The resort's future felt more exciting, more tangible than it had in years. And also more terrifyingly complex.

And Chase…

He was no longer just Eli's quiet, studious best friend, or even just the highly respected architect we'd hired. He was a partner. A man whose passion for his work was as palpable as the Florida humidity. And something else that hummed beneath the surface of every professional interaction. A low, unsettling, and undeniably intriguing vibration.

As I headed for the door, he was already returning the pencil behind his ear. "This is going to be great," he called after me without looking up. "I promise you."

I paused, my hand on the doorknob. The weight of his promise, of his belief, settled over me. "I hope you're right, Chase."

But as I walked toward the Kids Club to fetch Finn, a

different, far more unsettling thought formed. Saving Sunset Siesta was supposed to be the hard part.

What if Chase Ashworth himself was becoming the most complicated variable in the entire equation?

---

The next Coleridge to take center stage will be Harper in book two of the Siesta Sunset Series, BETTER THAN HOME. You might have picked up on some sparks between her and Chase, now it's time for those sparks to catch fire in this brother's best friend, single mom romance.

*Look for BETTER THAN HOME in early 2026!*

# Also by Erin Brockus

## SUNSET SIESTA SERIES:

*Sunset Charade:* A Sunset Siesta Novella

*Available free to subscribers

*Better than Never:* A Small Town Enemies to Lovers Romance

*Better than Home:* Book 2 coming early 2026!

## CALYPSO KEY SERIES:

### MAIN NOVELS:

*Visions of You:* A Small Town Single Dad Romance

*Because of You:* A Small Town Fake Relationship Romance

*Memories of You:* A Small Town Second Chance Romance

*Shades of You:* A Small Town Forbidden Romance

ASSOCIATED SHORT STORIES AND NOVELLAS:

*Traces of You*: A Small Town Rivals to Lovers Romance*

* Subscriber exclusive

## ISLAND ESCAPES SERIES:

*In Too Deep*: A Second Chance Romance

*Beached in Bali:* A Friends to Lovers Romance

*Betting on Paradise:* A Fake Relationship Billionaire Romance

Clock Strikes Paradise: Coming mid-2025!

## HALF MOON BAY SERIES:

**Dive into steamy small-town romance, where passion meets paradise!**

Award-winning author Erin Brockus writes steamy small town romances that transport readers to exotic, tropical destinations, and provide a perfect beachy getaway from everyday life. Her mature, relatable characters are impossible not to root for, and she weaves breezy romantic adventure into her stories, emphasizing scuba diving and the ocean.

Drawing on her twin passions for diving and travel, Erin infuses her characters and narratives with a sense of excitement and passion. Her idea of the perfect day involves sipping a cocktail on the beach after exploring the ocean depths.

Erin lives in Washington wine country with her husband, who is also a scuba instructor. She is currently hard at work on her next island adventure. When she's not writing, she enjoys running, mountain biking, or enjoying a good book with a cup of coffee.

www.ingramcontent.com/pod-product-compliance
Lightning Source LLC
Chambersburg PA
CBHW051438190726

48289CB00001B/245